DEVIL'S DANCE

ALSO BY MICHAEL A. BLACK

Chimes at Midnight

DEVIL'S DANCE

TRACKDOWN
BOOK 1

MICHAEL A. BLACK

ROUGH EDGES PRESS

Devil's Dance
Paperback Edition
Copyright © 2025 (As Revised) by Michael A. Black

Rough Edges Press
An Imprint of Wolfpack Publishing
1707 E. Diana Street
Tampa, FL 33610

roughedgespress.com

Paperback ISBN 978-1-68549-549-7
Ebook ISBN 978-1-68549-548-0

For my fellow veterans.
To all the men and women who have served.
To those who have yet to come home.
And to those who never will.
God bless and welcome home.

As flies to wanton boys, are we to the gods;
They kill us for their sport.

King Lear, IV, 1
William Shakespeare

DEVIL'S DANCE

CHAPTER 1

DECEMBER 24, 2015
SOMEWHERE ON THE OUTSKIRTS OF BAGHDAD,
IRAQ

The image faded and then became more distinct, like a mirage. Staff Sergeant Steven Wolf wiped his goggles as he watched the outline of the heavily black armored Hummer become clearer through the vestiges of the early morning dust storm. He wished it was a mirage. All of it: the Army, being part of the special six-thousand-man stabilizing force brought in-country to lead the coalition against Daesh, or ISIS, or ISIL, or whatever the hell they were calling themselves these days. Whatever it was, one thing was eminently clear: this "special mission" in Iraq sucked. This wasn't Wolf's first rodeo in the Sandbox, but this time, it was like boxing with one hand tied behind his back.

"Get your squad ready to meet up with some boys from the Vipers," Master Sergeant Lane had told him. His big index finger had tapped the map. "Zero-four-forty rendezvous here. Assist them in a raid on a house and give them safe passage out of the hot zone back into the green. I don't need to warn you about the unfriendly assholes in this area. But it's actually not supposed to be that bad. In fact, it should be a cakewalk coming back unless you run into some hostiles or some IEDs."

"Merry Christmas Eve," Wolf said.

Lane frowned. "Yeah, well, remember this ain't exactly the Holy Land, and nobody's celebrating Christmas out there, so watch yourselves. These orders came from the top."

"And shit rolls downhill," Wolf replied with a grin. "Besides, they're probably getting ready to rotate us back to Afghanistan anyway."

Lane smirked. "Probably."

Even though all of the American troops had officially pulled out in 2011, little by little, a small contingent of "peacekeepers" had trickled back in. Officially, they were there as "advisors" and were prohibited from engaging in any type of combat, but they all knew it would be dangerous until the last man's boots were out of Iraq.

It's all Indian Country, Wolf thought. *Until you're back on US soil.*

That's what Big Jim McNamara, "Mac," had told Wolf before he'd shipped out for his first deployment. It wasn't a reference to Wolf being part-Indian, but rather Army slang for hostile territory back in Mac's day in the 'Nam. McNamara, an Army lifer and a Green Beret, had been in more wars, conflicts, police actions, and hot spots than could be counted. He was retired now, but Wolf didn't figure things had changed much. The faces and the places changed, but the danger remained the same: dealing with another group of angry and resentful people, "indigenous personnel," in another hostile, foreign land where a whole lot of them were set on making sure you didn't make it back home. Back to the World.

Yeah, he thought. *It's all Indian Country, all right.*

Wolf had carried that bit of sage advice with him since his first tour years ago. Back when the war was still considered a good thing and not labeled "stupid" by the next wave of politicians. This deployment was number four for him, and hopefully, his last in the Sandbox.

Indian Country...

The advice and the mindset had kept him and the members of his platoon alive so far. He intended to keep it that way.

"Any questions?" Lane asked.

"Just one. What's this one about?"

Lane shrugged, the sweat making his dark face shine in the light of the ops tent. "Do we ever know for sure when it involves military intelligence and these PMC guys?"

PMC guys meant Private Military Contractors, in this case, the Vipers, one of the biggest private security outfits to hit the Sandbox since the war had officially started winding down. After the US had nominally pulled out in 2011, all the operational duties had supposedly fallen to the Iraqis, but that had proved more than a bit problematic. With the rise of ISIS, American troops gradually crept back, staying mostly in the background as "advisors" but really acting as a trip wire to protect what American interests were left in the Green Zone. In the intervening years, the PMCs had gradually assumed a lot of the stuff the military had once done, but their involvement was always in the shadows and without a lot of scrutiny. Now there was no telling what they were up to or why, at least not at Wolf's level.

"All I know is it's being coordinated by MI," Lane added. "Lieutenant Cummins."

MI...military intelligence. Wolf had dealt with Cummins before, a reservist with enough clout to land a cushy assignment in command ops for his deployment. Behind his back, the troops called him "blubber with a pair of bars." Despite a personal dislike for the man, Wolf had found him competent, sometimes a little too competent. He expected everything to go according to his "paper plans." In the Sandbox, things didn't always work out that way.

Wolf went to brief his team and tell them they were moving out.

An hour later, fully assembled, the body armor making him feel like a turtle, Wolf found himself winding through the deserted streets in the pre-dawn light. Lane had been right. This neighborhood looked mostly upscale, lots of stucco and bougainvillea. Ironic that even in an inhospitable place like this, plants flourished.

But it's still all Indian Country, he reminded himself as he continued looking for their hookup. And they were there, right on time: two PMC fortified black Hummers parked on opposite sides of the road. The farther one had five uniformed Iraqis with M-16s standing guard. Wolf noticed that they were wearing the emblem of the National Police as he and Spec Four Martinez stepped out of their Humvee.

Automatically, Wolf scanned for signs of danger: snipers, suicide bombers, recent digging that would indicate IEDs, or any locals standing by with cell phones, but everything looked deserted. He ordered the other five members of his team to deploy for perimeter security: Jenson with the SAW, Morgan and Thompson with their

M-4s.

A trio of three big guys got out of the Hummer across the road, which looked well-armored. No IED/Indian Country worries for them, or maybe they had faith that their Iraqi National Police team could handle whatever or whoever popped up.

It's good to have faith, Wolf thought with a smirk. He knew that despite the season, these weren't the three wise men in this desert locale.

Wolf recognized one of them: Lieutenant Cummins. He was clad in civilian clothes, his expansive gut obscuring the belt buckle. Wolf remembered wondering about the embroidered jump wings on the lieutenant's uniform when he'd first seen him in camp. The man had such a soft look to him, it was hard to envision Cummins doing push-ups and pull-ups, much less standing up, hooking up, and shuffling to the door. Waddling toward it, maybe. Or perhaps he was one of those PX heroes who'd never even strapped on a parachute.

The guy next to him was huge, maybe six-six, two-fifty. The body armor made him appear even more massive. He strutted more than walked, and Wolf somehow wasn't surprised to see him wearing cowboy boots with silver trim on the pointed tips. The sleeves of his tan shirt were rolled up, exposing massive forearms. A threatening red and black tattoo of a snake's head, replete with exaggerated twin fangs, was on the left one. The coils of the serpent wound around his arm so its open fanged jaws spread over the back of his right hand. He was slipping on a pair of latex gloves, which made Wolf wonder why not leaving fingerprints might be a concern. The third one was an Arab with bushy hair and a mustache with flecks of gray. Maybe forty. Big for a local, over six feet and at least a deuce and a quarter, but nowhere near the size of the giant with the cowboy boots. The Arab's eyes looked mean as hell, though.

"Sergeant Wolf?" Cummins asked as he approached, looking from Martinez to Wolf and at their names and ranks on their name tapes.

"Sir," Wolf replied.

Cummins nodded and motioned them toward the shelter of a nearby building, the edge of the latticework protecting them from the ubiquitous sand that surrounded them like fog. At least the temperature was better than the usual insufferable year-round heat. It felt almost cold.

"This fucking dust is everywhere," the big guy said as he leaned back in a stretch.

He had a Southern twang to his words, a good ol' boy who was a long way from home. Oklahoma or Texas, if Wolf's ear for linguistics was correct. But sometimes it was hard to tell.

"This is Lance Eagan," Cummins said, pointing at the big man. "He's with the Vipers. How extensively did Sergeant Lane brief you?"

"Not a lot, sir," Wolf said. "Just that we were to meet you here and provide security for a raid and an escort back."

"That's perimeter security only," Cummins said. "We're to let the locals handle things primarily."

Wolf nodded.

Eagan snorted. "Aw, hell, me and Nasim's boys coulda handled this with no sweat, Jack."

The big Arab grinned, showing a glimpse of gold inlays in his front teeth. Wolf also got the impression that the man's English was good, and he was probably acting as their interpreter. Eagan's familiarity with Cummins surprised Wolf more. Using the lieutenant's first name around here usually meant they were more than casual acquaintances.

Cummins frowned, then bit his lower lip. "The Vipers have been working with a contingent of Iraqi National Police forces led by Captain Nasim here. They've uncovered a nest of what we believe are ISIS sympathizers in the area. Let me reiterate, we're to going to observe and advise them only, and if necessary, call for support in mopping up."

Wolf saw something in the man's pale blue eyes. Uncertainty? Fear? He wasn't sure which, but he didn't like it. Both emotions lurked here in the air you breathed and in your sweat, but you had to control them. If you didn't, they would start controlling you. He hoped the lieutenant's judgment hadn't been overly compromised. Most of these private contractors were ex-military and combat-tested and weren't bound by elaborate rules of engagement. Wolf didn't like the idea of following their lead.

"These boys inside are some real hard cases," Eagan said. "And they may have friends. Be ready, and don't drop your guard."

"We're always ready," Wolf told him.

Eagan's tongue rolled over his chapped lips, and he looked amused.

The time for amusement was later, Wolf thought. *After business was taken care of.*

"Our ultimate mission is to recover a briefcase," Cummins said. "It's purported to contain some good intel. Let me be absolutely clear about this. If and when it's recovered after the initial assault, I'm to take charge of it. Should you somehow come into contact with it, you and your men are not to open it. Understood?"

Wolf nodded again. It wasn't like he could read

Arabic anyway. "How sure are we about this place? The intel pretty good?"

"Like we'd be here if it wasn't?" Eagan asked. He removed a circular can about the size of a hockey puck, popped it open, and sliced off a wad of tobacco. "Don't worry, boy. Me and Nasim's crew will handle things just fine. For you guys, it'll be kissin' cousins to a cakewalk."

"That's what people kept telling me before my first tour," Wolf said.

"Shee-it," Eagan said, and the big man grinned. "This boy's got him some spunk."

Wolf decided the accent was more Texas than Oklahoma.

Eagan placed the plug of tobacco inside his lower lip and squared his enormous shoulders. "Let's roll. The house we're looking for is in the next quadrant over."

All balls and swagger, Wolf thought as he watched the big man saunter back to the Hummer. *I just hope he doesn't get any of us killed.*

Pale, nascent light slid between the buildings as they wound their way through the deserted streets, the asphalt giving way to macadamized dirt leading to piles of rubble and broken-up buildings on either side. It was early, but that didn't mean there weren't all sorts of prying eyes behind the dilapidated frames and windows, watching and waiting for them to make a mistake. Or to drive by a buried IED.

Wolf deployed his secondaries at each end of the block, assigning them their quadrants and fields of fire. Jenson had remounted the M-60 on the turret and was ready in case anyone popped a round off at them. Ahead of them, Eagan seemed to know where he was going, driving with the same swagger and impunity he'd shown earlier. Of course, those PMC assholes had all the latest equipment, and it was always in perfect working order. They never had to worry about the cracked lenses in night-vision goggles or the dead batteries that were the rule rather than the exception for the troops. Their pay was a lot better, too. Wolf wondered whether it wouldn't be better to hire a bunch of mercs to fight the next war, like the French Foreign Legion. They were supposed to be a crack outfit. Of course, they'd had their lunch handed to them back in Indochina at Dien Bien Phu, but that had been a long time ago.

I'll have more time to ponder that idea once I get transferred back to Afghanistan, he thought with a grim smirk.

Wolf scanned the buildings on either side of the street. Most of them were two stories. Windows...lots of windows. Too many. A good place for an ambush.

The radio crackled in his ear. He'd reset it to the frequency Cummins had given him.

"Bravo, this is Alpha One," Cummins' voice said. "You read me?"

"Lima Charlie, Alpha," Wolf said, depressing the belt mic button.

"Our target is three houses up on the right. Blue doors. We'll make entry and secure the interior."

"Roger that," Wolf confirmed.

Let the Iraqis do the grunt work for a change, he thought. *But that's okay. This way, I won't have to worry about some oversized dude with cowboy boots covering my ass.*

He briefed his squad, telling them to be ready after the breach in case they were called to help clear. Jenson was to remain in the vehicle in a cover capacity.

"Shit, you guys have all the fun," Jenson said, grinning. This wasn't the first time they'd hit a house in Iraq, but hopefully, it would be close to the last. He thought about the scheduled withdrawal and knew they couldn't afford to be lax.

"Everybody stay on your toes," he said. "We're all getting short, and that's when our buddy Murphy usually makes his appearance."

The rest of his squad grunted. They were all well-acquainted with Murphy's Law: *Whatever can go wrong will go wrong.*

Wolf snapped his selection lever off SAFE and checked the snap-fastening his M&P nine-millimeter sidearm. That could stay fastened until he needed it. Hopefully, this thing would go down by the numbers.

The black Hummer ahead of them slowed, and Cummins's voice came through his earpiece again. "This is it. They're hitting it now." Wolf relayed the message to his guys, and they switched their radios to the common frequency.

The two black Hummers ahead of them slowed suddenly, and one turned and bashed into the front gate to the house. The other pulled to a quick stop behind it. The National Police team piled out and ran through the opening with their weapons at the ready, followed by Eagan, Cummins, and Nasim.

Martinez slammed the Humvee to a stop, angling the nose toward the ramshackle gate in front of the house to afford them maximum cover. They filed out, taking cover behind the vehicles. Wolf reminded Jenson to stay in place in the Hummer, ready with the SAW in the turret. Wolf waved them forward and heard the crack as the ram slammed home. He glanced through the broken gate. Inside a small courtyard, he could see the Iraqis bunched together like a bunch of amateurs, slamming the ram against the door. It shuddered but held.

Cummins's voice crackled over the radio. "Get your squad in here."

Wolf motioned his men forward. They could have just as easily slipped over the wall, which was riddled with holes and missing chucks, but they were wary of broken shards of glass bottles that could have been cemented along the top. One of the Iraqis slammed the ram again, and the door finally flew open. He dropped the ram instead of stepping back, and they looked like a bunch of squirming pigs trying to get into a poke.

Several rats scurried in front of them as they ran across the courtyard. Heavy rug-like drapes blocked the windows. Morgan was first to the door, which hung from a single hinge. He shoved it hard, and it clattered to the floor just inside. The interior looked dark and foreboding. Wolf slipped through the opening, flipping down his night-vision goggles. The main room was large, with a couple of tables and prayer rugs hanging on the walls. Wolf pointed to cover positions at each hallway juncture and listened for indications as to which way Cummins and Eagan had gone. He heard a commotion to the left and saw Cummins standing in the hallway holding a pistol, his arms flailing awkwardly at his sides in a "What now?" gesture. Wolf motioned for his team to check the adjacent hallway.

Move, he thought. *Got to keep moving.*

He heard one of his team say, "Clear," followed by another voice yelling that he had three foreign nationals at gunpoint in the south room. With methodical precision, they checked the rest of the rooms, finding no one. Wolf gave the all-clear and told Thompson to assist Morgan with searching and guarding the three Iraqis they'd found. Satisfied that none of them was armed, they bound the three men's hands behind their backs with plastic cuffs. A finely crafted leather briefcase sat on a table in the far corner.

Wolf keyed his mic and updated Cummins. "Looks like we've found your briefcase."

"Roger that," the officer said. "We're coming. Don't touch it."

Eagan sauntered in first and shone his flashlight around. Wolf jerked his head away lest the brightness of the beam made it seem like a bomb had gone off inside his night-vision goggles. He reached up and shut them off. It was light enough now that Wolf didn't need them anymore. The wad of tobacco distended the area below Eagan's lower lip. He spat on one of the hanging prayer rugs. Wolf looked to see Nasim's reaction, but if the Arab was offended, he didn't show it. Neither did the contingent of National Police who trundled after them.

"Where are the prisoners, Sergeant?" Cummins asked.

Wolf pointed down the hallway.

"We'll take it from here," Cummins said. "You and your men deploy outside."

"Sir, I don't think that's such a good idea," Wolf said. "I have—"

"You heard the man, sonny," Eagan said. "We got this one."

Wolf looked at him. The big man was grinning.

"I don't take orders from civilians," Wolf said.

The grin got bigger. "Then maybe you'd better start taking them from your betters."

Wolf said nothing. The two men locked eyes.

"Wolf," Cummins said. "That's enough. You and your men get your asses out of here. Secure the perimeter." He pointed at his radio. "Switch back to main mission frequency, and I'll call you when we're ready to disembark."

Eagan pointed at Nasim. "This here is an internal security matter, boy. Like the lieutenant told you, we'll handle it."

Wolf felt like knocking the big man into next week but didn't.

"I don't like to repeat myself, Sergeant," Cummins said. "Now get your men assembled outside."

"You got to learn how to work with the locals, boy," Eagan said, slapping Nasim on the shoulder as they headed down the hallway.

Fine, Wolf thought. *Let these assholes play it any way they wanted. Not that it matters that we saved their fucking asses.*

He clicked back to the main mission frequency and asked for a sitrep from those on the street.

"All clear so far, Sarge," Jensen said.

Wolf motioned for Martinez to go get the others. It wouldn't hurt to do a bit of reconnoitering in case some locals were out and about and maybe thinking to set an ambush for the return trip.

Their scanning and setup took a quick fifteen. Wolf felt sweat trickling down his sides and back. He began to notice furtive movements in the adjacent buildings and dark eyes peering down at them from above. He heard the tolling of a bell and knew it was time for morning prayers. That might give them a bit of a respite, but all around him, the enemy had the high ground. The longer they stayed in position, the longer he and his squad were sitting ducks. Damn, he wanted to get his guys out of there. How long was Cummins going to devote to this damn farce? They needed to take the prisoners out of there before the shit really hit the fan. He took a quick look around and switched his radio back to secondary frequency.

Before Wolf could speak, he heard Cummins's voice. "Both of them. The Lion and the Lioness Attacking the Nubians. Tell him the deal was for *both* of them." It sounded like he was in the middle of a conversation, not talking directly into the microphone.

He must not know he has an open mic, Wolf thought.

More voices, this time speaking Arabic.

"He say he only have one," another voice offered.

"Tell him we want both of them now," Cummins said. "Immediately. Or else."

In addition to sounding distant, the lieutenant's voice was strained, like a man tiptoeing on the edge of desperation.

"Take it easy." Eagan's slow Southern drawl. "All we got to do is put a little fear of God into them."

"We're wasting too much time." Cummins again.

"Aw, *shee-it*," Eagan's voice said. "Lemme speed things up, then."

In the background, Wolf could hear a bunch of muttering. "*Allahu Akbar, Allahu Akbar...*" The chant was being repeated over and over. Arabic for "God is great."

Suddenly, the chanting was overshadowed by a guttural yell. Something foreign and indistinct, followed by a more frantic chanting, then a keening moan.

"Christ, you're making too much noise," Cummins said.

"Who's gonna care?" Eagan asked.

More groaning.

Wolf was confused. *What the hell is going on in there?*

He tapped Thompson on the shoulder. "I'm going back inside. Make sure everybody maintains surveillance of their quadrants, and have Jenson keep the SAW trained on those windows." He pointed across the street. Thompson nodded, a tense expression on his face.

Wolf kept the secondary channel on and listened to the intermittent cries and moans. Someone was putting some systematic hurt on somebody. He moved cautiously through the door, not because he feared for his safety but because he wanted to catch this little play in progress. He rotated the selection lever to rock and roll—full auto—just in case. Still, Cummins was a lieutenant in the US Army. He slipped it back one to SEMI.

The corrugated soles of Wolf's boots made little sound as he went down the hall to the last room on the left, the one where they'd left the three prisoners. If Eagan and company were abusing them, Wolf didn't want it to be on his watch. Not so much because he held much sympathy for the Iraqis, but the last thing he wanted was to be embroiled in any Iraqi civilian brutality bullshit. One of the Iraqi policemen stood in the hallway, smoking a cigarette as he peered through the open door. He glanced up with a surprised look, saw Wolf advancing, and turned and said something in Arabic to those in the room. When Wolf was about three feet away, the Iraqi lifted his rifle and pointed it at him, shaking his head.

What did this asshole think he was doing? Wolf stopped and raised his own weapon.

Through the partially open door, Wolf could see movement in front of one of the kneeling men. The guy's eyes were closed, and Wolf couldn't tell if it was tears or sweat or a combination of both rolling down his face. Something flashed, and he heard Eagan's partner Nasim shout in Arabic.

It was more like a growl.

"*Allahu Akbar, Allahu Akbar,*" the kneeling Iraqi was chanting.

"We ain't asking him again." English. Eagan's Texas drawl.

Then Cummins's voice, sounding nervous, with, "No, wait."

The Iraqi in the hall turned his head toward the room and spoke again in Arabic, his rifle still leveled at Wolf's chest.

It was quiet for a few seconds, then Nasim's voice said, "We got problem in hallway."

"Aw, hell," Eagan said.

The voices were in stereo, one in his ear mic and the other coming through the open door. The Iraqi in the hall canted his head toward the room once more, and Wolf stepped forward. He swiveled his body out of the line of fire and reached out with his left hand, grabbing the Arab's rifle's barrel and shoving it to the side. The Iraqi stumbled slightly, and Wolf used the momentum to push him into the room as he pulled the M-16 out of his hands.

Inside the room, Nasim's fingers were twisted into the dark hair of one of the kneeling prisoners, pulling his head back as the silver gleam of the big knife in Eagan's hand knife drew across the man's exposed throat. A red line appeared and then popped open, emitting a crimson waterfall down the man's dirty tan shirt.

"What the fuck's going on here?" Wolf said, leveling his rifle at them.

The three captors' faces rotated toward him like the three monkeys, except theirs reflected a combination of shock, surprise, and anger.

Cummins moved forward. "Get the fuck out of here. That's an order. This is prisoner interrogation."

The mic in Wolf's ear screeched with a sudden and piercing noise: feedback from Cummins's radio coming too close to his with the open key as he moved forward. "Get out of here now!"

The jarring sounds in his ear threw Wolf off for a second. That was all Eagan needed. The big man dropped the knife and reached out, grabbing the barrels of the two rifles Wolf held and directing them toward the floor. Wolf pulled back, but Cummins reached out with both hands and grabbed Wolf's helmet, twisting downward. His head followed, then something exploded against the back of his skull. Wolf felt his grip on the rifle weaken and slip, then a plethora of fists and feet smashed into his back and sides, forcing most of the air from his lungs. He heard the crunching sound again as he fell forward, and when the dirty tiles of the floor rushed up to smack against his face, the world went black.

* * *

"Sarge, Sarge," a far-off voice said. It held an urgency that made Wolf struggle to clear his head. It still felt fuzzy. Automatic weapons fire echoed nearby. Distinctive. Piercing. AK-47s. M-4s in reply, then the chunking sound of the M-60.

That thing'll be good for tearing up some scenery, Wolf thought. But why were they firing? And where the hell were they?

He blinked and shook his head. He still felt groggy.

"What's going on?" he managed to ask.

Thompson's face seemed to have been pulled taut by invisible strings. "We gotta get the fuck outta here, Sarge. We're in a shitstorm of a firefight."

Wolf shook his head again, trying to clear it. Thompson was helping him up when the wave of nausea brought part of his early morning MRE churning up from his stomach. He bent over to puke.

"Where's Cummins?" Wolf managed to ask.

"Gone," Thompson said. "We called for support, but it's real bad out front. We're taking fire from all sides. Come on, Sarge."

Wolf felt Thompson's strong fingers digging into his arm, lifting him to his feet.

"The prisoners?" Wolf asked. "Where are they?"

"Cummins and that big fucker said you were guarding them when they took off with those Iraqi police. I came back and found all this." He gestured toward the right. Wolf turned his head, feeling a shooting pain up and down his neck as he moved. Three bodies lay on the floor, their hands still secured behind their backs with the plastic cuffs. It filtered back to him now. One lay on his back, his head surrounded by a halo of blood, a KA-BAR next to him. The second one was slumped over on his side, his face flat against the floor, his glazed eyes staring upward. A small, neat circular hole decorated his left temple. The third man was kneeling, the front of his legs dark with blood that formed a half-circle around his knees. Expelled shell casings lay off to the side.

"Shit," said Wolf.

"Un-huh. We came under fire right after Lieutenant Cummins and the other ones booked." Thompson frowned. "He told me they were coming back, and we were to guard the scene. When I didn't hear from you on the radio, I came in to check, and—"

The sounds of more rounds smacking into the buildings and the Humvee came from outside.

"Sarge, I called for support, but we got to get out of here now. Otherwise, we'll get cut to ribbons."

Don't start a fight you can't finish, Wolf thought. Sage advice from Mac. "Let's go."

Wolf managed to move his feet as the two of them half-staggered forward.

Stand up, hook up, shuffle to the door... The refrain played in Wolf's mind as he moved, Thompson guiding him through the aperture. Their shoulders banged into the doorjamb.

"My weapon," Wolf said, suddenly cognizant that it wasn't slung on his shoulder. He felt for his pistol. It was in its holster, but the strap had been undone.

"My weapon," he said again.

"I got your rifle," Thompson said. His voice sounded like it was coming through a tunnel. "We gotta go now, Sarge. Jenson's laying down suppression fire."

"Grab those shell casings." Wolf pointed to the brass on the floor.

"We ain't got time, Sarge," Thompson said as he forced him out the door. "Come on."

"Grab them, dammit. They're evidence of a war crime."

Thompson swore and leaned Wolf against the wall, then went back into the room and retrieved the two casings. He held his hand out toward Wolf. "Okay?"

Wolf nodded. He watched as Thompson pocketed the casings.

Another burst from the SAW ripped through the air, and Wolf's legs propelled him mechanically down the hall toward the dangling front door, zigzagged him across the courtyard, and got him to the open door of their Humvee. A burst of rounds dotted the ground a few feet away and Thompson forced him down, his M-4 sending a stream of hot rounds out the ejection port that bounced off Wolf's arm.

"Motherfuckers!" Thompson yelled. He aimed his rifle in an upward trajectory at the taller building across the street.

"Give me my rifle," Wolf said, but his ears had lapsed into sudden deafness, and he couldn't hear how his words sounded. After a few seconds, his hearing partially returned, accompanied by a constant ringing that made everything sound like it was being filtered through a pair of tin cans connected by a string. Rounds peppered the dirt around them. Or was it brass from the M-60?

Keep moving, keep moving, he thought. It sounded like a chant. Sort of like the one he remembered hearing before everything went black.

Allahu Akbar, Allahu Akbar.

"We're almost there, Sarge," Thompson said.

The front end of the Hummer lifted as a puff of yellow and red blew off the hood, and a concussive wave rolled over them just before the inky blackness returned.

CHAPTER 2

Wolf woke up before the morning buzzer sounded, knowing he had a good twenty minutes before the mandatory 0600 hours wake-up. He had no watch, nor did he need one. Just his internal clock. In the past forty-two months, he'd become very conscious of time.

Wolf started this morning the same way he'd started each of the previous one thousand five hundred and twelve days, counting his stockade time, since he'd been incarcerated: with push-ups. After knocking off fifty, he stood up and jumped, grabbing the edge of the I-beam. He let himself settle into a dead hang, then started his pull-ups.

As on all the other mornings, he heard the voices inside his head: the CID interrogator: *Sergeant Wolf, is it the best of your recollection that you still don't recall what transpired the morning in question?* The mellow tones of his JAG defense attorney talking, just prior to the commencement of his court-martial. *Consider the offered deal, Sergeant. It's pretty lenient, and we've got no real defense. Not with you claiming you can't remember anything in your own defense.*

In your own defense ...

What could you say when the truth was you couldn't remember jack shit, and you had been told that the ballistic information on the recovered rounds and shell casings confirmed they'd come from your military-issued sidearm? But there was nothing he could offer. Why was it so hard for them to accept that he couldn't fucking remember?

CRS, as my grandfather used to say, he thought. Can't remember shit.

Wolf lowered himself down to another dead hang. Another voice spoke in an all-too-familiar refrain. The prosecuting JAG attorney: *As part of the government's prima facie case, we will present irrefutable evidence that rounds were recovered from the bodies of two Iraqi nationals, one Captain Faroke Hussein Mohammed and Hassan Karem Ali of the National Police, as well as two shell casings, which were recovered by Specialist Nathan Thompson at the scene, came from the military-issued nine-millimeter Smith & Wesson pistol that had been issued to the defendant, Sergeant Steven Wolf...*

Dead hang. *CRS*. Pull-up.

The JAG prosecutor's voice continued inside Wolf's head: *And that a military-issued KA-BAR knife was also recovered at the scene, said weapon having been used to slice the throat of one...which had been wiped clean of any fingerprints...*

Dead hang, pull-up. *CRS*.

The stern face of the judge, decked out in his dress uniform, staring down from his bench flashed into view.

His defense attorney's soft voice whispering, cajoling. *Take the deal, Steve. Plead guilty to manslaughter and take the eight years. It's lenient. You'll be out in four. We got no defense. Not with that evidence and the gaps you've got in what you recall. Not with Lieutenant Cummins and that PMC guy, Eagan, testifying against you.*

And I still can't remember shit, Wolf thought as he brought his chin over the edge of the I-beam.

Cummins... That fat, lying son of a bitch.

The memory of the defense attorney's voice continued. *Lieutenant Cummins' recollection of the incident is vastly different. Both he and Eagan swear that the Iraqis were all alive when they left the building. So do the National Police officers who were with them. Essentially, it's six against one.*

Dead hang.

Fuck Cummins. Fuck Eagan. Fuck 'em all... All but nine, as the old Army prayer went.

Two for road guards, six for pall bearers, and one to count cadence.

And with the rest of your squad not providing us with anything we can use...

Even his own men couldn't back him up. It had been the ultimate nail in Wolf's Army-green coffin.

He managed nineteen more chin-ups before his fingers gave out. Dropping lightly to the floor, he spread his hands shoulder-width apart and began another set of push-ups. The voice inside his head started the questions again and he increased his pace to distance himself, concentrating on the numbers. It was all about the count. Only the count. He stopped when he reached one hundred.

Montell Gant, his cellmate, rolled over and grinned.

"Not even cutting yourself some slack on your last day, huh, bro?"

Wolf shook his head as he got to his feet. His upper body felt pumped and tight. He took a few moments to get his breathing back to normal before he smoothed the sheets and blanket, making as tight a bunk as he had in Basic years before.

"Too bad the Army don't realize what a gung-ho, strac super soldier you are," Gant said, stretching out and rotating his head. "They done lost themselves a real fire-pisser."

"Maybe they'll pardon me in time for the next war," Wolf said.

"Well, one thing we can count on. They always gonna be shooting black or brown people somewhere."

Wolf smirked as he slipped on his t-shirt and pants, then stepped into his lace-less sneakers. It would feel good to get his old civilian clothes back. He could wear his desert boots, jeans, and a sweatshirt. Anything but his old uniform, even if they'd let him. They'd busted him down to E-1, and there was no way he would leave here wearing slick sleeves. Maybe they'd give him a new suit like in those real old James Cagney movies. That and a ten-dollar bill.

Of course, he thought, *with inflation, it must be up to at least fifty*.

He'd certainly earned at least that much in the ebb and flow of monotonous and mundane jobs inside during the last three and a half years. He wondered if he'd have to walk into town to catch the bus. And if so, where would he go?

Darlene had written faithfully at first, then with less regularity. He'd sensed the distance in her tone increasing as time passed, and the ending salutations went from *love always*, to *love*, to just plain *always*.

Always what? Always going to wait?

Then the letters stopped coming. His mail came back marked *REFUSED*.

But how could he blame her? They'd lost the house to taxes after the first year, and Darlene had been forced to move back with her folks. Two months after that, the divorce papers came for him to sign. He did and sent them back. No harm, no foul. She was still young enough to start over. Not much future for an Army wife whose hubby had gotten himself tossed in the pen, along with a DD.

Dishonorable Discharge. Forfeiture of all rank, pay, and benefits. It wasn't much compensation for ten years of faithful service. Well, six, since he couldn't include the past four. Maybe he'd been *too* faithful and too willing to follow orders without question. Too stupid to trust, too unwilling to see.

But he still saw those faces every night. All three of them on their knees. Dark stubble-lined cheeks and chocolate brown eyes filled with terror, leaking tears, pleading with him in a language he didn't understand. Sure, they were Iraqis and probably the enemy, but they were also civilians, not combatants. They were on their knees, hands bound behind them. Not threatening. Cummins, Eagan, and that Nasim guy had been calling the shots.

But it was his word against theirs, and nobody had believed him. Especially when he said he couldn't remember what happened next.

You're saying you have no recollection? The prosecutor's voice started again. *Even if we take into consideration your statement, Sergeant, as dubious as it is, why didn't it cross your mind to question the legitimacy of this alleged action that you claim you witnessed?* It was some fucking Army major intent on getting his silver oak leaves by stepping on Wolf's face. *You do know that if an order is unlawful, it's your duty to question it, don't you, Sergeant Wolf?*

Of course, nobody believed him. With the credible lieutenant's testimony, as well as that of the big Texas shitheel PMC guy and an Iraqi National Police Officer backing each other's accounts up, Wolf's attorney more or less told him the prosecutors could easily make their case for the more serious charge of homicide. But the whole war was just a bad memory in everybody's mind at that point, and the DOD just wanted this ugly little incident brushed under the rug with the rest of them.

Wolf had considered fighting the charges, but in the end, he knew he couldn't win. Plus, that blank gap, the section he really *couldn't* remember, kept haunting him. It was like trying to present a jigsaw puzzle as complete with the center section gone. After getting assurances from his JAG lawyer that the rest of his squad would be in the clear as long as he took the fall, Wolf agreed to the offered deal.

The prosecution convicted him on conduct unbecoming and took his stripes, his pay, his benefits, and his self-respect. When the judge told him to stand and hear his sentence, it was the last time anyone addressed him as "Sergeant Steven Wolf."

They'd all been shipped back to the States. Good old Lieutenant Cummins had gone back to his civilian life as a lawyer or something, and Eagan went off to who knew where. At least the Iraqis, Captain Nasim and his National Police buddies, had stayed in Baghdad to fight their own country's war.

Gant swung his legs off the edge of the upper bed and jumped to the floor, holding out his hand.

"Well, no sense dragging this out," he said. "Take care of yourself out there, man. Remember, you ain't gonna have good old Montell watching your back no more."

Wolf took Gant's proffered hand and smiled. "I'm not sure where I'll end up, but we can keep in touch. Look me up when you get out."

"Shit, that ain't gonna happen anytime soon. You know how they love to keep a black man down."

The sentence was punctuated by the loud, electronic click that signaled the opening of the cell doors. Wolf and Gant exited and lined up against the wall.

Last forced march, Wolf thought. He wondered what it would be like on the outside, being able to go and come as he pleased. Then again, he had nowhere to go. The thought of going home, back to the rez, maybe to see his mom, seemed less than desirable. How could he face those people—his mother, his uncle, all of them? He'd gone away to be a soldier, a hero, only to return as a disgraced convict with a DD.

A whistle was blown and the line came to attention, then upon command, faced right. They began a slow shuffle forward, maintaining standard D and C discipline. The stench of the prison chow grew stronger as they got closer to the oversized mess. Another line was marching past them in the opposite direction, holding their paper plates. Wolf tried to look past this last prison meal. He'd be processed out after that, and then he could go to a fine restaurant somewhere.

If he had any money.

He doubted his mother or anybody from the reservation could afford to come pick him up. Maybe they'd have a bus to take the released cons to the train station or somewhere to get them out of here. Maybe—

He caught a glimpse of the huge white guy's shifting eyes as they approached each other from opposite directions. A big fucker, much bigger than Wolf, cupping his hand under that paper plate. Wolf could only guess what the hand held, but the eyes, they told it all. Seconds later, the big guy lunged, thrusting his left hand forward. Wolf's arm shot out, blocking the blow with his own left and smashing his right fist into the big man's nose. He grunted and jerked his head, and that was all the time Wolf needed to grip his assailant's hand and bend it back. A plastic shank fell from the involuntarily straightened fingers as Wolf forced the big man to his knees, his eyes still glaring upward as a curtain of crimson washed over his lips and mouth. His exposed white teeth looked like bone showing through an open wound.

"What you trying to do?" Wolf yelled as he twisted his adversary's hand upward, bearing down, forcing the big man to his knees and catching a glimpse of a red and black tattoo amongst the blue jailhouse graffiti on the man's forearm.

Before this adversary could answer, Gant stepped forward and delivered a solid kick to the big man's jaw, snapping his head back and sending the mandible sideways with a crack.

Wolf glanced around, and Gant pushed him back against the wall. The big man sank to the floor facedown, a widening puddle of blood flowing outward from either side of his thick neck.

Three guards were suddenly there, pushing everyone in sight against the wall, calling in the incident on their radios.

"Okay, what's going on?" the main guard asked. "Who started this?"

He glanced down at the prone figure and spoke into his radio's mic once more.

"We've got one down in Corridor Bravo. Send a stretcher." He removed his handcuffs. "All right, either you say who did it, or everybody goes."

Before Wolf could speak, Gant shouted at the guard, "No need for that. It was me. The white motherfucker tried to shank me. Guess he don't like brothers. Called me a nigger."

He pointed at the crude, pointed plastic shank on the floor.

A couple of the other black inmates eyed him with curiosity but said nothing.

Wolf stared at him, and Gant winked.

The message was clear. His cellmate was watching his back one more time.

As the guard pulled Gant's arms behind his back and ratcheted on the cuffs, the black man smiled.

"So long, super soldier," he said.

* * *

Wolf was the last man through the gates after pausing to shake hands with one of the guards who'd been decent to him. The rest of the newly released cons kept shuffling toward the gray bus that would take them into town. Some had people there in cars waiting for them, but mostly they just looked like a bunch of sorry-asses making the slow walk to their next stop. Broken men on the road to nowhere, and now he was one of them. Wolf moved to the end of the line with the rest of the losers, reflecting on the call he'd gotten a month ago from his mama.

"Pa's dead," she told him. "Went back to drinking and got in a wreck. Hit a cement porch up in Lumberton." The news had stunned him. She continued, "I'm sorry, Steve. I just can't get all the way out there to Kansas to meet you."

Wolf vaguely remembered telling her it was all right. They were dirt-poor as it was, and now that Pa was gone, it would probably get worse before it got better. But his little brother was there, and hopefully, he'd step up and take care of ma. His sister was in North Carolina, too. They were both a lot closer than he was now, and neither one of them was branded with a stain of dishonor. Better that he stayed as far away as possible, but where could he go?

The question kept repeating in his mind as he approached the open doors of the bus. He paused and took one more look at the Fort Leavenworth US Disciplinary Barracks. From here, the place appeared almost pretty, with an expanse of green and some sizeable trees giving way to a sturdy stone building looking like it could house a couple of battalions. The view was a lot different from inside those consecutive layers of fencing and concertina wire, especially when you didn't have the luxury of leaving when you wanted to. Now he was out. Free, but free to do what?

At least he could get a meal lined up and waiting without the worry of getting shanked. He wondered what the big man's motivation had been this morning. Wolf hadn't recognized him and didn't remember even seeing or talking to him before. But in prison, seemingly insignificant slights took on a whole new meaning, and debts were often paid through a convoluted system of passed-on favors owed and rewards given. Wolf wondered about Gant, too. The man had taken the hit for him, but Gant was in for the duration. Twenty-to-life. Robbery and assaulting an officer. Gant was basically a good man, though. A soldier. The kind you wanted next to you in a foxhole when the shit was hitting the fan. Funny how sometimes the guys you least expected turned out to be the ones that led the company. Maybe in another life, he would have won the Silver Star or something.

Another life, another time, far away from Leavenworth.

He paused and took a deep breath of the fresh air. It smelled different inside the walls. Out here, the air was nice and clean.

That was when he heard the twin toots of the horn.

Wolf glanced toward the source, a black SUV. A Cadillac Escalade. Arizona plates. He couldn't quite make out who the guy behind the wheel was, but he was wearing a cowboy hat. A white one. The driver's door opened, and Big Jim McNamara—Mac—stepped out and grinned.

Wolf couldn't believe it. What was he doing here?

Mac waved him over.

Wolf picked up his duffel bag and walked toward the SUV. McNamara stepped away from the door and extended his hand.

"As they never used to say back in my day, welcome home." He and Wolf shook. "Guess you weren't expecting to see me, huh?"

Wolf snorted. "You got that right. What are you doing here?"

"Waiting on you." He opened the rear door, grabbed Wolf's duffel bag, and tossed it inside, pausing to run his fingers over the swash of black paint where the prison officials had obliterated the rank designation in front of Wolf's name. He glanced at it and shook his head. "Don't miss a trick, do they?"

Wolf felt a flush of embarrassment. "So you going to tell me how you happened to show up at this particular time?"

"Your mama called me." McNamara slammed the door and motioned for Wolf to get in the passenger side. "Sorry to hear about your daddy."

Wolf nodded and got into the Escalade. It figured that his mother would contact Big Jim. He and Wolf's father had been in service together, and Mac had almost been a surrogate father to Wolf.

"Well," Mac said, "your hair's nice and short. I like that. Looks like you been keeping in shape, too."

"I did my best," Wolf said. "What's with the cowboy hat?"

"I settled in Arizona. Everybody who's anybody wears one there out there. We'll have to get you one. Of course, you being half-Indian, we'll have to get you one like Billy Jack's."

Wolf laughed. "I always hated those old movies."

McNamara patted the dashboard. "This is my baby. How do you like her?"

Wolf smirked. "Never figured you for a Cadillac man."

"Hell, after all them years of driving jeeps, deuce-and-a-halfs, tanks, and then those damn Humvees, I figured I owed it to myself." He slapped Wolf on the back and asked, "What's the first thing you want to do? Get drunk? Get laid? Get in a fight?"

"How about getting the hell out of here?"

McNamara smiled and shifted into gear. "We'll put at the top of the list."

Wolf appreciated the smoothness of the Cadillac's ride as they got on the highway and headed west. The miles passed in silence, and Wolf didn't ask where they were going. He didn't care, as long as it was away from Leavenworth. While the place hadn't quite been hell on earth, it hadn't been the Club Med either. He wondered again about the attack that morning and what had precipitated it but decided it was water best left under the bridge. He was out now and didn't have to worry about such things.

He did make a note to contact Gant at some point in the future to thank him for taking the blame. Perhaps that had been the intention: it had been common knowledge that Wolf was getting out. Being involved in a fracas, injured or not, would have delayed his release. Maybe even canceled it.

The silence continued, and he hoped that Mac wouldn't ask him the inevitable question. *So what was it like in there?*

He answered it himself: Too many bad memories, too many sleepless nights, too much time to sit and think and wonder and play "What if?" It was like being in a forward area with no weapons, waiting for the balloon to go up. All you could do was sit and wait...and wait...and wait some more. And then there were those absent memories, dancing elusively in some corner of his memory. What had happened during those voided, blacked-out moments in Iraq? The worst part was the frustration of not being able to recall the specifics.

"You hungry?" McNamara said, pointing at a rectangular blue sign advertising a list of restaurants and fast food joints.

Wolf wasn't, but the thought of having the freedom to go into some place, a real restaurant, sit at a table, and order whatever he wanted was suddenly very appealing to him. It had been a long time. Too long.

"Sounds great," he said. "But I don't have much in the way of money."

McNamara chuckled and steered toward the exit ramp. "For now, you just let me worry about that."

* * *

The waitress looked barely this side of sixteen, all blonde hair and dimples, with a burgeoning figure that was really going to be something in a year or two. Her nametag said Jenny. Wolf appreciated the surreptitious glances and bright smiles she kept throwing his way. Mac had insisted on pulling into the first place they saw after Wolf mentioned that he'd skipped breakfast at Leavenworth.

"Would you gentlemen like some dessert?" the girl asked.

McNamara lifted his eyebrows, and from his expression, Wolf figured his friend was going to make some rakish comment asking what the girl had in mind. But he didn't. Instead, he pointed at Wolf and said, "He will for sure. You got some of that apple pie with ice cream on top?"

"We sure do. You want some?"

"He does," McNamara said with a grin. "He's just coming back from what we used to call a hardship tour."

Wolf was still chewing his steak. He just wanted to enjoy his first outside meal in over two years, but Mac just wouldn't leave it be.

Jenny looked at Wolf, her eyes widening. "Wow, are you, like, in the Army or something?"

Wolf shifted what was left of the steak to his cheek and said through clenched teeth, "I used to be."

"Go on, show the little gal your tattoo." Mac tapped Wolf's left forearm. "Prettiest pair of jump wings you ever seen."

"Jump wings?" she asked. "What's that?"

Wolf flushed as Mac said, "Airborne. He used to jump outta airplanes."

"Wow, were you, like, in the SEALs or something?" She was obviously awestruck.

Wolf started to set her straight, but McNamara cut him off. "The SEALs are Navy. He was Army, but he was just what you call a Ranger. I was a Green Beret. Course, in the military, we say Special Forces."

Just a Ranger, Wolf thought. He was about to give Mac shit, then realized he wasn't a Ranger anymore. He was just a guy who used to be one, long ago and far away.

"Were you two in the war?" Jenny asked.

"Hell, yes," McNamara said. "A couple of 'em, in fact." He leaned forward and rolled up his sleeve, showing her a heart with a dagger through it under which was lettered, *DEATH BEFORE DISHONOR* on his beefy forearm. "I got plenty more of 'em, too. Maybe you'd like to see 'em sometime. Of course, some of them are in embarrassing places, so we'll have to wait till you're a little bit older."

The girl bit her lip as the hint of a blush crept up her neck.

"That apple pie sounds real nice, Miss," Wolf said.

She looked at him with a nervous smile and said she'd be right back.

He noticed McNamara licking his lips and watching her as she walked away.

"Hey," Wolf said. "Relax. She looks like she just got her braces taken off."

McNamara winked and leaned forward. "Yeah, well, I'm just trying to get you set up for number two on that list."

"What list?"

McNamara held up his hand and began ticking off his fingers, "Get a good meal, get laid, get drunk, get in a fight..."

"I already had my fight for today. Some asshole tried to shank me this morning."

Twin spaces formed between McNamara's eyebrows. "What? Who was it?"

Wolf shrugged. "Some big white guy."

"Anything come of it?"

"The guy's gonna have trouble eating solid food for a couple of months."

McNamara smirked, then his face turned serious again. "I'm surprised they let you out after that."

Wolf savored more of the coffee. It tasted much better than it had this morning behind the walls. "My cellmate took the blame for me."

"You and this guy been getting into it or something?"

"Not hardly. Never locked horns with him before."

"Then why'd he go after you?"

"Probably heard I was getting out and wanted to score some points with his Aryan buddies by shanking a guy that's half-Indian." Wolf set down his coffee cup. "Don't need a lot of reasons in that place."

"Just the same, I'll see what I can find out about it," McNamara said. "I still got some connections, you know."

"Why bother? It's behind me now, and I'd like to keep it in my rearview mirror." Wolf shoved another piece of steak into his mouth and was about to reply that he wanted to be in charge of his own list when he noticed a subtle change in his friend's expression. McNamara had insisted on sitting so his back wasn't facing the door, taking the seat Wolf wanted. "What's up?"

Mac's mouth tightened. "Trouble, maybe, or at least two guys looking like they're spoiling for it."

Wolf glanced over his shoulder and saw two bikers strolling by the front register, ignoring the Please Wait to be Seated sign. Big, bearded guys with weightlifters' bare arms and lots of tattoos. They wore filthy Levi jackets with the sleeves hacked off and a plethora of patches and insignias of motorcycle wheels with wings. As Jenny walked past them, they both swiveled around to ogle her, and Wolf saw *AMERICAN BREED* spelled out in white and black letters across their broad backs. One of them let out a low whistle.

The bigger of the two said, "I know what *I* want to eat."

The other guy, stockier and with an impressive set of triceps, punctuated his partner's comment with a growling laugh. "I'll be sure to leave you sloppy seconds, Coyle."

Coyle laughed, and the two of them plopped down in a booth a couple of spaces away from Wolf and McNamara, next to a family composed of a man, his wife, and two teenage girls, who looked like twins.

The one named Coyle leered at them across the way, his lips curling into a feral sneer.

"What the fuck you looking at?" he asked. "Ain't you never seen the American Breed before?"

Biker number two chimed in, "No, but I'll bet his

daughters have." He laughed. "Or at least they will pretty fucking quick."

"I wonder what charm school they graduated from?" Wolf asked as he cut another piece of steak and placed it in his mouth.

"Yeah," McNamara said. He squinted and got a serious look on his face. "Hey, I got to ask you, one troop to another, what the hell really happened over there? In Iraq."

Wolf shook his head, said nothing.

"Come on," McNamara urged. "It's just you and me sitting here."

Wolf shrugged, then set down his knife and fork. "Mac, I'm not lying when I tell you there's a part of it I just can't remember, no matter how hard I try."

McNamara's face twitched.

"It's the truth," Wolf said. "I really can't. The doc said it was due to the severe bash I got to the head. Erased the memory. It's like a blank spot. I can remember every-thing up to a certain point, and then everything after that, but I lost those crucial ten minutes. Didn't do me any good saying that at court-martial, but it's the truth."

"Yeah, well, I guess I should tell you I've had a lawyer looking into things for you."

"What?"

The two bikers made another loud, off-color comment.

McNamara pursed his lips, looked around, nodded, and stood up. "You know, I got to check on something. Be right back."

"Hey, wait. What do you mean, a lawyer?"

McNamara didn't answer. Wolf shifted in his seat and watched as his mentor got up, put his cowboy hat on his head, and sauntered down the aisle past the two lowlife bikers and the family trying to finish what had previously been a pleasant meal.

The father motioned for the waitress to come over. When Jenny got there, the man said, "We'd like to move to a different table, please."

"Hey, sweet cakes," the biker named Coyle said. "Which one of you three wants to sit on my face?" His tongue lolled out of his mouth, and he gave it an exaggerated wiggle.

Jenny turned and started to say something, but Coyle reached out and grabbed her around the waist, pulling her onto his legs. "In the meantime, how about a little lap dance to warm things up, baby?"

"Let me go!" she screamed. A middle-aged woman, evidently the manager, came from behind the register and threatened to call the police.

"Go fuck yourself, bitch,' the other biker said. "You touch that phone, and the Breed will be on your ass quicker than you can say 'blow job.'"

"Hey, Remmy," Coyle said, his hands all over Jenny's breasts, "I kind of like the sound of that."

Jenny screamed again.

Wolf looked around for McNamara but didn't see him.

He must still be outside, Wolf thought. *Just when I need him.*

Wolf stood, wiped his mouth with the paper napkin, and strolled over to the booth with the bikers. He stood looking down at them. They both had cruel eyes and expressions that looked like they were itching for a taste of violence.

"Why don't you let her go and get out of here?" Wolf said, keeping his voice even and calm.

"You talking to me?" Coyle asked. He squeezed

Jenny's breasts again. "Remmy, you think he's talking to me?"

The other biker laughed. "Shit, you got me. Mumbles some, don't he?"

"Get outta here, boy," Coyle said, staring up at Wolf. "Before I really mess you up."

"Leave the girl alone," Wolf said.

"You talking to me?" Coyle continued to fondle Jenny and laughed. "Hey, Remmy, you think this shitbird's talking to me?"

Wolf's eyes darted to the second biker, but he stayed out of grabbing range.

"I told you to get outta here," Coyle said. "You shit-for-brains faggot."

Wolf saw he was missing a few of his front teeth. He wasn't surprised.

Remmy laughed again.

Jenny squealed in distress.

Wolf looked down at Remmy. "Anybody ever tell you that your laugh sounds like a horse trying to pass a peach pit?"

"Say what?" Remmy's bulky frame shifted as he started to move out of the booth.

Wolf pivoted and smashed the heel of his left hand into the biker's nose. His head jerked backward, and Wolf grabbed a handful of the long, stringy hair, pivoting so he could slam the man's face on the tabletop.

Coyle pushed Jenny off his lap and lurched out of the confines of the booth. Wolf stepped back, waiting for the girl to get clear as the big biker moved forward.

"I'm gonna rip your head off and shit down your neck," Coyle growled.

Wolf's right foot shot out in a snap-kick that collided with Coyle's left knee. He stumbled forward, and Wolf smashed a left hook into his outstretched jaw. It was a perfect punch, and Coyle collapsed in a heap on the floor.

Remmy, his nose a crimson faucet, reared upward, slashing a buck knife he'd pulled from his belt at Wolf.

"I'm gonna cut your fucking balls off and feed 'em to ya," he yelled.

Wolf stepped back and avoided the man's arcing swing. Remmy swung his arm back as he rushed forward with the assurance of a man who'd brought a knife to a fistfight. This time Wolf timed the lunge and grabbed Remmy's knife arm with both hands, pivoting and using the heavyset biker's momentum to shove him forward, then back, twisting the arm with the motion. Wolf bore down on the man's wrist, forcing the hand back, and the knife clattered on the floor. As Remmy's eyes followed the lost weapon, Wolf brought a knee into his groin, then repeated the motion several more times, still maintaining his grip on the arm. He let go and Remmy sagged to his knees, at which time Wolf delivered a one-two combination of punches that twisted Remmy's face first one way, then the other.

As the second biker fell forward, Wolf turned and helped Jenny to her feet.

"You all right?"

"I'm okay," she said breathlessly. "Thanks to you."

"Great job," the man with his family added. He turned to the older woman, who was still frozen in place by the register. "Are you going to call the police, or what?"

Her head wiggled a nod and she started for the phone, but McNamara was walking back inside, holding up his cell phone.

"Don't trouble yourself, honey," he said. "I got that covered. Just wanted to step outside so I could get better reception, is all." He looked at the two fallen bikers, then at Wolf with a nod of approval. "Not bad. Not bad at all."

Wolf grinned. "You mean for *just* being a Ranger?"

"Aw, hell, I was just trying to help you out."

"Oh, yeah? How do you figure that?"

"I figured that little gal would feel sorry for you, and you'd get lucky." McNamara grinned back as he took out two pairs of plastic handcuffs. "Help me get these two trussed up, partner. I think these boys are worth some money."

"Money?"

McNamara stooped and flipped Coyle onto his belly, then looped the first set of cuffs over the man's wrists. "Do that one while I check something." He tossed the second set of cuffs to Wolf, who rolled Remmy over and twisted his arms behind him. Due to the guy's blocky physique, he had to pull and maneuver a bit. The semi-conscious Remmy groaned in pain, which didn't bother Wolf. In fact, it sounded like sweet music to his ears.

McNamara, now on his cell phone, was sorting through Coyle's wallet. "Yeah, his name's Coyle Weiner." He read off the date of birth and driver's license number. McNamara snapped his fingers at Wolf. "Gimme the other one's wallet, will ya?"

Wolf patted Remmy down and found two wallets. The one with the Harley Davidson wings obviously belonged to the biker. The other one had the identification and credit cards of a woman named Marcia Livingston. Wolf handed them to McNamara, who went through them, keeping one and dropping the other into the biker's vest.

"Probably stolen. The cops will probably want to take a look at that one." McNamara smiled. "Unless he's really a Marcia. Anybody want to check?"

"No, thanks," Wolf said.

McNamara took out Remmy's driver's license and read the information into his cell. After about fifteen seconds, he nodded. "Okay, brother, we'll be turning them over to the county police as soon as they arrive."

He hung up and smiled.

"You want to tell me what the hell's going on?" Wolf asked.

McNamara tucked the wallets back into the bikers' respective pockets and stood up. "Both these jokers got outstanding warrants. I figured as much when I seen 'em stroll in. Bikers are usually a good bet."

"A good bet?"

"I just talked to a local bail bondsman and told him I had them both in custody and that we'd be turning them over to the county cops." He paused and smiled. "All we have to do now is follow them to the lock-up and get verification so we can pick up our fee from the bail bond place."

"Bail bond place?"

"Yep," McNamara said, turning to Jenny, who was still wide-eyed and watching them. "Honey, we need to settle up right away. And I think my friend here will take that apple pie a la mode to go."

"Mac," Wolf said.

McNamara shushed him with a wave and smiled. "Don't worry none about the check. This one's on me."

"Thanks, but I'm still not sure what the hell's going on."

McNamara squinted and gave Wolf a sideways glance. "Ain't you figured that out yet? I'm what they call a multi-state bail enforcement agent, otherwise known as a bounty hunter."

Wolf was letting that settle in when McNamara

added with a laugh, "By the way, I was planning on broaching this subject later, but circumstances have brought things to a head a bit quicker than I planned."

"Broaching what?"

McNamara smiled. "How'd you like to go into business with me as a full-fledged partner? Unless you got a better offer going."

* * *

"Taylor versus Taintor, 1872," McNamara said, making chopping gestures with his hand. His eyes moved periodically to the Plexiglas window, where the girl behind the glass was processing their paperwork. "It established the right of recovery of an accused who's skipped out on bond. Don't you ever watch that TV show with Reno Garth?"

"Who the hell's that?" Wolf asked.

McNamara shook his head with a grin. "Never mind. Steve McQueen made a movie about bounty hunting, too. *The Hunter*. His last one, in fact. You remember Steve McQueen, don't you?"

"Only from the retro-TV cable show."

McNamara snorted. "Don't be sacrilegious. Anyway, all you need to do is come work with me as my partner. I'll get you set up with all the courses you need, community college and mail order stuff. Piece of cake. With your background, you'll be a natural."

"Explain to me again how this works."

McNamara took a deep breath. "When a shitbird like our buddy Coyle is arrested, he's eligible to be released on bond. That's court talk for money. He can walk as long as he guarantees that he'll be back in court to answer the charges. Because..." McNamara raised his eyebrows, "our great Constitution states that the son of a bitch is considered innocent until he's proved guilty."

"Believe me, I know all about that," Wolf said.

"I'm sure you do, but let me finish the civics lesson. Now, in all fifty states, excepting Kentucky, Illinois, and Oregon, you have what they call bail bondsmen. They're certified through the courts to guarantee the bond set in the case. They carry an insurance indemnification that allows them to sign an agreement stating that if somebody like good old Coyle misses his court date, they'll pay the court the full amount of the bond. In this case, fifty thousand dollars. Follow me?"

Wolf nodded.

"Good," McNamara said. "Now, because Coyle and his moron partner, Remmy, both blew off their scheduled court appearances, the judge issued warrants, and the bail bondsman is on the hook to pay out the bond or..."

"Go looking for them."

"Exactly. But seeing as how the vast majority of his clients are less than reputable individuals, he contacts a bail enforcement agent like me. It's my job to track down these assholes and bring them in. If I can do that within thirty days, the bail bondsman is off the hook for the full amount of the bail."

"And how does the bondsman make anything out of this?"

"The arrestee puts up some kind of collateral." McNamara jerked his thumb toward the door. "In this case, he's got the titles for their Harleys. He's sending a tow truck for them as we speak."

"Poetic justice."

"So, everybody's happy. The bail bondsman's saving money and keeping his insurance premiums down, and the two scumbags are in the hoosegow. He then pays me a recovery fee, usually ten percent of the bond amount, plus expenses in certain instances, for tracking them down."

"I'd hardly call what we did tracking them down."

"It's all in how you look at it. We saw an opportunity, and we acted on it."

"So, you're based here in Kansas?"

McNamara shook his head. "I'm based in Phoenix, Arizona, but I'll operate in all fifty states if need be, and then some." He leaned close and whispered, "Been south of the border down Mexico way a time or two."

"You have arrest authority in Mexico?"

McNamara smiled and nodded. "Sure. You just have to make sure not to get caught."

"Or?"

"Or you could end up on the bad side of a Mexicana jail, and them places make the worst of ours look like Disneyland North."

"You carry a weapon on these missions?"

"A Glock 17." McNamara patted his side. "Wouldn't leave home without it. Got me a concealed carry permit."

"Isn't that only good for Arizona?"

McNamara smirked and brought his finger to his lips. "Shh, don't tell nobody."

"So, you could've pulled it back there when that biker pulled the knife on me?"

"Coulda, woulda, shoulda. The story of my life." McNamara grinned. "But I was watching through the window. I was ready to nail him if things got bad, believe me, but I had to see for myself."

"See what?"

"If you could still handle yourself. I had to make an assessment."

"An assessment?"

"Yep." McNamara looked at him and raised an eyebrow. "So, how about it?"

"How about what?"

"How about going into business with me?"

Wolf's gaze went to the floor as he shook his head. "Mac, I appreciate the offer, but..."

"No buts about it. You're a natural. Look how easy you took out those two shitheads."

"That was different."

"Different, my ass. Like I said, with your background—"

"Background?" Wolf shook his head. "I've got a DD and a prison record."

McNamara snorted. "You got a helluva lot more than that. You won the Silver Star, for Christ's sake. And the Purple Heart and the DSM. They don't give them to just anybody."

Wolf shook his head. "I lost all that when I went into Leavenworth, remember?"

McNamara snorted. "Bullshit. You don't lose who you are or what you done, no matter what the damn record might be now. It don't matter what those dickless pencil-pushing assholes say."

It was Wolf's turn to smirk. "Tell that to the Department of the Army."

"I don't have to tell them shit. No matter what their fucking records say, it can't take away what you have in here." His fist thumped on his chest. "It don't change what you did. Or who you are."

Wolf pursed his lips as he remembered how they'd used razor blades to slice the chevrons off the sleeves of his uniform while he stood at attention. Slick sleeves, stripped of his decorations. Was that who he was now?

"You know I'm right, don't you?" McNamara said. "It don't change nothing. Nothing that really means something, anyway."

Wolf stared down at the dirty tiles on the floor, thinking about an old schoolboy riddle about a person being more than the sum of his parts. Where did the intangibles like truth and honor fit into the equation? What really defined who you were? He thought about them pulling the three rows of ribbons off the front of his blouse and setting them on the table next to his severed chevrons. Slick sleeves, no medals.

The girl behind the Plexiglas pressed a button that amplified her voice. "Your booking slips are ready, sir."

McNamara stood up and went to the window. When he turned around, he held the papers out toward Wolf. "All that's left now is for us to pass Go and collect our money. We'll split it fifty-fifty." He looked askance at Wolf. "That is, if you're in."

Wolf smiled at his old mentor. "Mac, looks like you've got yourself a new partner."

McNamara's laugh did little to reassure Wolf. Deep down, he wondered if he could really pick up the pieces and begin again after all that had happened. He knew he'd have to prove himself in this new arena, but if he did...*once* he did, he'd get back his self-respect.

And he pitied anybody who ever tried to take it away from him again.

* * *

"Why Phoenix?" Wolf asked, stretching in the passenger seat. They were back on the freeway, heading west with money in their pockets. Wolf felt better than he had in a long time.

"Easy," McNamara said. "It's within a road trip of two of my biggest markets, Vegas and LA. And the weather's always nice enough that I can get a flight out to New York or New Jersey or Miami if I need to."

"You go all those places on skip traces?"

McNamara laughed. "One of the perks to being the best in the business. They need someone bad enough, they send me on an expense-paid trip to someplace nice."

"What if they send you to Detroit or Gary, Indiana?"

"Yeah, sometimes to some not-so-nice places, too." He laughed. "But hell, way back in the day, I joined the Army to see the world, didn't I? Now I'm doing this to see the good old US of A."

Wolf smiled. "So, how'd you get on to those two jokers back there?"

"Tricks of the trade," McNamara said. He pointed at the Thermos in the cupholder between them. "Pour me another coffee, will you?"

Wolf unscrewed the cap. "Want me to drive for a while?"

"No way. Not till you get a license. You ain't covered by that overseas troop deployment loophole no more."

Wolf nodded as he handed over the steaming cup. There was a lot he had to catch up on. "What about those two biker assholes?"

McNamara sipped the hot brew and let out a satisfied "Ahhhh." He took another quick sip. "Like I told you, after you been doing this a while, you get a knack for knowing who's hot and who's not, just like walking into a crowded village. Bikers can usually be counted on for outstanding warrants. Part of their lifestyle. I sized them up, then went outside and ran their license plates. Came back with the warrants attached."

"Ran their plates? How?"

"Kasey did that." McNamara drank some more coffee. "She's got computer tie-ins to a bunch of information banks in different states. My little gal's a wizard with that computer. She's my ground support."

"Kasey?"

"Yep. She's in Phoenix." He set the cup on the dashboard and leaned to the left, then extracted his thick wallet out of his back pocket. After flipping open the laminated sections, he held it toward Wolf. A snapshot of a slender woman with angular features holding a baby. Her brownish-blonde hair was cut short around her face, looking almost like a helmet. The smile on her face looked forced.

"Pretty," Wolf said.

McNamara snapped the wallet shut. "Don't get no ideas. She's my daughter."

"Your daughter?"

"Yeah. Once upon a time, I had a life too, you know."

"So, that's your grandbaby?"

McNamara nodded, and his grin grew wider. "Great little guy named Chad. Gonna be a good soldier someday."

"I take it she's married?"

McNamara frowned. "The less said about her baby's daddy, the better. He's military. They're separated, getting a divorce." He leaned over and began working the wallet back into his pocket.

Wolf figured it was a good time to change the subject. He adjusted the seat back and asked, "You're sure you don't want me to drive, huh?"

McNamara shook his head.

"Okay," Wolf said, closing his eyes. "I think I'll get some shut-eye."

"There's more good news."

Wolf looked over and saw McNamara pointing at a sign that said *Welcome to Colorado*.

"We ain't in Kansas anymore, Toto," McNamara said. "We can stop and buy some marijuana in this state if you want."

"No, thanks," Wolf said. "Let's head south and get into New Mexico as fast as possible."

"Damn straight. Glad you said that."

Wolf chuckled and shut his eyes again.

They were not in Kansas anymore.

CHAPTER 3

THREE MONTHS LATER
THE LAW OFFICES OF FALLOTTI AND ABRAHAM
NEW YORK CITY, THE BOROUGH OF
MANHATTAN

Lance Eagan sat in the office's outer waiting area and evaluated the shape of the secretary's breasts, which were visible through the fabric of her white blouse. He wondered what she'd look like naked. She was a bit on the dark side, obviously mixed race, reminding him of Halle Berry. Her caramel-colored skin brought back memories of his missions in Central and South America. Lots of good times down there, all those caramel-colored girls waiting in line, eager to please him.

But this bitch had hardly looked at him twice.

Probably a dyke, he thought.

He glanced at his watch and ran his tongue over his teeth. Leave it to the rich prick of a lawyer to keep him waiting, like his time was so much more valuable than everyone else's. He decided to push the envelope a bit and stood up. The woman's dark eyes glanced toward him.

Eagan shot her one of his don't-fuck-with-me looks.

She quickly looked away, which amused him, but he still felt uncomfortable. Having his damn collar buttoned for this long bothered him, as did the damn necktie. He hated wearing shit like that. It went against his honed survival instincts to wear a ready-made noose around his neck for some adversary to grab. But this wasn't the battlefield.

This was the civilian world, and there were certain protocols that had to be followed, especially with a rich asshole like Von Dien. Looking professional, or at least what passed for professional in this world, was part of it. He had to look and sound good when he explained away the latest glitch in the current plan, and it wasn't even his fault.

If only his former boss, that asshole Stu Novak, hadn't taken the easy way out by blowing his head off, leaving the rest of the Vipers without any financial parachutes. No reserve money. Nothing.

Eagan was determined to land on his feet. With a few more big scores like this one and a little luck, he'd be forming his own PMC in a few months. And this time, he'd be the one sitting in a comfortable office and sending other ex-grunts over to some foreign land to shed blood and get shot at.

It was a matter of building his credibility. Plus, he still had his Viper contacts. Yeah, he needed to explain the botched hit on that slippery asshole Wolf at Leavenworth that Novak's stooge had fucked up, but hell, it had been a last-minute play that Von Dien had insisted upon. The guy suddenly got a hair up his ass about eliminating all the "loose ends" from the Iraq mission four years ago, now that the second half of his precious Iraqi artifact had resurfaced. It fit with the old rich prick's supposed obsessive/compulsive nature, but why had he felt it was necessary at this juncture? Hell, that thing in Iraq was, like, ancient history now.

Eagan considered this and came up with his own conjecture. Back then, they'd only recovered half of that fucking "treasure," and the rich asshole had been drooling ever since. Now that the other half had finally surfaced, Von Dien didn't want to take the chance that somebody working on an appeal for Wolf's case might take a look at what happened in Iraq and somehow be able to connect the dots.

No loose ends, even one as remote as a half-Indian grunt they'd framed getting out of prison. Eagan knew the sorry fucker didn't have a pot to piss in. He'd probably go back to whatever reservation he'd crawled off of and take refuge in a bottle. Indians were good at that. He looked at the girl again and caught her stealing a glance at him, and that made him feel better.

Who knows? Maybe she digs the swing after all.

"Is it going to be much longer?" Eagan asked.

He didn't add that he could come back later since they both knew he wasn't going anywhere. He'd spent his life working for rich bastards who held all the cards —and the money. But just maybe, after this little caper, all that would change.

"Let me see, sir." The caramel-colored honey picked up the phone and spoke into the receiver in a voice too low for Eagan to hear. When she hung up, she smiled at him and said, "Mr. Fallotti says for you to go right in."

Eagan nodded his thanks and strode to the door, which was solid-looking wood with a carved pattern of ornate flourishes. A metal plaque in the center was adorned with the lawyer's name. This guy went first class. Eagan took note of the arabesque design, thinking he'd have a similar one put on his door once he was in the money.

Entering the room, he saw three men inside. Marco Fallotti was seated behind a large mahogany desk. His charcoal-gray suit matched the gray flecks in his black hair. Eagan estimated Fallotti was in his late fifties, intelligent-looking, orderly, and methodical. Each stack of paper was meticulously placed, so they formed three even stacks, equidistant from each other and all the same height.

Eagan knew the type—one of those order freaks with over-attention to detail. Not such a bad trait for a rich man's lawyer. He watched as Fallotti stood and smiled, coming around the desk to offer his hand. The guy was going soft around the middle. Eagan shook it, making sure he exerted just enough pressure to project the latent power in his grip.

"Mr. Eagan, we're glad to finally meet you in person," Fallotti said. "May I present Mr. Dexter Von Dien the Third." He motioned toward an enormous man seated in a leather chair in front of the desk. The guy looked like a scaled-down version of one of those Buddhas Eagan had seen in the Far East. A head the size of a basketball set on top of a body of fat. He looked even softer than the lawyer.

Richer, too, thought Eagan.

Still, he had to remember above all else that this soft, rich freak was the connection to more money than Eagan could ever dream about. Play his cards right, and he'd be one step closer to setting up Vipers II and running it from someplace warm and sunny. Preferably foreign, too, and without an extradition agreement with the US.

The third man, obviously a bodyguard, stood next to Von Dien. At least the guy had that formidable look about him, the kind you got from walking the walk and talking the talk. His upper body was sufficiently broad, but Eagan knew he could take him if push came to shove. Guarding a rich prick was sure to put a few burrs on the sharpest blade, and this son of a bitch probably had to wipe the rich man's ass after he took a shit.

At any rate, he was certainly no undercover cop or Customs agent. Plus, as careful as Von Dien had been about checking references, Eagan didn't figure the rich bastard would get caught up in a law enforcement sting, even as anxious as he was to get his hands on the treasures.

Fallotti adjusted his necktie. "Dexter, perhaps we should have Harland wait outside?" The bodyguard's head cocked downward, waiting for his master's voice.

Von Dien's massive upper body swelled as he inhaled a deep breath, then he nodded, dismissing his man with a minimal gesture of his fingers. Maybe the guy was more of a gofer than a bodyguard. What kind of name was Harland for a tough guy? Whatever he was, he moved to the door and closed it quietly behind him.

"Please, Mr. Eagan, sit down." Fallotti indicated a chair opposite them. Out of the corner of his eye, Eagan caught the guy watching him, but it was like a fat meat merchant eyeing a tiger through the bars of a bamboo cage.

Good, he thought. *There's a bit of fear there.*

He looked at the lawyer, who had a fatuous smile plastered on his face. "Dex, this is Lance Eagan, the guy who did that work for you a few years ago in Iraq.

Remember we used Stu Novak's PMC, the Vipers?" He turned to Eagan. "Lance was Novak's, right-hand man."

Eagan nodded.

The Buddha made no acknowledgment.

Eagan kept his expression neutral.

They both know that I could break them in half if I wanted, he thought.

He was still standing, so he towered over them, knowing his size was intimidating to potential employers as well as potential adversaries. He had to be careful not to overplay his hand if he wanted to snare this well-paying gig. The elephant in the room was the ill-conceived and failed attempt to tie up that loose end at Leavenworth, but Eagan could hardly be blamed for that. It hadn't been his op.

"Sit down, Lance," the lawyer said.

Eagan kept his expression neutral and extended his hand toward the still motionless fat man. The slug made no move to accept it.

"Ah, Mr. Von Dien prefers to avoid contact with people in a non-clinical setting," Fallotti added.

A non-clinical setting? Afraid of germs? Eagan cocked a grin as he let his arm fall to his side. *Or just too good to touch the hired help?*

"Please, sit down," Fallotti said. "We have a lot to discuss."

"I'm sure we do," Eagan said, lowering himself into the chair. *Like how I'm gonna end up rich beyond my wildest dreams.*

"By the way," Fallotti said, "we were sorry to hear about Stu. He was one hell of a good guy. And one helluva a patriot."

Eagan nodded again, thinking, *I guess that's why he blew his brains out just before the G was going to indict him.*

Fallotti's smile seemed fixed. "I believe you also served in Iraq with one of my firm's junior partners," he continued, the smile still stretching his lips. "Lieutenant Jack Cummins."

Eagan nodded. He remembered Cummins as a grade-A fuck-up: fat, cowardly, basically incompetent.

"We acquired Jack a few years ago from the public defender's office shortly before he was reactivated by the military," Fallotti said. "When he returned from his tour of duty, we welcomed him back with open arms."

Some tour, thought Eagan. Military intel officer, setting up deals with a bunch of contractors and no doubt pocketing the extras. Eagan recalled how back in Iraq, Cummins had blown chunks after the one raghead's throat had been slit. Right before the shit had hit the fan.

"Jack was, for lack of a better term, our liaison with Stu," Fallotti said. "He was instrumental in setting up our little operations over there. As I'm sure you know, the Vipers' end of it went fairly well. But the matter got bogged down later on down the line."

Eagan nodded fractionally. The sooner this prick cut to the chase and laid it out, the better.

"We want Jack to work exclusively with you on this since you two have worked together before, and he knows all the principals." Fallotti tilted his head back and looked down his long nose at Eagan. "This is a rather delicate matter, and there are certain precautions that must be taken."

"Fine. I have no problem with that."

"So," Fallotti asked, his practiced lawyer's grin looking as unctuous as ever, "do you know why we invited you here?"

Pouring on the charm for the hired mercenary. Of

course, he fucking knew. He'd suddenly been cast as the only ex-Viper they could deal with, as distasteful as it probably was for them, after Novak blew his brains out. Their boy Jack wasn't up to doing the deed. Eagan knew they needed him to make it work, and that would make this little transaction all the more sweet and lucrative for him. Eagan mulled over what to say, but he'd never liked beating around the bush, even when discussing something just the other side of legal. Since Fallotti was Von Dien's lawyer, everything said here would be confidential. Attorney-client privilege for the rich man. It provided Von Dien with sufficient insulation. The man was nothing if not careful. Greedy, but careful. Still, he'd heard through the grapevine how connected Von Dien was.

Eagan cleared his throat. "When I was in Iraq with Vipers, as you know, the military was working with the international task force, trying to recover more of the stolen antiquities from the National Museum."

There was a subtle gleam in Von Dien's eyes. The fat man had turned into a venal Buddha. Just talking about the fucking stuff was probably giving him what passed for a hard-on for him. But the gleam set off alarm bells in Eagan's gut. He smiled. "Many of the most valuable artifacts are still missing."

Fallotti nodded. "Exactly."

Eagan paused to scratch his chin. Better to play it close to his vest. "When Stu approached me about this latest mission, he had very sketchy information. I believe you had several other individuals in the loop?"

Fallotti and Von Dien exchanged glances.

"Well," the lawyer said, his voice sounding like he was beginning a closing argument, "back before the war, there were certain items that had been paid for to

Saddam's government when he was in charge, of course, and were legitimately the property of Mr. Von Dien."

The horse's ass they were, Eagan thought, but he nodded in agreement.

"So," Fallotti continued, "after the regime change in the country and the unfortunate looting of the National Museum, retrieving his property became somewhat problematic when pursued through regular international business channels. Thus, we had to rely on certain individuals whom we subsequently discovered to be..." He paused and traced his thumb and index finger over the brackets on each side of his mouth. "Shall we say, less than reputable"

All this talk just to get him to get on board for something that was a little less than legal. Eagan kept his grin minimal. "The black market."

Fallotti cleared his throat. "Yes, but may I remind you that unlike here, the black market is considered a legitimate business entity in many Third World countries."

"Sir," Eagan said, figuring they'd go for the old enlisted man show of respect, "let's cut to the chase. I was the one that ramrodded the original mission in Iraq a couple of years ago, remember? If you need someone to help you recover this new property, I'm your man."

Fallotti and Von Dien exchanged glances again. Buddha's eyes narrowed. Eagan almost didn't catch the fractional nod.

"Good, good, Mr. Eagan," Fallotti said, his smile wide now. "I must say, I like a man who doesn't beat around the bush."

"Why don't you bring me up to speed, then?"

"As you may or may not know," Fallotti said, "I recently represented a client named Thomas Accondras."

He paused as if waiting to see if Eagan recognized the name.

Eagan kept his expression as flat as a glass of warm beer. Novak had given him some of the details, but they didn't need to know how much he knew.

Fallotti cleared his throat again. "Mr. Accondras was a graduate student who'd been studying Arabic and Middle Eastern. He's half-Saudi and half-Canadian." The lawyer's eyebrows rose. "And he was also an associate of Stu's."

Eagan had figured as much. Stu had mentioned he had a sure-fire way to get the stuff smuggled out of the country through a conduit in Jordan.

"Mr. Accondras was in the Middle East. Amman, to be exact," the lawyer continued. "Acting on behalf of Mr. Von Dien to recover his missing property." He paused and took a deep breath, the corners of his mouth turning downward. "Unfortunately, he was arrested as he tried to enter this country."

"What was he charged with?" Eagan asked.

"Mr. Accondras apparently had an outstanding warrant from a previous misunderstanding that happened some months ago in Manhattan. The matter was believed to have been settled, but, much to our chagrin, the case had never been properly resolved."

"What kind of case?" Eagan asked.

Fallotti shot a quick look at the Buddha, then back to Eagan. "Aggravated Criminal Sexual Exploitation of a Minor, but he assured us of his innocence."

A short-eyes, Eagan thought. These pricks don't give a shit who they deal with as long as the job gets done.

"He was arrested as he tried to enter this country from Canada," Fallotti said, "I was immediately notified and managed to get him released on bond. We were unaware of it at the time, but Mr. Accondras had the item shipped to himself when he was in Toronto."

"A priceless artifact in the hands of postal morons," Von Dien chimed in. "*Canadian* postal morons."

Eagan said nothing, silently appreciating this guy Accondras for his foresight and temerity. If the jerk hadn't taken the proper precautions, these two assholes would probably have left him hanging him out to dry as soon as they got their hands on the goods.

"One of our main concerns in using him," Fallotti said, "was to have a layer of insulation between him, the artifact, and Mr. Von Dien."

Eagan nodded. He recalled hearing that the rich man had been called on the carpet by some governmental watchdog group several years ago for being involved in purchasing stolen Middle Eastern artifacts. His lawyers had gotten him out of it with a fine and a slap on the wrist. This guy Accondras was set up to be the fall guy this time if things went wrong.

"Needless to say," Fallotti continued, "this entire matter had to be handled with the utmost discretion. I secured the services of a reputable bail bondsman, who guaranteed the million-dollar bond the judge assigned."

"A bail bondsman?" he asked.

Fallotti compressed his lips, then said, "As I mentioned, it was essential to keep a layer of insulation between Accondras and us."

By "us," Eagan knew he meant the rich prick.

"And that's where things started to go a bit off-course," Fallotti said. "Instead of surrendering the artifact to us as he'd promised, Mr. Accondras disappeared."

Smart move, Eagan thought. He obviously wanted to up the ante now that his back was against the wall.

"He's missed his first court date," Fallotti said. "I

managed to get a two-month continuance regarding the extradition hearing, but he's no longer in the United States. The court date's coming up in about ten days."

Eagan emitted a low whistle. "A hundred grand up in smoke. I'll bet the bail bondsman isn't too happy about that."

Von Dien made a hissing sound of disgust. "That idiot's happiness is inconsequential."

Fallotti jumped in, as eager to keep the fat Buddha calm as if he were balancing an egg on the tip of a razor blade. "That's not really an issue. We've already made arrangements to cover his losses. And we actually know where Accondras is."

"The pathetic cretin is trying to renegotiate our deal," Von Dien said. His eyes took on a new hardness.

The bagman turneth. Eagan kept his expression neutral.

"Believe me," the fat Buddha said, "I don't take kindly to those who choose to cross me, Mr. Eagan."

Was that supposed to be a warning? Eagan gave him no reply, not even a fractional nod.

Never let them see you sweat, he thought. Never show weakness, especially to some rich fat cat who thinks he could buy and sell you like a piece of beef.

"You said you know where he's at?" Eagan asked.

"Yes," Fallotti said. "We have located him in—"

"Mex-i-co," Von Dien chimed in, drawing out the three syllables like he was reciting a distasteful word.

"His parents, or rather his mother and stepfather, own beachfront property in a resort area down there," Fallotti said. "It caters to rich foreigners and is very well-protected. Armed guards patrol the area and the beachfront."

"Protection from the filthy Mexican riffraff," Von

Dien said. "At least it gives me some hope that the artifact is there and safe."

"So, you think he has it there?" Eagan asked.

"We do, but we're not exactly sure where he's keeping it. He doesn't get on that well with his stepfather, so we're not sure if he'd keep it on the premises."

"Maybe a safe deposit box in a bank?" Eagan asked.

Fallotti shrugged. "Again, we're not sure. After his brush with the authorities up here, he's purportedly a bit paranoid."

"And he's willing to make a deal?"

"He's been fairly open about contacting us," Fallotti said. "To renegotiate things, as he put it."

The lawyer quickly glanced at Von Dien, whose expression hadn't changed from a look of total disgust.

"We sent a private detective down there to keep tabs on him," Fallotti said. "Accondras is there, but he's keeping the whereabouts of the artifact a secret. Our man hasn't been able to locate it."

"You should have never trusted that greasy little son of a bitch in the first place," Von Dien said. His words were laced with irritation.

"So you need someone to grab him," Eagan said. "And find out where he's stashed the item."

"Exactly," Fallotti said. "And persuade him to relinquish it."

Working everything through a third party, Eagan thought. Someone to take the fall should anything go wrong.

Von Dien emitted a hissing breath. "Where else could it be? It's his only insurance."

Eagan nodded, keeping his expression totally neutral.

That added a new element to the mix. Dealing with the

policía south of the border could be tricky. They could be bought, but they also didn't play fair, especially if they got wind that there was a lot of money involved. He'd have to add some layers of insulation of his own to the mix.

"What about the Mexican authorities?" Eagan asked. "Are they going to be involved in any way?"

Von Dien made the hissing sound again. "Do you think I want to risk having such a valuable piece fall into the hands of some grubby, filthy Mexicans? They're so corrupt down there, they'd merely turn around and demand their own payoff. I trust them as far as I can smell them."

"Just what is this artifact that you're talking about?" Eagan asked.

The two of them exchanged glances, then Von Dien's head made the slightest of movements.

"It's half of a piece called the Lion and the Lioness Attacking the Nubian," Fallotti said.

Eagan raised an eyebrow. "The second part of the item we removed from Iraq a few years ago?"

Fallotti nodded. "The Lion. The most valuable part."

"As I recall," Eagan said, "it wasn't that large."

"Two matching hand-carved ivory plaques inlaid with gold, jewels, and mother of pearl," the fat man said, his voice sounding almost breathless, like a teenager describing his first copped feel. "Not that large, but priceless to the right buyer."

Fallotti licked his lips. "A few days ago, Accondras contacted my firm, saying he wanted to negotiate a new deal."

"For an exorbitant amount that I wouldn't mind paying," Von Dien said, breaking in. "But I am not naïve enough to believe that if in fact he does still possess the item, he will make good on his promise to return it to me."

Return it to me? Eagan almost chuckled. As if the fucking thing belonged to this rich prick in the first place.

"We'd been in contact with Stu Novak on a related matter a few months ago," Fallotti said.

The botched hit on Wolf at Leavenworth, no doubt, Eagan thought. Stu had mentioned that it had been a last-minute clusterfuck of a request.

"And when the news of Mr. Accondras' possible whereabouts came to light last week, we attempted to contact him again. That's when we heard the unfortunate news of his death."

"And you were told that I was running the Vipers now," Eagan said, leaning forward. "So you want me to discreetly grab Accondras, find out where he'd got the artifact stashed, and get it back for you." He made it a statement rather than a question. "Anything else?"

The venal Buddha nodded. "Two things. First, there's the matter of verifying its authenticity."

"That shouldn't be a problem," Eagan said. "I know a guy. He used to be affiliated with the Iraqi National Museum of Art."

"An Iraqi?" Von Dien's lips curled downward as if he'd smelled something unpleasant. "Can he be trusted?"

Eagan nodded. "I've worked with him before. In fact, he's the one we used over there a few years ago to get the first half of the artifact."

The rich prick seemed to consider this. "And he is…" He let his voice trailed off.

"Available?" Eagan asked as if he could read the asshole's thoughts. "He's actually in this country now.

Stu brought him over, claiming political asylum. I got his number."

Fallotti nodded and flashed a slight smile.

"What's the name of this private detective you've got down there?" Eagan asked.

"Jason Zerbe. Shall I call him and advise him you're coming?"

"Hold off on that for the moment," Eagan said. "We need to set up some ground rules."

"Ground rules?" The lawyer's forehead furrowed.

"Yeah." Eagan paused for maximum effect, making sure he had their full attention. "I've worked south of the border before. You're absolutely right about the Mexican police being corrupt and basically worthless, so what we need is to put the stamp of legitimacy on this operation."

"Legitimacy?" Fallotti asked.

"Absolutely not," Von Dien said. "I thought I made it clear that I wanted this matter to be handled discreetly."

"It will be," Eagan said. "But I'm not going to take any of my guys down there to run a covert operation without a contingency plan in place. A plan we can run as a cover story should things go wrong."

Fallotti squinted. "I'm not following you."

"You said this Accondras skipped out on his bail, right?"

The attorney nodded.

"Then it's simple," Eagan said. "We'll use a subterfuge. Put me in contact with his bail bondsman, and we'll set things up to make it look like he sent a couple of skip tracers down there to pick up his errant client."

"I don't know," Fallotti said. "Sounds risky."

"As risky as Accondras' parents making a stink about some gringos coming down there and abducting him? Eventually, the shit's gonna hit the fan, pardon my

French, and it's all gonna get traced back up here. Is that what you want?"

Fallotti's eyes darted toward the rich prick. "He's got a point."

"He certainly does," Von Dien said, his obese face softening a bit. "Mr. Eagan, I commend you on your foresight. I like a man with foresight. Eliminates a lot of potential problems. But about these skip tracers, as you call them... Can they be trusted?"

"Leave that to me. Do we have a deal?" Eagan said. "If I agree to this, I run the show. And my services don't come cheap."

Von Dien sat in silence for several seconds.

Fallotti glanced at the fat Buddha. Eagan could almost see the avarice gleaming in the rich prick's eyes. Finally, Von Dien nodded at the lawyer. "Do it." Turning to Eagan, he added, "Whatever it takes. Just bring me that artifact."

"I will," Eagan assured him.

"One more thing." Von Dien's eyes shifted to Fallotti.

"Mr. Von Dien is understandably concerned about this not leading back to him," the lawyer said. "At some point down the road."

Eagan glanced at Von Dien and then Fallotti. "No loose ends?"

"Exactly," the lawyer said. "No loose ends."

CHAPTER 4

JUST OUTSIDE OF PHOENIX, ARIZONA
FIVE AM

Wolf worked his way up the winding path on the mountain, feeling the sweat pouring off him in the early morning heat. It was four miles to the top, then four miles back down. Going down was a little harder on the knees but easier overall than going up—if anything could be considered easy in the escalating temperature of the desert. Still, it was nothing compared to Iraq, the ultimate Sandbox.

In the three months or so since he'd been back, he hadn't done much besides run and work out and go to school. He'd done nothing in the way of bounty hunting after moving into a makeshift room above Mac's garage. It was small, but after spending close to four years in an eight by ten cell, it seemed luxurious. He had his own bed, a small kitchen, his own shower and toilet, and a separate entrance from the house.

All he needed now was someplace to go.

At Mac's insistence, he'd started to get his life back in order. He'd gotten his driver's license and a passport and enrolled in a couple of night courses, Introduction to Law Enforcement and English 101, at the community college. He didn't even mind taking the bus to get there. It was a reminder of his freedom. Sometimes Mac would suggest Kasey could give him a ride when she was going to her classes at the university, but Wolf usually declined. She wasn't a bad-looking girl, mid-to-late twenties with the slim, angular build of a natural athlete, but she hardly went out of her way to speak to Wolf. She seemed more than a little resentful that her father had brought him into their circle. Her snide comment the day they'd met still rang in his ears. "Well, it looks like Dad finally got the son he always wanted."

Nothing like making a guy feel welcome, especially when he was already feeling like a freeloader. But he knew she had a rough lot to plow: a single mom with a small kid and a worthless ex, not to mention having grown up with Mac as an absentee father due to his many deployments, something he'd repeatedly mentioned as one of his life's biggest regrets. She'd been a late blessing from his second marriage, another one that had ended badly, but despite that, Mac had said his relationship with his only child had improved dramatically in the last year. More importantly, her son Chad seemed to be holding up well under it all. Whenever Kasey wasn't studying or working on the computer, she was doting on her kid. She was something of an exercise fiend, too, getting up early to do a run or ride her bicycle. Wolf had offered to run with her early on, but she'd shut him down, saying she preferred to run alone.

"It's one of the few times I have to think," she'd said.

He'd gotten the hint.

Most nights she wasn't in class, she went out to dinner with Rodney, the lawyer who was handling her divorce. Wolf suspected the guy was handling a little more than just that.

But that doesn't concern me, Wolf thought, although he kind of pitied Rodney. Who'd want to be caught playing hide the salami with Big Jim McNamara's daughter?

Besides, Wolf had made up his mind that until he got himself squared away and was back on his feet, any thoughts of romance were out of the question. He *had* gone for coffee once with Consuela Ruiz, the pretty Mexican-American girl he'd met in his English class, but that was at Mac's urging after he had seen them talking outside the building a few days ago. Mac had approached him the next day and asked who that "pretty little gal was," and Wolf had told him.

"Ruiz, huh?" McNamara raised an eyebrow. "You know, I think you'd best ask her out for coffee after class next time."

"What, are you playing matchmaker now?"

"She sounds like a hot *tamale*." Mac's grin seemed to hold something more than mere wishful thinking on behalf of his friend and protégé. "Show some interest in her. Speak a little Spanish to her. You still know how to do that, right?"

"*Sí, mas o menos.*"

McNamara winked. "Well, do that, then. Ask about her family, where she lives, stuff like that. Girls like that."

This struck Wolf as odd. "Why? You thinking of asking her out after I do?"

McNamara flashed him a lascivious smile. "Not me. I'm all business."

That seemed like a strange reply to Wolf, but he dismissed it.

The coffee chat had gone well, and he'd thought about asking her out on a real date but had decided against it. He was still basically broke, living off the largess of McNamara and feeling guilty that Mac was treating him like family.

Plus, as far as going out with a girl, it had been a long time. Too long.

In some ways, he regretted that he hadn't taken Mac up on his offer to do a stopover at a "gentleman's club" outside Las Vegas, but a quick lap dance by some bored hooker wasn't what Wolf wanted. He was holding out for something more meaningful. Something real. Something special. Something he'd lost. But only when he felt the time was right.

It all added up to be another wall between him and the rest of the world. No matter which side he found himself on, he felt like an outsider.

No, "outsider" wasn't the right word. "Freeloader" was more like it.

Mac had picked him up from Leavenworth, fed him, clothed him, paid his tuition, and even offered to pay for a plane trip back to Lumberton to see his mother, which Wolf had declined. He wasn't ready to see her or go back home. Not until he had reestablished himself. Not until he felt redeemed, if he could ever feel that way. The guilt lingered in him, and he wished he could put it in a locked box in his mind and forget about it. But he couldn't. The only thing he'd been able to forget was the exact sequence of events during those crucial few lost minutes in Iraq, and that hadn't been intentional. If only he could remember them. Maybe they would provide an answer.

He wondered, too, about Mac's motivation. Why was he doing all this? What was in it for him? Did he really want Wolf as a partner in his bounty hunting business, or was he looking, as Kasey had said, for a surrogate son?

Wolf pushed the thoughts out of his mind as he rounded the curve and saw the white post signaling the four-mile mark. Almost to the top. His fingers traced the marker as he completed his circle and paused to take a drink from his water bottle before heading back down.

Just like making the halfway point in your deployment tour in the Sandbox, he thought. *It's all downhill from here.*

* * *

Wolf heard the light tap on the door as he was drying himself off after a shower. He figured it was Mac but slipped the towel around his waist in case Kasey was with him, then yelled, "It's open."

McNamara walked in with a grin and a laptop. "I hope you're not dropping your guard, leaving your door unlocked when you're taking a shower, then walking around half-naked and unprotected."

Wolf chuckled and tossed the towel on the sofa.

"Nothing to steal in here," he said. "And I figure if any unauthorized personnel violated the perimeter, you'd have them in your sights as soon as they come down the road from the highway."

McNamara smiled. "Depending on an old man like me to protect you?"

"You ain't that old." Wolf slipped on his underwear and t-shirt. "Besides, I'm depending on you for just about everything else, right? Also wondering exactly how I'm going to pay you back."

McNamara made a dismissive gesture and set the laptop on the small kitchen table. "You learning anything in them classes?"

"Yeah. In the classic literature section, we're studying about a guy named Sisyphus."

"What did he write?"

"He didn't have time to write," Wolf said with a grin. "He spent most of his time pushing a big rock up the side of a mountain, only to have it roll down the other side when he got to the top."

McNamara snorted. "Sounds like he musta been an Army lifer. Anyway, I got me an idea since you're almost finished with your first college course in the law."

"It was a short course." Wolf smirked as he pulled on his socks and pants. "And I'd hardly equate it with Harvard law school."

"You young college fuckers are all alike," McNamara said. "It's a good basic background for getting you established as a bail enforcement agent. Say, I forgot to ask you how your date went with that little hot *tamale?*"

"It wasn't much of a date. All we did was go out for coffee."

"You try speaking some Spanish to her? I heard those Latina chicks like that."

"I have to keep in practice, don't I?"

"You offer to see her home?"

"How could I do that? Give her a ride on the handlebars of my bicycle? I don't have a car, remember?"

"We start making some good pinches, we'll rectify that." McNamara winked. "Besides, if it's a matter of you achieving number two on that list, I'll let you drive the Escalade."

"Number two?"

"Getting laid," McNamara said. "Wouldn't want you to forget how it's done."

Wolf frowned. "I think I can remember."

McNamara grinned. "You give her a little goodbye kiss after the coffee?"

"No, I didn't." Wolf shook his head. "But you ought to know. I saw you driving by."

"You did?"

"Yeah, I figured you were you checking up on me."

McNamara compressed his lips and said nothing for several seconds, then, "Never mind. Let's go into Phoenix and go see Shemp. He finally got back to me after all these months."

The way he said "Shemp" made Wolf wonder how much Kasey's father approved of his daughter's choice of a beau.

"Rod?" Wolf asked. "Got back to you about what?"

"I contacted him a while ago, asking him to look into your case."

"My case? You did?"

McNamara nodded. "And wish you wouldn't call him 'Rod.' Remember, he's dating my daughter."

Wolf nodded. He wondered what news Shemp had and if it would be good or bad.

Bad, probably, Wolf thought.

But he was curious just the same. Maybe, just maybe…

"Now get rid of that damn t-shirt," McNamara said. "Put on one of those nice polo shirts I bought you." He fingered the collar of his sleeveless camouflage BDU blouse. "Ain't you never heard of the saying, 'The clothes making the man?' You never get a second chance to make a first impression."

"Just who am I supposed to impress?"

"You'll see."

As they went down the stairs into the garage, McNamara threw a quick punch at Wolf's old Army duffle, which he had hung from a cross-beam. He'd filled it with sand and now used it for his heavy bag work. The black paint they'd used at Leavenworth to disguise his name and serial number was almost all beaten off.

"You keeping in shape with all this stuff?" McNamara asked, glancing at the speed bag in the corner. He'd bought and erected it as a surprise after he'd seen Wolf working out.

Wolf pivoted and shot a quick hook-kick into the speedbag.

"With a little luck," McNamara said, "you'll be doing that to some prospective bounty's head pretty soon."

"Can't wait."

McNamara grunted in approval. "Say, my contact at Leavenworth finally got back to me on that son of a bitch that pulled a knife on you."

"It wasn't a knife, it was a shank. A filed-down pointed piece of plastic. They make them out of tooth-brushes or anything else they can find."

"Yeah, well, whatever. His name's Eric Phipps. Ring any bells?"

Wolf shook his head.

"He was a new arrival," McNamara said. "Last visitor was his lawyer."

"What was he in for?"

"Aggravated assault on an officer. Doing ten to fifteen."

"Figures," Wolf said.

"You still got no idea what it was all about?"

"Inside, it could be anything. Somebody stepping in front of somebody else in the chow line, an imagined slight in the athletic yard…"

"Sounds like some rules of engagement I wouldn't care for. Glad you're outta there."

"That makes two of us," Wolf agreed.

As they went outside and headed for McNamara's big Escalade, Kasey pulled up in her silver Toyota Celica. McNamara slowed and watched with grandfatherly pride as Chad waved to him from the rear car seat.

Kasey got out and walked over to give her father a hug. She gave Wolf a quick nod, then turned to open the door and remove her son.

"You guys going somewhere?" she asked.

"Yeah," McNamara said. "We're going to see your lawyer friend."

"Rod? What about?"

McNamara shot Wolf a look and rolled his eyes.

"Just some legal stuff. Then I thought we'd go try to drum up some business from Manny. You get a chance to run that guy I asked you about?"

"I did," she said, taking the baby into her arms. "Come on into my office, and I'll give it to you."

Wolf started to turn, but McNamara quickly put a hand out and flipped him the car keys. "I'll get it. You just go start up the beast there and make sure that air conditioning's on high by the time I get back."

Wolf watched the two of them head for the house, where Kasey maintained her computer and office files. He wondered if he was ever going to quit feeling like an outsider.

But at least I'm getting to start up the Escalade, he thought.

* * *

The office of Rodney F. Shemp, Attorney at Law, was on the top floor of a five-story office building down the street from one of the courthouses. They had to call up to the suite first to get the special code to use the elevator. McNamara swore and shook his head.

"What kind of a wimp would have a system like that?" he asked.

"A careful one," Wolf said. "Considering the type of clientele he deals with."

The office was fairly spacious. A pretty girl with auburn hair sat at a desk devoid of anything except a phone and a computer monitor. She looked up, smiled, took their names, and purred into the phone.

After she told them to "Go right in," Mac winked at her and tipped his hat.

She blushed.

Always the ladies' man, Wolf thought.

Shemp's office had numerous wooden filing cabinets, and the lawyer was hunched over a traditional mahogany desk with his shirt sleeves rolled up. He stood and offered his hand, first to McNamara and then to Wolf. He looked to be in his early thirties and had a full head of brown hair, an athlete's build that was starting to go to seed, and a friendly smile that remained frozen on his face as they sat in the two chairs in front of the desk. McNamara removed his cowboy hat and set it on the corner of the desk.

"Nice to meet you, Mr. Shemp," Wolf said.

"Please, call me Rod."

Wolf shot a quick glance at McNamara, who was leaning forward, massaging his temples.

"Well, Steve," Shemp said, clearing his throat, "I've had a chance to go over the transcripts of your court-martial in depth."

Wolf thought the man's smile looked nervous and got the feeling whatever the lawyer was going to say wasn't going to be promising. Of course, who wouldn't be nervous having his girlfriend's father show up when there was bad news on the horizon?

"I knew this was going to be an uphill battle," Shemp continued. "Appeals usually are."

He's trying to let me down easy, Wolf thought.

"I didn't find much in the way of improper procedure. That means our chances for an appeal and a reversal are—" He clucked sympathetically. "Kinda slim."

Wolf nodded, saying nothing. This wasn't anything he hadn't heard before.

McNamara muttered "Shit" under his breath.

"On the bright side, your Army lawyer was able to avoid more serious charges with the plea bargain. But your plea to conduct unbecoming and negligence in causing the death of the Iraqi civilians, even though you did it under the auspices of an Alford plea, still stands as a conviction on your record."

Hearing it recounted, it all seemed like a bad dream to Wolf now. Back then, he'd gone on faith, way out of his element in the courtroom, acting on what he'd hoped was the best advice. It was definitely somebody else's battlefield.

"What the hell's an Alford plea?" McNamara asked.

Shemp took a deep breath. "It's basically pleading guilty while maintaining your innocence because the prosecution has more than enough evidence to prove you guilty."

"Sounds like a lot of lawyer horseshit to me," McNamara said.

Shemp emitted a nervous laugh. "But despite your guilty plea, at least there was no allocution on your part."

"Allo-what?" McNamara asked. "Will you speak English, for Christ's sake?"

"Allocution—an admission of guilt in open court,

hence the Alford plea. It stems from an old case in North Carolina where a man pled guilty to avoid the death penalty but maintained his innocence. It went all the way to the Supreme Court."

Wolf nodded. "I wasn't going to admit to something I didn't do," he said. "Besides, I actually was telling the truth. A lot of it was a blank. Still is. I honestly can't remember parts of it."

"A head injury can do that sometimes," McNamara said. "In time, it might come back."

Shemp glanced at him, his head bobbing like one of those flocked dogs on a dashboard. "Oh, absolutely."

The three of them sat for a moment in awkward silence, then McNamara heaved a disgusted sigh. "Ain't there anything more you can do for us?"

Shemp compressed his lips. "Well, after reading these transcripts, I am a bit surprised your lawyer didn't try to take this to trial. I think the prosecution's case would have ultimately been difficult to prove."

"He was a newbie in JAG," Wolf said. "Besides, this was the Army, and you had three non-combatants dead at the tail end of an unpopular war. He told me if I was smart, I'd take the deal, avoid the shitstorm, and serve my time."

"By doing that, he lost the chance to cross-examine Lieutenant Cummins," Shemp said. "I've reviewed his deposition, and it left a lot of openings."

"Cummins was a reservist," Wolf said. "He had already been released back to civilian life by the time we got to the court-martial. My lawyer said the Army wanted to save time and money not having to fly him back." He shrugged. "Like I said, it was the Army."

Shemp's lips contorted. "Bad advice, I'm sorry to say, Steve. The same for this other fellow, Eagan, and the

Iraqi national, Nasim. They weren't very effectively cross-examined at the preliminary hearing, and their depositions aren't stellar either." He leaned back in his chair, trying to look nonchalant, but Wolf could tell he was tiptoeing around the eggshells.

"So, that's it?" McNamara asked, getting to his feet. The expression on the big man's face said it all; he was not very pleased with his daughter's boyfriend.

Shemp sprang forward, as eager to please as a wallflower trying to impress the parents of his first prom date.

"Rest assured, I can and will continue to review this case. I think we might possibly have a chance to build an appeal on the grounds that the defense counsel rendered ineffective assistance."

"So, he's got a chance for a reversal?" McNamara asked.

Shemp sighed and looked at him. "Well, we've got a shot at it, but the best we could hope for is a new trial at this point."

"And what are the chances of that?"

Shemp bit his lower lip. "As I said, the prosecution's case was essentially their word against yours initially, but they had the corroborating statements of numerous individuals, one of them an officer, that directly contradicted yours." He paused and blinked twice. "Well, what there was of your account, and you not being able to recall some of the details cast doubt on your credibility."

McNamara leaned forward and slammed his hand on the top of the desk. "This man's a decorated veteran, and you're calling him a liar?"

Shemp held up his open palms in a calming gesture.

"Mr. McNamara, please," he said. "I'm just the messenger here."

"Yeah," McNamara said, his face reddening. "Well, it sure don't look like you're much of a lawyer."

"Mac," Wolf said in a tone of rebuke.

McNamara heaved a sigh and stepped back.

A flush of pinkish scarlet crept up Shemp's neck to his cheeks.

"However," he said, "they wouldn't have offered the deal if they weren't worried about some aspect of the case. If we could come up with new information or a counter-witness, it would make a big difference."

"How the hell are we gonna find a counter-witness when this happened over in Iraq four years ago?" McNamara asked.

"Well..." Shemp let his voice trail off.

"I guess I should have followed my instincts at the time and fought it," Wolf said. But he remembered that he had also been promised that by him taking the heat, the rest of his team wouldn't be touched, and they'd been through enough. Martinez had been killed, and Thompson had lost a leg in that IED blast. He hadn't wanted to drag anybody else down with him in an unwinnable fight. "Sometimes, you get bad advice."

"Sometimes you do," Shemp agreed. "It would help if you could give a more complete account of what you remember."

Wolf shook his head. "Believe me, I wish I could."

"So, what you're saying is you can't do nothing for him?" McNamara asked.

Shemp looked like somebody'd kneed him in the balls. The corners of his mouth twisted down, and he cleared his throat. "As I said, I'll keep looking into it, but it's going to take some time. And there's no guarantee that we'll be successful."

McNamara frowned, and he shook his head. "What

about clearing his record then, with one of them expungements?"

"We couldn't do that without a reversal, and as I said, to do that, we'd need some new evidence."

"So, it's pretty hopeless?" Wolf asked.

"Well, I'll go over it again and look for a possible procedural error," Shemp offered.

"How about the chances of a CC permit?" McNamara asked.

Shemp compressed his lips and shook his head.

McNamara frowned.

"Thanks, Rod," Wolf said, getting to his feet and offering his hand. "How much do I owe you?"

Before Shemp could answer, McNamara jumped in again. "Shit, you don't owe him squat. He ain't done nothing for you." He paused to put on his hat and squinted in the attorney's direction. "Like I said before, Rodney, this is a *family* matter."

"Sure, Mr. McNamara. No problem." Shemp smile was nervous again. "No charge."

"Rod," Wolf started, "I can't do that—"

"Sure you can," McNamara said as he moved toward the door. "Come on, let's go see Manny and maybe get a line on how to make some money."

Wolf nodded his "thanks" to Shemp as they shook hands.

"So much for us getting you that damn concealed carry permit anytime soon," McNamara muttered as he thrust open the glass doors that separated the building's interior from the parking lot. "And I thought I told you not to call that asshole Rod."

"He doesn't seem like a bad guy."

McNamara snorted. "Shee-it."

Outside, away from the coolness of the air conditioning, Wolf felt sweat collect in his armpits. He waited while McNamara hit the remote to unlock the doors of the Escalade.

As they got in, Wolf noticed a black Hummer parked down the block. He couldn't see well, but he thought he saw a flash of movement behind the heavily tinted windows.

The Escalade felt like an oven on medium-high. McNamara turned it on, rolled down the windows, and flipped on the air, shaking his head and growling the whole time.

"What do you expect?" Wolf said. "It's Phoenix. It's supposed to be hot, isn't it?"

"Shit, I ain't thinking about the heat. I'm just wondering what Kasey sees in that damn guy. 'Shemp.' What the hell kind of a name is that?" The big man shook his head. "He never even served. You don't think he's secretly gay, do you?"

Wolf chuckled. "Gay? Because his name is Shemp? Or is it because he's a lawyer and he didn't serve in the military?"

"You know what I mean, dammit. I just don't want her to get mixed up with another loser who's going to break her heart down the line."

"He seems all right," Wolf said. "Kasey could do worse."

"She already has." McNamara shook his head again. "Yeah, well, I guess he is an improvement over that shit-bird she was married to."

"You mean the Army guy she met, right?"

McNamara shot a disapproving frown at Wolf, then sucked his upper lip behind his lower one. "Yeah, dammit, but it was my own damn fault. Never being around. Always being deployed overseas somewhere, fighting somebody else's goddamn war." The creases in his big face deepened as he talked. "She was raised by her mama, and when she passed four years ago, I shoulda seen it coming. Kasey and me, we were strangers. Flesh and blood, but strangers just the same."

"You're being pretty hard on yourself, Mac. She looks like she's turned out all right."

"No thanks to me," McNamara shot back. "No thanks to me." He sighed and fell into a morose silence.

Wolf figured it was better to let this conversation die and leaned back to contemplate his bleak prospects. At least some cool air was finally beginning to filter in through the vents.

* * *

Emmanuel Sutter's bail bond business was sandwiched between a game shop and a laundromat in a run-down strip mall. A yellow sign with big black letters spelled out *BAIL BONDSMAN* in the front window. Wolf sized up the proprietor as he shifted his bulky frame forward from behind an expansive desk. It was hard to place his age, but he looked to be on the far side of forty and was well over three-fifty, weight-wise. He wore his hair in a shaggy bob that that hadn't been in style for a few decades and had a trail of crumbs down the front of his short-sleeved mauve shirt. His smile looked as genuine as a politician's handshake, but he had what appeared to be a genuine Rolex on his expansive left wrist. Wolf saw a chrome-covered snub-nose revolver riding in a pancake holster along the right side of the big man's belt. A half-eaten pastry and a Styrofoam cup of coffee with a mutilated plastic lid sat on waxed paper on top of a clutter of official-looking forms. Despite the guy's excessive weight, he had big hands and arms, indicating he wouldn't be a pushover in a fight.

"I'd offer you something to eat, but my nephew Freddie's out getting us lunch now," Manny said, wiping his hand on the solid-looking gut pushing out his belt. "So, this is the guy you been telling me about, huh?"

"Right," McNamara said. "Steve Wolf."

"Looks like he could handle himself pretty good." Manny squinted and stretched his open palm across the desk. "You part Mex or something?"

Wolf shook the man's hand. It felt soft as a baby's behind. "Half-Indian."

"Indian?" Manny grinned. "I take it you mean Native American rather than a dot-head?"

"Cherokee on my mother's side," Wolf said. "My father was white."

Manny nodded in approval. "Yeah, well, I always said there ain't no better trackers than Injuns." He glanced at his watch, took another bite of the pastry, and added, "No offense."

"None taken," Wolf said. He'd long ago given up letting ignorant statements from bigots and idiots bother him.

Manny shifted to look at McNamara. "Where's that fucking Sherman with my goddamn lunch? That's the last time I have him go out for Chinese."

"Sherman?" McNamara said. "I thought his name's Freddie?"

Manny smirked. "It is, but I call him Sherman just to piss him off." He took another bite of the pastry, shifted the load to his cheek, and asked, "So, how'd it go with the mouthpiece?"

"Don't look good for that concealed carry permit," McNamara said, "but he's working on it."

Manny smirked. "Ain't they all? In the meantime, what you gonna do? Wait for a Presidential pardon?"

Wolf said nothing, surprised the guy knew so much about the situation.

McNamara shrugged. "Don't expect it'll slow us down none."

"No, I guess not. Could be a problem down the road, but as long as he's working with you?" Manny curled the side of his lip, obviously trying for a commiserating sneer. "And as long as the lawyer says he's working on it."

Mac nodded. "Like I said, we can handle it for now. I was hoping you had something for us. Maybe something easy and quick."

Manny's chuckle sounded like a toilet flushing, resonating inside the massive chest. "Easy and quick, I can do myself."

"Come on," Mac said. "You been tossing all the big ones to fucking Reno."

Manny flashed a crooked smile. Wolf noticed bits of the pastry stuck along the man's gumline.

"Whaddaya want me to do?" Manny said. "The guy's a celebrity now with that MMA thing he's got going and that cable TV show. And there's talk of putting him in the movies."

"Shit, I've forgotten more about tracking a felon than that joker's ever learned," McNamara said. "Now, what you got for us?"

Manny compressed his lips and squinted like he was contemplating which bone to throw to one of his dogs. His big fingers sorted to go through the piles of forms on his desk, causing the coffee cup to teeter. Wolf's hand shot out and grabbed it before it spilled. Luckily, the plastic top didn't come off.

"Hey, nice catch," Manny said, the half-smile and phlegmy chuckle reappearing. "You got quick hands."

"You ought to see him use them," Mac said. "Like I told you, we can handle whatever big-money skips you got."

Manny nodded, accepted the coffee cup from Wolf, and set it on a metal filing cabinet adjacent to his desk. He pulled open a drawer, and his fingers ran over the tops of a section of files. "I don't know, some of these guys are kinda rough, and with him not having a piece..."

"What difference does that make?" Mac said, patting his side. "I got one."

Manny nodded his head. "You know, I just got a little something that might help him. You can try it out for me." He pulled open a drawer and withdrew a sleek cylindrical plastic object about the size of a flashlight. It was bright yellow and black, matching the bail bondsman sign in the window.

"What's that?" Mac asked. "One of them sex toys?"

"No." Manny frowned, holding it up and pressing the button on top. "It's a Taser."

An arching strip of electrical current crackled between two metal prongs on one end.

Mac nailed him with a sharp look. "Don't you know you ain't supposed to point a weapon at somebody you're not intending to use it on?"

Manny chuckled again. "Relax. It's got a cartridge that fits on the front." He held up another piece of plastic shaped like a hood. "Shoots out fifteen feet. It can take down a Brahma bull. Or you can use it up close and personal for what they call a drive stun." He flicked the arc again, then handed it to McNamara. "Here, take it. Try it out. Of course, you want him to officially carry it, he's got to get certified. They're having a certification class at our annual conference this weekend."

McNamara frowned. "I told you before, I ain't going to that damn thing."

Manny's grin was wide, showing that the food stuck along the gumline still hadn't dissolved. "Why not? Don't you wanna see who's gonna get the Bounty Hunter of the Year award?"

McNamara's frown deepened. "We both know who's gonna get it, which is why I'm not going."

Manny shrugged. "Suit yourself, but remember, Kemosabe, Tonto here still has to get Taser-certified. Sooner better than later."

"We'll make it later, then," Mac said, holding the Taser in his big hand. "You got a couple of them cartridges to go with this?"

Manny held up his palm. "Of course, but I'll wait till he's gone through certification before he gets those. As it is now, you can use it as a stun gun. So start thinking about going to the conference."

McNamara shook his head and stuck the Taser in the pocket of his blouse. "Okay, I'll think about it. Now, what you got for us?"

"Just what you wanted." Manny smiled as he ran his tongue over his front teeth, making a sucking sound. "An easy pinch."

"I don't want easy. I want something where we can make some money. What about that Mexican dude, Ruiz, with the hundred-thousand-dollar bond?"

"Luis Ruiz?" Manny shot him a quizzical look. "How'd you hear about him? Freddie?"

"Never mind how I heard," McNamara said. "I been working some angles on that one."

Manny shook his head. "I don't know. That one's no

pushover. Besides, he's been laying low. Reno's been trying to track him for a week and ain't been able to find nothing."

McNamara held out his hand. "Sounds like it's just what we been looking for."

* * *

Eagan sat facing the bar, staring at his reflection in the big mirror on the rear wall lined with glasses and bottles. Somebody had given it a spit-and-polish job. You could actually see yourself in barroom mirrors now, probably a result of the New York Clean Air Act. You could also watch, in an unobtrusive fashion, who came and who went. He sipped his bourbon and branch water. It would be his last drink until the op was completed. A rule of his: no drinking on the job. He thought about the meeting he'd just had and the one yet to come. Four years seemed a long time to wait for the second half of a pair of carved trinkets, but then again, this Von Dien guy was used to waiting, so a little bit longer wouldn't hurt. If anything, it would make him more appreciative when the goods were delivered.

Eagan thought again about the quarry being in Mexico and how that added another set of complications to the retrieval.

After taking another sip and feeling the burn, he considered the possibilities.

Extraction and retrieval would be more accurate.

Insulation, he thought. *That's all I am to those fuckers. Just another layer of insulation.*

He made a mental note that he needed to be careful as well. Get some insulation of his own.

Two more guys entered the bar. One of them was Cummins, his head swiveling as he searched the room.

Eagan told the barmaid he'd be moving to a booth, then stood, picked up his drink, and headed to the place he'd reserved when he'd walked in. The barmaid pivoted and made a show of giving the wooden surface of the tabletop a quick wipe with her towel. Eagan sat with his back to the door this time and watched as Cummins struggled to squeeze in behind the shelf of the table.

Christ, the simple effort of sitting down seemed to have winded him. Eagan doubted he could depend on him if the shit hit the fan, but he didn't intend to. He reaffirmed his previous conviction to get his own layers of insulation, just like in Iraq. He snapped his fingers and motioned at the waitress. She stepped back toward them.

"So how you been, Jack?" Eagan asked. He extended his big hand over the tabletop.

"I been okay," Cummins said, wincing as Eagan squeezed his hand.

"What you drinking?"

"I'll take a club soda," he said, then shook his head. "No, strike that. Give me a perfect Manhattan, okay?"

She nodded.

"It's five o'clock somewhere, right?" Cummins asked, shrugging. "Besides, I doubt I'll get called back to meet with any clients. The boss wants me to ride shotgun with you on this until it's done."

"Just like in the Sandbox, huh?"

"Yeah." Cummins laughed. "You don't know how many strings they had to pull to get me that assignment over there for that brief little foray."

"Fortunes of war," Eagan said.

The girl smiled and turned her eyes toward Eagan. "You want another B and B?"

He shook his head and turned to Cummins. "Slip her a twenty."

Cummins lips parted. "Come again?"

"Do it," Eagan said, transferring his attention to the other man. "She's been holding this booth especially for us." When Cummins sat there immobile, Eagan snapped his fingers again.

Cummins pursed his lips, removed his wallet, and started sorting through it. "I'll have to add it on to the tab. Not sure I have one."

"Oh? Let's see." Eagan reached across the table and snatched the open billfold. His large fingers pulled out a fifty and handed it to her. "Here you go, honey. Keep the change and see that nobody bothers us, okay?"

She licked her lips. "Sure."

He watched her ass as she walked away.

"This was supposed to be on the firm's dime," Cummins said. "I would've left a nice tip on the bill."

Eagan felt like reaching across and bitch-slapping one of the other guy's fat cheeks, but he knew he'd accomplished what he wanted to: he'd reestablished his dominance by using a dash of intimidation.

"You can still do that," he said. "In fact, you will. I don't know too many women in this town. I might want to come back later when she gets off work."

Cummins emitted a short, disgruntled sound.

Eagan shot him an icy stare, letting the silence settle over the other man like an embracing shroud.

The fat lawyer licked his lips. "Ah, I assume the boss brought you up to speed this morning?"

Eagan shrugged. "More or less. He said you'd fill in the rest of the blanks."

Cummins nodded and was just about to speak when the barmaid brought two drinks, settling the frosty martini glass in front of Cummins and another B and B in front of Eagan.

"On the house, big guy," she said, giving him a wink.

"Thanks, babe. We'll be putting your tip on the tab," Eagan said before she walked away.

That seemed to frustrate Cummins, but all he did was purse his lips again.

"You're supposed to be filing in the gaps," Eagan said.

Cummins frowned, nodded, and took a swig of his drink. When he set the glass down, his face looked flushed. "Okay, how much did Mr. Fallotti tell you?"

"Enough to know that the other half of what we got for them in the Sandbox didn't end up where it was supposed to."

"Yeah, after all that planning and work." Cummins smirked. "Not to mention three dead ragheads." His smirk stretched into a grin. "Yeah, good thing we had good old Sergeant Wolf and his boys to take the heat for that one." He snorted a laugh. "What a putz. Took a horseshit plea bargain and went bye-bye. He's lucky they didn't have me as a prosecutor in JAG, or he'd a gotten life."

"I'll bet he's still counting his blessings." Eagan grinned. "Especially after almost getting shanked on his last day at Leavenworth."

Cummins frowned. "Stupid fuck-up. And after Stu assured us that it would go off without a hitch." He grabbed the glass and drained it. The ice clunked when he slammed it down on the tabletop. "I told them that was a dumb move. Wolf's just a wart on a barfly's ass. He can't do shit."

"So, why'd the big man want him iced anyway? As you said, it ain't like he can do anything."

"Word got back to us that somebody'd hired a lawyer

to look into Wolf's court-martial case," Cummins said. "Possible appeal."

"Somebody? Who?"

"I don't know. Some two-bit lawyer outta Phoenix or someplace." Cummins lifted the glass and then realized it was empty. "Nothing's gonna come of it."

"Then why was the big man worried about it?"

"Victor Delta's always worried about the little shit. He's very meticulous. In fact, you could say the son of a bitch is obsessive-compulsive sometimes."

"Victor Delta?"

"That's what I call him." Cummins giggled. "Stands for VD. Get it?"

Eagan got it all right, and he wasn't amused. He knew Cummins wouldn't dare say anything disparaging to Von Dien's face, which made this fat prick a backstabber. Eagan hated backstabbers. He almost regretted that he'd gone along with Cummins's plan to make old Sergeant Wolf the fall guy back in Iraq. Almost... The dumb fucker made too good of a patsy, and he was part-Indian at that. They were born to be used, abused, and discarded.

Cummins waved, trying to get the attention of the waitress, but she seemed to be distracted, talking to another customer. His frown deepened, and he swore under his breath. "He's paranoid about loose ends. Doesn't like leaving any."

Good to know, Eagan thought. *It's something we share.*

It also reaffirmed something for him to keep in mind: that to a rich prick like Von Dien, he was another one of those loose ends, as expendable as a used condom. And so was this fat fuck.

"But our buddy Wolf's on the back burner for now,"

Cummins said. "Victor Delta's going bonkers about this current situation."

"The artifact."

"Right," Cummins said. "When the second half surfaced, they made the mistake of sending the wrong flunky to do the job." His eyes moved to the untouched bourbon in front of Eagan. "Ah, you gonna drink that?"

Eagan shook his head and pushed the glass across the table.

A fat lush as my go-between for the mission and the money, he thought. *Better make sure I have a contingency plan.*

"Thomas Accondras," Eagan said. "The grad student."

"Yeah, that's the guy, or should I say the mule?" He brought the bourbon to his mouth, took a delicate sip, and set it down. "You know, I'd better not be mixing drinks, or I'll get diarrhea."

Christ, Eagan thought. He must have a weak belly.

He didn't remember this fat idiot being such a pansy-ass, but their association in Iraq hadn't been that lengthy. Novak had set everything up, including working with Cummins.

"So anyway," Cummins continued, "this guy Accondras assured us he had all the right connections. Everything was set until he showed up here and got pinched on an outstanding warrant." He motioned for the waitress again, and when she came over, he said, "Gimme another one."

She left.

Eagan noticed that the alcohol was affecting Cummins pretty rapidly. A man who couldn't hold his liquor? That could indicate carelessness. He hadn't noticed that back in Iraq, but there hadn't been any booze available then, either.

He studied Cummins. There was a lingering sheen of panic under all that blubber, further evidence that the man would not be dependable in a crisis—not that Eagan needed any after the way Cummins had blown his cool four years ago. He'd practically been reduced to a pile of melting Jell-O after Eagan had sliced the one camel jockey's throat open.

Cummins shrugged and toyed with the empty glass, then leaned forward, lowering his voice. "We had this whole thing worked out. The plan was for Accondras to bring the item here, then turn it over to us after he'd passed Customs."

"How'd he get it through Customs here?"

"He didn't say but claimed he had it all worked out." Cummins drank some more from the glass. "Turned out he'd stashed it in Canada. Wanted to be paid up front before delivering it."

"Smart move."

"He got his tit in a wringer before even approaching us." Cummins' lips curled into a half-smile. "Got his ass arrested. Called us for bond."

"Which your firm arranged through the bail bondsman."

Cummins nodded. "The old fart's paranoid. Insists on several layers of buffer material so nothing can be traced back to him."

"How'd Accondras ship it through Canadian Customs without attracting attention?"

"He was affiliated with some museum up in Canada. Unbeknownst to us, he'd already shipped it there, along with a bunch of other Arab junk. He flew back there and was supposed to pick it up and bring it to us on the sly."

"And then he got busted."

Cummins glanced around before giving a quick nod. "That's when things started to get screwed up. When

Accondras got arrested, we immediately signed on to represent him. As soon as we got his bond posted, he went back up north, took the item, which, like I said, he'd shipped to himself before he got here, and then beat feet for his old man's place in Mexico."

"The judge didn't take his passport?"

Cummins smirked and rubbed his thumb and first two fingers together. "He apparently had two of them."

"And you're sure he's got the item?"

Before Cummins could answer, the waitress returned and set an icy glass in front of Cummins. She smiled and winked at Eagan again, and he felt a stirring in his groin. She took the empty glass and left.

Cummins swallowed more booze, then said, "Says he does, and we got no reason to doubt him. We received an anonymous email with a picture of it from Mexico. He then called on a burner phone, demanding a higher payoff. An enormous amount to set him up for life."

"What about this private dick you've got down there? He figure out where the thing is?"

"Zerbe's been on him like stink on shit. Supposedly. But he claims he ain't made no moves. He's got it stashed down there, that's for sure."

"You trust this guy Zerbe?"

"No reason not to." Cummins brought the glass to his mouth again and almost drained it. "Aaahhh, that's good."

"One thing's bothering me," Eagan said. "If money's no object, why doesn't the old man just pay the asshole what he wants?"

"I think they're figuring Accondras might be gonna welsh on the deal. He'd be stupid not to. It's his only insurance policy. He knows we can't afford to alert the authorities about him for fear of losing the item. And he also knows that once it's not in his possession anymore, his ass is grass."

"Just one more loose end to be tied up."

Cummins snorted in agreement.

"Any possibility he might sell it to somebody else?" Eagan asked.

"It's always possible, but I doubt it. I mean, where could he unload something like that? It's not like you could put on eBay." Cummins shrugged. "No, it's his insurance policy. His ace in the hole. And now he's sitting pretty down in Mexico."

"With an outstanding warrant for a failure to appear case that's coming up in about ten days."

Cummins looked at him over the rim of his glass and nodded. "They ain't so concerned about that. The bail bondsman will be out the money, but we'll make good on it. They just don't want it traceable back to us."

"It won't be," Eagan said. "Either to you or Victor Delta."

Cummins's eyes narrowed. "You got an idea about how to handle it?"

"Yeah." Eagan slid out of the booth and straightened. "Come on. I want you to introduce me to this bail bondsman."

CHAPTER 5

PHOENIX, ARIZONA

"That's it," Mac said as he pulled to the curb and pointed at a one-story tan stucco house farther down the block.

"That's his house?"

"Actually, it's his mother's sister's place."

"Why did Manny say the guy was so hard to find?"

McNamara smiled. "Hard to find for the amateurs. Not for Sherlock Holmes here."

Wolf rolled his eyes.

"Anyway, don't question my methods," Mac said as he took out his cell phone and pressed a button. "Yeah, we're there. What else you got?" He listened, nodding and grunting. After a moment, he stared at the house, his eyes narrowing. "All right. Check you later. What? Yeah, yeah, I will be."

Wolf lifted an eyebrow. "Care to share?"

"Just checking in with Kasey. She'll alert the cops if we need 'em."

"She's worried?"

McNamara shook his head slightly. "Sometimes she's worse than her mother was."

"What's the plan?"

"You go knock on the front door and announce yourself. I'll be waiting at the back when he tries to make his break. Talk to them in Spanish to keep them off-guard."

"Announce myself? And what makes you think they're going to open the door for the likes of me?"

Mac compressed his lips like he wasn't sure of his answer, then said, "They will. You got that real familiar look."

"Huh? What are you talking about? I don't know these people."

McNamara shrugged and adjusted his hat. "You never know. You're a nice-looking young fella. Say you're a Jehovah's Witness or something."

"And that's going to make them open the door? They're probably Catholic."

"All right. Say you're a cop or something."

Wolf frowned. "And if they ask to see some identification?"

"They won't."

"But if they do, I'm an ex-con, out on parole, impersonating an officer of the law." Wolf shook his head. "I don't want to end up back in the joint."

Mac blew out a slow breath, then reached into his pocket, pulled out a thin black wallet, and handed it to Wolf. "Here, take mine."

Wolf opened it and saw an ID card behind a plastic holder in one section and a shiny miniature gold badge on the other. *BAIL ENFORCEMENT AGENT* was imprinted around the state seal. A velvet protector was between the two sections.

"This has your picture on it," Wolf said.

"Well, put your thumb over it," McNamara replied, opening the door.

"What are you gonna use?"

"I got this one." McNamara held up a gold star within a circle that had the same imprint as the smaller badge.

"I don't know about this," Wolf said.

"Aw, hell. Just yell 'Bail enforcement agent.' Make a lot of noise. All you have to do is make enough racket to send old Luis running out the back." McNamara held up a booking photo of a sullen-looking Hispanic male in his forties. "But make no mistake, this shitbird's dangerous. He's one of the original gangbangers with the Los Lobos. Wanted on two warrants for auto theft and possession of a controlled substance. He also had two arrests for weapons violations." His mouth twitched. "You want me to give you a bullet-proof vest?"

"You got one?"

McNamara nodded. "Got two."

"You gonna wear one?"

"Shit, no. Too damn hot."

"Then I'll pass, too," Wolf said. "You know, you still haven't told me how we found him so easily."

"Don't question my methods. Just flush him out and leave the rest to me. Here." He handed Wolf the Taser.

"What do I want with that?"

"Maybe you can light the fucker up."

"No, thanks."

"Humor me." Mac shoved the Taser at him. "Keep it for shits and giggles."

Wolf stuck the Taser in his back pocket, hoping he wouldn't have to use it.

McNamara slipped out of the car and leaned back inside. "Give me a couple of minutes to get set up on the other end. And remember, this one's worth a pretty penny to us." He turned, then stopped. "Ah, I'm gonna have to talk to you afterward about this. Something I gotta tell you."

"What?"

"Later," McNamara said. "We gotta get this done quick."

Wolf wondered what the hell Mac had meant as he watched him amble down the sidewalk past the tan house. He went two houses down, then angled to his right, cutting through someone's yard toward the backs of the houses.

Wolf waited for another minute before he got out. He adjusted the rearview mirror and caught a glimpse of a midnight-black Hummer parked down the block behind him. He remembered seeing one earlier.

The same one?

Undercover cops, maybe? Doubtful that they'd be driving something like that, but it could be a confiscated vehicle. The windows had dark tint, so Wolf couldn't tell if it was occupied.

Dismissing his concerns, he got out of the Escalade and walked toward the door. The sun shone overhead, and he could feel the sweat starting to seep through the fabric of his polo shirt. No wonder Mac had told him to wear something nice and professional-looking. He smiled to himself, wondering if this whole thing was a mistake, and went toward the front door. A green Toyota Corolla was parked in front. Wolf thought the vehicle looked familiar somehow, but he couldn't place it. There was an ornate display of three-foot-high plastic religious icons in the front yard under a large picture window. Two window air conditioning units hummed mightily on the side of the house, adjacent to a driveway with an overhanging roof. A big Honda motorcycle leaned against a beat-up brown pickup that looked like it hadn't been moved in months. He took a deep breath, held Mac's credentials in his left hand, and rang the doorbell.

Inside, he heard chimes, then voices in Spanish. The door opened, and a heavyset Hispanic lady looked at him through the fine mesh of the screen door with suspicious dark eyes.

"*Bueno?*" she asked.

"*Está aquí Luis?*" Wolf said in as loud a voice as he could manage.

"*Luis?*" The woman's eyes narrowed. "*Porque?*"

Aw, hell, Wolf thought. He held up the badge case and yelled, "Bail enforcement agent."

The woman's eyes widened, and she yelled a torrent of Spanish over her shoulder.

A moment later, a pretty, much younger woman came into view.

"*Porque, mama—*" She paused and looked at him. "Steve?"

As the younger woman stepped forward the light, Wolf discerned her features. It was Consuela Ruiz from his English Lit class. No wonder the name had sounded familiar. He felt stunned and angry. Had Mac known about this? If he did, and Wolf was now sure that was the case, he was going to have to talk to him about it.

"What are *you* doing here?" Consuela asked. Her voice took on a high-pitched whine. "What do you want with *mi tio?*"

"Is he here?" Wolf managed to ask. His voice sounded weak. He felt like a shitheel.

"Of course, he's here," Consuela said. "He's my uncle. He has been staying here. What's this about?"

Before Wolf could answer her, there was a commotion inside, and he saw the flash of a man running toward the back of the house. It had to be him. Wolf pivoted and ran across the front of the yard, tripping over a three-foot-tall icon of Jesus in the process. "Halt!" he yelled to alert Mac. "Bail enforcement agent."

The door on the side of the residence was thrust open, and the male turned sharply and ran toward the motorcycle. He pulled it away from the truck and started to roll it toward the street, kicking the starter. Wolf saw McNamara running at full speed toward them, but he was still about twenty feet away. His face was scarlet, and his Glock was in his right hand, the gold badge flopping around his neck. He made a grab for Ruiz, but the fugitive stiff-armed him, and McNamara tumbled to the ground.

The motorcycle's engine came alive, and just as Ruiz lifted his leg to straddle the seat, Wolf rounded the front of the pickup and tackled him. The momentum carried them and the motorcycle to the ground. The bike's engine continued its high-pitched whine as Wolf struggled to pin Ruiz to the sandy earth. The wiry Hispanic proved tougher than he looked, kicking and punching the whole time. Wolf cocked his arm back to deliver a punch and heard a woman scream from behind him, "Don't you dare hit him."

It was Consuela. A vision of her pretty face flashed in his mind's eye.

Ruiz brought his foot back and tried to kick Wolf in the balls. Luckily, the blow was off-center. Wolf grunted in pain but managed to deliver a half-assed punch south of the border to the smaller man's gut. Ruiz writhed in commiserating agony.

Consuela swore at him in Spanish and then in English.

Wolf repeated his punch, this time able to add a bit

more oomph to it. Ruiz grunted again. Wolf felt long fingernails rake his cheek. Before he could react, McNamara was there, pushing Consuela back. Her flailing arms knocked his cowboy hat off his head.

"Where's that damn Taser?" he yelled.

Wolf reached into his pocket and pulled it out, jammed it against Ruiz's belly, and gave him a good jolt. The man stiffened like a board.

Consuela screamed.

Her mother was next to her now, hurling more invectives in Spanish, which Consuela was echoing in English.

"*Policía*," McNamara yelled. "*La migra* too, dammit." He thrust a set of handcuffs toward Wolf. "Can you get him cuffed?"

Wolf jammed the Taser into his belt, grabbed the cuffs, flipped Luis onto his stomach, pulled the smaller man's arms behind his back, then ratcheted the handcuffs into place.

Moments later, the two women backed off slightly, and Wolf and McNamara were able to get Ruiz to his feet and walk him across the sandy front yard toward the Escalade. McNamara stopped to retrieve his hat. The two women followed, with Consuela taking the lead, calling Wolf every name in the book and then some in both of the languages she spoke.

"You kiss your mama with that mouth?" McNamara asked.

Wolf held the Taser against Ruiz's side as he pushed him into the back seat and got in after him. McNamara tipped his cowboy hat to the ladies and got into the driver's seat. Shaking his head, he said, "That little college girl's a real spitfire, all right. Wonder what she's like in bed?"

"Hey, man!" Ruiz exclaimed. "That's my niece you talking about."

"Shut up and try to figure out how you're gonna make bond this time," McNamara said with a grin. "Cause I don't think Manny's gonna post it for you."

Ruiz kicked the back of the driver's seat and Wolf secured him in place with the seatbelt and snapped it closed. "Take it easy." He held up the Taser and pressed the button to send a warning arc.

The Hispanic slumped in the seat with a look of raw hatred on his face.

Wolf looked at Mac. Why hadn't he been straight with him from the beginning when he'd encouraged him to take Consuela on a date?

The words replayed in his memory.

"You'd best ask her out for coffee after class next time." Mac had been insistent.

"What, are you playing matchmaker now?"

"Not me. I'm all business."

All business. What he should've said was he was all about gathering intel.

Wolf thought about that pleasant conversation in the student union over coffee. It was the closest he'd been to a woman in a social setting in years, and he'd felt awkward and shy. Still, he'd enjoyed it very much, even though all they had done was talk. He remembered seeing McNamara drive by as he was escorting Consuela to her car. At the time, he'd put it off to Mac being nosy, but now he knew better. Mac had set the whole thing up so he could follow her. That was how he had known where she lived. He must have known, or at least had a pretty damn good idea, that Ruiz had a sister and figured he might be hiding out there. Wolf felt a sudden twinge of disappointment. He felt used. Couldn't Mac have been straight with him? Told him what the plan was?

It was something he was going to have to straighten out. He owed Mac big time, but he didn't like being deceived. But this wasn't the time or place. Not in front of her no-good fugitive uncle.

Luis Ruiz spat a mixture of curse words in Spanglish.

McNamara shifted into gear and was just starting to pull away from the curb when a huge black flash zoomed in front of them, accompanied by a screech of brakes. It was the black Hummer, and it had the Escalade blocked in. The passenger-side door of the Hummer swung open and a massive African American man jumped out, his right hand on a sawed-off shotgun dangling from his shoulder on a sling, his left displaying a gold badge with a circled star like Mac's. He moved forward with a wide stride, a wider smile stretching over his lips. He wore a sleeveless BDU blouse, and his arms looked like twin pythons.

Another figure, this one a white guy with a spiked mohawk and cauliflower ears, slipped around the rear of the Hummer. He had a big semi-automatic pistol in a tactical holster and wore the same type of star affixed to a leather tag on a chain around his thick neck. Clad in a black leather vest, this guy looked equally well-muscled, although he was not as overdeveloped as the black man.

They didn't look much like undercover cops.

The white guy pulled open the driver's door of the Escalade, grabbed the steering wheel, and put his face an inch or so from McNamara's.

"Hey, Big Mac," the man said. "I think you got something that belongs to us."

"What you talking about, Reno?" McNamara said.

"And you better get out of my face and move outta our way."

"I don't think so, old man." Reno grinned. "Don't you move either, jailbird, or Herc will ventilate this hunk of junk with some double-ought buck."

The black man raised the shotgun.

Wolf said nothing, evaluating his chances of making a countermove. Nothing appeared feasible. He wondered if Mac was going to pull his gun.

"Jailbird?" McNamara said. "Why, you son of a bitch. This man's a decorated war veteran, which is more than I can say for the likes of you two."

"That ain't the way I heard it." Reno smirked. "Get out now, and keep your hands up where I can see 'em."

McNamara didn't move.

"I said—"

"I heard you," McNamara said in a low, even tone. "Go fuck yourself."

Reno shrugged. "Suit yourself, Big Mac." His right hand reached inside the vest and came out with a pistol-shaped Taser that made a popping electrical sound. A cloud of tiny shards of paper exploded inside the Escalade and Mac's body stiffened, lurching upward. The black guy was beside Reno, covering Ruiz and Wolf with the shotgun.

"Keep that one covered, Herc," Reno said as he pulled McNamara out of the driver's seat his body, still shaking, his hat tumbling onto the street. Twin lengthy wires extended from the front of the square plastic barrel and hung in front of Mac's chest.

Herc, the black guy, pulled open the door. "Keep your hands where I can see 'em, small fry."

Wolf eyed him as he raised his hands and watched

with concern as the one called Reno lowered Mac to the street. Wolf saw that the guy's pistol was a 1911 .45, but it had a lot of gold leaf trim. Not a standard Colt, that was for sure. Then Wolf saw the emblem; it was a Kimber. *Mucho* bucks.

Still holding the Taser, Reno bent down and grabbed McNamara's Glock out of its holster. He straightened, shoved the Glock into his belt, and looked at Wolf.

"You ain't packing, are you, jailbird?"

Wolf shook his head slowly.

"That fits with what I heard," Reno said. "Ex-cons can't get no concealed carry permit." His lips pulled back in a feral grin. "But keep your hands up just the same."

He kicked McNamara's side, rolling him onto his back. Mac groaned and started to come around. Reno stepped over him and pulled the keys out of the Escalade's ignition. "Get Ruiz."

"Reno," McNamara said. "You son of a bitch."

"Shaddup," Reno said and jammed his boot on top of Mac's chest.

Herc let the sawed-off drop on the sling so it hung by his right side. His left hand reached down and came up with a big Bowie knife, which he used to slice the shoulder strap and seat belt. Ruiz's eyes widened as the knife came within millimeters of his body.

Reno stepped around, pulled Ruiz out of the back seat, and slammed him against the car. Then he looked at Wolf. "You slide your ass across the seat and get out, too. Try anything, and I'll give old Big Mac here another ride with the Taser."

Wolf did as he was told, his eyes never leaving the other man. When he stepped out, Reno said, "Check him."

Wolf thought about making a move, but with Mac on the other end of those wires, it seemed like too much of a risk. Besides, both these jokers were armed, and neither seemed very stable.

Herc slipped the Bowie knife into a leather sheath on his belt and ran his left hand over Wolf's body. It was a half-assed search at best, but he found the Taser in Wolf's belt. He handed it to Reno, who put it into his own pocket.

"That's all he got," the black guy said.

Herc shoved Ruiz toward the Hummer. The lean Hispanic's hands were still cuffed behind him. The black man grinned, his white teeth looking like a bright ivory keyboard in contrast to his dark skin. He shoved Ruiz into the back seat of the Hummer, buckled him in, slammed the door, and came sauntering back. McNamara appeared to be getting back to normal now, and he gripped the wire extending from his chest as he started to sit up.

"Leave 'em be," Reno said, still brandishing the Taser. "Unless you want another ride."

He gave the trigger a brief squeeze, and McNamara stiffened again.

Reno leaned over, his hands on his knees, and laughed. "Let's face it, Big Mac. You were way out of your league on this one, trying to compete with the best. And that's what you get for stealing our pinch."

"*Your* pinch?" McNamara asked. "It was *ours*."

Reno laughed again. "Manny musta told you we been tracking him for the better part of a week, so we got first dibs. Don't know how you found him before we did, but thanks for locating him for us." He straightened and motioned to Herc. "Well, as much as I'd like to stay and chat, we got a bounty to collect on. The clock's ticking."

"Hey, give me my keys," McNamara said. "And my piece."

Reno patted the handle of the Glock. "I been meaning to check one of these things out, but I think I'll stick with my Kimber." He took the keys out of his pocket, flipped them in the air, caught them, and threw them over the top of the Escalade. "Those shouldn't be too hard to find for a good tracker like you." His lips peeled away from his teeth in a mocking smile. "Nice Caddie, but Herc here is gonna do a little safety inspection on your tire."

The big knife appeared in the black guy's hand again, and he moved to the right rear tire of the Escalade and pressed the point into the tread. Seconds later, the tire began to emit a hissing sound.

"Reno," McNamara said. "You're a no-good son of a bitch."

Reno tsked. "Big Mac, face it. You're getting old. You're starting to repeat yourself."

Herc laughed, re-sheathed his knife, went around the driver's side of the Hummer, and got in.

"You can't do this," Wolf said. "This is armed robbery."

Reno laughed. "Not really. Just a little property dispute. Besides, my brother's a lieutenant on the PD. You got any complaints, take them to him."

Wolf glanced at McNamara, who gave a brief nod.

Reno disconnected the cartridge from the Taser and yanked the barbs out of McNamara's pectoral muscles. He grunted in pain. Reno smirked, winding the wires around his fingers as he sidled to the still-open door on the passenger side of the Hummer. "And stay outta our way, or next time, we'll smash your hat."

"What about my gun?" McNamara asked.

"I told you, I prefer my Kimber. It's a real man's weapon." Reno paused at the rear bumper. "I'll tell you what. I'll leave your polymer piece of shit with Manny, along with your other stuff. But you really ought to consider retiring, Big Mac. Oh, wait, technically, you *are* retired, ain't you?" He slammed the door of the Hummer. Wolf couldn't see through the darkly tinted windows, but he heard raucous laughter.

Herc followed, grinning as he went around and got into the driver's seat. The Hummer roared away, leaving Wolf and McNamara inhaling an effluvium of exhaust fumes.

Wolf started to help Mac to his feet, but the older man shook him off.

Wolf understood that Mac's pride was hurt worse than his body. Stooping, he grabbed his hat from the street and brushed it off.

"You all right?" Wolf asked as he handed the hat over.

"I'm all right, dammit," McNamara said. "That son of a—" He stopped and ran his hand over his clothes. Two small spots of blood stained the fabric of his shirt where the prongs had hit him.

"You sure you're okay?" Wolf asked.

"Shit, yeah. Just some injured pride."

Wolf took his cell phone out. "I got his license number. Should we call the cops?"

McNamara shook his head. "I heard this ain't the first time he's pulled shit like this. Just the first time with me."

"So, what are we going to do?"

"I'll settle up with those assholes in my own way."

"I take it you know them?"

McNamara nodded. "Reno Garth and his partner, Black Hercules. That's his stage name. They both fight in them MMA matches on the side. Got some kind of TV program, too, and a reputation that makes it look like they're the best in the business. In reality, they're the kind that gives the profession a bad name."

Wolf processed this information, wondering how he'd fare going toe-to-toe with either of them. They looked formidable, but he was already formulating a plan of attack.

"Well," McNamara said, "looks like they won this round."

"You sure you don't want to call the cops?"

McNamara shook his head. "It'd only be our word against theirs. Besides, his brother'd just get it swept under the rug."

Wolf didn't like it, but he figured it wasn't his call to make. Nor did he feel it would be a good time to discuss how Mac had deceived him about Consuela, even though Luis Ruiz was gone. If this partnership was going to work, Wolf would eventually have to confront him about it, but now was not the time. He hooked his thumb toward the Escalade. "You got a jack in there?"

"I expect," McNamara said. "Never had to use it, though."

"First time for everything," Wolf said.

"And hopefully the last one, too," McNamara replied.

* * *

GRAHAM'S BAIL BOND SERVICES
QUEENS, NEW YORK

Theodore "Teddy" Graham looked like a living skeleton wearing wire-rim glasses as he sat perched behind a large gunmetal-gray desk awash with paperwork. His hair was snow-white on the sides and gone on top. He'd tried to compensate with a bad comb-over, which would have given Eagan a good chuckle had the office not been so damn small and smelled of mold and cigarettes. An overflowing ashtray was perched on top of a stack of papers.

"Yeah," Graham said. "That bastard Accondras is gonna cost me a pretty penny, that's for fucking sure. You know how much I had to post for his ass?" His voice had a husky, whispering quality like each word had to be forced out with an emphasizing breath. "A million-dollar bond, ten percent of which is a hundred thou. All down the drain if he don't show up next week, and I don't guess that he will, right?"

"Teddy," Cummins said, "I already told you the firm's good for it."

"Yeah, right." Teddy snorted in disgust. "You know how big a hit the bail bond business took after that crazy fucking governor forced that motherfucking bail bond reform act through the legislature? Burglary, manslaughter, stalking, robbery. Christ, they're giving the fucking shitbirds Knicks tickets just to show up for court."

"It'll be repealed soon enough," Cummins said.

"Fuck that. Paying me under the fucking table's the least you can fucking do after begging me to post the asshole's bond so you guys wouldn't be officially involved. Fine and dandy, but what about the increase in my bonding insurance premiums after taking a hit like that? Where will you guys be when *that* fucking bill comes in?" He snorted. "Not to mention the damage to my rep. Word gets out that somebody put one like that over on Teddy Graham, it'll be bad for fucking business."

"What would you say if we told you we got a solid lead as to where he's at?" Cummins asked.

Teddy snorted again. "I'd like that even better. Where?"

"Mexico."

Graham frowned. "Shit. Might as well be in the Emerald-fucking-City. Even if the Mexican cops could pinch him, they're too fucking easy to pay off down there. They'd want to cut in and start their own action. He'd never make it back across the border."

"Maybe," Cummins said. He cast a sly look at Eagan. "Or maybe not."

Teddy glanced at them, pursed his lips, and bumped his glasses up on his nose. "I'm listening."

The asshole's got a beak like a Heeb, Eagan thought. Doesn't fit with a name like Graham, but he sounds like a Jew-boy.

"But," Cummins said, "like us posting the bond, we can't be officially involved, see?"

Teddy smirked. "So, in other words, you need me to hire someone to go down there and grab him for you?"

Cummins nodded.

Teddy barked a harsh laugh. "This is New York City, pal. Nobody up here knows Mexico turf. How the hell am I supposed to find some bounty hunter who wants to risk going down there and taking a chance on ending up in some spic prison, much less smuggling a fugitive back across the border?"

"What if I told you we've got that angle covered?" Cummins asked.

"How?"

"I run a PMC called the Vipers," Eagan said. "Give me forty-eight hours, and I can set up an op south of the border that'll be in and out without any problems."

"A PMC? What the fuck's that?"

"Private military company."

Teddy's mouth gaped. "You mean, like black helicopters and that kind of shit?"

Eagan nodded. "I've got personnel who can get down there undetected, but I need a legitimate bail enforcement agent to go with, just in case."

"In case of what?"

"When we get the fugitive back across the border," Eagan said, "we'll need someone to turn him over to the proper authorities."

Teddy's head rocked back and forth for several seconds. "So, you need some licensed skip tracers to bring the son of a bitch back here and turn him over to the cops?"

"Right," Eagan agreed.

Teddy glanced at Cummins. "Your firm bankrolling this?"

The lawyer nodded.

Teddy canted his head to the side, licked his lips, and smiled. "Then color me interested."

"Good. I thought you'd say that."

"But I still don't know nobody I can send down there with you," Teddy said. "At least, nobody that knows that region."

"The National Bounty Hunters' Convention starts the day after tomorrow in Las Vegas," Eagan said. "Ever heard of it?"

Teddy smirked. "Yeah. So what?"

"You going?"

Teddy shook his head. "Wasn't planning on it. Got too much shit to handle here. Plus, I can't afford no trip to Vegas, as much as I'd like to get out of this shithole."

"I'm sure if you *did* go out there," Eagan said, "you'd

be able to find somebody who could fill the bill for what we're looking for, right?"

"Maybe." Teddy raised an eyebrow, rubbed his chin with his bony fingers, and nodded. "Yeah, matter of fact, I do know a guy who's got an operation out west. He'd probably be able to put us onto somebody who could do the job."

"Not us," Cummins said. "*You* gotta handle this. We'll be flying under the radar."

"Why's that?"

Cummins took in a deep breath. "Let's just say that the firm's concerned about the PR aspect."

Teddy smirked. "Okay. So, what else?"

"What else?" Cummins asked.

"Yeah, butterball," Graham said, lifting his hand and rubbing his thumb and forefinger together. "What else is in it for me?"

Cummins smiled, leaned forward, and grabbed a pen from the jar on Teddy's desk. He scribbled a figure on a piece of paper. Teddy looked at it, and the grin widened. "Yeah, that'll work. Plus, you also agree to cover the bond forfeiture and the cost of my new insurance premiums if the snatch and grab down there ain't successful."

"Done," Cummins said, holding his open hand toward Graham. "And we're throwing in an expense-free trip to Vegas."

* * *

**BAIL BOND OFFICE OF EMMANUEL SUTTER
PHOENIX, ARIZONA**

Fifty-nine minutes later, they were standing in Manny's office, and Mac was hovering over the bail bondsman's desk. Freddie, the nephew, got up and went into the bathroom as soon as he saw them come through the door.

"Reno been here?" McNamara asked.

Manny looked down. "Yeah." He opened the drawer and placed Mac's Glock and handcuffs on the desk. "Left these here for you."

Mac grabbed the Glock first, removing the magazine and pulling back the slide to check the round in the chamber. "You can start by explaining how Reno showed up to steal our collar."

"Steal?" Manny rolled his shoulders. "I told you up front he was working on the case, too. This is a free-enterprise system."

Mac pointed his finger at him. "You tipped him we were on to Ruiz, didn't you?"

Manny's chair squeaked in protest as he leaned back. "Hey, Mac, I can't afford to get in the middle of something like this. Reno called me. Asked what you were doing here. He musta seen you come in. I told him you came in looking for an assignment. That's all."

"Bullshit."

Manny's face blanched, and he held his hands up palms-outward. "Hey, Reno's no dummy. He's good. That's why he's gonna be named Bounty Hunter of the Year. Say, you going to the conference, ain't ya? Everybody who's anybody's going to be there."

"Including you?"

Manny nodded. "All packed. Just starting to tidy up here so I can catch my flight." He opened the drawer in the center of his desk and shuffled through the clutter.

"Here, I got a couple of extra tickets somewhere. I'll give 'em to ya for what I paid for 'em."

McNamara's face twisted into a scowl and he swept the papers off Manny's desktop.

"Hey! What you do that for?" Manny looked genuinely wounded. "I told you, I didn't sic him on you intentionally. Reno was working the case before you. Maybe he was already setting up on the guy's place when you guys got there."

"You told us he'd been looking for him for a week," Mac said. "How'd he know where to go all of a sudden?"

Manny held his hands out in a who-knows gesture. "Jeez, you got me. How'd you figure it out?"

Yeah, Wolf thought. *How did you?*

"Reno couldn't find his ass with both hands and a map," McNamara said, glaring at the bail bondsman. "Somebody tipped him we were on Ruiz's trail."

"Like I said, it wasn't me." Manny flashed a nervous smile.

McNamara continued to glare at the other man. Wolf wondered if his friend was going to belt him. Finally, Mac took a deep breath, and his body relaxed.

"This ain't right, and you know it. We did all the work, and he stepped in and stole our arrest. And you had no right to tell him anything about Steve here. He's a veteran, not a jailbird."

Manny shrugged again, flashing a crooked smile. "Hey, Mac, I'm sorry, okay? I tell you what." He opened the drawer again and set another Taser on the desktop. "Keep this one. Let Tonto here use it."

"'Tonto' means stupid in Spanish," Wolf said, his anger rising.

"Sorry, pal. Native American, okay?"

McNamara balled his fists. "Maybe you and me better step outside."

Manny held up his hands again. "Hey, being politically correct ain't exactly in my DNA, you know. But I'm a lover, not a fighter. I'll even toss you a couple of easy pinches."

"I don't want your charity," Mac said. "I want Reno."

Manny's eyes widened. His mouth opened, but no sound came out.

"Where's he at?" Mac asked.

"How should I know?"

McNamara started to go around the desk. Wolf wondered again what Mac was going to do. The bondsman rolled his chair backward until it collided with the wall and crossed his arms in front of his face. "Okay, okay, okay. He came by here to collect his check, then left."

"Left for where?" Mac asked.

"Vegas, okay? Him and Herc are going to the conference, just like I told you. He's up for Bounty Hunter of the Year."

"Shit." Mac stopped and looked down at the other man, inhaled deeply, and turned toward Wolf. "Let's go pack our bags. We're going to Vegas."

Wolf nodded. "Sounds like a plan. Always wanted to see that place."

"Hey, wait a minute," Manny said. "If Reno finds out I told you—"

"He won't," Mac said. "Unless you call him and tip him again."

"Me?" Manny's upper lip was covered with sweat. "I wouldn't do that."

"You'd best not if you know what's good for you."

"Hey," Manny said, "what you gonna do?"

Mac said nothing. He turned and pulled open the door, motioning for Wolf to follow.

Wolf nodded to Manny as he turned and left.

In the parking lot, Wolf asked, "What *are* we going to do?"

"I'm gonna collect a debt," Mac said. "Those two sons of bitches owe me for a seat belt, a tire, and a new shirt, not to mention that ten grand recovery fee."

CHAPTER 6

MCCARRAN INTERNATIONAL AIRPORT
HOURLY PARKING AREA
LAS VEGAS, NEVADA

The three of them sat in the air-conditioned comfort of the spacious limo, drinking iced drinks from the car's built-in wet bar. Eagan could tell the New York bail bondsman, Teddy, was close to being half in the bag. Bringing the skinny creep along to lubricate the way for hiring some experienced skip tracers who could serve as a buffer for their excursion down to Mexico was a necessary evil.

Teddy had admitted that his contacts were all in the Big Apple, not west of the Pecos or wherever the fuck they needed to be. But the fugitive from a chemo ward did mention that he knew a fellow bail bond guy out here who could put them on the right track. That would be good enough.

Eagan knew all he needed was a couple of expendable bounty hunters as a subterfuge while he took Accondras to a safe spot and interrogated him. Still, that part had to be handled carefully and with finesse. Accondras had to be kept alive until Eagan had the authenticated artifact in his hands.

The bounty hunters would also take the blame later when things inevitably went south. Their activities to grab a fugitive with a warrant would obscure why Accondras was really grabbed. It would be put off to the exploits of the overzealous bail enforcement agents who had gone into Mexico without proper authority to grab a wanted fugitive and came in conflict with the Mexican police.

At least, that would be the assumption once the bodies were discovered. The shit-kickers were expendable. Accondras, too. No way any of it could be traced back to Von Dien and his stupid artifact. No loose ends, which was just what Fallotti and Von Dien wanted.

Fine with me, Eagan thought. The bonus money Von Dien had said he wouldn't mind paying for the artifact had sweetened the pie.

Eagan still had the Vipers' LLC account and routing numbers in the Caymans. Once the money was deposited there, the rich prick could have his little piece of petrified crap. The Lion Attacking the Nubian. Eagan didn't care about it, as long as that big deposit ended up in his bank account with no repercussions. If he played it right, this could be his last job. He'd be set for life.

He glanced at his watch again. Nasim's flight was due in from Toronto about twenty minutes ago. The limo driver had been dispatched to stand with a sign by the escalators leading to the baggage claim carousels. Once the gang was all here, they'd head to their hotel.

Eagan had mixed feelings about dealing with that camel jockey again. The last time had turned into a real clusterfuck, but what choice did he have? Nasim was the only one who could authenticate the fucking artifact. After that was done, he could pound sand up his Iranian ass as far as Eagan was concerned.

Then again, Von Dien had casually mentioned that Nasim could turn out to be another of those loose ends. That could be arranged, but there was something else. If Nasim was a liability, Eagan figured he was, as well. He'd have to make sure that he held onto the artifact until he got paid in full and then some. Disappearing to parts unknown would then be the next step. He'd have enough money to buy his own island.

"Where's this convention again?" Cummins asked. He reached over and refilled his glass from the limo's built-in bar.

Eagan noticed that Cummins was a bit tipsy too. He was on his second drink. Eagan was the only one of the three who wasn't drinking alcohol. There'd be plenty of time for partying once the mission was done.

"It's at this new hotel," Teddy said. His pale skin showed more creases than an opened fan. "The Leprechaun, or something Irish like that."

"The Shamrock," Eagan said.

Teddy grinned, causing another set of facial wrinkles to appear. "You got it."

Eagan said nothing. This human skeleton was wearing thin. As soon as he made the right introductions, Eagan would jettison him. Then again, maybe a more final solution was called for. The guy could be classified as another of those loose ends Fallotti had talked about.

Whether they let the Big Apple bondsman live or not was immaterial to Eagan, but it would put him in the good graces of the boss if he showed some initiative. All he wanted was the recovery fee for the fucking artifact. It was his ticket to a new start somewhere on a beach with a couple of half-naked, good-looking broads and an endless supply of rum and Cokes filled with ice.

"You sure about this guy you're going to introduce us to?" Cummins asked. He was starting to slur his words. Eagan was going to have to have a little talk with the former lieutenant. Instill some missing military discipline into his overweight carcass. Eagan watched him sip his drink.

He doesn't know it yet, Eagan thought, *but the party's over*.

"Manny Sutter," Teddy said. "His first name's Emanuel, but everybody calls him Manny."

"Emanuel. A good Biblical name," Cummins remarked.

Teddy nodded, the wrinkle-framed simper still plastered drunkenly on his face.

"He works this area a lot. Knows everybody out this way, even though he's based in Phoenix." Teddy shrugged, and liquid sloshed over the rim of his glass. "But Phoenix ain't actually that far from Vegas. It's drivable."

Eagan caught a flash of movement outside and stiffened. A pair of gloved knuckles rapped on the window, and the door opened. Nasim's dark face appeared in the opening, his mouth stretched into a wide grin. "Long time, no see."

Eagan smiled back at him. "Looks like the gang's all here. Climb on in, and we'll get this show on the road."

* * *

HOOVER DAM

BOULDER CITY, NEVADA

"They put this new bridge in so you don't get to drive over the dam anymore," Mac said, pointing to the right.

Wolf looked at the massive, sloping structure as they drove onward. It looked like a misplaced castle wall sandwiched between two cliffs. Beyond it lay a huge body of water. Lake Mead, Mac had told him, "The largest manmade lake in the world."

"Where's the place where you can step over the line into another time zone and lose an hour?" Wolf asked.

"By that second little turret," Mac told him. "You gain one, stepping back."

"If only time was always that easy to manage," Wolf said, thinking back to the endless days that had been divided into different segments: wake-up bell, standing morning cell check, breakfast, laundry drop, physical activity period, shower time, new clothes pick-up, lunch, back to your cell.

The monotony was occasionally broken by optional counseling or academic classes, but coming and going was always coupled with constant danger lurking around the next corner. That attack on his last day had just been one of many. Still, its timing was still an enigma to him.

Most fights arose from the constant posturing, the need to prove yourself tougher than the other guy, or the need to keep something like your body parts from being used and abused by somebody who thought they were bigger or stronger or tougher than you. Fights were commonplace, and Wolf had initially had his share, but as his reputation grew inside the walls, the challenges became virtually nonexistent. Nobody wanted to mess with him.

The last attack by the bald-headed gorilla had come out of the blue. Had somebody been trying to settle an old grudge before he shipped out? Possibly, but Wolf had been a loner, aligning himself with no one in particular except Gant, who'd been his cellmate for the better part of a year.

They went their separate ways in the yard, though. Gant chose to sit with the other blacks, and Wolf went for a run or did some katas to remind everyone, cons and guards alike, that he was one very dangerous man. Plus, his fluency in Spanish won respect from the Hispanic gang contingent. Everybody pretty much left him alone.

Pretty much.

Especially after he'd backed Gant when they'd been cornered behind a tower wall on clean-up duties. The white Aryans had been looking to exact revenge for the shanking of one of theirs by a black inmate. Six big white guys with shaved heads and crude swastika tattoos had ordered Wolf to back off as they approached Gant, two of them with their shanks drawn.

It had taken Wolf less than twenty seconds to disarm and knock down both armed goons. Then he and Gant, who was the light-heavyweight prison boxing champion, had made short work of the other four assholes. After that, a truce had been called, and the gang leaders had decided upon another means to settle the matter. Maybe that last attack had been an eleventh-hour attempt at belated payback by the Aryans.

"You look deep in thought," McNamara said.

"Just thinking about doing time." He wondered if he'd ever get that new trial and be able to clear his name. One thing he did know; he liked the idea of putting people behind bars a lot more than being behind them himself.

They were on a long stretch of a freeway now, with a cluster of buildings cropping up in the distance. "We in Vegas yet?"

"Closing in on it. The hotel we're going to is on the Strip. Maybe we'll have time to do a little sightseeing. I'll take you to the old downtown section called Fremont Street. We can stop and take in the light show on that canopy or even do a zip-line ride across the street."

Wolf shook his head. "I'm more interested in why we're here in the first place. How are we going to give that Reno guy some payback?"

McNamara's grin faded. "You think you can take him? Remember, he does that mixed martial arts stuff. That big black guy does, too."

"Then we'd better stop and buy a baseball bat."

McNamara chuckled. "Hit him with that, and it'd probably just make him madder."

"I notice you brought your gun with you. You authorized to carry in this state?"

"Sure I am," Mac replied. "As long as I don't get caught."

"So, what is our plan?"

McNamara didn't answer. Instead, he took the next exit and got off the freeway. "There's this place called the Neon Boneyard where they keep all the old signs from the hotels they tore down."

"The plan?"

"Just trying to give you a little historical perspective. You ain't never been here before, have you?"

"The plan," Wolf repeated.

McNamara chuckled. "Damn, you are one tenacious son of a bitch." He swung into a gas station and drove up next to a pump. "Out of state bounty hunter rule number one: don't run out of gas."

"What's number two?"

"That's easy." Mac's grin creased his face as he opened the door and got partially out. "Always have a plan."

* * *

THE SHAMROCK HOTEL AND CASINO
LAS VEGAS, NEVADA

The bright lights of the smoky casino greeted the four of them as they walked into its air-conditioned comfort. The hot climate outside had reminded Eagan of Iraq, but the Sandbox had been much worse. Of course, there he didn't have to worry about sweating in a business suit. Here, it was a different story. He had to appear professional, not formidable, and totally in control. Never let them see you sweat, especially when you're wearing a suit and tie.

The constant dinging of the various slot machines merged into a dissonant background like an audible curtain. The odor of burning tobacco renewed his urge to go buy a can of chaw, but he'd given that up years ago. He didn't like anything, even a craving for nicotine, having control over him.

The motif of the hotel was Irish. The Shamrock had everything cast in various shades of green, with statues of leprechauns peeking around each corner and oversized four-leaf clovers adorning the back of every chair. Even the cocktail waitresses' outfits were green and black, their boobs almost spilling out of their push-up bras and the high-cut pants pulled tight, exposing a good portion of netted nylon over their asses. Teddy's grin went from ear-to-ear, and Nasim eyed every scantily clad girl in sight. He seemed to have regressed into a traditional Muslim posture since their last meeting, refusing any alcohol in the limo. That could be good, or it could be bad. Imbibing always added to the possibility of a screw-up, but religious zealotry could be a wild card as well. Still, this was a long way from Mecca. Eagan figured he could keep the Arab occupied once things got rolling by getting him a start on his seventy-two virgins while he was here, although finding someone of that status in Sin City might prove a bit challenging.

Cummins was still sweating as he walked, even after they'd stepped inside, and Eagan wondered if the fat fucker was going to keel over. He was definitely a weak link in the chain.

As he lasts long enough to get my paycheck forwarded to the right account, Eagan thought.

"The convention center's this way," Teddy said, pointing at a set of escalators bisected by an extended staircase. Eagan estimated it to be at least two hundred steps to the top. A huge sign at the bottom of the stairs read NATIONAL BAILBOND ENFORCEMENT CONVENTION UPSTAIRS. Eagan slapped Cummins on the shoulder and asked if he wanted to race up the stairs.

"You kidding me?" Cummins shook his head. "No way. Be my guest."

Eagan considered it, then decided against it. While he had no doubt he could beat the escalator with ease, the prospect of being winded overrode the momentary tactical advantage of standing at the top looking down at the rest of them. Besides, he was venturing into unknown territory here and didn't want to stand out too much. He paused, gave one of the cocktail waitresses a twenty for four green paper derby hats, and handed them out.

"Put these on," he said, eyeing the ceilings for PTZ cameras. The hats would make them somewhat less distinguishable. "Get in the spirit of things."

Teddy smirked and slipped his on, followed by Cummins and finally Nasim, who looked leery.

"I think the first thing I'll do is get laid," Teddy said.

"Wrong," Eagan countered. "Your gonads can wait. The first thing you'll do is find us that guy you were talking about. The one with the connections in this neck of the woods."

Teddy frowned but nodded. "All right, all right. Let's get up to our room, and I'll see if I can find his number and give him a call."

Eagan nodded and stepped onto the escalator behind the three of them, continuing to scan the walls and ceilings for the ubiquitous cameras. He knew they were providing a video trail he had no hope of controlling, but the hats would help. Just four more drunken idiots here for a good time. What happens in Vegas stays in Vegas.

Hopefully.

Low-key was the way to go. For now, anyway. Later, when they were in the field, or at least in a place with no cameras or police around, he would be more assertive.

CHAPTER 7

LAS VEGAS, NEVADA

As they proceeded toward Las Vegas proper, Wolf took in the brown mountains in the distance that reminded him of his tours in Afghanistan and along the DMZ in Korea. An explosion of houses sprang up on both sides of the roadway, with all sorts of homes in basins between the uneven landscape while others sat up on escarpments.

The residential buildings gave way to commercial structures ranging from the standard array of gas stations and chain stores to rows of low motels, hotels, and casinos. The occasional vacant lot had clusters of election posters lining the sidewalk, extending back into mosaics of papers, plastic bottles, and other urban detritus.

They passed under a viaduct where a couple of homeless people had erected two blue plastic curtains to form tents. A pile of feces resided on the sidewalk between them as odiferous demarcation.

The Third World's gaining ground on us, Wolf thought. Even here in Sin City.

At least in the Sandbox, they'd had good latrines. At Leavenworth too, although those always held the potential for danger and violence.

The road morphed into four lanes bisected by a grassy median. Wolf saw that the street sign proclaimed Las Vegas Boulevard. After passing the iconic angular Welcome to Fabulous Las Vegas Nevada sign, a white ellipsoid edged in gold and topped by a flashy red eight-pointed star that hovered over the lettering, the building got higher, and in the distance, a still taller skyline was visible. Rows of stores and smaller structures gave way to bigger and bigger high rises.

A small private airport extension was on the right, and a few football fields over, a jet plane soared into the late afternoon sky.

The street expanded to six lanes, and an X-shaped wedge of tall white-topped high-rise buildings trimmed in gold marked what Mac said was the beginning of the Strip. The hotel was set back from the street behind open metal gates, and a wide private drive gave way to sculptured lawns, trees, and gushing fountains.

It looked like something out of a theme park. Next to the ornate gold-colored windows decorating the sides of the huge wedge of buildings lay a shiny black pyramid that looked like a glistening version of an ancient Egyptian fantasy, replete with a huge faux sphinx in front.

An old-fashioned castle framed by brilliant blue- and red-topped turrets lay on their left, and an older beige-colored hotel, the Tropicana, was on the right.

Across the street, an ersatz Statue of Liberty stood prominently in front of a miniaturized Manhattan skyline, and opposite that, the MGM Hotel beckoned with a quartet of reflective bright-greenish buildings with flashing billboards advertising shows, fights, and who knew what else. The statue of an immense golden recumbent lion kept watch over the busy intersection.

Wolf tried to take it all in, but it was overwhelming.

"Man, this place is something," he said, thinking it was a monument to American excess.

McNamara chuckled.

"It sure is, ain't it?"

"Looks like Disneyland for adults," Wolf commented.

"That's a good comparison. Lots of pretty gals around, too." McNamara clucked his tongue. "We still have to work on number two on your list, too, don't we?"

Wolf thought back to number two, get laid, then shook his head. He wasn't sure about that one at the moment. It had been a long time since he'd been with a woman in an intimate context. Although he hated to admit it, he found the idea at this point. "I thought this was all about business."

"Hell, it is," Mac said. "But that don't mean we can't take some time off to enjoy ourselves a little bit."

Wolf said nothing. Enjoyment took money in this town.

And at present, he didn't have very much of it. The last thing he wanted to do was to keep sponging off his friend and mentor. He already owed Mac way too much.

"How about I start earning my way a little more before we talk about that?"

McNamara snorted. "You will be as soon as we catch up to Reno."

Wolf didn't like the sound of that. Not that he was

afraid of him. He was confident he could hold his own against either Reno or the black guy, Herc.

Both of them were big and had the weight advantage, but Wolf had seen the way they'd moved—muscle-bound and slow, especially the big black guy. Speed and endurance would be the keys to fighting them, though hopefully not both at once. That and delivering solid kicks to their knees. No matter how big they were, once the supports were knocked out of place, the whole house came crashing down.

He'd faced many a bigger foe in the cell blocks, bathrooms, and prison yard at Leavenworth, where there were no rules except one: survive. And the times he'd fought in the ring, it had been his experience that the guys with the big muscles ran out of gas sooner rather than later. His wind was pretty good from running up and down the mountain on a regular basis.

Still, taking on two professional fighters would likely prove problematic, especially considering that MMA fighters trained for five-minute rounds.

But he owed Mac, even if it meant getting his ass kicked. He'd just have to give as good as he got. There wouldn't be any rules on the street, either.

McNamara turned right and headed down to the next intersection. The heights of the buildings lessened, with fewer tall buildings on the left and more of the airport and planes on the right. After a quick left turn at the next intersection, they proceeded down a street that was slightly less populated by the ubiquitous flow of vehicles.

"The convention hotel's down a ways," McNamara said. "At the Shamrock."

"Maybe it'll bring us luck," Wolf said. "You're Irish, right?"

"Scots-Irish, just like the Duke."

"The Duke?"

McNamara sighed. "John Wayne."

"That gonna help us get a room there?"

"Kasey already took care of that. Got us a nice suite at a place down the way. It's called Motel Six. I'm sure they'll leave the light on for us."

Wolf laughed. They'd both slept in worse. "As long as the roof don't leak."

"Right," Mac said, shifting lanes to the sound of protesting horns. "We'll park at the Shamrock and do some recon first."

"If we can get there without an accident," Wolf said.

McNamara snorted. "We'll get there, all right. Then we'll do some settling up."

After turning into a parking garage and going over a series of speed bumps, McNamara accelerated up the ramp that wound between rows and rows of parked vehicles. They seemed to ascend forever, but finally, they emerged from the penumbra of the last covered level onto the uppermost one in the fading sunshine. Finding a place large enough to accommodate the Escalade proved a bit tricky, but they settled on an isolated space at the far end of the lot. McNamara secured his Glock in the special metal case between the seats and locked it.

"You going to feel a bit undressed without that?" Wolf asked.

McNamara smiled. "Nah. Like I told you, the clothes make the man."

They walked across the open roof area toward a set of elevators. The temperature was similar to Phoenix's: sunny, hot, and dry. They were still dressed for traveling in comfort in jeans, t-shirts, and gym shoes, but after parking, they'd both slipped on their loose-fitting BDU blouses. The garments had been specially modified with additional inside pockets and epaulets to accommodate clip-on mini-mag flashlights. Additionally, the sleeves had been removed for extra coolness. Both garments were camo-patterned, with Wolf's being gray and white and McNamara's having dark tiger stripes.

The height of the parking structure gave them a bird's eye view of the profusion of surrounding buildings. Across the street, the fronts of several hotels displayed flashing neon lights as well as statues, cultured landscaping, and exotic designs. An immense Ferris wheel with plastic capsules large enough to accommodate half a dozen people rotated at an infinitesimal pace.

McNamara pointed out several other hotels and landmarks, then tapped his knuckles on the wall by the elevator button. "I forget what this here place used to be called. It's been bought and sold and remodeled so many times."

The indicator light dinged, and the doors opened.

"Hit the button marked casino," McNamara said. "You gotta go through there to get to anyplace else in the hotel."

"Figures," Wolf said. "This place is all about business, too."

The car descended, stopping at every level on the way down. An assortment of middle-aged tourists got on, as well as a pair of beautiful women, one blonde and one brunette, whose heavy makeup and tight clothes labeled them as working girls. Both were busy texting and paid Wolf little attention.

Maybe working on number two on that list might be in the cards after all, he thought wistfully. *But these chicks are way out of my league unless I can somehow grab a windfall at an overripe slot machine.*

But even then, the idea didn't really appeal to him much. The specter of his bleak financial situation and unpaid debts edged out all other considerations at the moment. Also, his disastrous attempt at reentering the dating scene with Consuela still loomed large.

Baby steps, he thought.

The elevator stopped, and after the doors opened, everyone shuffled out. McNamara made a show of ogling the blonde girl's low-cut display of ample cleavage, then held up his index and middle fingers, mouthing "Number two" and pointing at Wolf.

The corridor gave way to a longer section with a pattern of green and white tiles on the floor. The walls were lined with plaster figurines in recessed slots, each peeking through four-leaf clovers they held in different positions. Each frozen impish face displayed a conspiratorial wink. The corridor widened into a walkway with shops, restaurants, and snack stands every few feet. They came to another open expanse, and McNamara headed toward a pair of long escalators, over which a gold sign flashed the lighted letters spelling CASINO.

Looks like it's getting close to showtime, Wolf thought as he mentally began to formulate the first moves he would use on each of his opponents. He wondered how effective they'd be.

"Remember, we're here for recon only," McNamara said as if he'd read the concern on Wolf's face. "Not to go toe-to-toe with Reno and King Kong's little brother."

"That's not very politically correct of you," Wolf said.

They were almost at the bottom of the escalator now.

McNamara laughed. "Yeah, you're right. I wouldn't want to insult the anthropoidal species by associating that moron, Herc, with one of them."

Wolf knew Mac didn't have a prejudiced bone in his

body. They'd both lived and served with men of all races, creeds, and colors and had killed quite a few variations of each one as well. In the combat brotherhood, nobody cared what your ethnicity or religion was, only that you had each other's backs.

They stepped off the escalator, and Wolf saw row after row of brightly lit slot machines clustered in bunches with comfortable-looking padded chairs in front of each. A cacophony of ringing sounds, each signifying a pull of the lever, drowned out any music or conversation. Cigarette smoke hung in the air and irritated his lungs. He'd been around tobacco all his life, but he'd never used it despite the ritualistic significance it held for some tribes in the Native American community. The smell of it bothered him.

He saw a guy perched in one of the seats, cigarette in one hand, drink in the other, staring intently at the spinning symbols inside the three slotted vents before him. They stopped in a mismatched pattern, and the man reached up and punched one of the buttons. The symbols started their spins again.

Interspersed between the clusters of slots were tables housing card games and craps. One black guy reached into his pants pocket and tossed two hundreds on the green felt surface. He rolled the dice between his palms, held them in front of a gorgeous woman to his right, and waited for her to blow on his hands. She did, and his arm shot outward.

Wolf saw the dice hit the opposite end of the table barrier and land with four dots facing upward. Snake eyes. The dealer used a long rake to sweep the bills toward her.

McNamara clucked sympathetically and turned to say, "You don't always break even in this town."

Obviously, Wolf thought. Not that he had any money to gamble with anyway. His thoughts returned to Reno and his buddy. Even though Mac had downplayed the idea of a confrontation, it would be prudent to remain vigilant.

Spot them before they spot us, he thought.

McNamara pointed at an oval-shaped bar and slid onto an open stool where he had a more or less clear view of the rest of the casino. Two large four-leaf clovers were suspended over each end of the bar, and a cocktail waitress in low-cut green satin and fishnet stockings stood a few feet away from them, holding a silver tray. She smiled, and Wolf smiled back. The bartender came over and set three drinks on the tray, and she winked as she turned away, her jiggling breasts barely contained by her lime-green décolletage.

Grinning, McNamara flipped the bartender a bill and ordered two beers.

"Nothing like the sight of a pair of well-filled cups, is there?"

"Depends on what they're filled with," Wolf said.

Mac laughed. "Yeah, you're right about that."

The bartender set the steins down, and McNamara picked his up, took a sip of the froth, and swiveled to face the crowd. Wolf did the same but didn't touch his beer.

A large banner had been strung across a hallway leading to another section proclaiming WELCOME NATIONAL BAIL ENFORCEMENT AGENTS CONVENTION.

"So, what's the plan?" Wolf asked. "Look for Reno and company?"

"Nah, that son of a bitch can wait." Mac took another sip, but it was a dainty one. "Right now, I'm just recon-

noitering. Looking for familiar faces. Manny's supposed
to be here, too. Maybe he can introduce us to some new
bail bondsmen out this-a-way."

A trio of guys in leather vests with lots of tattoos and
armbands with RENO RULES printed on them sauntered past, obviously trying to look tough. They were
heading toward the area designated by the banner. One
of them gave Wolf and McNamara the once-over as they
passed and whispered something to the guy next to him.
That one looked, then smirked.

Yeah, we're here, Wolf thought. Back in Indian
Country.

* * *

Eagan checked the long hallway on the second floor as
the nice-looking woman in the business suit led the four
of them to the meeting room he had reserved. The hall
ran parallel to the main floor of the casino, and several
windows provided glimpses of the throngs of people
below. Teddy looked like a human scarecrow next to this
new bail bondsman, who had to tip the scales at close to
four hundred. The guy looked like a throwback to the
seventies, or at least what Eagan knew about that period.
The two of them walking side by side down the hall
made Cummins appear small. The son of a bitch was
looking winded just from carrying the briefcase with the
pertinent information in it. Eagan hadn't liked dealing
with him in Iraq, and he didn't care for it now. He would
have preferred to handle this negotiation himself, but
Cummins had a better grasp of the particulars. Plus,
Fallotti's law firm was paying the bills, so for now, he'd
let Lieutenant Blubber handle things.

"Here it is," the woman said. The brunette had a slim

figure with nice legs. Eagan allowed himself a moment to consider what she might look like without all those clothes. He smiled and shook his head when she asked if they'd like anything else.

Inside were four chairs positioned around a table. Cummins entered first and set the briefcase on the tabletop.

Eagan noticed there was a bit of moisture around his flabby neck.

How had this guy ever made it through basic training, much less OCS?

But that had been a while ago, and Cummins had only been a reservist.

Lieutenant Blubber held out his hand toward the other behemoth and introduced himself.

"I'm very glad to meet you, Mr. Sutter," he said. "Teddy has told us a lot about you."

"None of it good, I imagine." The big face twisted with a wry grin. "And please, call me Manny."

"Okay, Manny," Cummins said as he lowered his obese frame into one of the chairs. "Sit down. Take a load off."

Manny descended with the care of a big man who knew better than to flop into any chair that might need reinforcement. As it was, the black leather chair emitted what sounded like a groan. Teddy the human skeleton took a seat next to Cummins. Eagan walked around the table and positioned himself so he was facing the door.

"So, what gives, Teddy?" Manny asked. "You said on the phone that you needed some help on a skip trace."

Teddy flashed a quick glance at Cummins and Eagan, then smiled.

"Yeah, I got talked into taking on a risky client," he said. "And it looks like he's left me high, wide, and handsome. I stand to lose a hundred grand if he don't show for court next week, and word is he won't."

Manny chuckled. "A hundred grand? What'd he do? Rob the New York Mint?"

Teddy snorted. "I wish. You heard what's happening in the Big Apple, ain't ya? They got this new law where they're letting people go without posting any bond. Stuff that used to be my bread and butter: burglary, stalking, manslaughter... And they're giving them game show tickets to show up in court. It's nuts."

"Christ," Manny said. "I hope that don't happen out in Phoenix."

"It's probably coming the way things are going, pal." Teddy emitted a series of hacking coughs, then got himself under control. "Anyway, this kind of forfeiture could ruin me."

"And the turd's out this way somewhere?" Manny asked.

The skin of Teddy's face seemed to flatten out over the angular bones of his skull. "We got a line on him. He's in Mexico."

Manny blew out a heavy breath. "Shit. You're fucked, then."

Teddy leaned forward, becoming almost animated. "Don't say that. Like I said, things are going to hell in a handbasket in New York. I need some dependable skip tracers who can slip down there and bring this shitbird back to me."

Manny's face contorted and he leaned back in his chair. It gave off a dire metallic squeak.

"I don't know. It ain't so easy going down there now. The cartels, lots of crooked cops to pay off. You might end up spending a whole lot of money and get nothing."

Teddy's tongue flicked over his lips. He cast a furtive

glance at Eagan, then looked at the other man. "We know where he'd hiding. It's in a *gringo* resort. Lots of foreigners living there. Should be a piece of cake."

"But then you got to worry about bringing him back through the border," Manny countered. "That's not gonna be easy."

"As porous as our southern border is?" Cummins asked. "Even with the new additions to the wall, we have that angle covered."

Manny shifted in the chair, focusing on the lawyer. "What's the name of your law firm again?"

Cummins took a breath, then reached into his shirt pocket. He took out a business card and handed it to Manny. "Fallotti and Abraham. We do a lot of work for a very exclusive clientele."

Manny accepted the card, glanced at it, and slipped it into his pocket.

"So, what's your connection to all this? You representing the skip?"

"Hardly." Cummins straightened and assumed a posture of righteousness. "We represent the family of the victim."

"Victim?" Manny's face contorted again. "What'd this guy do?"

"Child molestation," Teddy said.

Manny's expression twisted into one of revulsion. "A *short-eyes*? And you posted bond for that piece of shit?"

Teddy glanced at Eagan again.

Stick with the story we rehearsed, Eagan repeated mentally and willed Teddy to hear the unspoken words.

"I told ya," Teddy said. "Things are stone-cold crazy in New York now. I can barely keep my head above water. And this shitbird supposedly came from a real good family."

"Why didn't *they* post bond for him, then?"

Teddy rolled his eyes. "It was all handled through a third party. Claimed they had all their assets tied up and couldn't come up with the cash, so they put up some bullshit stocks and bonds as collateral. Turns out they ain't worth shit. Next to nothing. And now I'm left holding the bag."

Manny seemed to consider this, then looked askance at Cummins.

"You still ain't told me how Fallotti and Abraham's involved."

Cummins cleared his throat and smiled. It looked forced.

Come on, thought Eagan. *Don't choke on us now, you fat slob.*

"As I said, we represent the victim's family. They want justice to be done. They hired us to assist with the prosecution. Not officially, of course, more of a behind-the-scenes involvement. The suspect's family does have substantial assets abroad, including a residence down in Mexico where the suspect is staying. We've hired a private investigator who's located him down there."

Eagan watched as Manny's large frame relaxed.

"You mentioned you had the border thing covered?" he asked.

Cummins flipped the twin catches on the briefcase, lifted the lid, and removed a sheaf of papers.

"Let's just say that we've engaged the services of Mr. *Smith* here." Cummins extended his open palm toward Eagan. "He runs an organization that has special capabilities, one of which is flying helicopters. They have experience in transporting individuals to and from different areas."

Manny gave Eagan the once-over, then his lips curled back in a half-smile, exposing some of his crooked teeth.

"Why don't *you* go down and get him, then?"

Eagan said nothing. They were still on track as far as their cover story and plan, and the ball was still with Cummins.

"They're strictly a transportation entity," Cummins explained. "Your men can go down there and grab the target, bring him to a designated area, and Mr. Smith's group will take him back across. Your men can then proceed back through the checkpoint as if nothing happened. The plan is foolproof."

Manny emitted a long breath, then brought his finger up to scratch his ear.

"And how are my men, as you call them, gonna get credit for the pinch?"

"I'll see they get the ten percent," Teddy said quickly.

"And we're willing to pay a bonus as well," Cummins added. He plucked a pen out of his pocket and scribbled a figure on the hotel tablet on the table.

Manny's eyebrows rose when he glanced at it.

"What do I get for arranging all this?"

"You get Teddy and our eternal gratitude," Cummins said. "And..." He scribbled another amount on the tablet, circled it, and held it toward Manny.

The huge man smiled.

"I think I got just the guys for you," he said, taking out his cell phone. "And one of them's about to be named Bounty Hunter of the Year."

* * *

"Well, well, well," a voice said from behind them. "You get your tire fixed, Big Mac?"

Wolf turned to see Reno Garth in a buckskin jacket with decorative fringe hanging in patterns from the sleeves and in a V-shape across the front. Underneath it, he wore a light-blue shirt and a string tie with a bulbous plastic slide. Suspended inside it was a dead scorpion.

As Reno's grin pulled his lips back, Wolf noticed that the man's front teeth looked way too perfect to be real. Obviously, he held his guard a bit too low in the octagon. There were ridges of scar tissue over both eyebrows, and both ears were even more cauliflower than Wolf remembered from their brief encounter. Of course, that time he'd been more focused on other things.

The big black guy, Herc, was next to him wearing a tuxedo, complete with a knotted bowtie. His smile was so wide that his teeth looked like a miniature piano. The upper arms of the tailored garment were stretched by the man's massive upper arms.

McNamara smiled at their adversaries.

"As a matter of fact, I did," he said. "As soon as I get that seatbelt your gentle here damaged fixed, I'll be sending you the bill for both."

Reno's smile didn't change, but Herc looked puzzled.

"Gentle?" he said. "What you mean?"

"Relax," McNamara said. "It's a compliment. Didn't you ever read *The Maltese Falcon*?"

"Huh? What you talking about?"

McNamara shook his head and clucked sympathetically. "You should really try to expand your horizons, big fella. Especially if you're gonna go around calling yourself Hercules."

"That's *Black* Hercules to you, sucker."

McNamara affected surprise, then exaggerated his Southern accent. "You're a black guy? Shucks, I heard of y'all. Mind if I check under your watchband?"

The big son of a bitch is as tense as a coiled spring, Wolf thought.

He shifted his body off the stool and stood, ready to slam the beer stein into the black man's face should he make a hostile move. They were close, so the subsequent strike would have to be quick and to a vital area, like a ridge hand to the throat.

The black man's head swiveled toward Wolf.

"What?" Herc said. "You want something, small fry?"

"You know," Wolf said, "I'm getting real tired of you calling me that."

"Herc, relax," Reno said, still smirking. "These two are just jealous, that's all. We stole their pinch, flattened their tire, and there ain't squat they can do about it."

"We'll see about that," McNamara said. "But it *is* good advice."

"Damn right, it is," Reno said. The smile on his face was fading.

"So I suggest you take it," McNamara said. "Before we put a hurt on you, messing up your ill-fitting gorilla tux and his Roy Rogers jacket."

"Gorilla?" Herc started to edge forward, but McNamara jammed his right hand into the lowest pocket of his BDU and extended a protuberance in the big man's direction.

"I wouldn't do that," McNamara said. "I got me a nice little Bond Arms two-shot derringer in my pocket here. Forty-five caliber, too. Make a real nice hole in that pretty ruffled shirt of yours."

Reno put his arm in front of the black man, and Herc stopped.

"You wouldn't dare," Reno said. "Not in here in front of everybody."

A smile curled McNamara's lips back. "Wouldn't I?"

Reno's face twitched. "How do we know you ain't bluffing?"

"First of all, I never bluff. And second, the nicest thing about this particular derringer is that the barrels are all interchangeable. That means I can blow two holes in each of your big old chests, then remove the barrels and switch in my second pair right quick. I drop the old barrels down a sewer hole, and *voila*. No ballistics that are traceable back to this gun, even if they catch me with the weapon on me."

Herc's face was livid. Reno kept his open palm pressed against his partner's huge chest.

"As big as you are," McNamara continued, "you'd be a tempting target that would be way too hard to miss."

"You ain't gonna do nothing," Herc said. "They got cameras in here, motherfucker."

"The cameras are watching the tables, boo," McNamara said. "I could put one round in each of you and get up and walk away before anybody'd care to notice." He smiled. "And then you wouldn't be able to get your little award, would you, Reno?"

Reno's smirk twisted into a sneer and he turned, pushing Herc away from the confrontation. "Come on, let's get outta here. I don't want to mess up getting that award." He spat on the floor next to McNamara's stool. "These two ain't nothing."

"I'll be coming for you, sucker," Herc shouted as he gesticulated by pointing the fingers of both hands at them. "And I'll be coming real soon."

"Yeah? Well, keep threatening me in public, why don't ya?" McNamara said, his grin widening. "I'm sure somebody's got a cell phone video of it by now with real good sound."

Herc looked like Mr. T on a rampage in a Rocky

movie, but the mohawked Reno kept pushing him away. He reached to his belt, pulled out his cell phone, and looked at it.

"Come on," he said. "He ain't nothing. And somebody's calling me." Reno cocked his head around and said over his shoulder. "We'll be settling up for this one, Big Mac. Just you wait. You too, jailbird."

Mac smiled as they trundled off, then he swiveled and winked at Wolf.

"That went a long way toward making up for that earlier humiliation," McNamara said.

"You weren't really gonna shoot him, were you?" Wolf asked.

"Yep. Right through the heart." Mac pulled his right hand, index finger still extended, out of his pocket. "Only I lied about having two shots with this one."

Wolf grinned. "Remind me never to play poker with you."

"Well, if you ever do," Mac said, reaching into the lower left side pocket of his BDU blouse and withdrawing the handle of a derringer so briefly that Wolf only caught a glimpse. "Just remember, I never bluff."

* * *

Forty minutes later, Eagan sat in his suite in the hotel and sipped a club soda as he contemplated the op thus far. He was far from satisfied. Things seemed loose, and he didn't like loose. He'd been less than impressed with Reno Garth and his muscle-bound associate after they'd been summoned to the conference room by the Arizona bail bondsman. "The Bounty Hunter of the Year," as fat Manny had introduced him, seemed like a blowhard with a mohawk and an old-style king-of-the-cowboys fringe jacket than a professional. And the guy's partner, Black Hercules, looked like a gorilla in a tuxedo. He wondered if they had the smarts to follow instructions and not screw up. Eagan had asked them if they knew how to go to coordinates on a map, and the one called Reno had looked at him like he'd just been asked a question about nuclear physics.

"We can provide you with a GPS," Cummins interceded.

That could work as long as they retrieved the instrument from them after they'd dropped Accondras at the LZ.

It seemed simple enough. All they had to do was grab Accondras from his parents' villa—and the private dick, Zerbe, was supposedly working that angle—bring him to the pre-planned location, then get their payoff. That their payoff would be in lead instead of Benjamins would be their problem. Once they'd committed to doing this job, they became one more loose end that had to be tied up before the rest of the Viper crew could make it back to safe soil. He wondered, however, if they'd be missed. Being Bounty Hunter of the Year carried a certain notoriety in the skip tracer circuit.

Maybe bringing them into the deal wasn't such a good idea after all.

Eagan also knew he needed that layer of insulation to protect him, Fallotti, and ultimately Von Dien from any subsequent scrutiny should things go wrong. Of course, if Reno and Herc were caught by the Mexican police, they were registered bounty hunters trying to apprehend an actual fugitive wanted on a legitimate warrant. They would rot in some Mexican jail with nobody to pay to get them out. But the Bounty Hunter of the Year?

Maybe somebody would, he thought. And that could lead back to us.

Eagan blew out a slow breath.

Cummins seemed satisfied, but it had been his lack of foresight and piss-poor planning that had forced the scrambled cover-up back in Iraq that had framed Wolf. It worked out well that Nasim had set up that IED. Came in handy to add a bit of punctuation to Wolf's patrol escort. But the whole thing was sloppy, even though Lieutenant Butterball had claimed to have all the bases covered. This time, Eagan wasn't going to be left holding the bag. He had no IEDs to detonate here.

His cell phone buzzed, and he glanced at the number.

Speak of the devil, he thought, and pressed the button to answer the call.

"You ain't gonna believe it," Cummins said. He was panting and out of breath and his voice sounded panicked.

"Slow down," Eagan said. "Believe what?"

"Wolf. He's here."

"What? Where?"

"Here in the hotel. I just saw him. I went downstairs with Manny for a celebratory drink, but I had to go take a piss first. When I came out, I saw Manny talking to two guys, and one of them's Wolf."

"What? You sure it's him?"

"Goddamn right, I am."

"He see you?"

"No. When I saw him, I ducked behind a pillar and called you."

Another fuck-up. But if Lieutenant Blubber could be believed, this one could be salvaged. But how the hell did Wolf, of all people, suddenly get on the scene, and what was he doing talking to that Manny guy? Could he have somehow gotten wind of them?

"Eagan?" Cummins said. "You there?"

"Yeah. They still talking to him?"

"Don't know," Cummins said. "I hightailed it outta there. Want me to go back and look?"

That wouldn't do. Lieutenant Blubber was about as stealthy as a hungry St. Bernard in a butcher shop. It was better to operate on the assumption that Wolf, however he had gotten there, hadn't seen Cummins and didn't know why they were there.

But that fat fuck, Manny, did.

"No," Eagan said. "Get your ass back up here without letting them see you."

"But—"

"I don't want to hear any fucking buts. Just do it. I don't care if you have to walk out the front exit and circle around to the employees' entrance. Don't let them see you. You got it?"

"Yeah."

"Good. Now do it."

Eagan hung up without waiting for a response.

Some fucking Army officer material, he thought. And in military intelligence, no less. That gasbag couldn't find his way out of a men's room with two entrances. He scrolled through his cell phone lexicon and pressed the button for Teddy's number. It rang several times, then went to voice mail.

Eagan thought about leaving a message but decided against it. Instead, he went to his room phone and dialed the front desk. The skeleton had mentioned that he wanted to get laid. Maybe he was waiting for some pussy.

When the receptionist answered, he asked to be

connected to Mr. Graham's room. The phone rang once and Teddy picked up, sounding anxious.

"We need to talk," Eagan said.

"Ah, can't it wait? I'm expecting company."

Eagan figured that meant he was waiting for a hooker or for room service.

"No, it can't. I need you to call your buddy, Manny. We got to see him. We got a problem in the making."

"Huh? What kind of problem."

"I'll explain when you get to my room."

"But I got a girl on the way."

"So call her back and tell her you'll be a while. When we're finished here, I'll buy you two of them. Call that fat fucker Manny back right now, and tell him we got to see him immediately. Alone. And find out who those two guys he was just talking to are."

"Huh? What two guys?"

Eagan took a deep breath before he answered. This was like running a football play with a bunch of players who didn't understand the game.

"He was just down in the bar talking to—" He stopped. Better not to try to explain it right now. "Never mind. Just get your ass down to my room. Now."

Teddy was silent for a few seconds, then heaved a sigh and said, "Okay. On the way."

He sounded like a teenager who'd been stood up on his first date.

Eagan terminated the call and came up with a new idea. Maybe this thing was salvageable after all.

He quickly dialed Nasim's cell and waited. The last thing in the world he needed now would be for that camel jockey to go prancing around in the casino and have Wolf see him. The Arab answered on the second ring.

"Where are you?" Eagan asked.

"In my room. It is almost time for *Maghrib*."

Maghrib. Sundown prayers. This fucker was more devout than Eagan remembered. Or maybe it was just being caught up in the Western glitter of Las Vegas.

Brings out the Muslim in the best of them, Eagan thought.

"There's a problem," he said. "A significant one. I need you to stay in your room, out of sight, until you hear from me. If you need food, order room service. Understand?"

"Yes."

Eagan resisted the temptation to say *"Insha'Allah,"* Arabic for "And so it goes," fearing Nasim would take it as sarcasm. He still needed the towelhead to authenticate the artifact. Instead, he repeated a few banalities and said he would re-contact him shortly, after things were safe.

Someone knocked on the door. Eagan reached it in three steps and pulled it open.

The human skeleton stood there, looking even more emaciated. Losing his chance to get some professional tail seemed to have drained him even more.

"You get a hold of your buddy, Manny?"

"Yeah," Teddy said. "He asked me what's up and where you wanted to meet."

"Okay, call him back and tell him you'll meet him in the conference room in ten minutes. Makes sure he comes alone. And ask him who those two guys he was talking to in the bar a few minutes ago are."

Teddy winced, then shrugged. He took out his phone and poised a finger above the screen. "What am I supposed to tell him again?"

Christ, thought Eagan. He repeated his last instructions and ended with, "Tell him there's a problem that just came up with our business proposition. Tell him it involves money."

Teddy nodded and made the call.

As Eagan listened to Teddy's side of it, there was another knock on the door. Eagan opened it and saw Cummins face, red and wet with perspiration.

Eagan pulled the fat man inside and glanced up and down the hallway.

Nobody.

"He didn't see me," Cummins assured him.

Teddy was talking on the phone, but Eagan could hear little of the conversation. After a series of grunts, the skeleton hung up.

"Okay, he's on the way," Teddy said.

"He say who those guys were he was talking to?"

"Yeah, a couple of bounty hunters he knows."

"Bounty hunters?"

"Yeah. The guy's name is Big Jim McNamara. Him and his new partner. They're from Phoenix."

Phoenix. So that was where Wolf had landed after getting out of Leavenworth. His mind worked, then it came to him. It was all about tying up those loose ends, and this one had been dropped in his lap. It was too good to pass up.

"They any good?" Eagan asked.

Teddy shrugged.

"Ask him," Eagan said. He scrolled on his phone and pressed Dan Reynolds' cell. He was one of the few Vipers with formal education and was well-spoken. He used to be part of Stu's sale pitch meetings. Reynolds answered after three rings.

"You got a suit or a sports jacket with you?" Eagan asked.

"No, why?"

"Go down to the gift shop and get a nice dress shirt and a necktie," Eagan said. "Something conservative. And some bandages to cover the Viper tattoo on your hand. Then double-time it to my room."

"Roger that," Reynolds said.

He was a bright, dependable guy who looked enough like a lawyer to pass for one, except for the damn tattoo. It was going to take a bit of crafting, like pulling off a quarterback sneak on the one-yard line, but it could work.

If I can keep juggling all these balls in the air, Eagan thought

CHAPTER 8

LAS VEGAS, NEVADA

"But I thought you'd decided on using Reno and Herc?" Teddy asked.

"Changed my mind," Eagan replied.

Teddy blew out a long breath. "Well, I don't know if he's gonna like that. Manny already told them they got the job."

Eagan frowned. "I'll talk to Reno. I got his cell number. I'll call him and tell him we've got him some helpers."

Teddy shook his head. "But Manny said the four of them don't like each other. Bad blood."

That was even better. It would make things easier.

"I already said I'd take care of Reno." Eagan felt his anger rising. Dealing with these idiots was always irritating but necessary. "Just don't tell Wolf and his buddy anything about Reno."

"But what if these other guys ask questions? Maybe they seen me talking to Reno and that big black guy?"

Eagan thought about that. It was a possibility. After a few seconds of consideration, he said, "All right, if they ask, tell them Reno's having second thoughts. Like, he's afraid to go down to Mexico."

Teddy's mouth pulled tight. "I don't know. I hear that dude Reno's pretty tough. He's an MMA fighter and prides himself on being a professional badass."

"I'll handle him."

"But what if he don't go along with that?"

"Just do it. I told you, I'll handle him." Eagan thought about it some more. It could be just what the doctor ordered, another layer of insulation between him and Accondras' abduction. It certainly couldn't hurt.

Teddy shrugged. "Okay, if that's the way you want it."

"That's the way I want it," Eagan said. "When Manny gets here, take him down to the casino, find Wolf and his buddy, and offer them the fucking job."

Teddy turned, then halted. "How will I know who the hell they are?"

"Have Manny call them. I'm sure he has their number."

Teddy frowned. "I don't like it. What if he don't buy it? Word might've gotten around that you already hired Reno and Herc."

Eagan blew out a slow breath. "Just do what I fucking told you. I'll take care of the rest."

Teddy shrugged and rolled his eyes. "And I was about to get laid."

There was a knock at the door. Eagan strode over, opened it, and saw Reynolds standing there, holding a white plastic bag.

"Got the stuff," he said.

Eagan pulled him inside, looked out, and glanced up and down the hallway.

No sign of Manny yet. He closed the door. Reynolds was already slipping off his polo shirt. The Viper tattoo extended down his forearm and encroached on the top part of his right hand.

"Hey, he's got a tattoo like yours," Teddy said.

Eagan ignored him and ripped open the box of Band-Aids. He thrust the torn box toward Reynolds, who began peeling the adhesive strips and placing them over his tattoo.

Cummins peered down at the process.

"Reynolds," Eagan said, "you're going to be playing a representative of the law firm of Fallotti and Abraham for this little interlude. Jack here will brief you on what to say."

Cummins nodded at Reynolds, who grabbed the folded shirt and began removing the securing pins.

Teddy's face scrunched. "You ain't coming with me like before?"

"No. Wolf can't know that Cummins and I are involved."

"Huh? Why not?"

"We've got history. Bad history."

"I don't know," Teddy said. "This whole thing's starting to stink pretty bad."

"It'll work," Eagan said. "Throw some dough at them." He gave Teddy a wad of cash. "Buy them all some drinks. Remember, say you called Manny because Reno was having second thoughts, like he's afraid to go down to Mexico. If they don't like each other, they'll jump at it. Reynolds can give Wolf just enough info to get him down there."

Teddy's cell phone rang, and he answered it.

"Yeah, Manny," Teddy said, his skeletal face turning

toward Eagan with a smile. "Where you at? We gotta talk."

* * *

"Where the hell did Manny go in such a hurry?" Wolf asked.

McNamara shrugged. "Don't know, but I told him I was expecting him to steer us onto some new clients."

"I wonder what him and Reno were talking about earlier?"

They'd seen the heavyset bail bondsman emerge from the elevators with Reno and Herc. When the two bounty hunters had departed for the convention floor, Mac had caught Manny's eye and waved him over. After a brief conversation, during which Manny seemed particularly evasive, the bail bondsman had gotten a call and abruptly departed.

"I guess we'll just have to wonder about that. Something was off, though." He stopped, his eyes widening. "Oh, Lord. Lookie there."

He rotated his stool to face the bar as a trio of elegantly dressed women, one white, one Hispanic, and one black, wound their way through the slot clusters and gaming tables toward the bar area. Wolf regarded the one closest to him, the tallest of the three. She had a mane of auburn hair that hung down to the mid-back of the blazer of her black pantsuit. Every curve was deliciously accentuated. She was holding hands with the equally stunning Hispanic female on her left, who was clad in a metallic gold jacket and white pants. Her dark hair was cut short, ending just below her jawline, and she had the features of a fashion model. The Latina's head canted to the left as she talked to an equally gorgeous African American, who was wearing a purplish-red cape over a blazer with slits down the sleeves and a white tank top. Her black pencil-leg slacks stopped perfectly at her ankle, failing to reach a pair of shiny stilettos so high Wolf wondered how the hell she could walk without losing her balance. Her hair, which Wolf thought looked fabulous, was pulled up in a high ponytail, and her gold hoop earrings gave her an *I Dream of Jeannie* look.

Wolf let his gaze wander upward again but stopped on the bluish-green eyes of the red-haired woman, who immediately halted.

"What are you looking at, sonny boy?" she asked.

Wolf thought he heard the trace of a Southern accent. Embarrassed at being called out for staring, he smiled. "Nothing, ma'am."

"Ma'am?" The woman rolled her eyes and glanced at her companions. "I'm going to have to take this damn outfit back to my fashion designer."

The Latina smirked.

"Honey," the black girl said, "that ain't the question you should be asking. It should be, 'Do you like what you see?'"

How could I not? Wolf thought but felt it was better to remain silent.

"Hey," McNamara said, rotating on his stool with an accompanying chuckle. "Like old Dino used to say, you can't go to jail for what you're thinking. Can you, Dolly?"

The redhead's lips went from a challenging sneer to a surprised smile. "Well, Big Jim McNamara, as I live and breathe." She stopped and threw her arms around him, pushing her ample cleavage against his chest as she planted a kiss on his cheek. "Why didn't you tell me you were coming to the conference? We could've met for drinks or something."

"Or something?" McNamara flashed a grin and tipped his fingers off the brim of his hat. "That sounds promising."

"One of these days, I'm gonna have to get you a Texas hat, darling," she said.

When she leaned back, Wolf saw she wasn't as young as he'd initially thought. He put her in her late thirties, maybe early forties.

The woman released her embrace, and each of her companions also gave McNamara a tight hug and a kiss. The black girl wiggled against him conspicuously. "How's my big boo daddy?"

McNamara cast a quick glance at Wolf and winked.

"I ain't really her daddy."

Wolf chuckled and stood up, wondering how Mac knew these three lovelies.

McNamara turned his head toward Wolf, the grin still frozen on his face. He had three smears of red lipstick on his cheek.

The redhead gave Wolf the once-over. She was almost as tall as he was, and he noticed she was wearing flats. "So, who's this young studly, Mac?"

"Who, him?" McNamara chuckled again. "This is my new partner, Steve Wolf."

"Wolf?" she asked with a laugh. "Is that his name or his disposition?"

"Both," McNamara said. "Steve, these fine-looking young ladies are Ms. Dolly Kline, Brenda Carrera, and Yolanda Moore." He pointed at the redhead, the Latina, and the black woman in sequence. "The three prettiest and meanest bounty hunters in the whole state of Nevada. We worked together on a couple of cases."

"That's M-O-O-R-E for me, boo," the black girl said. She smiled, and Wolf saw her flawless white teeth.

He raised his eyebrows. "You girls are bounty hunters?"

"Well, why else would we be here, sugar?" Dolly said. She glanced at McNamara. "Good help that hard to find, Mac?"

"You'll have to excuse him. He just got back from a hardship tour," McNamara said. "They call themselves the P Patrol."

"And that P don't stand for pink, sugar," Dolly said with a wink.

"We were going to spell out the word," the Latina said. "But we figured that'd get the feminists on our case."

Wolf flushed with embarrassment, realizing what word she meant.

"Why don't you let us buy you gals a drink?" McNamara said. "Or two."

"Hell," Dolly said, "maybe even three or four. I'm gonna need all the fortification I can get to sit through that rubber-chicken dinner and see them give that award to that asshole Reno."

McNamara stood up and snapped his fingers to attract the attention of the bartender. "Whatever these ladies are drinking," he said. "And give us two more beers."

Dolly ordered vodka with a lime twist. Brenda, the Latina, ordered the same, and Yolanda asked for a chardonnay.

As they moved to a table, Wolf caught a pleasant whiff of perfume and a glimpse of a tattoo on the right shoulder blade of the black woman as she brushed back her cape.

"Why didn't you call me and say you were coming?" Dolly asked.

McNamara shrugged. "It was sort of a last-minute decision. But if they were going to give the award to you, I wouldn't have missed it for the world."

Dolly smiled and squeezed his hand. "Same here, sweetie. Can you believe they're giving him Bounty Hunter of the Year?"

"He probably paid somebody off," Brenda said.

"Don't mean shit anyway," Yolanda added.

They sat at a table, and a waitress brought their drinks. McNamara slipped her a bill and told her to keep the change.

"That's my boo bear," Yolanda said. "Always generous and always a gentleman."

McNamara smirked. "Well, not always on the latter."

The three women snickered, and Wolf wondered about their past history. Apparently, there was a lot Mac hadn't told him.

The conversation continued, with Dolly explaining how McNamara had helped them nail a particularly elusive and dangerous skip in Arizona and insisted on driving them back to Las Vegas to turn him over.

"And he wouldn't even accept a portion of the money," Dolly finished. "Needless to say, we were very grateful."

"He was such a gentleman," Brenda said, smiling. She wore black Versace glasses that Wolf suspected were non-prescription and just for show.

"So we treated him to dinner at the Peppermill," Yolanda said. "And then some."

McNamara glanced at Wolf and winked as if to imply that wasn't all they'd treated him to. Before Wolf could speculate on what that might be, Mac's cell phone chirped with an incoming text. He glanced down at it.

Eyebrows rising, he looked up. "Damn, it's Manny."

He held the phone toward Wolf.

The screen said, **Need to talk to you ASAP. 9-1-1.**

* * *

Wolf was disappointed to leave Ms. Dolly, as he'd found out she liked to be called, and her two gorgeous partners in bounty hunting, but Mac had told him it involved a possibly lucrative new job offer. Business always overrode pleasure, his partner had told him, unless the two intertwined.

"He say what it was about?" Wolf asked.

Mac shook his head. "Just that it involved big money."

They met Manny and his three associates in a restaurant called the Lucky Charm just off the main floor of the casino. After Manny made the introductions, Theodore Graham, a bail bondsman from the Big Apple, and Mr. Reynolds from some law firm, they were seated in a secluded booth in one corner. The lighting was low, and Wolf felt like a spy in one of those old espionage movies: five men meeting in a dimly lit location to discuss a mission. The two bail bondsmen looked like the polar opposites of one another. Manny was huge and morbidly obese, while the new guy, Teddy, looked like a set of bones in a skin suit. The third guy, Reynolds, had a firm handshake and a rugged look to him that didn't quite fit the law firm tag. Apparently, Mac didn't think so either.

"You don't look much like a lawyer," he said.

"Actually, I'm not." Reynolds flashed a quick smile. "I'm a paralegal and work for the law firm's special investigations team."

Wolf noticed that the guy had several bandages covering the top of his right hand.

An injury? He wondered what had caused it if the guy worked in an office.

"So, what's this all-important job you wanted to see us about?" McNamara asked.

Manny and Teddy exchanged looks. The skeleton spoke. "We need a couple of good and dependable bounty hunters to do a job."

"That so?" McNamara asked. "Where? New York?"

"No. Mexico."

"Mexico?" Mac squinted. "That's like dancing with the devil down there."

The two bail bondsmen exchanged glances again.

"I heard you were the men for the job," Teddy said.

"Who'd you hear that from?" Mac asked.

Wolf was content to let him do the talking, but the more he heard about this deal, the less he liked it.

"From Manny here," Teddy said. "He speaks very highly of you."

McNamara glanced at the heavyset bail bondsman and frowned.

"I'll bet he does."

Manny shrugged and flashed a shifty-looking half-grin.

"They play by a whole different set of rules down south of the border," McNamara said.

"Look, I know it's dangerous," Teddy said. "But Manny says you guys are the ones for the job."

McNamara smirked and looked at Manny. "That so? What about Reno? We saw you talking to him."

Manny's mouth gaped in what might have passed for a self-deprecating smile.

"Well, yeah. I did talk to him and Herc, but it got back to me that he wasn't too crazy about going down there."

"My associates at the law firm expressed some reservations about those two as well," Reynolds added.

"Who are these associates?" Mac asked. It was evident that he was leery of this new guy, and Teddy as well. "And why ain't we talking to the top man?"

"Mr. Fallotti's in New York," Reynolds said. He handed over a card that read Fallotti and Abraham Attorneys at Law. "Due to the nature of this transaction, he wishes to add a bit of circumspection to the negotiation process."

That did sound like legalese to Wolf's ear, but he still had an uneasy feeling.

"Look," Teddy said. "These guys are some heavy hitters outta New York, I can assure you. Flew me out here on a private jet, limo service to the hotel. All first class." He rubbed his thumb and forefinger together. "They got bucks. Big bucks."

"Okay," Mac said. "Talk. We're listening."

Teddy and Reynolds took over, giving them the tale about Accondras skipping on bail and being due in court in Manhattan in eight days.

"The recovery percentage of the bond is ten percent of one hundred thousand," Teddy said. "It's all yours."

"And the family of the victim is well off," Reynolds said. "They'll be offering a bonus of twenty-five thousand in addition to the bond recovery fee."

The amount shocked Wolf, but he showed no reaction.

"That's a lot of money," McNamara said. "It seems like you're in a pretty big hurry, too."

"Christ, yeah," Teddy said. "Like we said, the fucker's due in court next week."

"We also intend to serve Accondras with a civil

subpoena regarding a lawsuit at that time," Reynolds said. "There's a time constraint on filing that."

"So, you know for sure where this shitbird is down in Mexico?" Mac said.

"We do," Reynolds said. "We hired a private detective who's located him."

"And all we have to do is grab him and bring him back?" Mac continued.

"Grab him and bring him to this location," Reynolds said. He spread a map on the tabletop. "We've engaged the services of a private pilot to meet you there and transport the defendant back to the States."

"Who's this pilot?" McNamara asked.

"I'm not at liberty to say," Reynolds told him. "But you won't have to accompany him. Your only responsibility will be to do the drop. We'll arrange separate commercial transportation to Mexico and back for you and Mr. Wolf."

McNamara stared at the man. "If we accept, when do we get paid?"

"Immediately," Reynolds said. "Accept the job now, and we'll be glad to deposit half of the agreed-upon amount in your bank account before you leave, as well as give you a credit card and expense money for down there. You'll be paid the rest upon completion of the delivery. On scene, if you prefer."

"Hey, these guys are legit," Teddy said. "Like I said. First class all the way."

"Yeah." Manny nodded in affirmation. "They already took care of me for setting the meeting up."

McNamara squinted at him. "For which one? This one, or when you introduced them to Reno?"

Manny's head jerked back like he'd been slapped.

"Hey, Mac—"

"Don't bother denying it," McNamara said. "He was your first choice, wasn't he?"

Manny blew out a slow breath. "Look, that was…" His voice trailed off, and he shrugged. "Well, after all, he *is* Bounty Hunter of the Year. They'd heard of him, is all."

"Yeah," Teddy said. "And like we told ya, he was kind of wishy-washy about going to Mexico."

"You saying he turned it down?" Mac asked. "Or that he wanted more money?"

"Let's just say," Reynolds chimed in, breaking into the conversation, "that he seemed a bit squeamish. Additionally, my firm was less than satisfied with Mr. Garth's qualifications and requested to interview someone whom Mr. Sutter felt would be more qualified."

"Right," Manny said. "I mean, your boy here speaks Mexican, don't he?"

Wolf's hackles rose when he heard the pejorative.

"It's Spanish, not Mexican," McNamara said. "And he's nobody's 'boy.'" He glanced at Wolf and slid out of the booth. "We'll discuss it and get back to you."

"I'm afraid that won't do," Reynolds said. "We have set certain things in motion already. We need a definite commitment now."

"You'll get our answer shortly," McNamara said.

He stood up and motioned for Wolf to join him.

Wolf slid out of the booth as well, and the two of them walked toward the restrooms.

"Well, what do you think?" McNamara asked when they were out of earshot of the others.

"I don't know, Mac. Sounds a little hinky to me."

"Hinky? How so?"

Wolf shrugged. "We're not getting the whole story. I'm just wondering what's being left out."

"Yeah, me too." McNamara's mouth worked, then the

muscles of his jaw tightened. "But this would be a good chance to show up that damn Reno. Especially if word gets around that he turned it down because he was scared. Bounty Hunter of the Year, my ass."

Wolf was worried that Mac was letting his dislike of Reno override his better judgment.

"What about all that stuff you mentioned about going south of the border?" Wolf asked. "The dangers?"

A smile cracked McNamara's face. "Hell, I know all about stepping over them borders to get the job done. You do too, I expect."

"Yeah. But—"

"You do it once, it gets easier after that. We just got to be careful, is all. This won't be the first rodeo for either of us."

Wolf was still uneasy.

"What about weapons? Didn't you once say that if they catch you with a gun down there, they lock you up and throw away the key?"

"Until somebody can grease the right palms."

"So, we won't be able to take any firepower with us?"

"True, but we get enough money for expenses from this Reynolds guy, maybe we can buy whatever we need when we get down there." He grinned. "We just can't afford to get caught. Besides, this is a chance to make some real money and show Reno who the real Bounty Hunter of the Year is. Those two still owe me for a shirt, a seat belt, a tire, and a pinch."

"I don't know about this, Mac."

"Well, the recovery percentage of the bond is ten percent of one hundred thousand. That's ten thousand bucks in case your math's not working." McNamara clucked his tongue. "Plus, there's that special bonus of twenty-five grand being offered by the family. Thirty-five large split two ways, right down the middle, for a couple days' work. That's seventeen-five for each of us."

Wolf didn't feel right about the fifty-fifty split.

"Look, I appreciate the offer," he said. "But you should take more than—"

"You'll be taking the same risks I will. Plus, you speak Spanish. You do this, and we'll call it even between us." He laughed. "And this way, you'll have some money, and I'll be able to start charging you rent."

Wolf was touched by his friend's generosity. How could he let him down?

"That *is* a lot of money for a quick trip down to Mexico," he said.

"Damn straight," McNamara said. He focused on Wolf's face. "Well, whaddaya think?"

Wolf still had a very uneasy feeling in the pit of his stomach. Something about this whole thing bothered him, but then again, he'd been on a lot of missions where the risks were greater. Much greater. So had Mac. Plus, he owed this man more than he could ever repay, and he sensed this was one Mac really wanted.

"I say, let's go south of the border," Wolf said. "Down Mexico way."

McNamara smiled. "That's what I was hoping you'd say. I wasn't relishing the thought of going down there all by my lonesome."

* * *

Eagan watched Cummins as the fat lawyer made the final arrangements to have the advance money deposited in McNamara's bank account.

Trackdown, Incorporated, an interesting and appropriate name for a bail bond enforcement agency. He still wondered how Wolf had gotten hooked up with this place so quickly after getting out of Leavenworth, though. Eagan had figured the dumb Indian would go back to the rez, or whatever pathetic place he came from and drown himself in booze while contemplating his pathetic little life, or what was left of it. The piece of shit had turned out to be way more resilient than anticipated. Maybe Victor Delta had been right in wanting that loose end tidied up, and now, that particular avenue had suddenly opened up for him. It should be worth a bonus.

His cell phone buzzed with a text. It was Reynolds.

All set. Monies deposited. Instructions given.

Their departure?

As specified. Anything else?

Negative, Eagan texted back. **Come back up here but don't let anyone follow you. Bring Teddy.**

Everything was in motion now. Wolf and his buddy would be off to Mexico the day after tomorrow, and Accondras would hopefully be delivered within a few days. Then it was a simple matter of extracting the location of the artifact from him, and that shouldn't be very problematic.

In fact, Eagan thought, it might even be pleasurable.

He enjoyed breaking people, using enough pain to ensure that the desired information was obtained and verified while the subject was still breathing. Wolf's intrusion four years ago had messed up the synchronization. If he hadn't barged in, Eagan was certain that he and Nasim could have gotten the location of the other half of the artifact right then and there.

Instead, it had turned into a clusterfuck.

No matter, he thought. Everything comes to he who waits.

And now, this quest had turned into something even

more lucrative. Something that he wouldn't have to split with the late Stu Novak.

A knock on the door jarred Eagan out of his reverie. He went over, opened it, and saw Reynolds and Teddy.

Reynolds nodded at him as they entered, reaffirming the instructions in the text.

"Go back to your room and pack up," Eagan said. "We're getting out of here."

Reynolds nodded and turned to leave.

"Outta here?" Teddy said. "Why? We got it all set up, just like you wanted."

Eagan put his arm around the other man's shoulders and walked him over to the wet bar. The guy felt so frail. Eagan could probably kill him with one blow. Maybe two, if the son of a bitch was stubborn or tougher than he looked.

"Not you, Teddy," Eagan said. "Just us. We're just going to a different hotel, is all. You can stay here, and I'll make sure you get those two babes I promised you."

"Yeah?" Teddy's emaciated face lit up. "Now?"

"Soon," Eagan said. "Have a drink."

Teddy's face twitched. "Ah, I don't know. I got other things on my mind if you know what I mean." He flashed what Eagan took to be a lascivious grin.

"Just one won't hurt." He uncapped a bottle of whiskey, filled the two shot glasses sitting on the bar, and motioned for Teddy to take one.

The thin man shrugged and picked up the glass, bringing it to his mouth and taking a dainty sip.

"Oh, come on," Eagan said. "Bottoms up."

He hoisted his glass and brought it to his mouth but didn't drink any of it.

Teddy did likewise, and Eagan set his glass down and grabbed the bottle.

"Here, let me freshen that up for you."

After refilling Teddy's glass, he set the bottle down, then placed his arm around Teddy's shoulders again. This time, he steered him toward the door. The hallway was empty, and Eagan turned away from the elevators. They walked down the long corridor toward a large window at the end. He'd noticed that the only PTZ camera on the floor was mounted by the elevators; there were none along the hallway going toward the stairway exit.

"Hey," Teddy said, still holding the glass. "The elevators are back that way."

Eagan nodded and smiled.

"We've got one more thing to discuss," he said. "We can take the stairs."

"The stairs? Come on. Who do you think I am, Charles Atlas?"

Charles Atlas?

Eagan vaguely recalled those nostalgic comic book ads of the scarecrow guy being insulted by the beach bully, only to reemerge as a muscleman and the hero of the beach. He smiled at the memory as he reached into his pocket and removed a pair of thin leather gloves.

"You'd rather save your strength for those two babes, huh?" Eagan slipped the gloves onto his hands. They fit like a second skin over his big hands.

Teddy's face cracked into a wide grin. "You got it. What's with the gloves?"

Eagan responded with a series of miniature nods, which he hoped looked reassuring, as he pressed his hip against the crash bar of the stairwell door. He pushed the door open and held it for Teddy.

"Let's just step in here for a second while I ask you something," Eagan suggested.

Teddy rolled his eyes and stepped into the stairwell.

The platform had a zigzag of descending and ascending stairways set into the walls. Eagan scanned the area for cameras and, seeing none, took out his pocket comb and held it to the metal doorjamb, preventing the door from closing all the way and locking them in the stairwell. When he turned back, the smile had vanished from his face.

A look of uncertainty eroded the smile on Teddy's face. Some of the whiskey spilled over the edge of the glass he still held between his fingers.

"Whaddaya want?" Teddy asked, his voice cracking.

"I need to be sure you didn't mention anything about me to that Wolf guy."

"Huh? Are you nuts? You told me not to, so I didn't."

Eagan nodded.

"I have to make sure you don't," he said.

Teddy huffed and reached for the door handle. Eagan grabbed his wrist and squeezed.

"Careful," Eagan said. "If that door closes all the way, it locks automatically. Then you have to walk down to the first floor to get out."

"Let go of my arm," Teddy said, wincing from the pressure on his arm. "You're hurting me."

"We wouldn't want that," Eagan said, releasing him. "Would we?"

Before Teddy could answer, Eagan brought his open right palm up and slapped the thin man's left shoulder, sending him sprawling. The glass slipped out of his grasp and shattered on the hard cement platform. Teddy took a couple of exaggerated steps, then managed to regain his balance.

"What the fuck's wrong with you? You son of a bitch. I coulda slipped and fell down the fucking stairs."

"Shoulda, woulda, coulda," Eagan said as he took a substantial step forward, carefully avoiding the spilled drink and shattered glass, and shoved Teddy's shoulder. The thin man screamed as he tumbled pell-mell down the hard stairs, grunting in pain as he bounced off each step. He flopped down hard on his back on the first landing and groaned.

"Help me," he muttered. "Please."

Eagan descended with steady but unhurried deliberation. He was surprised that somebody as out of shape and unhealthy-looking as Teddy had survived the fall and remained conscious. It would be entertaining to see if he could do a repeat performance. Stopping by the prone man's head, Eagan bent down and pulled him to his feet.

Skin and bones, he thought. No muscle at all.

He walked Teddy over to the edge of the second stairway, grabbed the thin man's right hand, and pressed his fingers on the slickness of the metal banister. When he was sure he'd left some good recoverable prints, he released the bondsman, letting him teeter on the precipice for a few seconds before giving him the merest shove. His face struck the fifth step from the top, leaving a crimson smear, then he somersaulted the rest of the way down. The grunts ceased about halfway, but his momentum carried him to the next landing.

He lay there in a fetal position, not moving.

Eagan went down to make sure he was dead.

No breathing, no pulse.

He touched the thin man's half-open eye to make sure.

No reaction.

As he straightened, he marveled at how resilient the skinny son of a bitch had been. Eagan thought about calling up fat-ass Manny and seeing what kind of bounce his corpulent frame would produce going down the stairs face-first, but that would have to wait. He'd find out on the mop-up trip to Phoenix.

After all, he thought, it would be too coincidental if two out-of-town bail bondsmen met their accidental demises at the same conference and in the same hotel.

* * *

SUITE 1836
LAS VEGAS, NEVADA

Wolf found himself temporarily alone in the huge hotel suite as he looked out the window at the sea of sparkling lights in the darkness. He reviewed the events of the long day.

After agreeing to do the job in Mexico, he and Mac had left the conference to check into their hotel. The Motel 6 was a far cry from the luxury of the Shamrock, and they were sharing a room.

"Hell, this is almost a throwback to our Army days," Mac had said. Then he'd decided to call Dolly and offer to take her and her partners out on the town.

"Unless you want to go to that rubber-chicken dinner and see Reno get that damn award," he added.

"Not on your life, darling," Dolly said, her voice so loud that Wolf could hear it from several feet away. "We done did all the rubbernecking we're going to do at that place. I got better things to do with my time."

Mac laughed and whispered something into the phone that Wolf couldn't discern, then hung up.

"Looks like we got us some dates tonight," he said.

"She asked if I was bringing my handsome new partner along."

"Was she talking about your handsome new *broke* partner by any chance?"

McNamara chuckled, then read Wolf's concern. "What's the matter?"

Wolf said nothing, wondering if he should tell Mac how deeply indebted he felt. The constant and growing indebtedness hung around his neck like a metaphoric millstone.

McNamara took a step closer and laid a big hand on the other man's shoulder.

"Listen, Steve, I kind of ramrodded you into this Mexico thing. I know it's dangerous, but it's a chance to make some good money real fast."

Wolf nodded. "It's not that. You've been great. Better than I deserve. But—"

"But what?" Mac asked. "If you're still worried about being broke and how you're gonna pay me back, we can start keeping a ledger if it'll make you feel better."

"It's not all about the money," Wolf countered.

"Then what is it?"

Wolf thought about bringing up that he resented how McNamara had used his association with Consuela to locate Luis Ruiz, but he thought better of it.

"I'm still working on getting you number two on that list, boy." McNamara laughed, then frowned at Wolf's subdued reaction. "Say, you're not still upset about that little ploy I used back in Phoenix with that Latina chick, are you?"

Wolf was silent.

"Well, it was just the way things worked out, is all." McNamara shrugged. "When I first encouraged you to go out with her, it was innocent enough. I wasn't even sure who she was in relation to that skip I was tracing, even though she had the same last name. But I figured if you could get in good with her, we might be able to use the Latina connection down the road. Then I went by looking for you and just happened to see you walk her to her car, so I figured, what the hell, and followed her. It was a lark and a hunch."

"Looking for me? Why?"

McNamara shrugged. "Just making sure you were keeping outta harm's way."

"Harm's way?"

"Yeah. I didn't want you to get hooked up with the wrong kind of gal."

"So you followed her?"

"Well, yeah. And once I saw where she lived, I had Kasey do some computer backtracking and found that was the same address old Luis had used on a credit card app eight years ago. He'd since moved." McNamara shrugged again. "Anyway, it was all pure coincidence."

"Yeah, sure."

"It was, dammit." McNamara cracked a smile. "Would I lie to you?"

Wolf smirked. "That's what I've been wondering since we left Phoenix."

McNamara clucked his tongue. "Well, get that thought outta your head and start thinking like a professional bounty hunter. And tonight, we're going hunting for some trim."

"Trim?"

McNamara winked.

"Like I said, Dolly specifically asked if I was bringing you along, so let's not disappoint the lady."

So they hadn't.

After a steak dinner and several rounds of drinks at a

place down the street called the Peppermill, Wolf was looking forward to going back to their undersized room at the Motel 6. The strain of the long drive and the events of the day were weighing on him, and it was closing on midnight.

But Ms. Dolly and the P Patrol had other ideas and seemed intent on demonstrating that the three of them were easily capable of drinking him and Mac under the table. It was no contest, though. After a glass of wine with the steak, he'd switched to club soda or pineapple juice for the remainder of their stops. The pending quest to Mexico and the bad blood displayed by Reno and his partner made Wolf want to remain ready and alert. He'd never cared for the vulnerable feeling of an alcohol-induced haze impinging on his ability to defend himself if the need arose. So he tagged along, watching the three gorgeous women imbibing and laughing at Mac's corny jokes. A half-dozen or so bars later, they found themselves back at the Shamrock, and Ms. Dolly had insisted they come up to her suite for a nightcap.

"Wait till you shee this place from the inshide," she said, her words slurred from all the booze.

Mac grinned and said it sounded like an offer they couldn't refuse, holding up two fingers as he and Wolf ushered the women into an open elevator. Wolf wasn't sure if the fingers meant victory or number two on the list.

He had mixed feelings about both.

Ms. Dolly pressed several wrong buttons before Brenda laughed and pressed 18.

"She always knows what button to press," Ms. Dolly had confided.

McNamara winked again, and Wolf wondered what that meant. The car rose, stopping twice before reaching the eighteenth floor. The corridor was furnished in the same Irish-style motif, with green and white wallpaper and decorative wall lamps in the shapes of four-leaf clovers on the walls. The overhead fluorescent lights made the place as bright as day.

Ms. Dolly had obviously spared no expense on the suite. It had two bedrooms with a large party room between them, with a fully stocked wet bar, a sink, a counter, and a huge table in the center.

If you moved the table, Wolf thought, you could hold a dance competition in here. Or maybe on top of it if you didn't.

Once inside, Ms. Dolly and Brenda headed for the bedroom on the right, and Yolanda had veered to the one on the left.

"We'll be right back," Ms. Dolly had told them. "Nature calls."

"Hey, she's calling me, too," McNamara said.

"Well, come on, sugar," Ms. Dolly said, placing her arm around his neck and pulling him with her and Brenda. "We don't mind sharing."

McNamara started to go along but stopped, plucked his cowboy hat off of his head, and set it on Wolf's.

"Take care of this for me," he said with a sly wink.

The door slammed behind the three of them, and Wolf found himself alone in the expansive suite.

He'd hardly drunk anything during the prolonged barhopping, so the need to empty his bladder wasn't that pressing. Taking off the hat, he set it on a nearby sofa and moved to the big window.

The curtains had been drawn, but he separated them and gazed at the dappling of white lights interspersed with colored dots. The huge Ferris wheel he'd seen on the way into town was several hundred yards away and was doing an incremental rotation, the oval globes now illuminated by purple lights. Beyond that, slashes of bright neon sliced through the darkness, advertising hotels and stores, and seemed to extend to the distant mountains, which were barely visible in the moonlight. The moon hung full and round in the sky against a canopy of black velvet. There was too much light below to see stars.

How many nights had he looked up at them from all those different places?

The nighttime celestial display had always made him feel small and insignificant, yet they had somehow filled him with hope and ecstasy.

That was one of the things he'd hated most about Leavenworth; he couldn't see the sky at night.

At least in a combat zone, the sky was available for viewing.

For the most part, anyway.

Ironic, he thought. *In Iraq, half a world away, I only had to look up to see the stars, and here in Vegas, the best I can do is look around to see the artificial ones.*

He was wondering where the rest of this night was heading when he heard a door open behind him. Yolanda had come out of the bedroom on the left. Ms. Dolly, Brenda, and Mac were still in the one on the right. That door remained closed, although he could hear Ms. Dolly's distinctive honeyed-whiskey laugh through the door.

In the reflection of the window, Wolf saw Yolanda pick up Mac's cowboy hat and place it on her head as she came up next to him.

"What are you looking at?" she asked.

She was close enough that he could smell the mixture of perfume, body musk, and something else. He couldn't figure out what that third scent was, but it was as pleasant as the other two. The combination sent a shiver down his spine.

"The moon," he said. "And the absence of stars."

Her fingers drifted over the back of his neck.

"Pretty, ain't it?" she asked.

Wolf's eyes moved to the faint reflection of them in the glass, and he noticed she only came up to just above his shoulder. She'd been almost as tall as he during the barhopping. He looked down and saw that she'd taken off the cape and her stilettos. When he glanced at her face, she smiled.

"Where's your cape?" Wolf asked.

She shrugged. "Didn't think I was gonna need it in here. Why?"

"I was going to ask you what color it was."

"Why? You colorblind or something?"

He shook his head. "I just couldn't tell if it was supposed to be pink or red. You know, like Supergirl's."

"Actually, it's fuchsia."

"What about your shoes?"

"Louboutins. And they were killing my feet."

"I was going to ask you how you could walk in them."

"Practice, boo. Practice." She took off Mac's hat, set it on Wolf's head, and brought her hand up to slap at her hair several times.

Wolf raised an eyebrow, thinking about how delicate her features were. A button nose and a pair of dark eyebrows artfully angled against mocha skin so smooth it looked like an elegant painting by a master. Her brown eyes locked onto his.

"That thing looks good on you," she said, touching the brim of the hat. "You grow up in Arizona?"

He shook his head. "Lumberton, North Carolina."

She raised her eyebrows and tilted her head. "So, your name really Wolf?"

"It is."

"You part-Latino or something?"

He shook his head. "Half-Indian."

The dark eyebrows arched again. "I never been with a real live Indian before. Or do you say Native American?"

"Native American was coined by some guilty white liberal," he said. "We call ourselves Indians."

Her heavy red lips moved back over those perfect white teeth.

"Yeah, just like African American," she said. "Never been to Africa in my life."

"I have."

Her brown eyes widened. "For real?"

He nodded.

"In the Army?"

"Yeah."

"So, what was it like?"

He blew out a slow breath, wondering how much he should tell her. He didn't want to say the wrong thing, give her the wrong idea. It had been so long since he'd been with a woman, and she was beautiful.

"Well," he began, "the parts I saw weren't the best places. A lot of desert, a lot of slums, a lot of really poor people."

She snorted a laugh. "Sounds like the low-income sections of Vegas."

He was trying to think of something clever to say when her arms encircled his neck and she stood on her tiptoes to kiss him. The first one was quick, almost like a glancing blow, but her face lingered close to his, and their mouths came together again.

This time it was slower, pressing together with a firm

readiness, lingering before the inevitable parting. Her tongue flickered briefly at first, then slowly rotated over his. His arms encircled her body, and he drew her closer. He was surprised by how firm her body felt, tight and solid like an athlete's except for the softness of her breasts, which were pressed against him.

The taste of her was exquisite as well, mixing with her scent, which was now a swirl of perfume, muskiness, and—he finally placed it—cocoa butter. They stayed entwined for several long, slow, delicious seconds. Wolf began to harden, and a flash of anxiety hit him.

It had been so long...

Would he be able to perform?

He drew a couple of breaths, doubt gnawing at him. He felt like he was about to run a fifty-yard dash but didn't know if his legs would move. But he didn't want this to be fast; he wanted to savor every moment.

How much about himself should he tell her?

In his head, he heard himself say, "I've been in prison." Would that be like pouring a glass of ice water over everything?

She separated her body from his but kept hold of his hand and pulled him toward the bedroom door on the left.

"Come on," she whispered, her voice pitched low.

His feet felt like lead weights.

She paused, and one of the dark eyebrows rose. "What's the matter? Don't you want to?"

He did, more than anything, but the self-doubt hung over his head like a swinging pendulum.

"What about the others?" he managed to say.

"Don't worry about them." The trace of a wicked-looking smile graced her lips. "Dolly and Brenda are bi.

They like to share, and they're taking Big Jim along for the ride."

That sent another bolt of fire through him. He took a deep breath.

"It's been kind of a long time for me," he told her.

The wicked smile grew more intense. "Well, I'm sure you didn't forget how, did you?'

"No."

"Okay then." She pulled him closer to the open door, and he moved along more readily now.

"I—"

"Shhh." She brought a finger to his lips. "Don't talk."

The feel of her hand on his face erased all doubts and concerns.

"And remember, baby," she said. "What happens in Vegas stays in Vegas."

CHAPTER 9

Wolf watched as McNamara stooped to hug his grandson and then stood to embrace his daughter. Her blue eyes never strayed from Wolf as she stared over her father's shoulder, and the look was pure malevolence.

He tried a quick smile and wondered, *Why does she hate me so much?*

It was clear that Kasey blamed him for this upcoming foray into Mexico, even though, in reality, Wolf had been a reluctant volunteer. But he felt it was a whole lot more. She'd been icy toward him since Mac had brought him to Phoenix from Leavenworth. The words came back to him: *Looks like he finally got the son he always wanted.*

That had to be it, the reason why she disliked him so much, but there was little he could do about it.

She probably thinks I'm the one dragging him to Mexico, he thought. *When it's actually the exact opposite.*

But trying to explain that to her would only be wasted breath. At this point, all he could do was go along as backup and try his best to keep Mac safe and sound.

The added pressure bore down on him like a weighted vest.

Still, Mac had been to hell and back more times than you could count, so it wasn't like he was shadowing a newbie. But all that had been a while ago, and after recalling that incident with Ruiz, as well as Reno and Herc, Wolf couldn't help but wonder if his friend and mentor had lost a step.

Father Time caught up with everybody.

Pushing the doubts out of his mind, he recalled the pleasantness of the night before last. It was definitely the stuff that memories were made of, and Mac sure hadn't seemed like he was lacking in any way. Although the next morning after Mac had rousted him out of bed, he'd asked Wolf to do the driving.

He recalled the mischievous grin on his mentor's face as he'd walked both Ms. Dolly and Brenda into the bedroom and closed the door. Sure, he was tired the morning after, but who could blame him?

McNamara had pushed open the bedroom door of Yolanda's room, rousted Wolf awake, tossed him his clothes, and said they had to get moving.

"And what the hell did you do with my hat?" he asked.

"What the hell time is it?" Yolanda muttered, her voice creaky with sleep.

"Zero six-thirty," McNamara said. "Time for reveille."

He thrust open the drapes, flooding the room with a bright dose of sunlight.

Yolanda pulled a pillow over her head and muttered profanities.

After finding his cowboy hat on the floor under

Yolanda's black silk outfit, Mac had grumbled something about them being behind schedule, placed the hat on his head, and tipped the brim as he looked at her.

"We'll stop back here in Vegas when we get back from where we got to go," he said and left Wolf and the girl alone.

"Where you going?" she asked, pulling the pillow away to look up at him.

"We got a job south of the border," he said as he was slipping into his pants.

"Mexico?"

He nodded.

"Not too smart, boo. They play by a different set of rules down there."

"So I've heard," Wolf said. He stood and pulled his t-shirt on.

The night had been one of infinite delights, and he hoped Mac's admonishment that they'd be back would turn out to be true. He wanted to see her again.

"Ah, could I, like, maybe have your phone number or something?" he asked.

She turned onto her side, holding the sheet to cover her breasts, and reached for a small purse on the nightstand.

He was amused by her sudden display of modesty after they'd spent the night together. But the fairer sex had always been a conundrum to him.

Withdrawing a business card from the purse, she rubbed her hand over her face and heaved a sigh.

"Oh, I shoulda taken the time to wrap my hair better," she said. "I probably look a fright."

"You look beautiful."

"That's nice to hear in the morning." She smiled. "Give me a pen."

Wolf patted his pockets and came up empty. Turning, he saw a desk with a pad of hotel stationery in the middle, along with a monogrammed ballpoint. He grabbed it and handed it to her.

As she was scribbling something on the back, three loud knocks came from the other side of the closed door, accompanied by McNamara's booming voice.

"You almost ready in there? You ain't engaging in any more hanky-panky, are you?"

"Give me a minute," Wolf called.

"Okay, minute-man, but hurry up. It's a long drive back to Phoenix."

Yolanda finished writing something on the back of the card and handed it to him.

"My cell," she said. "Call me sometime."

Wolf smiled, and for the first time since getting out of Leavenworth, he felt like a winner. He slipped the card into his pocket and leaned down to kiss her.

Even though it was a lips-only peck, Yolanda having said that she had "morning mouth," it brought back the pleasant memories of last night. He wished he could crawl back under the sheet.

McNamara's voice intruded again. "Let's go. We got to ship out."

For all his early morning rooster-crowing, when they got back to the Escalade, Mac tossed him the keys and got into the passenger seat.

"You drive," he said. "I gotta get me some sleep."

"But I don't know the way," Wolf said.

"The navigation system's built in." He reclined the seat and placed his hat over his face. "I already entered the address."

He was snoring by the time Wolf pulled out of the parking garage.

Now, barely thirty hours later, they were packed and ready to board a plane for Cancun International Airport.

First-class and commercial, Wolf thought. The thin bail bondsman had been right. Whoever was behind this had money and plenty of it.

McNamara released the embrace and stepped back from his daughter. Her eyes still bored into Wolf with obvious malice. He felt like telling her that he was an unwilling participant but knew it would do little good. McNamara grabbed the extended handle of his carry-on suitcase and began walking toward the escalators that led to the TSA checkpoint. Wolf went to follow with his backpack as well and felt a sudden tug on his arm. He turned back and saw the intense emotion in her eyes.

"You'd better *not* let anything happen to my *father*," she growled.

She spat the third and ninth words with special emphasis.

He was at a loss to reply. All he could think of to say was, "I'll do my best." He realized a second later how trite and superficial that had sounded. There was so much more he wanted to say to set things right: that he hadn't wanted to take this job in Mexico in the first place, that her father was a man who made his own decisions, that he probably would have gone down to Mexico alone if Wolf hadn't agreed to go with him.

There was much more, but he couldn't find the words.

He winked and waved at little Chad, then followed in Mac's footsteps toward the gates. McNamara was already about forty steps ahead of him.

After showing their boarding passes and IDs at the first stop, they went through the rest of the screening without any problems or delays.

As they sat on the bench to lace up their footwear, both of them having chosen to wear Army desert boots, McNamara grunted and elbowed Wolf.

"This whole thing irks me every time I have to go through it," he said. "Them damn Arabs. You know, all this rigmarole of having to take off our shoes is because you young guys didn't kick their asses hard enough when you were over there."

"Well, if I ever get a chance to go back," Wolf said, "I won't make that mistake again."

McNamara chuckled and jumped to his feet. Wolf couldn't remember the last time he'd seen his friend so energized.

"Hell," McNamara said. "I was just kidding. I'm real proud of the job you all done. That was some good soldiering."

Except that I ended up in prison with a DD, Wolf said to himself.

He tucked the ends of the laces into his boots Army-style and got up. Since they were not planning to stay long, they had only carry-ons with a couple changes of underwear and an additional set of clothes. Wolf trailed behind once again as they walked to the gate.

Reynolds, the guy from the law firm, had given them everything they would need initially: a couple of burner phones with international SIM cards, an anonymous credit card, and an envelope containing instructions about who to call once they landed. The information seemed a bit on the light side, but Reynolds had come through on the money transfer and put half the agreed-upon amount in McNamara's business account as a show of good faith.

First class all the way, that bail bondsman Teddy had said. Wolf wondered if he was nervous about them bringing back this missing felon. Wolf also wondered about their quarry. So far, all they knew about him was that he was wanted in New York on a warrant for child molestation.

Taking indecent liberties with a minor.

That could mean a lot of things, and none of them were good.

Despite the presumption of innocence being constitutionally guaranteed, the charge disgusted Wolf. The man had fled rather than stand and defend himself, which usually indicated a person was guilty as hell. But having seen firsthand how short-eyes were treated in prison, Wolf couldn't blame him for running. But there would be no remorse in making sure he was turned over to the proper authorities.

That was another thing Wolf had found troubling. According to the instructions Reynolds gave them in Vegas, they only had to snatch the offender and bring him to an airfield, where he was to be turned over to a group working directly for the law firm. He'd be flown back to the US, no problems with messy explanations at the border, no problems with extradition. It seemed like an unnecessary step in the process and of questionable legality. Then again, time was of the essence, according to what Reynolds had told him, and a lengthy extradition process would certainly slow down any court proceedings back in New York. The handoff seemed under-the-table, but so was this whole bounty hunting thing at times.

When the law broke down or didn't function, McNamara had told him on the long ride from Leavenworth, somebody had to step in and do something.

An easy snatch, then a handoff. Things could be worse. And the pay was good.

Wolf had asked Reynolds for a copy of the warrant, some pictures of the suspect, and more information about him.

"All that will be provided to you by our operative in Mexico," Reynolds had said.

Lots of unanswered questions, thought Wolf. And lots of questions to be resolved.

* * *

SOMEWHERE OVER THE GULF OF MEXICO

Eagan reclined in the comfortable seat of the Lear jet as it flew toward their destination. This was his first trip to Belize, and hopefully, it would be his last. Although the cabin was fairly spacious, it still felt cramped to his over-sized form. He glanced at Cummins, who was looking more nervous by the minute.

Maybe the porker doesn't like to fly, Eagan thought. Probably spent most of his time in military transports shitting his pants or sitting on the toilet. But Eagan didn't need to him for the grunt work. There were four of his own men, Vipers, as well as Nasim, so the fat lawyer was only there to manage the money transfer. He was extra weight as far as Eagan was concerned. So were those two bozo bounty hunters. Cummins had been delighted when he heard the details of Eagan's plan.

"You do have a point," the shyster lawyer had said. "You know how Victor Delta feels about loose ends. It'll be easier to take them along thinking that they're in on the capture instead of trying to deal with another set of bodies here in Vegas."

Of course, I had a point, Eagan thought.

Although Teddy's mishap appeared to have been

attributed to an unfortunate trip down the stairs, with alcohol as a contributing factor, having Reno and his partner show up with a couple of bullet holes in their brains would be bound to arouse suspicion. Especially with one of them being Bounty Hunter of the Year. And even though those two muscle-bound morons were dumber than a box of batteries, they were tough enough and skilled enough not to go down easily. That was why he'd insisted on taking along the four Vipers. For now, Reno and Black Herc were all smiles, thinking that they would take charge of the prisoner from Wolf and his buddy and transport him back to the US.

"It's a way of covering our tracks thoroughly," Eagan had explained to them the previous day. "We're staging in Belize, so there'll be no official record of the two of you ever setting foot in Mexico. Plus, you'll collect the bonus when we land Stateside."

"And we'll be stealing another one from good old Big Mac," Reno had said. "They do all the work, and we get the glory."

"And the money," Herc had added.

Eagan had laughed along with them while thinking these two idiots had taken one too many blows to the head. It was almost too simple. In one fell swoop, he'd eliminate all the loose ends, not only for this op but the Iraq fiasco as well.

Yeah, he thought. *I like dealing with morons.*

Reynolds knew what all the parties looked like and would be a familiar face to offset any suspicions on the part of Wolf and McNamara at the drop, and Kunish, Harper, and Wells were all combat-tested and capable. Plus, Kunish could sub as a helicopter pilot should anything happen to the guy who was lined up down in Belize.

Reno and his black buddy would serve a purpose, too. They thought they'd be going down to steal the perp from Wolf and McNamara. However, Eagan had had Zerbe spread a bit of pre-mission intel about the possibility that a couple of trouble-making *gringos* might be smuggling weapons into Mexico. The authorities would be on the lookout for them.

Later, when all the bodies were discovered, it would look like the *gringos*, who would be identified as American bounty hunters after Accondras, had shot it out with each other and perished. All the loose ends tied up in a nice little bow.

It would be a quick in-and out mission. After they had the artifact in their possession, everything else, and every*body* else, could be jettisoned when they were on this jet back to the US. Von Dien—Victor Delta—would get his precious Lion Attacking the Nubian, or whatever the hell it was.

The Lion, Eagan thought, remembering Fallotti's phraseology. *The most valuable part. Kiss my ass.*

It wouldn't be long before he was on his way to an extended, luxurious, and perhaps permanent vacation somewhere in the Caribbean. He couldn't care less about the rich old fart and his expensive trinkets.

He rotated his neck to take out some of the kinks and caught Cummins staring at him. Their eyes locked, and the fat lawyer looked away.

The thoughts of a possible double-cross flashed in Eagan's mind, but he quickly dismissed them.

No, the old man wants the artifact too much to risk trying to cut me out, he thought. *But after he has it...*

He pushed that thought out of his mind. He was at least safe until after Victor Delta had the thing in his greedy little hands. And if he was planning something, he would have sent someone much more capable than Cummins to supervise the transaction.

He began to feel more assured. There would be no double-cross, at least not until everything was complete.

But after that, Eagan knew he could very well become one of those loose ends that would eventually have to be tidied up.

* * *

CANCUN INTERNATIONAL AIRPORT, MEXICO

The touchdown was smooth and uneventful. McNamara had slept through most of the relatively short flight, and Wolf felt reassured. Even though he'd been unable to grab a combat nap, it was a good sign that his mentor had sidelined his over-eagerness and was regaining his combat legs.

Nothing was more reassuring than seeing a troop flying into a hot zone so relaxed that he was dozing on the way there. It was the ultimate insouciance. Wolf shook him awake as the plane banked to make its final descent. A couple thousand feet below them, a mosaic of mostly white buildings on a thin ribbon of white sand bisected the azure water.

"Damn," McNamara said. "Looks mighty pretty, but so did the 'Nam until we touched down."

Wolf thought about the Sandbox. It had never seemed very pretty to him.

Neither was the touchdown that followed. The big jet bounced on the runway, and the grating sound of the brakes being applied sounded like a novice plumber trying to clamp shut a leaking faucet. Wolf put his hands on the back of the seat in front of him.

McNamara laughed. "Don't tell me you're a nervous flyer."

"Just a nervous lander," Wolf said.

"Well, at least there's nobody shooting at us."

Not yet, Wolf thought, but he kept further repartee to himself.

Since they'd traveled light, with only Mac's carry-on and Wolf's Army backpack, they were able to bypass baggage claim after getting their passports stamped and their IDs' checked. They each received a document the agent said had to remain with their passports at all times.

"I don't remember doing all this on my last trip to foreign soil," McNamara said with a wry grin. "All I needed then was my military ID card."

Wolf nodded in agreement, but out of the corner of his eye, he saw the agent who'd stamped their passports reach for a phone as they walked toward the long line that led to Mexican Customs.

"Don't tell me we got to stand in another line," McNamara said. "This is getting more and more like the Army by the minute."

"Well, maybe we'll luck out and get the green light to go right through."

Wolf studied the congestion ahead. An array of uniformed men, each with an officious air about him, was seated behind large gunmetal-gray desks. Each desk had a metallic box with two lenses on the front edge. The lenses were illuminated by either a red or green light. The lines inched forward. The people near the front were separating into two distinct groups: those who got a green light signal to proceed without being checked and those who received the red light, which apparently meant their possessions had to be inspected. The people in the red-light section were forming into a series of mini-lines, each one halting as the man behind a desk went through the suitcases and paperwork of each tourist.

A traffic signal for pedestrians, Wolf thought.

The light on the desk in front of their line was solid red, and the agent behind it seemed to be moving with a particularly meticulous monotony.

"Something tells me there's more than a couple of red lights in our future," McNamara said. "It's a known fact that the line you're not in always moves fastest."

Wolf said nothing as the man at the desk finally finished questioning the tourist, handed him back his paperwork, and motioned for him to proceed into the airport. He then reached out and tapped the top of the metallic block, changing the red light to green momentarily.

The person several people ahead of them walked to the desk and stood next to the red light. Wolf assumed the next available position in the line and used the wait time to review the situation. The fugitive they were tracking was named Accondras, Thomas. He was thirty-three years old, five-ten, one hundred and eighty pounds, dark complexion, and lived at a seaside resort with his parents.

They had no picture or other information about him, and they were supposed to meet up with some private detective Fallotti and Abraham had hired to locate him. The detective, Zerbe, was supposed to give them the rest of the details, including a map with the coordinates of where they were supposed to drop the fugitive for transport back to the States.

Pass Go and collect your two hundred dollars, Wolf thought, remembering his childhood experiences playing Monopoly.

No matter how many times he played, he could never seem to win. Hopefully, this real-life game would be different.

The man behind the desk handed back the person's passport and motioned them through. He pressed the button changing the red light to green.

Almost time to start jumping through those hoops, Wolf thought.

The three couples ahead of them looked like members of some kind of fraternal organization, and they all received a green light. They bustled toward the main terminal in a flurry of laughter and back-slapping.

"Finally," McNamara said and started walking toward the exit. "I was getting pretty tired of standing behind those yo-yos."

The red light flashed, and a uniformed policeman held up his hand and spoke to him in Spanish. "*Espera. Tiene que ir ahí.*"

"Huh?" McNamara said.

"Looks like one of those red lights just popped up," Wolf said. "He's telling you to go over there."

A red light flashed for him also, and he put a hand on Mac's shoulder to guide him toward the long metal tables where the luggage was inspected.

McNamara started whistling the old Sinatra tune, *South of the Border*. Wolf recognized it from one of the CDs the man had played over and over on their way to Vegas.

"I was hoping for another song," Wolf said.

"Which one?"

"How about *Nice and Easy*?"

McNamara chuckled. "Best to keep it in mind as we go through this."

"Does it every time," Wolf agreed.

One of the agents, a thin man in a tan uniform whose nametag read PEREZ, motioned for them to place their bags on the table, then held his hand out for their passports and IDs.

Wolf handed his over, and McNamara did the same.

"*Gracias,*" the man said, accepting both offerings. He squinted as his eyes swept back and forth, obviously comparing the photos on the IDs to their faces.

"It's me," McNamara said. "You might recognize me from *Soldier of Fortune* magazine."

"What?" Officer Perez said.

"*Lo siento. Mi amigo solamente estaba haciendo un chiste,*" Wolf said, recalling the way the other guy had eyed them when they had just deplaned.

Perez seemed taken aback by Wolf's use of Spanish. His reply was laced with sarcasm. "And obviously *se especializa* in telling jokes that are not funny. I speak English."

He motioned for them to open their suitcases.

"And take that off as well," he said, pointing at Wolf's backpack.

They complied, and the Customs agent went through their bags with meticulous care, going so far as to call one of his assistants to take the empty luggage to be x-rayed.

"Do you have any weapons?" Perez asked.

"None to speak of," McNamara said, flashing a grin and jerking an extended thumb in Wolf's direction. "But he knows karate, so his whole body's a weapon."

"I am not amused," Perez said. "Now, answer my question."

"No, we don't," McNamara said, his expression turning serious. "What's this all about?"

Perez glared at him, ignoring the question. "And what is the purpose of your trip to Mexico, *señor?*"

McNamara started to say something, but Wolf interceded and held up his hand.

"*Señor*, let me apologize for my friend's impatience," he said. "We had a rather rough flight. We're only tourists to your great nation."

Perez appraised him, scrutinized the credentials again, and raised an eyebrow.

"So you are here for pleasure? Not business?"

"*Sí*," Wolf said. "*Solamente las actividades diversiónes.*"

Perez frowned. "Speak English, please. Have you been to my country before?"

"Our first time," Wolf said.

"Nice place," McNamara added. "Or so we've heard. Wouldn't know it by this reception, though."

The agent's mouth tightened into a frown. "Then let me acquaint you with our laws. We are very strict about bringing and carrying weapons in Mexico."

"Weapons?" Wolf asked.

Perez's head tilted as he assessed them again. "I haf to tell you, you do not look like typical *turistas*. To me, you look more like *alborotadores.*"

"What?" McNamara said.

"Troublemakers," Wolf said, smiling. "Nothing could be farther from the truth."

"Yeah, we're only looking to see the sights," McNamara said. "Maybe meet up with a couple of pretty *señoritas.*"

The Customs agent's frown deepened and he was silent for a few more seconds, then said, "There are many *Americanos* who come down here for such purposes. But they usually bring more clothing than one change of clothes."

"We heard you got good tailors down here," McNamara said. "And cheap, too."

Perez's nostrils flared. "I ask you again. What *es* your purpose for coming here?"

Something had alerted the officials. Did they stand out that much?

Wolf kept his expression neutral. "Just what we told you."

"Well, let me repeat that bit of advice." His eyes went from Wolf to McNamara. "We haf very strict laws here in my country. If you haf come here to cause trouble, or to engage in some illegal activities, consider this very carefully. Actions haf consequences."

"They always do," Wolf said.

This wasn't going very well already. He felt like turning around and getting on a plane back to the States.

A man brought the backpack and the suitcase back, set them down, and shook his head.

"Such *es* life," Perez said. He handed them back their passports and paperwork. "Enjoy your stay in Mexico."

"If everybody's as friendly as you," McNamara said, "I can see that this trip's gonna be a real blast."

"A poor choice of words, *señor*." The agent looked askance. "Just remember what I told you about obeying our laws. Okay?"

"*No nos olvidaremos,*" Wolf said.

McNamara grinned and cocked his thumb toward his own chest. "Whatever he just said goes double for me. You've been real *muy lindo.*"

The agent recoiled slightly and handed their IDs back, then stepped aside but pointed to his eye. "*Tenga cuidado, señores. Vamos a estar mirando.*"

"I wonder what that dude's problem was?" McNamara asked as they walked into the main terminal.

"It almost sounded like somebody tipped them off we were coming," Wolf said.

"Who'd do that?"

Wolf shrugged. "Maybe somebody who's setting us up to fail?"

The question lingered between them like a pending debt.

"Say, where'd you learn that Spanish?" Wolf asked. "*Muy lindo.*"

McNamara snorted a laugh. "I was quizzing Brenda back in Vegas on how to say some stuff in Spanish. Pretty slick, huh?"

"Real slick," Wolf said. "Officer Perez was very impressed. You told him he was real very pretty."

"Oh, shit. I did?"

Wolf chuckled. "Well, you probably weren't his type anyway. Now, what's this guy Zerbe supposed to be wearing again?"

"A white Panama hat and sunglasses." McNamara blew out a quick breath and glanced behind him. "I hope that guy didn't get the wrong idea."

The description fit at least a dozen or so men in the vicinity. The area was crowded, and lines of uniformed limo and bus drivers stood waving signs with various names printed on them. Off to the side, Wolf spied two people: a slender, waspish looking Mexican with several days' growth of beard, next to a heavyset Caucasian in a Panama hat, sunglasses, and an off-white sports coat. The Mexican's eyes were darting around the crowd, and they locked onto Wolf's.

Bingo, he thought, when he saw the Mexican slap the guy in the Panama hat.

Wolf and McNamara approached the ungainly pair,

the man in the sunglasses offering no acknowledgment, the Mexican grinning broadly.

"You are *El Lobo*?" he asked. "*El* Wolf?"

"I am," Wolf said. He looked at the man in the Panama hat. "You Zerbe?"

The man gave a barely perceptible nod, then motioned for them to accompany him. He turned and began pushing through the crowd toward the front entrance. Wolf and McNamara followed, the little Mexican falling into step next to them.

"*Bienvenido a Mexico*," he said. "*Me llamo José.*"

"Well, *Josie*," McNamara said, obviously mispronouncing the man's name. "It's been more like *malovenido* so far."

The little man's eyebrows rose in unison. "You espeak Spanish?"

"*Pepino*," McNamara said with a wink.

José's brow wrinkled, and he looked confused.

"He means '*poquito*,'" Wolf said.

Mac glanced at him and raised an eyebrow.

"Brenda taught me a little bit more than I let on," he said.

"I'll bet she did," Wolf said with a smile. "'*Pepino*' means cucumber."

McNamara grimaced. "I hope he didn't get the wrong idea either. But it wouldn't be the first time I made an ass out of myself trying to speak a foreign language."

After pushing through the crowd of people, they got to a set of glass doors. As soon as they were out of the air conditioning of the airport, the heat and humidity embraced them like a moist cloak. Wolf felt the familiar surge of adrenaline since it somehow reminded him of his first touchdown in Iraq. The heat had been different there. Dryer. No moisture in the air. This was more tropical, and he wondered if this was how Mac had felt when he'd touched down in Southeast Asia many years before. Zerbe stepped to the curb and pressed a button on his cell phone. As he whispered into it, Wolf noticed the phone was a burner. The same type of burner Reynolds had given them.

After a brief conversation that Wolf couldn't hear, the PI stuck the burner in his pocket and began walking down the sidewalk, waving for them to follow. A long line of lime-green taxis, mostly old Volkswagen Beetles, sat along the curb. Zerbe walked at a brisk pace, which was surprising for a man of his bulk. When he stopped, Wolf saw a heavy wet ring of sweat seeping through the underarms of his sports jacket. He lifted his arm and waggled his fingers, and an orange and white Volkswagen van with tinted windows pulled forward, honking at a few pedestrians to get out of its way. The people scattered, and the van came to a stop.

Zerbe pulled open the front passenger door and got in. José pulled open the sliding side door and told Wolf and McNamara to get inside. He then grabbed their suitcases, moved around to the rear of the vehicle, and lifted the hatch. José reappeared and said, "I do. I do for you."

Wolf and McNamara got into the rear seat area of the van and waited.

José finished jamming the luggage into the back, slammed the hatch shut, and then squeezed into the seat next to Wolf. The man's body odor was pungent.

It quickly became apparent that the vehicle's air conditioning was fighting a losing battle against the omnipresent humidity. Zerbe leaned back in his seat, took off his hat, and began fanning himself.

"Welcome to the hottest fucking place in the world," he said as the van took off. He had a distinct accent that Wolf had trouble placing. It almost sounded British, but Wolf didn't think it was, nor did he want to ask.

"We both been in hotter places," McNamara said. "A lot hotter."

"So I've heard," Zerbe replied.

"Reynolds tell you that?" McNamara asked.

"Who?"

"Reynolds. The guy we met in Vegas. Works investigations for the law firm."

Zerbe stuck his index finger along the underside of his nose, then nodded.

"Oh, yeah. Right." He patted his pocket and took out a pack of cigarettes, then shook one out and placed it between his lips.

Zerbe flicked a lighter, and the oppressive stench of cigarette smoke filled the interior.

I hope this is going to be a short ride, Wolf thought.

The driver accelerated and used his horn almost constantly until they reached a busy street and pulled out into traffic.

"This is Paco," Zerbe said, pointing at the driver. A smoky breath escaped with his words. "Him and José here are my two right hands."

"You can never have too many of those," McNamara said.

"Especially in this place." Zerbe drew deeply on the cigarette. "So, we got you in a hotel down the way here. It'll serve as your base of operations. As soon as we get there, we can go over things."

"Sounds like a plan," McNamara said.

Wolf said nothing. The noxious odors and irritating smoke were bothering him, but he was trapped in the middle of the seat and couldn't crack a window. He hoped it wouldn't take long to reach where they were going.

After about five minutes of speeding, honking, abrupt braking, and quick turns, they arrived in front of a tall high-rise building. The van pulled underneath a long overhang that offered a welcome bit of shade from the bright afternoon sun. Zerbe slid out of the door. "The guys'll get your bags. Give 'em a tip, would ya?"

He walked toward the revolving glass doors. The sign over them said *Bienvenido al Hotel Casa Blanca.*

Wolf could hardly wait to get out of the vehicle and breathe some fresh air. As he tried to shake off the remnants of the interior of the stuffy van, he caught a whiff of something else: salt. The sea air smelled fresh and clean, and he took a deep breath.

Zerbe was already pushing through the doors. Wolf glanced at McNamara, who was right behind him. He wondered if Mac felt as uncertain about this as he did. He also knew that once they'd landed here, they'd reached the point of no return. They had to see this thing through, but that didn't mean they couldn't abort if necessary. Wolf had no intention of ending up in a Mexican jail, waiting for some law firm in the US to get them out. But hopefully, it wouldn't come to that.

He thought about Kasey's last words to him. *You'd better* not *let anything happen to my* father.

Wolf had no intention of letting that happen to either of them if he could help it. But the added responsibility of watching both their backs and being without weapons and a known support system felt like an unwelcome load of free weights in his backpack. At least the hotel looked first class.

He entered the first open triangular space of the revolving door and pushed the shiny brass handrail. As the door rotated, it was like going from the oven into the refrigerator. The air conditioning embraced him like an ice shower, and he immediately felt the cooling sensation on his skin. It was a far cry from a tent or a Quonset hut on the far side of the globe. The floor was tiled in red marble that led up to a long desk that shone like black onyx. Huge pots on either side of it sported pointed, cactus-like plants, and the wall behind the desk was a pale green with bright blue oval housing scripted yellow letters spelling out the hotel's name.

From behind the desk, a pretty woman in a black business suit greeted them in perfect English. Zerbe went to the elevators and stood off to the side, smoking.

So much for a smoke-free environment, Wolf thought.

After showing their IDs and presenting the credit card Reynolds had given them, the woman tapped some keys on her computer and then gave them each a key card in a small cardboard folder. José and Paco came through the doors, towing the suitcase and the backpack. They made a show of placing the items on a hotel cart and José pushed it toward them, stopping a respectful distance away. Paco stood by the door.

"You can obtain some pesos from the ATM machine over there," the woman suggested.

McNamara's brow creased.

"For the tip," she said.

"Oh, okay," McNamara said. "But, ah, maybe you can show me how to use it? I'm kind of technically challenged."

The woman smiled. "But of course."

She moved from behind the desk, and Wolf saw Mac check out her legs in the tight skirt. He glanced at Wolf and winked.

Technically challenged, my ass, Wolf thought. *He just wants to check out hers.*

Wolf strolled over to Zerbe, who was extinguishing his cigarette in a sand-filled metal ashtray. There were half a dozen butts sticking out of the mound of white granules. Zerbe reached in his pocket and took out his cigarette pack again.

"Would you mind not smoking?" Wolf said. "It's giving me a headache."

The heavyset detective was still wearing his sunglasses, so Wolf couldn't see his eyes, but the twitch of his jaw and tightening around the mouth told the tale as he slipped the pack of smokes back into his shirt pocket. He turned and jabbed the elevator button.

"What room you guys in?" he asked.

Wolf looked at the cardboard folder. "Seven-nineteen."

"Okay, I'm in six-oh-eight. Call me when you get settled in. I'll get my stuff out of the safe in my room and be there shortly."

Wolf nodded, and the elevator doors opened. McNamara's laughter carried across the lobby, and Wolf saw that he was still at the ATM with the pretty desk clerk. The two Mexicans stood there with the luggage cart. Zerbe got into the elevator, and the doors slid closed.

Wolf wasn't sorry to see the creepy PI depart. There was a lot not to like about the guy: his cigarette smoking, his shifty appearance, his body odor...

And anybody who wears sunglasses inside, Wolf thought, *either thinks they're a movie star or is hiding something.*

Presently, McNamara sauntered over after giving the two Mexicans a handful of pesos each.

"How much did you give them?" Wolf asked.

"Aw, hell, I don't know. It looked like enough, judging

from the smiles they both had." McNamara shrugged. "What does it matter anyway? I put it on that special credit card. We're not paying that bill."

Wolf wasn't sure a bill wouldn't be forthcoming down the line, one way or another. He pressed the button. The two Mexicans were in conversation by the lobby doors, and when the elevator doors opened, José pushed the cart toward them. Paco left.

"*Esperan, por favor*. I take it up to your room, *señores*," José said, a glint of white teeth showing in his unkempt, bearded face.

Wolf acknowledged that in Spanish.

The Mexican's smile broadened. "Ah, you espeak Spanish, eh?"

"*Poquito*," Wolf said, not wanting to reveal his fluency. It was always better to let them think you knew less rather than more, at least until you knew all the players and what their positions were. Wolf wasn't sure where this guy fit in.

Seven-nineteen was almost adjacent to the elevators. The cart rolled easily over the plush gray carpeting, and their room turned out to be equally elegant, except for a lingering odor of cigarette smoke mixed with disinfectant.

It had a spacious anteroom with a chair, a sofa, a fairly large table, and a flat-screen TV. A wicker basket full of fruit and bottled water sat in the middle of the table. A refrigerator was next to a bureau, upon which sat a coffee maker and a glass cabinet with individual bottles of alcohol, soft drinks, and candy bars.

There was a small hallway, off which was the black marble-walled bathroom, complete with a walk-in moon shower with translucent walls, a fancy toilet, and a sink and cabinet that extended up from the floor. Wolf glanced at his reflection in the mirror as he carried his backpack and Mac's suitcase into the bedroom. It had two king-sized beds, two dressers, a desk, a TV, and a pair of chairs.

McNamara trailed behind him and emitted a low whistle. "Almost as good as Ms. Dolly's room at the Shamrock."

José came prancing into the room, and Wolf shot him a wary stare.

The reedy Mexican raised his hands and smiled.

"I take de cart back down, den I wait until eet *es* time to come back."

"Come back for what?" McNamara asked.

"Zerbe say you want to talk about de plan," José said.

Wolf wondered how many other people were in on this plan as the little man scurried out the door. He started to mention his concern, but McNamara's loud voice cut him off.

"Man, would you take a look at this bathroom? Look at that shower. I almost want to go find me a girl and put her in there so I can watch her through that glass. Can't wait to try it out."

He stepped inside the bathroom, and at the same time, he motioned for Wolf to follow him. McNamara opened the shower door, turned on the water full force, and stood next to the steady flow. He gestured for Wolf to come closer.

"I'm gonna check out both rooms for bugs," McNamara whispered, holding up his smartphone.

Wolf nodded. He hadn't thought about the possibility, but it made sense. He'd had an uneasy feeling since first hearing about this op and was glad Mac seemed to share his wariness.

Leaving the shower running, McNamara stepped out

and activated the app on his smartphone. Wolf watched as his friend went around each room with assiduous care, monitoring the screen on his phone and ducking to glance under tables and lamps. Wolf did his part by joining in and picking up various pieces of furniture. He also scanned the picture frames, vases, and other decor for micro cameras. After a thorough search that took the better part of fifteen minutes, they'd found nothing out of the ordinary. McNamara went back into the bathroom and shut off the water.

"Well," he said, "at least we now know Big Brother ain't listening in."

"Where'd you get that bug tracer?"

"Kasey. She's up on all the latest computer gadgets and is always ordering them and setting them up for me." He held up his smartphone. "Took me a while to get used to using this thing, but it kinda makes me feel like James Bond."

"Pretty good for a guy who's so technically challenged he needs help using an ATM machine."

McNamara smiled and shook his head. "Yeah, that little gal's *muy lindo*, ain't she? I wouldn't mind sticking around here for a couple of days after we've finished and taking her out to dinner."

"Remember, it's *'linda'* for her," Wolf said. "And if you do, don't drink the water."

He went to the phone and dialed the front desk. When the girl answered, he requested to be put through to Mr. Zerbe's room. The PI answered after three rings.

"You ready for that meeting?" Wolf asked.

"Yeah. Give me a couple minutes, and I'll be up there."

His words had a slight slur, and Wolf wondered if the PI had been sampling his room's little courtesy bar's offerings. So far, despite the luxurious accommodations and the front money, this operation had a lot of less-than-impressive players. It was like finding a swath of corrosion under the hood of your new car. The sooner they got this one done and got out of here, the better. He wondered if Mac felt the same way.

"Sounds like he's had a couple from his mini-bar," Wolf said after hanging up the phone.

"Shit," McNamara said. "I hope we didn't sign on with a bunch of drinkers and dopers."

"Dopers?"

McNamara's face twisted into a half-smile. "My first tour, back before I was Special Forces, I was with an infantry company. They dropped a bunch of us into Indian Country to set up a base camp. I was green and scared. Turned out that about half of the company was dopers, going out to smoke that shit on patrol instead of beating the bush looking for Charlie."

Wolf shook his head in disgust. He'd experienced similarly disappointing things during his time in the military, but not to the extent Mac had several decades before.

"One night, the VC hit us," McNamara continued. "I was on watch. Looked through my starlight and saw them coming like a human tsunami from all sides. Half of them idiot dopers had been smoking their shit instead of watching their posts. They were incapable of fighting, at least not effectively."

"Shit," said Wolf. "What happened?"

"We got overrun. Lost a shit-ton of men, but we managed to hold them off. The LT called in a couple artillery strikes on our own position. By the time the Cobra gunships came in, the pilots barking like dogs and using them M-60s, it was pretty much over with. I made up my mind never to trust another doper, be it pot, drugs, or booze."

"Good words to live by."

McNamara's smile was wistful. "I was a sixteen-year-old enlistee. Lied about my age. Got me a couple of medals and re-upped on the condition that I could go to jump school. Then went on to Ranger school, then Special Forces. Got my Green Beret and went back." He sighed. "Stayed in way longer than I probably should have. Ended up costing me both my marriages and a lot more."

Wolf felt the pain of Mac's loneliness. "You and Kasey seem close."

McNamara seemed ready to say something else when a knock on the door interrupted. McNamara strode over to open it, but Wolf couldn't help but notice his friend's quick brush at his eyes as he moved past him.

"It's me," a familiar voice said through the door.

McNamara checked, then opened the door.

Zerbe stood there, minus the hat and the white sports coat but still wearing the sunglasses. He was holding a large manila envelope. A cigarette dangled from his lips.

"Anybody ever told you that you smoke too much?" McNamara asked.

The overweight PI stepped inside and took a long drag on his cigarette. After exhaling, he took it out of his mouth and held it up.

"Got an ashtray?"

Wolf saw a ceramic dish on the bureau and handed it to Zerbe. He crushed out his cigarette and set the ashtray down. Taking out his burner phone, he punched in a number. After a few seconds, the other party answered, and Zerbe muttered, "Come on up. Seven-nineteen."

He hung up and went to the table, opening the flap of

the envelope as he plopped down in one of the chairs. "José's on his way."

"We need him on this part?" Wolf asked.

Zerbe turned toward him, saying nothing.

Wolf tried to read the man's expression, but the sunglasses were off-putting. Upon closer inspection, they appeared to be prescription lenses.

"How much you know about Accondras?" Zerbe asked.

"Not much," Wolf said. "We were told you would meet us down here and bring us up to speed."

"Well, then," Zerbe said. "Let me do that."

He removed a sheaf of papers from the envelope and spread them out on the table.

A quick knock echoed from the door. Wolf stepped over to it and looked through the peephole. The diminutive Mexican was on the other side, and he too was smoking.

After opening the door, Wolf nodded at José. As the smaller man smiled, Wolf plucked the smoke from his lips and carried it to the ashtray.

"*No fume*, eh?" José asked.

Wolf crushed out the butt, and McNamara pulled out the chair opposite Zerbe. José plopped down on the sofa and crossed his legs. Wolf remained standing but moved closer to the table.

"Let's get to it," McNamara said.

Zerbe placed an 8x11 photograph of a man's face on the center of the table.

"This," Zerbe said, "is Thomas Accondras."

CHAPTER 10

CANCUN, MEXICO

Sweat ran down Wolf's sides under his loose-fitting BDU blouse as he sat wedged next to the window in the rear seat of the microbus. McNamara was next to him, and José was kneeling on the floor between the front and rear seats. Paco was driving, and Zerbe was in the front passenger seat.

The combination of the heavyset PI's oppressive body odor mixed with that of Paco and José made for a very odiferous ride. Wolf couldn't wait for it to be over but reflected that in his time, he'd smelled worse. It was nothing compared to a stack of dead bodies in the desert heat or people torn open by an IED, but the proximity of the diminutive Mexican was unsettling. He constantly placed his hand on Wolf's knee as he leaned toward the window and pointed out various landmarks and people.

"*Mira,*" he said. "Dat is one of de armed guards. Dey carry machine guns and let no one into de *Palacios Dorados.*"

Palacios Dorados, thought Wolf. Golden Palaces.

As Zerbe had described it, the place was a well-guarded subdivision housing rich foreigners who'd purchased oceanside property in Mexico. A solid brick security shack sat in the center of a private cobblestone road. Wrought iron gates were suspended from a twelve-foot brick wall that extended along the roadway and into the distance, with a coil of concertina wire along the top. Wolf caught a glimpse of the houses beyond the gates and saw that they did resemble small palaces.

"On de beach side," José continued, "dey carry machine guns, *también.*"

Wolf pushed the little man's hand away as he repositioned himself. The air was barely breathable, and the air conditioning was practically nonexistent.

"*No me toca,*" he said. "Don't touch me."

José snorted a laugh. "*Lo siento, pero no me piensa que soy un cundango.*"

Wolf wasn't familiar with that word. "*Qué?*"

"*Cundango,*" José said with a sly look. "You know, queer."

"What the hell are you two talking about?" McNamara said.

Wolf realized he'd lapsed and revealed to José and the other two that he was more fluent in Spanish than he had first let on.

Bad tactical move, he thought. Never show your cards until the hand's over.

"Hey, Zerbe," he said. "Either crack a damn window or toss the butt. It's getting kinda nauseating back here."

If the PI heard him, he gave no indication.

McNamara reached forward and clapped him on the shoulder.

"That goes double for me, pard," McNamara said. "I got a low tolerance level for smokers of all kinds."

Once again Zerbe made no reply, but this time stubbed out his cigarette in the ashtray, which was over-flowing. Paco glanced at him with a questioning look. He had a cigarette dangling from his lips as well.

"Yeah," McNamara said. "You too, *amigo.*"

Zerbe grunted something, and Paco rolled down his window and tossed out his cigarette.

"As you can see," Zerbe said, pedantry lacing his voice, "trying to get inside that place to grab the son of a bitch is pretty much out of the question."

"So we gotta wait till he leaves the compound," McNamara said. "Any idea when that might be?"

"As a matter of fact," Zerbe said, turning in his seat and grinning, "I do. Tonight."

"Tonight?" The space between McNamara's eyebrows squeezed into twin horizontal lines. "We got to move on this tonight?"

"That's correct," Zerbe said.

McNamara was silent for a few seconds, then he glanced at Wolf.

"That Reynolds fella told us we'd have a few days to scope things out," McNamara said.

"Plans change." Zerbe lifted his hands in a what-are-you-gonna-do gesture. "We're on a tight timetable, and the window of opportunity is very limited. If we don't move tonight, the opportunity could be lost."

"And if we move too soon," McNamara said, "without a good, solid ops plan, a lot more could be lost. Namely, us."

"Listen," Zerbe said, "I've been down here sitting on this guy for the better part of two weeks. Believe me, we're not going to get another chance like this. I've got it all worked out. Nothing can go wrong."

"Where have I heard that before?" McNamara asked.

Where, indeed? Wolf thought.

The more he heard, the less he liked this.

José shifted to a seated position on the floor and took out his phone.

"You want me to call Salvador, *jefe*?" he asked.

Zerbe nodded.

"Who the hell's Salvador?" McNamara asked.

Zerbe held up his palm.

McNamara obviously wasn't pleased with the man or his gesture, but he said nothing.

Wolf was seriously considering trying to convince Mac to scrap this mission and this unsavory trio, but they'd gone too far.

José started gabbing into the phone, laughing and uttering words so rapidly and pronouncing them so sloppily that Wolf couldn't understand what was being said or get a feel for the conversation.

If they don't want you to understand them, he thought, *you won't, no matter how good you think you speak the language.*

José laughed again and muttered a few more words before terminating the call. He looked up at Zerbe. "All set, *jefe*."

"Let's go down to the market and get some tacos," Zerbe said.

Paco nodded, and they sped down the street.

Wolf and McNamara exchanged glances again as they sat in silence. The trip wasn't long, but it was punctuated by sudden stops, weaving in and out of lanes, and an almost constant blaring of horns. Through the window,

Wolf watched the sea of brown faces they passed: men, women, and children walked alongside the road or pulled carts stacked with fruits, clothing, or electronics. It reminded him a little of the streets of Baghdad, at least until IEDs had made the treks too perilous to appreciate the indigenous color. Here, whenever they stopped, people ran up to the side of the van, extending their wares.

"Kind of reminds you of downtown LA, don't it?" Zerbe asked with a smirk. "In the old days back in Johannesburg, we'd just shoot the bastards and leave 'em lay."

So he's South African, thought Wolf.

"How long did you say you had Accondras under surveillance?" McNamara asked.

Zerbe shrugged.

"About ten days. My job was just to locate him and keep an eye on him until you guys arrived."

"Who you working for?" McNamara asked.

The PI didn't answer for several seconds. "The same people you are."

Wolf had taken a distinct dislike to this Zerbe character and read that McNamara had the same misgivings.

Paco suddenly jammed on the brakes, and everyone shifted forward with an abruptness. He rolled down the window to yell and curse, then wheeled around some obstacle in the road.

"We're almost there," Zerbe said.

"Thank God for small favors," McNamara said with a grin. "And I was actually thinking about renting a car down here, too."

"Not advisable," Zerbe said. "Plus, you've got to buy Mexican insurance."

They felt the van veer to the left and go over a huge bump. At first, Wolf thought they'd run over someone, but José looked up at him and winked.

"*Un tope*," he said.

"Speed bump," Zerbe added.

Wolf had heard tales about them down here but never experienced one until now. It made him long for the stable suspension of a Hummer.

After moving off the pavement and onto what felt and sounded like a gravel roadway, the van came to a stop. Wolf saw they were in some sort of open-air market with rows of tents and vehicles. The sharp odors of hot peppers and meat being cooked wafted to them as they opened the doors. It felt good to stand and stretch after being cramped in the vehicle. Zerbe walked toward a couple of tents, José and Paco following. They stopped in front of one of the tents, where a squat Mexican woman shuffled a chopped meat, green and red vegetables, and dough in a pan over an open flame. Zerbe said to José, "Order me four *durados* and a can of soda." He passed the slim Mexican a handful of pesos and looked askance at Wolf and McNamara. "Get whatever you want, but I'd advise against overdoing it. We can't afford to mess up our timetable because somebody's got the shits."

"You don't have to tell us twice," McNamara said.

Both he and Wolf ordered two tacos and bottled water. After watching the food being prepared and listening to José extol the virtues of the cooking of *la señora*, they joined Zerbe at a wooden picnic table at the far edge of the clearing. It was fairly isolated.

José set a paper bag with Zerbe's food on the table, then sat on the far edge of the bench and began devouring a burrito. Wolf glanced around and saw Paco standing about fifty feet away, eating and apparently keeping an eye on his van.

Zerbe unwrapped his first taco and bit into it, chewed, and then nodded appreciatively.

"Best damn food in this shithole," he said.

If the pejorative offended the little man, he didn't show it.

Neither Wolf nor McNamara ate.

"All this running around serving any purpose?" McNamara asked. "So far, all we've seen is the mini-fortress where this guy's hanging out. You say it's his parents' house?"

Zerbe took another bite and nodded as he masticated. Running his tongue over his teeth, he grabbed the soft drink can, wiped the top with his coat sleeve, opened it, and took a swig. In this heat, Wolf doubted it was very cold.

"Salvador's on the way," Zerbe said.

McNamara rolled his eyes. "I ask again, who the fuck's this Salvador?"

José chirped a laugh, expelling some partially chewed food.

"Salvador?" he said. "He *es un padrote grande.*"

Wolf understood this description but remained silent.

Let's see how they're going to frame it, he thought.

Zerbe shot José a quick look, and the little man shrugged and bit off another piece of his burrito.

"Salvador is a man of many talents," Zerbe said. "He's a local legend around here." He paused as if considering how to phrase the rest of his description. "He's rather well known to the permanent American and European residents in *Palacios Dorados.* You might say he arranges things for those who have…unusual proclivities."

"*Un padrote grande,*" José said, expelling more food

particles. Wolf edged farther away from him. "*Muy grande.*"

"He's a pimp, then," McNamara said.

Wolf was glad Mac was able to read between the lines despite the language barrier.

"Yes," Zerbe said. "And he's our key to your getting Accondras."

"I'd like to know how it's *our* key to *us* getting him," McNamara said.

Zerbe smirked. "Listen, my job was just to locate him. Set things in motion for some pros to come down here and do the snatch. So far, you guys haven't shown me shit."

McNamara took off his cowboy hat and handed it to Wolf.

"How'd you like me to shove those last two tacos up your ass?" His expression made it clear he was prepared to do just that.

Zerbe's eyes were still concealed behind the thick green lenses, but Wolf was sure they were wide open now.

"Hey," Zerbe said. "Take it easy, will ya? I been cooped up down here for ten days, tracking this piece of shit. Then I get word Fallotti's sending down two pros to grab him. I'm just doing my job."

McNamara stared at the other man for several seconds, then blew out a breath.

"I'm tired of you giving us the runaround. You got a plan? Let's hear it."

The tip of Zerbe's tongue shot out and wet his lips.

"Accondras is inside that exclusive area," he said. "Armed guards on all sides. Concertina wire on top of the wall."

"So we noticed," Wolf said.

"Well," Zerbe replied, "getting inside there is virtually impossible."

"You told us that before," McNamara said.

"So, the only way to grab him is to get him to come out. Salvador is our way to do that." Zerbe picked up one of the tacos, looked at it for a moment, then dropped it back into the paper bag. "Accondras and Salvador are known to one another. You're familiar with Accondras' sexual preferences?"

Mac shot a quick glance at Wolf, who nodded.

"*Le gusta los niños,*" José said. "*Muy joven.*"

"So we've heard," Wolf said.

"Well," Zerbe said, wiping his mouth on the inside of his sleeve, "tonight, he'll be going out to partake in a bit of his perverse lechery."

Wolf and McNamara exchanged glances, their faces revealing their disgust and disapproval.

"How reliable is this information?" McNamara asked.

"It's taken me, or rather our employer," Zerbe said, "quite a tidy sum of money, in the form of bribes, to come across this connection."

"Connection?" Wolf asked.

Zerbe shifted his gaze to him.

"Right. Salvador has gotten him some fodder for his excesses in the past, and he's scheduled to do so again."

"Tonight?" Wolf asked.

"Tonight," Zerbe confirmed.

"How do you know he'll be coming out of the place?" McNamara asked. "What's to stop the pimp from bringing the kid inside the compound?"

"He's done it this way before," Zerbe said. "He doesn't get on well with his stepfather and can't afford to get kicked out of the house."

"And you're sure about this?"

Zerbe nodded.

"When's this supposed to be going down?" McNamara asked.

"In a few hours, actually. At dusk. Nobody likes to travel at night, especially the tourists and expatriates. Even though Cancun is not known for violence like the rest of Mexico, it can still be a dangerous place."

"A nest of vipers," Wolf said.

"What?" Zerbe asked.

"That's the Mayan translation for 'Cancun.'"

Zerbe shrugged. "If you say so."

"A few hours," McNamara said, looking at his watch. "Give me a time."

"Time is relative here," Zerbe said. "Suffice it to say that we'll be able to name our time and location."

McNamara frowned. "You better lay it all out for us. And quit being so mealy-mouthed."

The PI pursed his lips. "Okay, this is the way it'll go down. José contacts Salvador and gives him the where and when. We'll already be there, setting up on the location. Once he comes out, José calls me and follows them." He pulled his burner partially out of this pocket. "When he shows up expecting to see a little bare behind, you two step out of the shadows and grab him."

"And exactly where is this supposed to take place?" McNamara asked.

"It is near a place called *El Meco*. The ancient Mayan ruins. There's a smattering of slum housing almost adjacent to them. A lot of them are vacant. Pay somebody a few pesos to rent their shitty little shack for a few hours, and nobody gives a damn what you do in there."

"*Garida de apañar*," José said with a lascivious grin. "*Para el baile de diablo.*"

McNamara looked at Wolf.

"Den of iniquity," Wolf said. "Loosely translated. "For the devil's dance."

"So Accondras is going there to meet this Salvador guy," McNamara said. "Thinking he's gonna be getting his rocks off sodomizing some poor kid and then planning on beating feet back to his compound, of which he's afraid to leave after dark."

"Discretion is often unwisely supplanted by desire," Zerbe said.

"What is it you're not telling us?" Wolf asked.

Zerbe raised an eyebrow.

"If he's living behind a wall covered with concertina wire and has armed guards to keep the locals at a distance, and everybody's afraid to travel at night," Wolf said, intentionally drawing out his question, "then it stands to reason that even if he lets his desires supplant his discretion, he'll be taking some precautions. He gonna be armed?"

Zerbe laughed. "I doubt it. This guy's what you'd call a real pussy. A lightweight, albeit a crafty one." He pulled out the lapel of his dingy white sports jacket and snared his cigarette pack out of his pocket. After shaking one out, he put it between his lips. José was quick to lean over with his lighter and flicked the wheel. It ignited with a sharp burst. The PI leaned his head forward and stuck the end of the cigarette into the yellow flame. "He'll most likely have a guard with him."

"An armed guard?" McNamara asked.

"Yes, but it's doubtful the guard will accompany him into the house where he thinks he's going to find the boy."

"What kind of weapons this guard gonna have?" McNamara asked.

After taking a long drag, Zerbe let the smoke embrace his words. "A sidearm, most likely. Possibly something a little more substantial. An old Uzi or perhaps a shotgun."

"And we have nothing." Again, McNamara's reply was more of a statement than a question. "Can you get us a couple of guns?"

Zerbe shook his head. "Only the police, the cartels, and a few thugs have guns down here. It's difficult, not to mention extremely risky, but I'm working on it."

"Working on it?" McNamara said.

Zerbe nodded.

"Well, work a little harder," McNamara said. "We ain't going into this thing unarmed. What you're asking us to do sounds pretty risky."

"Isn't that what you're being paid for?" Zerbe said. "And, you'll have the element of surprise."

"*Surprise*," McNamara said, emphasizing the triteness of the word. "Against a guy carrying an Uzi or a shotgun, that ain't gonna count for a whole lot."

"Plus, I'm not too eager to maybe have to take out some guard who's just doing his job," Wolf said.

"Hey, you guys are supposed to be the pros," Zerbe said. "How you do it is your business. But this house we got set up for the..." he paused, smiled, and then continued, "liaison has a rear window. Just jump him once he gets inside, take him down, and carry him out the back. Me and Paco will be waiting down the alley with the van. We shove him in and take off for the rendezvous without anybody being the wiser."

"What about this Salvador fella?" McNamara asked.

Zerbe shrugged again as if striving for nonchalance, but it fell a bit short.

"I'll pay him off beforehand. He'll escort Accondras

and the guard to the house, give them the key, and collect his dough. Then he'll be gone."

"What if Accondras wants the guard to come inside with him?" Wolf asked. "To check things out."

"I don't suppose he will," Zerbe said. "He didn't the last time."

"That's a whole lot of supposing," McNamara said. "What if he starts yelling? That'll bring the guard in real quick."

"Lock the door behind him. I'll bring you a Taser and some duct tape to cover his mouth."

"A Taser," McNamara said.

"Yeah," Zerbe said. "They work great. You ever used one?"

McNamara and Wolf exchanged glances, and Mac smirked.

"Yeah," he said. "I know all about 'em."

"And *suppose*," Wolf said, exaggerating the word, "we are able to take this Accondras down inside without a problem or a sound. How are we going to get him out of town?"

"I already told you that. Bring him down the back alley to where we'll be waiting with the van."

Wolf kept his tone flat. "And then we'll drop him at a prearranged location."

"For which I have the coordinates," Zerbe said. "I was told you both have map-reading skills, and I'll have a GPS device if you're worried."

Wolf glanced at Mac, wondering what his thoughts were. It was his play to make or not. Wolf was having severe misgivings but said nothing. There was no way he was not going to back his friend and mentor.

"You said *gringos* are afraid to drive at night around here?" McNamara asked.

"Let's just say it isn't advisable," Zerbe said.

"Then how the hell are we supposed to get back here from this dust-off zone?"

Zerbe took another long drag on his smoke before replying, "Paco can drive you back."

"And you'll be with us?" McNamara asked.

Zerbe nodded. "All the way."

McNamara and Wolf exchanged glances. *All the way* —the Airborne creed.

Both of them smirked.

McNamara stared at the diminutive José, then glanced at his watch. "What time's this little illicit rendezvous set for?"

"I tol him *seis por la noche*," José said. "Eet will be getting dark by *siete*."

McNamara stood up, stretched, and readjusted his hat on his head.

"Okay, let's go check out this *garida de apañar*," he said. He started walking toward the van at a quicker than normal pace and motioned for Wolf to join him.

"Whatcha think?" he asked when Wolf caught up.

Wolf considered his answer carefully. He didn't like it, any of it, but he didn't want to let Mac down.

"Your call," he said. "But it sounds like it could easily turn into a clusterfuck."

"Yeah," McNamara agreed. "With us caught smack-dab in the middle."

Zerbe and José were still a good distance behind them and certainly out of earshot.

"It's not too late to back out," Wolf said.

McNamara glanced at him. "That what you want?"

"I got your back," Wolf said. "Whatever you choose to do."

McNamara gave a quick nod and smiled.

"I never doubted that." They strode for several more steps in silence, then Mac said. "Looks like we're gonna be dancing with the devil ourselves tonight."

* * *

VON DIEN WINTER ESTATE SOUTH BELIZE

Eagan watched as the trio of luscious Latinas cavorted in the pool, along with the two bounty hunters. The backdrop was a conflation of succulent green vines, blooming bougainvillea, wildflowers, and assorted trees spreading out into the verdant and seemingly infinite forest. Eagan knew that somewhere in the thick shrubbery, a high, electrified fence topped with barbed wire prevented unauthorized intrusions by man and beast. It was the kind of place men like him dreamed about. Not much different than Saddam's luxurious mansions, which had been scattered around Iraq. Eagan had luxuriated in them on his first tour while still a grunt in the Army. It had been a brief taste of a lifestyle very foreign to him and one he'd realized he would never see again unless he made some severe changes in his life. So after his hitch was up, he went back to Iraq, but not in uniform. There was far better money to be made in a PMC and only a contractual obligation that could be broken without any military consequences. The Vipers and good old Stu had afforded him a chance to hop into the fast lane and make some real dough, and then the nice little gig of "recovering" the artifacts had fallen into his lap.

One of the girls laughed and toyed with her bikini top.

Go ahead, he thought. Take it off, baby.

Her nipples were visible through the thin, wet fabric anyway.

It would keep his two problematic idiots occupied and unsuspicious for the short term.

The group of Vipers—Reynolds, Kunish, Harper, and Wells— were, by contrast, all business. They sat at a nearby table checking and cleaning their rifles, and Nasim was cleaning his Glock 19 as well. They all were wearing latex gloves. Eagan and each of the Vipers had sidearms, which were also Glock 19s. Weapons standardization was the first step on a well-run mission, so he had two more Glocks for the bounty hunters. Eagan had opted to go with AK-47s, the cheap SKS Chinese versions, for the rifles. Easy to come by and easier to leave behind. They could just drop them and run when the time came. Weapons of that sort were virtually untraceable. Plus, the loose-fitting design and ruggedness made them functional in virtually any climate or terrain. Eagan figured it would be dusty in Mexico. Good old Kalashnikov had known what he was doing when he'd come up with the design for that one. It was the most copied rifle in the world.

Eagan scanned the rest of Von Dien's plush Belize mansion, looking for Webber, the helicopter pilot. He worked exclusively for Victor Delta's corporation, whatever the hell that was. More than likely, it was just a front for the billionaire's riches. Eagan couldn't imagine the wrinkled-up Buddha had the skills or business acumen to have made that much money by himself. Probably inherited it from his family.

But none of that mattered, as long as the right amount of cash was deposited in the Vipers' Cayman account once the job was done. And hopefully, it would include a large bonus for tidying up all those loose ends. It was going to be a very comfortable vacation for him that would most likely extend into an early retirement of drinking rum and Cokes on some Caribbean beach and chasing the girls.

A tinkle of laughter sounded from the pool. The big black guy was flexing his biceps, and one of the girls, now topless, was seeing how the cup of her bikini fit over his bulging arm. The other guy, Reno, had another of the girls sitting on his shoulders.

If they only knew what was coming, Eagan thought.

But he had to keep his eye on the ball. It was one thing to let those two jokers play around, but a good leader crossed all the Ts and dotted all the Is, so the mission ran smoothly and without any hitches. No surprises, not like that goat-fuck in Iraq. He'd depended on that idiot Cummins too much on that one. That was a mistake he wouldn't make again. If he didn't need the fat asshole to facilitate the contact and make the final money transfer with Victor Delta, Eagan would have jettisoned him a long time ago.

He smiled.

Victor Delta, Eagan thought. *I wonder what the old man would say if he found out about Cummins' nickname for him.*

"Okay, that's great," Cummins said as he talked on the phone. "Keep me posted."

He terminated the call and turned to Eagan with a smile.

"It's all set. They're gonna move on Accondras in about five hours. By nineteen-forty or so, they'll be at the landing zone, and we'll have him in our custody."

And probably after about twenty minutes more, Eagan thought, *I'll have pried the location of the artifact out of him.*

His thoughts turned to the best technique to use. It had to be expedient and painful but not potentially disfiguring or immediately lethal. It all depended on where the son of a bitch had hidden the damn thing. Judging from the size of the other half, which they'd gotten in Iraq, it could easily fit inside a safe deposit box. When the two halves of the artifact were placed together, it wasn't much bigger than a good-sized cantaloupe.

A safe deposit box was a good bet. Even though the son of a bitch was living in that gated community, with armed guards patrolling, it seemed doubtful to Eagan that he'd chance leaving the artifact there with an adversarial stepfather watching his every move.

Then again, a safe deposit box would limit accessibility for Accondras should he need to retrieve the artifact quickly and unobtrusively, so it was equally possible that he'd be secreting it someplace else, maybe even on his person. Either way, Eagan would find out and quickly. And maybe, since he'd be dealing with a pussy child molester, just the implication of force might be all the persuasion that would be needed. But where was the fun in that? No, he'd put a little oomph into the initial venture to ensure truthfulness and cooperation.

If they had to hold him until banking business hours the next day to get into some vault, it meant that any persuasive measures would have to spare the hand he used to sign his name. It probably would be better if the asshole could walk, too, and had no facial disfigurements, but that left plenty of other body parts to work on. And after they had it, the son of a bitch was expendable. His body could be dropped with the rest of them for the scene setup. That would entail keeping everyone alive until the artifact was verified so the times of death would roughly coincide.

Not that the Mexicans would do much investigation, but there was always a danger that the US authorities might stick their noses in. The FBI, maybe. So things had to look explainable: a dispute between some American bounty hunters over a wanted subject that resulted in everybody getting shot.

All the little loose ends tied up in a pretty bow, Eagan thought. That ought to be good for a nice bonus from Victor Delta.

Death in the desert.

But all this was speculation. He wouldn't know anything for sure about where the artifact was until it was just him, Accondras, and the special equipment.

More feminine laughter tinkled from the pool, accompanied by splashing. Another of the girls had removed her top. Cummins pushed up his thick glasses on his nose and leered at her bare breasts.

"Hey, keep your eye on the ball," Eagan said. "Has he got everything else set up?"

Cummins pursed his lips. "He says he does. Two vanilla-looking vans, all gassed up and ready to go. He's got the LZ prepared, too."

"Where's Webber?" Eagan asked. "I want to make sure that helicopter's gassed up and ready to go too."

Cummins pointed toward the far end of the huge house.

"The helipad's over there. But don't you want to hear what Zerbe's got set up?"

"I don't care what he's got set up as long as he gets Accondras, Wolf, and his buddy to the LZ on time. You said he's estimating nineteen hundred for that?"

Cummins bumped his glasses up on his nose again and nodded. "That's what he said."

"All right. We ship out in two hours. I'm going to go check with Webber and get the rest of my gear."

"The rest of your gear?"

"Yeah," Eagan said. "A pair of pliers and a ball-peen hammer."

He could hardly wait.

CHAPTER 11

CANCUN, MEXICO

A nest of vipers.

The words kept running through Wolf's mind as the van sped through the early evening traffic. José was stationed outside the gate of the *Palacios Dorados* on a motorcycle, waiting for Accondras and his bodyguard to depart. A quick phone call to Zerbe would confirm that the game was on. For his part, Zerbe reiterated that he would be there but was staying in the background.

"Like I said, I don't do the rough stuff," he said.

Wolf noticed that the man still wore the same soiled and sweat-stained white sports coat, light-blue shirt, Panama hat, and sunglasses. Not that there would be much ambient lighting, but the PI stood out like a painted fence post on a country road. That was all right. Wolf hated that he and Mac were depending on this character as much as they were. Wolf trusted Zerbe about as far as he could throw him and his two Mexican sidekicks even less.

The bodyguard was another wildcard in the game. According to Zerbe, it wasn't a question of if the guard would be armed, but rather what kind of gun or guns he'd be carrying. That upped the stakes quite a bit. Wolf didn't like the idea of going up against an armed man in a situation like this, especially some guy who was just doing his job, even if that job was guarding a scumbag. Taking out an innocent bodyguard didn't sit right with him, and he couldn't imagine it sat any better with Mac. Still, how innocent could the guy be if he was escorting a child molester to what they assumed would be the rape of a minor? The sympathy factor lessened, but the danger didn't. They were in deep water now—Indian Country—and they had to figure out a way of dealing with every contingency.

The van slammed over another *tope*, and McNamara swore.

"Your boy sure loves to hit those damn things, don't he?" he asked.

Zerbe didn't answer. He had an unlit cigarette between his lips. Wolf wondered how long it would be before he made a move to light it.

"What kind of weapons did you get us?" McNamara asked.

Zerbe shook his head and pointed at Paco, then at the black plastic garbage bag down by his feet.

Mac glanced at Wolf, who frowned. This wasn't looking good.

The van slowed for another turn, then accelerated again as the sound of gravel beneath the tires became evident.

Paco made a left turn so rapidly the car bottomed out, jarring the occupants and stirring up a huge dust cloud.

"You trying to send smoke signals?" McNamara looked at Wolf and winked. "No offense."

Wolf managed a grin. "Well, we *are* in Indian Country."

Mac smiled and clucked his tongue.

"We're almost there." Zerbe pointed at a cluster of small houses that butted up against a patchy mixture of whitish sand and spots of green. "You wanted to approach it from the other side, right?"

"Right," McNamara said.

Paco hit the brakes hard, skidding to a halt and stirring up another cloud of dust on the roadway. Zerbe lit up his smoke and got out as Wolf and McNamara exited. As usual, Paco remained with the van. The neighborhood looked much the same as it had a few hours earlier, except far less crowded. A hundred yards or so in the distance, beyond the cluster of small houses, Wolf could see two triangular monuments of gray stone extending out of a sea of greenery. Each had a flat, square top. The angular sides contained large rows of centered steps. He momentarily thought about the Mayans and their vanished empire.

Cancun. He wondered how many vipers they would meet tonight.

Despite the sight of three *gringos* walking, people paid them little mind as they faded into the local landscape.

That didn't surprise Wolf.

Mac's wearing his big cowboy hat. I could almost pass for a Latino, and Zerbe looks like your typical shady Anglo reprobate prowling the sleazy back alleys.

"Not so many people right now," McNamara said. "Must be getting close to siesta time."

Zerbe was right on their heels, carrying a black plastic garbage bag and struggling to keep up as they wound through the alleys, taking the same circuitous route they'd painstakingly plotted during their first trip there. He was still wearing the dark sunglasses, and Wolf wondered how the hell the man could see well enough to avoid tripping. The spaces between the houses were a maze of dirt paths covered with fine gravel, which made a slight crunching sound as they walked. The ubiquitous smells of cooking meat and hot peppers hung in the air, along with conversation, laughter, and Mexican music. As they continued, the sounds and smells became less distinct and the houses more dilapidated.

"Anybody live around here?" Wolf asked.

"This area's mostly uninhabited," Zerbe said. "Lucky for us."

Wolf caught a glimpse of Mac's face. It looked grim and intense.

"I'll feel better about this when he shows us those weapons," Wolf said.

"Yeah, me too," McNamara said. "And I wish we knew what kind of firepower we will be going up against."

"I've got the stuff for you," Zerbe said. "In the bag here."

As they approached the last house in the row, Wolf stopped and held up his fist. McNamara halted, and Zerbe managed to slow his gait by skipping a bit and doing a little dance.

"That's it over there, right?" Wolf asked.

Zerbe grunted in agreement.

Wolf flattened against a low wall and took a quick peek. The structure was unlighted and perhaps fifty feet away from them. The squat stucco building had a roof covered with half-circular red tiles descending in an oblique slant. Several rows had broken or missing tiles, and there was a film of dust and dirt over the window next to the front door. Wolf could make out a dingy shade hanging on the other side of the filthy glass.

"Where's this Salvador character at?" McNamara asked.

"He should be along shortly," Zerbe said. "He's going to call me as soon as Accondras calls him."

"You mentioned you had something for us?" Wolf asked.

Zerbe nodded and reached into the side pocket of his sport jacket. He withdrew a black and yellow pistol-shaped Taser with a square barrel.

"The cartridge is good up to fifteen feet," he said. "You snap it off the end, and you can use it as a stun gun as long as you're touching the target."

McNamara gestured for Wolf to take the Taser. He unsnapped the cartridge from the end of the barrel and pressed the trigger. Electric current sparkled in the darkening twilight.

"It's fully charged," Zerbe said. "Put new batteries in this afternoon."

Wolf replaced the cartridge and stuck the Taser in the right pocket of his BDU blouse.

"What else you got for us?" McNamara asked.

The end of Zerbe's cigarette glowed bright red, and ashes dropped from it as he nodded and held up the bag. Whatever was inside made a knocking sound. After glancing around, Zerbe opened the top and dumped the contents on the dirt pathway. It was a roll of duct tape, two pairs of cheap-looking handcuffs, two butterfly knives with four-inch blades enclosed in thin, wooden handles, and a set of round nunchucks, also made of wood.

"That's it?" McNamara asked. "Where's our guns?"

Zerbe took a few steps back. "Like I told you, they're

real hard to get down here. Plus, if you get caught with them, they toss you in jail until you can buy your way out. You're better off without them."

"You said this bodyguard's gonna be armed." McNamara frowned. "Nothing like bringing a couple of knives and a Taser to a gunfight."

Wolf picked up the nunchucks and tested the chain, which seemed sturdy enough. It'd been a long time since he'd practiced with them, but they could be a formidable and silent weapon.

"Which knife do you want?" asked McNamara.

"Does it matter?"

McNamara checked each pair of handcuffs, making sure they were operational and that the ratcheted bottom half moved smoothly through the top portion. Satisfied, he handed one pair to Wolf, then picked up the two blades and tested their balance.

"Balisong knives. These things look like they came straight from the Philippines."

McNamara flipped the first one open with practiced ease, bouncing the rotating half of the thin wooden handle and the top of the blade against the back of his hand. He caught the other half of the handle, locking the extended knife blade. He gripped the side of the blade and tried to wiggle it; it moved substantially. McNamara flipped the knife closed with another flick of his wrist and handed it to Wolf. "That one's loose as a goose."

He repeated the movements with the second knife. This one had almost no play in the blade housing.

"You take that one," Wolf said, slipping the handcuffs into his left BDU pocket. "It looks a little more solid."

McNamara glanced at him, his eyebrows rising in doubt.

"You sure?"

Wolf nodded. "I've got these." He stepped away and whirled the nunchucks in continuous arcs, looping the front portion back and forth on either side of his forearm before spinning it alongside his body and then slapping it to a stop under his armpit.

"Hot damn," McNamara said. "Just like old Bruce Lee." His grin quickly faded and he added, "But this ain't Hollywood, and it ain't gonna do much good against a bullet. We need some firepower. Where's our guns?"

Zerbe shook his head. "I told you. No can do."

"Then maybe we should just call this whole damn thing off," McNamara said.

Wolf could see the concern in Mac's face and felt the same way, but he also knew how much his friend wanted this one.

"You got keys for the handcuffs?" Wolf asked.

Zerbe nodded and reached into his pants pocket, withdrawing two small keys. Wolf took them, and stuck one in his boot, and gave the other one to McNamara. He tested the locks on the cuffs, which were operational. He then jammed a portion of cuffs into his waistband.

"This guy might be easier to control if we had leg cuffs," McNamara said. "You got any more?"

Zerbe shrugged with an accompanying shake of his head. "That's the best I could do. Use the duct tape."

McNamara frowned and glanced at Wolf.

This whole thing's unraveling like a ball of yarn in a roomful of cats, Wolf thought. *How are we going to pull it off without getting real rough?*

The possibility of having to kill the bodyguard surfaced in Wolf's mind once more. Even if the guy was unsavory, as he'd surmised earlier, it wasn't particularly pleasing. He couldn't justify dealing out death as he had in the Army. This wasn't Afghanistan or the

Sandbox, and Cancun wasn't a combat zone. At least, not yet.

But he couldn't let Mac down, so there was little or no choice.

"I guess we can see how it goes," Wolf said. "Like he said, we'll have the element of surprise, and he's probably not going to want the bodyguard coming into the house with him."

"I don't know." McNamara shook his head. "I'm starting to have some real bad vibes about this." He turned to Zerbe and jabbed a finger into the PI's chest. "You weren't straight with us about the guns you were supposed to get."

"Hey, I tried. Did the best I could. Honest."

"The best you could." McNamara's tone was heavy with sarcasm. "That don't seem like too much right about now. How do we know the rest of this plan of yours isn't just as messed up?"

Wolf saw the sweat beading up on the PI's face. The odor wafting off his thick barrel-like body had the pungent tang of fear.

"It's not," he said. "You gotta trust me. I got a lot riding on this, too."

"Not as much as we have," McNamara said. "We're taking all the risks."

"It'll go down like clockwork," Zerbe said. "That guy Accondras is a fucking pussy, I tell ya. All you gotta do is Tase him and take out that guard."

"That's *all* we gotta do, huh?" McNamara asked.

Zerbe shrugged. "I never was much good at the muscle stuff. That's why they hired a couple of pros like you."

Flattery was the last resort of the desperate, Wolf thought.

Mac didn't seem to be impressed either.

"Well, let me tell you something, bud," McNamara said. "Him and me, we track people down for a living. If we find out you ain't been playing it straight with us, I'll personally track *you* down, no matter where you are, and make you wish you never were born."

Zerbe's head bobbled up and down in fractional nods, but he said nothing.

As they stood there, his cell phone chirped.

"That's gotta be Salvador," Zerbe said, nerves causing his voice to crack. "Or José."

* * *

HELIPAD AT THE VON DIEN ESTATE
BELIZE

Eagan watched as the bounty hunters, Cummins, Reynolds, Harper, Wells, and Nasim, all sat and belted themselves in. They all had their gear and their weapons stacked neatly in front of them, their hands glossy in the new latex gloves. No fingerprints, just like in the Sandbox. Eagan had told Kunish to sit in the co-pilot's seat and familiarize himself with the craft in case he had to take over. It was a big Sikorsky S-92 with plenty of room to seat them all comfortably, and it had a quiet zone feature that made conversation possible. The pilot, Webber, said it went for about seventeen mill. Surprisingly, he didn't seem to mind Kunish being up front. In fact, he welcomed the company. The helicopter pilots' brotherhood was alive and well, even when flying something this expensive.

Seventeen million, Eagan thought. Webber had mentioned that Victor Delta had a fleet of them.

Christ, the old Buddha was one rich bastard. Perhaps an adjustment to the bonus would be in order.

Eagan got the impression this wasn't Webber's first foray across the Belize/Mexican border. Reno and his buddy, Black Hercules, looked ill at ease. Maybe they'd noticed that everybody, all the Vipers, were wearing body armor, while they had none. But he'd shown them the two fully loaded Glock 19s, which had made it clear that they were part of this whole thing.

They didn't know neither gun had an internal striker, nor would they until the time came. The impotent Glocks were an appropriate metaphor for the two buffed-up, steroid-fueled MMA-fighters-turned-bounty hunters: all show and no punch. He smiled at the two of them and flashed them the thumbs-up. They smiled back.

Yeah, he thought. *That's the price of doing business, chumps. The payoff's right around the corner.*

The rotor blades came to life and began a slow rotation, then picked up speed. Cummins was fumbling with something he was trying to pull out of his ditty bag.

If I didn't need that fat pussy to complete the money transfer, Eagan thought, *I'd toss his ass out the door right now.*

His dislike for the man grew by leaps and bounds the longer this ungainly partnership lasted.

As the craft rose from the helipad, leaving the lush tropical scene below them, Eagan checked for any recent texts on his cell phone.

He had a new one. **Pigeons en route will advise.**

It was from Zerbe.

Eagan texted back, **And the other pigeons?**

Fed as prescribed. Will advise.

The "prescription" was that Wolf and friend were to

be given only enough equipment to complete the abduction of Accondras. Eagan felt they should be easily able to do that, but he didn't want them to have firearms to fall back on when the real fun began.

He took a deep breath.

The clock had started.

The estimated flight time was thirty-eight minutes, going over the Caribbean Sea and then heading inland to just south of Cancun and north of Puerto Morelos at the site of the now-abandoned hotel. Newman would be waiting there with the vehicles. Once they touched down, he'd leave Kunish behind with the chopper while the rest of them proceeded to the prearranged coordinates.

They were in for a big surprise once the Vipers rolled up and took charge. Eagan was looking forward to seeing Wolf's face. Maybe he'd mark him up a bit. But then again, the fucking half-breed was supposed to be a badass. At least, that was the word when he'd been in Leavenworth, and he had survived the shanking attempt. Eagan thought about it some more. Did he have time for such a pleasant diversion?

Maybe it would be more fun to see how Wolf paired up against the other two bounty hunters. Those guys were professional mixed martial arts fighters. He thought back to tales he'd heard about the Nazi guards in the concentration camps making the Jews fight each other to the death. It might be fun to watch. The payoff was going to be death for all of them once they had the artifact anyway, but he had to keep the four bounty hunters alive in the short term. At least until Accondras delivered the location of the damn artifact.

Then the authorities would find a nice little desert shootout where all the parties had died.

Business before pleasure.

No loose ends.

The helicopter banked, revealing a lush blanket of greenery five hundred feet below them. Eagan adjusted his earpiece and microphone.

"How's everything looking, Webber?" he asked, more to verify the communication system was working than to inquire about the flight.

Webber's reply came through crystal clear in Eagan's earpiece. "Looking real good, sir."

"Roger that," Eagan said. "Advise when we're within range."

The noise of the accelerating rotors drowned out all other sounds, but Eagan caught a glimpse of sudden movement out of the corner of his eye. The stench came seconds later as Cummins fumbled with a paper bag he was holding in front of his face. The fat jowls expanded, then he heaved a burst of vomit through the bag's open top. The unsteady movement of the chopper made catching all the discharge impossible, and some of it dribbled down the front of Cummins's body armor.

Blowing chunks again, Eagan thought. He'd done it before in Iraq.

The rest of the Vipers sat stoically, not showing any emotion at the disgusting loss of control. All except Nasim, who caught Eagan's eye with a sly wink and a smile.

Eagan nodded in agreement.

Yeah, he thought. Still a weak sister. Just like back in the Sandbox.

* * *

NEAR EL MECO

CANCUN, MEXICO

Wolf took an immediate dislike to Salvador, who sauntered up to them in the narrow alley with a young boy about seven or eight in tow. The man was whip-thin and had gold edges around his discolored front teeth. He brought a cigarette in a long holder to his lips and drew deeply, causing the embers to glow. The boy whimpered, and Salvador reached down and slapped him.

Wolf was about to protest when McNamara reached out and grabbed Salvador's arm.

"Do that again, and I'll shove that fucking cigarette up your ass."

Salvador looked perplexed, but Mac's intention needed no translation. The thin Mexican shrugged but still held the youth's arm.

McNamara turned to Zerbe.

"What the hell's this shit? You didn't say anything about a kid this young being involved."

"Relax," Zerbe said, the corner of his mouth pulling back in a half-assed smile. "Can we help it if Accondras insisted on seeing the merchandise before taking the plunge?"

"*Es el mismo tipo de joven*," Salvador paused and shook his head. "Same as de last time. Why you care?"

McNamara took in a deep breath. He was silent for several seconds, staring at Salvador, then transferring his gaze to Zerbe.

"Where'd this kid come from?" McNamara asked.

"Does it matter?" Zerbe asked. "He's hardly a virgin, and anyway, I told you he's not going to be hurt. He's just the bait."

McNamara glanced at Wolf, who was silent. He wasn't liking this any more than Mac did, but in his heart, he knew there was nothing they could do to change the situation. They'd both seen disturbing and despicable things on the other side of the world, and they knew their power to change most of them was nonexistent.

"Hey," Salvador said. "You pay me now. *Primero*."

Zerbe reached into the inner pocket of his sports jacket, removed an envelope, and handed it to him.

Salvador clenched his teeth around the cigarette holder and accepted the envelope with his left hand. His right still held the boy. Leaning down, he whispered something to the youth in Spanish, then released his grip on him. The kid just stood there, unmoving. Salvador used both hands to count the money in the envelope, then shoved it into his pocket.

Wolf caught a glimpse of the boy's sad, vacuous stare and wondered if the child had been drugged. He was on the verge of stupor.

I can't change the world, he told himself again. *But I can try to avoid any more collateral damage. Ride it out, but make sure the kid doesn't get caught up in any crossfire.*

Then again, neither he nor Mac had any guns, so how could he?

It added a new complication to the plan and made dealing with the armed bodyguard even more hazardous and complicated.

"You got a key to the house?" McNamara asked.

Salvador reached into his pocket and produced a long skeleton key. It looked ornamental. McNamara grabbed it and told Zerbe he and Wolf were going to check out the house.

"Good idea," Zerbe said. "I was told you guys were pros."

There was a sarcastic lilt in his tone, and Wolf felt

like belting him. He was angry at Mac, too, for getting them into this mess, but most of his anger was directed inward. It was his fault for messing up in Iraq, getting tossed into prison, and now going along with this ill-conceived plan. He should have done a better job of talking Mac out of it.

He followed his mentor to the door of the house, and Mac slipped the notched end of the key into the lock and twisted. The door opened, and Wolf immediately took note of the locking mechanism. It was a small rectangular wedge of metal that slipped into a bracketed metallic encasement in the doorjamb. The wood of the frame looked like it had seen better days.

About as sturdy as a cargo hatch secured by rubber bands and duct tape.

He surveyed the rest of the structure. It was composed of two dust-covered rooms separated by a dangling blanket with numerous holes worn through it. A dilapidated broom leaned against one wall, and three piles of swept detritus were lined up in the corner. The room they were in had apparently once served as the kitchen, dining, and family room. The remnants of an ancient rusted stove, still wearing an odiferous patina of burned grease, rested on a pile of bricks next to a dust-covered window. The other room was the sleeping quarters and contained a filthy mattress and two canvas cots. A dirty pillow, its case stained with several different shades of discoloration, resided on the mattress. Another crud-encrusted window was set in the far wall, perpendicular to the mattress. It was about three feet off the floor.

The honeymoon suite for a child rapist, Wolf thought. *Garida de apañar.*

It was a good thing they were taking this scumbag,

Accondras, out of the game. In the long view, it wouldn't change things much down here, but it would be one small step toward a better world.

McNamara clapped him on the shoulder. Wolf saw the sad expression on his friend's face.

"Go ahead and say it," McNamara said. "I really screwed up getting us into this, didn't I?"

Wolf said nothing.

McNamara pursed his lips. "Damn, that kid out there's not much older than Chad."

The mention of Mac's grandson was abhorrent in their current situation.

"Let's keep the kid out of it as best we can," Wolf said. "Ideas?"

McNamara exhaled and glanced around. He went to the window and managed to lift it about a half-inch before the upper edge collided with a metal pin embedded in the frame. Mac gripped the pin and pulled it loose, then raised the window to its uppermost position. He was then able to slip the pin back into the hole, securing it there.

"Just like the Holiday Inn," he said. "But it don't cost as much."

Wolf was glad to see his friend's tenebrous mood had lessened, at least for the moment.

McNamara leaned his head out, then ducked back inside.

"Looks like another alley leading to our rendezvous place," he said. "Best we incapacitate the son of a bitch in here with the Taser, then toss him through the window. We can slip the kid outta here, too, and we'll meet Zerbe down the way."

Wolf smiled. "Whaddaya mean, 'we,' white man?"

McNamara chuckled. "You got a better plan?"

"I'm thinking about the bodyguard. If he hears something, that front door, even if it's locked, will offer about as much delay as your first girlfriend's underpants."

"So, what you're saying is one of us stays in here," McNamara said. "And the other one takes out the bodyguard."

"That's the way it's got to be," Wolf said. "We can't afford to leave an armed assailant out in front of the place."

McNamara compressed his lips again.

"Dammit," he said. "Why'd I get us into this thing? I let my wanting to get one up on Reno overload my better judgment." He looked at Wolf. "I'm sorry, Steve. We can just slip out this back window now if you want, and we'll get the hell out of this damn country on the next plane out."

"And miss out on the chance for a big payday?" Wolf said, trying to sound more confident than he felt. "Plus, there's that kid. I don't want to step out now and leave him to get mauled by that asshole Accondras."

McNamara took a deep breath, then nodded.

"I look more like a Mexican than you do," Wolf said. "You stay in here with the Taser and take out Accondras. Throw him out the back window and head for Zerbe and Paco and the truck. I'll take out the guard and come meet you."

"And what if he's got an Uzi?"

Wolf shrugged. "Then I deal with it. One way or another."

McNamara shook his head, but a sudden harsh-sounding knock on the front door was accompanied by Zerbe's guttural voice.

"Hurry it up. They're here. Salvador's got to go meet them now."

Wolf and McNamara hurried to the door, and Mac handed the key back to the thin Mexican. The man's expression was a mixture of smugness and disdain.

Lucifer personified, Wolf thought.

"So, what's your plan?" Zerbe asked.

Wolf looked at Salvador. "Get your money from Accondras and let him take the boy inside. We'll make the grab inside and shove him out a back window."

The Mexican nodded.

"We don't want the boy getting hurt," Wolf said. "Where can we drop him?"

Salvador expelled a short burst of air out of his mouth. "Any place. *No importa*."

"It's *importa* to us," McNamara said. "Tell him not to say anything once he's inside, and we'll let him out the back window."

With a frown and a shrug, Salvador addressed the boy in Spanish. The words hardly seemed to register on the youth's face. Wolf listened to the one-sided conversation, and for as much as he could follow, the man had repeated the instructions almost verbatim.

"Are we fucking done yet?" Zerbe said. "I can't be seen here."

Wolf told him to go back the way they'd come and have Paco move the van to the designated position out of sight down the alley. "Wait there until we get there."

Zerbe frowned. "Of course. How long do you think it'll take?"

"Hopefully, not long," Wolf told him.

Zerbe nodded and looked at Salvador. He waggled his fingers at McNamara, who stepped back inside the house. Salvador pulled the door closed, slipped the key into the lock, and secured it.

"*Es* good," he said, shaking the door before grabbing

the boy's arm and pulling him back down the alley. Wolf was repelled by the youth's situation and silently debated the prudence of taking the pimp out if the opportunity arose. The unctuous son of a bitch deserved a beating at the very least, but Wolf decided not to push it. There was nothing he and Mac could do to change things.

They were in Indian Country.

I can't save the world, he told himself again.

* * *

CANCUN AND NORTH OF PUERTO MORELOS

Webber set the chopper down as softly as if he were stepping off a staircase. The guy was good. It helped that Newman had popped smoke and set up some landing lights, but still, it was a good endorsement of the helo pilot's skills.

But there was also something else to consider. Somebody could have seen this thing land. Beyond the immediate LZ, perhaps fifty yards away, Eagan could hear waves washing up on the shore. The moon was bright, and the three ruined stone pyramids with the box-like shapes at their peaks were shrouded in darkness. A crumbling section of stone wall fifteen or twenty feet tall separated two of them.

The distant lights of the nearest city or town were at least several kilometers away, but the sight of the helicopter, lit up like a Christmas tree, descending into parts unknown could have alerted the locals. Maybe even the cops or the cartel boys, or both. In any case, leaving only Kunish and Webber with the chopper now seemed too risky.

It was their ticket out of here, and he wasn't sure

when they'd be taking off. It all depended on breaking Accondras and recovering that damn artifact. If it was readily accessible, the task could probably be accomplished in a few hours at the most. If not, they'd have to play a waiting game until they could get on the chopper and beat feet back to Belize.

They exited the helo, and everyone ducked instinctively as the rotors slowed. Eagan peered into the night and took a moment to appreciate the ubiquitous darkness before activating and flipping down his night-vision goggles. The green-tinted world became visible, and he saw Newman walking toward them. A van was parked between the broken-down wall and the largest pyramid. With the night-vision goggles in place, Eagan could appreciate just how large the structures were.

It must have taken a lot of slaves to erect those big bastards, he thought. And a lot of human sacrifices on their altars.

He scanned the parked vehicle.

It looked like there was only one.

Shit.

He'd told that goddamn Newman to get two. He flipped the goggles up onto his forehead.

Newman stopped and extended his open palm toward Eagan.

He grasped Newman's hand and exerted a bit more pressure than he normally did.

When Newman grimaced, Eagan smirked and released his grip.

"I thought I told you to get two vehicles," he said.

"Sorry, boss," Newman said. "The other driver I had lined up crapped out on me. Showed up drunk. You know how fucking undependable these goddamn beaners are."

Eagan thought about that and nodded. It would make for tight quarters and maybe even two trips to and from the set-up site, but it was doable. He nodded in acknowledgment but silently relegated Newman to the top of the most expendable list.

"I assume you've done some reconnoitering," Eagan said. "Correct?"

"Yes, sir," Newman said. "This was the best clear, flat area for the chopper. There's a bunch of stone ruins over that hill, and this hole in the ground you gotta watch out for."

"Hole in the ground?"

"Yeah." Newman shook his head. "I was glad I came out here during the daylight hours. The hole's about twenty-five feet in circumference and maybe eighteen feet deep. You don't see it coming, you'll tumble right over the edge. Got a pool of water down at the bottom, but I don't know how deep it is. Not sure if it's saltwater since it's got twin waterfalls on each side."

"Marvelous." Eagan let his tone tell Newman that was way more information than he wanted.

"Okay," he called in a loud voice. "Everybody form up by the van. And turn on your radios if you haven't done so already."

A quick commo-check showed that everyone was reading him loud and clear.

"Okay," Eagan said into his mic. "Slight change of assignments. Wells, you stay here with Kunish and the pilot. Set up a perimeter and protect this bird. It's our only ticket out of here."

"Too bad they didn't spring for some Claymores," Wells said.

Eagan smirked. "You fuckers have AK-47s. I'm sure you can protect it from curious cops or cartel shitheads should they happen by. Speaking of which, we're only going to be about fifteen or twenty klicks from here, but there's no repeaters, so these radios won't cover that range. Use your burner phones to keep me posted about any problems."

Wells and Kunish nodded and began walking back to the helicopter.

"Remember, don't take off without us," Cummins called to them. He sounded nervous, and the fun hadn't even started yet.

The pussy has spoken, Eagan thought.

He herded the remaining six toward the vans, the adrenaline thrill of what was yet to come beginning to course through his veins.

CHAPTER 12

NEAR EL MECO
CANCUN, MEXICO

After familiarizing himself with the area around the house, Wolf slipped back inside through the open window and joined McNamara. They stood in the unlighted front room on opposite sides of the door. Wolf couldn't shake his uneasiness. There were too many variables and not enough planning. He'd been in far more dangerous situations before and worked with less.

So had Mac, but never with so little logistical support. If things went bad, they couldn't count on Zerbe. He'd made it clear that he was going to wait in the van with Paco, and the whereabouts of slimy José were anybody's guess. Wolf trusted the lot of them about as much as a quartet of wheels without lug nuts on a car.

At least their intervention tonight would spare the boy more indignities at the hands of Accondras. That was something positive that could be accomplished, not that it would make much difference for the kid in the long term.

But it was something.

Wolf thought about the youth's situation and of the dull, hopeless expression in his eyes. It reminded him of the countless despondent children he'd seen on the other side of the world—hungry kids cheated out of the joys of youth, with no hope for the future. His hatred of the situation and this op grew; he couldn't wait to get out of here.

Most likely, Mac felt the same.

The musty smell of the place was starting to grate on him when he heard voices. McNamara perked up, too. He gestured at the window, and Wolf pulled the shade away from the frame ever so slightly.

Four men and the boy approached. One was Salvador, and another appeared to be Accondras, judging from the pictures and description they'd be given. He looked like he'd put on some weight, but Wolf was certain it was him.

The other two men were Mexican nationals and looked hard and competent. Wolf could tell they both had handguns concealed under billowing flowered shirts, and the larger one carried something wrapped in a blanket that looked to be the shotgun Zerbe had mentioned.

Two guards... That added a new layer of complications to the situation.

But at least there was no Uzi.

The four men stopped about fifteen feet from the door. Salvador still held the youth's arm. They were engaged in a muffled conversation.

"There's two of them," Wolf whispered. "Two guards."

"What!" McNamara exclaimed. "Shit. They armed?"

"Yeah. Looks like two handguns and a shotgun."

"This gets better all the time," McNamara said. "And all we got's a Taser, two butterfly knives, and a pair of nunchucks." He took a deep breath and let it out. "How about we just say fuck it and slip out the back way?"

Wolf thought about it, then asked, "What about the kid?"

McNamara slowly nodded. "Guess we're in, then."

"You pay me now," the waspish pimp said in a low voice. "You take him, then I go."

Accondras was wearing a camo backpack that appeared to have some items inside. Wolf wondered what they could be and thought about the possibility that the child molester might be armed as well. Accondras reached into his pocket, took out some pesos, and began counting them out.

The two guards stood there with amused smirks on their faces. They were obviously privy to what was about to go on, so the thought of taking them both out didn't seem as objectionable as it had before.

Accondras stopped counting the money and looked at Salvador.

"Why are you sweating so much, *amigo?*" Accondras asked.

His voice was high-pitched.

"*Es muy caliente,*" Salvador said. "Very hot."

Accondras stared at him for a few seconds, and Wolf began to wonder if the man suspected a double-cross. Then he looked down at the boy, who was still passive, and resumed counting pesos into Salvador's outstretched palm. Shifting his back toward the two guards, Accondras leaned closer to the pimp. When he spoke, it was in a low tone, but Wolf could still discern it.

"What do you want me to do with him after? Same as last time?"

Salvador blew out a derisive breath. "*Sí*. Same as last time. Leave him in there, and I will send somebody to get rid of the body."

Get rid of the body, same as last time.

Wolf was sickened by the thought and more determined now than ever to put a stop to what was about to happen.

"He's planning on killing the boy after he's through with him," Wolf said, keeping his voice low.

"Fuckers," McNamara said. "How you want to play it?"

"Can you handle Accondras by yourself in here?"

McNamara grinned. "Does a bear shit in the woods?"

Wolf grinned too and handed McNamara the Taser. "Wait till he comes in and locks the door behind him. Tase him in the other room, then take him out the back way. The boy, too."

"What about you?"

"I'm going to sneak out the back way now and take out those two guards."

"Two armed men by yourself?"

"Hopefully, they'll just think I'm a drunken Mexican and take me for granted."

"Pretty risky."

"We got no choice," Wolf said. "If something goes wrong in here and they break through that door, we'll be sitting ducks."

McNamara's mouth tightened into a thin line, but he nodded. "Guess we don't have much choice, do we?"

They heard Salvador say in a loud voice, "Here *es* de key. Enjoy yourself, my friend. Until next time."

He was signaling them. Apparently, he had no

compunction about betraying Accondras since he had his money.

No honor among thieves or pimps, Wolf thought. Good thing.

He motioned Mac toward the second room, and they darted behind the suspended curtain. They'd left the window pinned open, and Wolf went to it and slipped one leg through the opening. He looked at McNamara.

"Good luck, top," he said.

McNamara smiled. "Been a long time since anybody called me that. A longer one since I deserved it."

Wolf held out his hand, and they shook. As he slipped out the door, he adjusted the nunchucks under the left side of his shirt, then took off at a run, the sandy earth grating beneath his boots. After passing three houses, he stopped and spun around a corner. The space between the two structures led to the alley he wanted.

Partway down the dank passage, he paused and shot a quick peek around a corner. Accondras was dragging the boy inside the house about thirty feet away. He tried to estimate how long it would be before he entered the bedroom and Mac hit him with the Taser.

Thirty or forty seconds, he thought. Definitely under a minute.

His foot bumped something, and he saw that it was an empty glass bottle that had probably once held tequila.

Perfect.

He bent down and grabbed it with his left hand, hoping the crust of dirt wouldn't be noticeable in the moonlight, then stepped into the alley and began walking toward the two guards. One was leaning toward the other one, his back toward Wolf. A flash of light signaled they were taking a smoke break. The shotgun was leaning against the front wall of the target house.

Smoking on sentry duty, Wolf thought. Careless.

The guard facing him looked up, his eyebrow rising as he stared in Wolf's direction. The bounty hunter adopted an uneven gait, bringing the bottle up and then cocking his arm as if he were taking a drink. He tightened his grip on the glass neck. One of the guards said to the other, "*Un borracho.*" "A drunk."

Good, Wolf thought. They're buying it.

Now, if only the ruse would allow him to get a few steps closer.

"*A donde vas, chingado?*" one of the guards said in a harsh tone. "Where are you going, fucker?"

Not too friendly a bunch, Wolf thought.

He tightened his grip on the bottle.

A few more steps...

Doubts began to flash in his mind. His hair was way too short. His clothes didn't fit your typical Mexicano. His boots were regulation Army desert-style terrain footwear. Add them all up, and he was wearing an emblem on his chest that advertised he didn't belong here.

One more step closer.

The second guard half-turned, his face cracking in amusement.

"*Piensas tenerlo algunas dinero?*"

"You think he has any money?"

They're planning on rolling me, Wolf thought. Good. Bring 'em on.

Another step.

He began singing *Cielito Lindo* in a loud voice. It was the one Mexican folk song he remembered, but he didn't know all the words.

Of course, he didn't need to.

The closest guard reached out to grab him, and Wolf stumbled to the side to avoid the man's outstretched arms.

A sudden grunting moan emanated from inside the house. One guard's face pivoted toward it. Wolf took an exaggerated step to the side, then moved in front of the alerted guard and swung the bottle in an arc. The solid cylindrical glass struck him across the bridge of his nose, but because the blow had been a backhanded motion, it hadn't carried a lot of power, so Wolf pivoted and delivered a quick overhand punch to the man's now-bleeding nose. The man took a half-step backward and brought both hands to his face.

Wolf's back leg shot out in a snap-kick to the second man's exposed groin. His legs were wide apart and provided an inviting target. Wolf felt the instep of his boot connect with a whipping motion, and after a second or two's delay, the man crumpled.

The first guard had recovered enough to pull back his shirt, exposing the handle of a large semi-automatic pistol in a leather holster affixed to his belt. Blood was streaming from his now-twisted nose, pouring over his thick mustache and down his chin. White teeth glinted between twisted lips, looking like bone glimpsed through torn flesh.

Wolf's left hand seized the man's wrist, stopping his draw, but the gun edged out of the holster, and the man's fingers curled around it. Wolf slammed a ridge hand into his adversary's throat, and the man gave an abrupt gurgle.

Keeping his left hand securely on the man's right wrist, Wolf pivoted and delivered two knee strikes to his abdomen. Each one sounded like a cardboard box being stuck with a baseball bat. The guard began to drop, his limp fingers abandoning his grip on the firearm. Wolf let him fall but followed him down, pulling the gun out of its holster as the man hit the ground.

The second guard rolled onto his side and started to pull his weapon. Wolf's right hand curled around one of the nunchucks, and he whipped the Okinawan bludgeon out of his belt and lashed out with it. The round stick whirled downward and crashed onto the second man's forearm. He cried in pain, and the gun slipped out of his fingers.

Wolf whirled the nunchucks again, but this time, he smashed the second stick against the guard's right temple. The man rolled over in a writhing heap. Wolf shoved the first gun into his waistband on the right side. He then stooped and picked up the second handgun, placing that one on the left. Both guards were still breathing but unconscious.

Probably better than they deserved, he thought as he remembered their amusement and indifference at the fate of the boy. These two were hardly men of honor.

Wolf grabbed the shotgun and thought about tossing it onto a nearby roof.

Fingerprints. Couldn't afford to leave those behind. With that, he shifted the rifle to his left hand and retrieved the bottle with his right. Taking two long steps, he heaved the bottle over the rooftop, then took off in a fast gait. He thought about checking the house to see if Mac and the boy and Accondras had made it out of there all right but decided against it.

I got to believe they did. He worked his way to the next narrow opening in the row of houses.

So far, he hadn't seen anybody, but that didn't mean nobody had seen him. Slowing down, he edged sideways through an opening, feeling layer after layer of sticky spider webs attach themselves to his face. Finally, he broke free and emerged into the alley. Pausing to look both ways, he caught movement about thirty yards to his left.

Two shadowy figures trundled down the alley, one oversized, the other seemingly stunted.

The boy was running alongside Mac, who had Accondras slung over his shoulder like a sack of potatoes.

* * *

NO MAN'S LAND
SOUTHWEST OF CANCUN

Eagan sat in the front passenger seat and watched the weak beam of the headlights bounce over the decrepit ribbon of asphalt that extended before them. The roads in Iraq had been better maintained, at least initially. Newman seemed to be doing a good job of avoiding the major potholes and cracks, as well as swerving to avoid the occasional stumbling pedestrian or wayward animal. The man knew the route and was a competent driver, so Eagan mentally took him off the shit list. For now, anyway.

All of the Vipers were expendable in the final analysis. Eagan would do his best to make sure they all got paid, but there was no way they were going to be in on his retirement bonus.

Newman slowed abruptly, and it shook Eagan out of

his reverie. Seconds later, the van bounced over a huge bump in the road, causing everyone in the vehicle to bounce.

"What the hell?" Cummins yelled. He was seated on the floor, directly in back of Eagan. "Did we hit something?"

"Yeah," Newman said. "A Mexican speed bump."

"Jesus Christ." The lawyer was still shaken up.

Eagan smirked.

"Relax, Cummins," he said. "At least it wasn't an IED."

"Might as well have been," Cummins said. "I hurt my damn tailbone."

That made Eagan want to laugh, but he needed the asshole to complete the funds transfer after the deal was completed.

Then I'll never have to see that son of a bitch again, Eagan thought. He turned to Newman.

"How much farther?"

"Not far," Newman said. "Maybe five minutes. I'll keep an eye out for another speed bump."

Eagan grinned. He was starting to like this guy.

* * *

NEAR EL MECO
CANCUN, MEXICO

Wolf caught up with McNamara and the boy after a quick sprint and called out to him. Mac slowed to a stop and leaned against a nearby wall, out of breath. Wolf saw that Mac's face was red with exertion and covered with sweat.

"Shit, this is taking more out of me than I figured," he

said. "How about you carry this sack of shit for a while? I'm plum tuckered out."

Before Wolf could answer, Accondras yelled, "Who are you guys?"

McNamara bent and dropped the other man to the ground. He landed on his side, but his hands were cuffed behind him, and he emitted a loud gasp. The backpack was still affixed to his body.

"Be careful, you idiot," Accondras said.

The boy was staring at him.

Wolf stooped and put a hand on the youth's shoulder.

"*Como se llama?*" he asked.

"Carlos," the boy said.

"Okay, Carlos," Wolf said, speaking with slow deliberation. "*Esperas aqui con nosotros. No sermos dolerlo.*"

The boy looked up and nodded. Wolf thought the kid's eyes looked less dazed than before.

"You can't do this to me," Accondras yelled. "I haven't done anything. Help!"

"Shut your damn mouth," McNamara said, his words coming out in gasps. "Or I'll knock it down to your ass."

A look of terror filled Accondras' eyes, and he screamed, "Help me, help me!"

McNamara balled his fist up and cocked his arm but didn't throw the punch. The intimidation was enough to quiet Accondras. McNamara reached into the pocket of his BDU blouse and pulled out the roll of duct tape, pulled off a long strip, and smacked it over Accondras' mouth. He shook his head and worked his jaw, rubbing it on his shoulder, trying to dislodge the tape.

"Give him another shot of the Taser," Wolf suggested.

"Wait," Accondras said, having gotten his mouth free. "Don't use that thing on me again. Please."

"Then shut the fuck up," McNamara said, straightening and looking around. "What's the status of our two friends?"

"Down for the count," Wolf said.

"Dead?" McNamara asked.

Wolf shook his head.

Accondras said nothing and continued to rub his chin against his shirt in an apparent effort to get rid of the rest of the duct tape.

Wolf glanced back the way he'd come.

"We better get moving," he said. "It shouldn't be too much farther."

"What you gonna do with that?" McNamara pointed at the shotgun.

It was a twelve-gauge pump-action. Wolf depressed the release and worked the fore-end, ejecting four stored rounds. With the breech locked open, he walked across to a narrow passageway between two buildings and used his blouse to wipe the barrel and stock. Then he tossed the shotgun into the expanse.

"Got two pistols, too," he said.

"Better ditch them," McNamara said. "It'll be bad enough if we get caught with this old boy here, but if we're armed, it'll put us behind bars down here for a real long time."

"Who's paying you?" Accondras said. "Is it Von Dien? One of his flunkies?"

McNamara looked down at him. "I thought I told you to shut up."

"It's gotta be that fucking Fallotti, right?" Accondras said. "That son of a bitch is a no-good liar." His words were coming out so fast that they all ran together. "I have what they want, and they're going to pay me a lot of money. Let me go, and I'll cut you in on it. They're no good, I tell you. No good."

"And I suppose you're Little Lord Fauntleroy," McNamara said. "We're bail enforcement agents, and we're arresting you for an outstanding warrant outta New York, asshole."

"What?" Accondras said. He gathered his thoughts, then laughed. "You dummies. Uncuff me, and I'll give you double, triple what they're paying you."

"That ain't how it works," McNamara told him.

The boy had been staring at the supine figure as he ran his mouth. He suddenly stepped over and kicked Accondras in the face. The man screamed, and McNamara pulled the boy away.

"Now, now, none of that, Carlos," McNamara said.

"You going to let that little piece of shit do that to me?" Accondras said. A stream of blood wound down from a cut on his cheek.

"One more word outta you, asshole," McNamara said, still holding the boy, "and I'll shove this Taser all the way up your ass and press the trigger."

Accondras made a sound somewhere between a pant and a huff, but he said nothing more.

Wolf pulled out the two pistols. Both were Taurus models PT92s. He dropped the magazines and racked back the slides. A 9-mm round popped out of the chamber of each one.

Wolf flipped down the takedown levers on each and field-stripped them, removing the slides, barrels, springs, and the flashlights attached to the rails. He flipped one of the flashlights to Mac and pocketed the other one. After ensuring that the four of them were still alone in the alley, he threw each part in a different direction over the tops of the nearby houses, then went over to Accondras and knelt beside him.

"What you got in your pockets?" he asked, jamming

his fingers into the man's pants. He found a large roll of currency in the right pocket. There was nothing in the other one. Wolf shone the light on the roll. It looked like a substantial amount of pesos. Setting it on the ground, Wolf pushed Accondras onto his side and began unzipping the backpack. "How about in here?"

"Leave that alone," Accondras yelled. There was a new urgency in his voice. "That's my private property."

"Shut up," McNamara said.

Wolf pulled the backpack open and saw it mostly contained crumpled newspaper. He pushed his hand farther inside and found something hard wrapped in one of the newsprint bundles. He probed further, but nothing felt like a weapon.

"No, no!" Accondras started bucking and kicking his legs.

"Settle down," McNamara said, placing his foot on the other man's face. Accondras sputtered and coughed.

Wolf found what appeared to be a passport, but it was hard to tell in the darkness. He re-zipped the backpack and asked for the duct tape. McNamara handed it to him, and Wolf extended the roll, wrapping it several times around Accondras' arms, legs, and ankles. When he'd finished, the heavyset fugitive was trussed up well enough to prevent any untoward movements.

"Let me go," he said. "I've got money, and I'm gonna get lots more. I'll pay you anything you want."

Wolf ignored the man's pleas and slipped the duct tape into his blouse pocket. He picked up the roll of currency he'd taken from Accondras and held it toward the boy.

The youth's eyes widened and he grabbed for the money, but Wolf closed his fingers over it.

"*Carlos, escuchame,*" he said. "*Este hombre y Salvador serán matarlo. Comprende?*"

The boy's eyes never left the money. He nodded.

Wolf handed it to him but retained possession as he issued one more admonishment: "*Tomalo. Todo. Es suyo. Pero no vaya con Salvador otra vez. Nunca.*"

"*Sí,*" Carlo replied. "*Comprendo.*"

Wolf released his grip on the money. The boy pulled it to his breast and began to dart away but stopped. He looked at Wolf and then at McNamara.

"*Gracias,*" he said and disappeared between two buildings.

"Well," McNamara said. "At least we got that part right."

"Yeah. For now, anyway." Wolf pulled Accondras up and straightened him, then squatted and hoisted the bound man onto his shoulder. "Now, let's get the hell out of here."

A pair of red brake lights flashed at the mouth of the alley about a hundred yards away. A motorcycle pulled up, its headlight illuminating the path before them. It had to be José. At least, Wolf hoped that was who it was, and not some Mexican cop. They increased their pace, and Wolf started to feel the strain of running with Accondras on his shoulder. He wondered how Mac had done it.

Suck it up, he thought. Almost there.

"That's them," McNamara said. "Can you make it?"

Wolf's words came out spaced between each step: "Did…that…bear…shit…in…the…woods?"

* * *

Eagan shone his light around as he surveyed the area where the exchange was supposed to be made. It was a flat, circular section between low stone walls about three feet high made out of uneven white flagstones.

Off to the right was a decrepit pyramid that looked like a glorified rock pile and appeared to have been constructed out of the same flagstones. The dark shapes of more buildings flanked the access road that led into this section from the main road. Placement of snipers and a react team would be easy. There was plenty of cover. He turned to Cummins. The two bounty hunters, Nasim, and the three Vipers stood off to the side.

"Zerbe check in yet?" Eagan asked.

"They're on the way," Cummins said. "Right on schedule. Five to ten mikes."

His use of military terminology amused Eagan and reminded him of the screwed-up mission in Iraq four years ago. Cummins had been trying to prove his combat-zone creds then too, but after the shit hit the fan and the shooting started, the fat son of a bitch had practically pissed his pants.

"Weapons?" Eagan asked.

Cummins shook his head and pulled out his phone, scrambling to send another text.

What an incompetent asshole, Eagan thought.

Nasim stood there grinning, his eyes locked on Eagan's.

"Okay, you heard the man," he said, figuring the wording would give Cummins a faux boost in self-esteem. He was still the key to the money transfer. "Harper and Newman, deploy there and there." He pointed at embankments about thirty feet away that were reinforced by more stone walls. "Keep ready in case things go south, but under no circumstances do you open fire on any personnel inside the van. Our target must be taken unharmed. Clear?"

The two Vipers grunted their assents.

Eagan turned to Reynolds. "Okay, you approach them from our van, which will be parked facing them. They'll be arriving on this road, so they should be stopping here, where Zerbe tells them. The two of them know you from the briefing you gave in Vegas. Proceed over to their vehicle and keep them occupied. Try to draw them out, and then—"

"No guns," Cummins said. "Zerbe just texted me."

Eagan hated to be interrupted, and he glared at the heavyset lawyer. After letting the silence resonate, he continued. "As I was saying, try to draw them out of the vehicle. If not, no sweat. The main thing is to keep them distracted."

"What about us?" Reno asked. "Where are those Glocks you showed us?"

Another interruption. Eagan couldn't wait to jettison these two bozos.

"Glad you asked." He reached into his ditty bag, pulled out the two Glock 19s, and handed a weapon to each of the bounty hunters. "While Reynolds is keeping them distracted, you two sneak up from over there." Eagan pointed to the ungainly stack of rocks to the left of the access road. "Approach their vehicle from the rear and get the drop on them. Our man on the inside says neither of them is driving or in the front seat, so they won't have visual capabilities from the mirrors. Take charge of the target and remove him from the vehicle."

Reno and Herc exchanged glances and smiled.

"Sounds like a plan," Reno said. "Just like we done them up before."

"Just try not to shoot anybody," Eagan said.

"Relax," Reno said. "We know what we're doing."

"We're professionals," the other one said.

The black guy pulled back the slide of the Glock a few centimeters to check if a round was in the chamber. Reno did the same, and upon glimpsing the glint of brass, let the slide ease forward.

If they only knew, Eagan thought.

CHAPTER 13

NEAR EL MECO
CANCUN, MEXICO

The van sped through the dark streets, dipping and weaving and occasionally slamming on its brakes. Beside them, Wolf could hear the high-pitched buzz of José's motorcycle escort.

"I'm sure glad you had the foresight to dump those weapons," Zerbe said, half-turning to look back on them from the front passenger seat. "On the off-chance we do get stopped by the local constabulary, it'll make things a lot simpler. A small bribe, and we'll be on our way."

"*Un mordida,*" Paco said, grinning.

"Down here," Zerbe continued, "you get caught with a gun, it's off to jail without passing go for a long, long time."

"*En el gran carcel,*" Paco chimed in again, "*Es muy duro.*"

"You guys are fools," Accondras shouted. "This whole

thing's a setup. Let me go, and I'll make you both richer than you ever dreamed."

"Why don't you put some of that damn duct tape over his mouth?" Zerbe said. "I'm getting tired of smelling his breath."

That was like the pot calling the kettle black, Wolf thought, considering how foul Zerbe's breath and body smelled.

Nevertheless, McNamara peeled off a strip of tape and slapped it over Accondras' lips. The bound man immediately began to work his jaw to try to dislodge it.

"You get that off of there," McNamara said, "and I'll have to seriously consider breaking your jaw."

Accondras stared up at him, then stopped moving.

The van bounced over a huge bump, and Accondras' lower body flipped up and came down hard on the metal floor. He emitted an extended moan.

"Let's see if we can make him a little more comfortable." Wolf took out his Balisong and flipped it open.

"Hey," McNamara said. "You got the knack of that down real good."

Paco hit another bump, then slowed a bit to execute a right turn. The noise from the tires told Wolf they'd transferred from asphalt to gravel.

Wolf grabbed the closest strap securing the backpack, slipped the blade underneath, and began sawing. Accondras' eyes widened, and he shook his head.

"Relax," Wolf said. "I'm not going to cut you."

Accondras continued to shake his head violently and began working his jaw in a frantic motion.

Wolf cut through the first strap and grabbed the second one.

As he was slicing through it, he heard Paco grunt, *"Por ahí. Mira."*

The buzzing of the motorcycle diminished as if it had slowed appreciably. Wolf looked up. Between the front seats, he could see through the windshield. They were entering a maze of rickety old stone buildings. The area in the center was a flat expanse about sixty yards wide. There were more stone structures along the perimeter, giving the flat area an almost circular shape.

El Meco, Wolf thought. The ancient Mayan ruins of a lost civilization.

Cancun…the nest of vipers.

* * *

Eagan watched the other van as it pulled onto the winding road leading to their position in the center of the flat expanse.

Finally, he thought.

The sour smell of Cummins's sweat wafted to him as the lawyer squatted next to him. Nasim was on the other side and smelled equally foul.

Maybe I can use the funk to break Accondras down faster, he thought with a grin.

"What if they're armed?" Cummins asked. His voice was high and nervous.

"Zerbe says they're not."

"What if he's wrong?" Cummins was silent for about ten seconds, then said. "We can't afford for Accondras to get wasted before we find that artifact."

"Relax, for Christ's sake." Eagan was getting very tired of this gasbag.

"I gotta go to the bathroom," Cummins blurted. He turned and waddled off

To the bathroom?

Eagan suspected Cummins was having another gut-check crisis, just like back in Iraq. The fat prick was yellow to the core.

Good riddance. He smirked.

Nasim grinned as well.

He keyed his mic. "Get ready. It's showtime."

* * *

Wolf could see a man walking toward them, silhouetted by the headlights of the vehicle parked behind him. It was a very deliberate and non-threatening approach, but Wolf didn't want to drop his guard. He now regretted abandoning those weapons. It would have been safer not to go into this handoff unarmed.

One mistake after another, he thought.

But there was little he could do about that now.

He tossed the backpack to the side and squatted next to McNamara.

"Looks like this one went pretty easy," McNamara said. "All things considered."

Wolf nodded, but something didn't feel quite right. He senses the same unease in Mac. While they had pulled it off with relative smoothness, it had seemed almost anticlimactic.

Accondras continued to thrash about as best he could, his eyes darting back and forth, but the duct-tape gag seemed to be holding. His breathing was becoming labored, and sweat poured off him.

Wolf found it hard to feel much sympathy, but at the same time, in the Army, he'd always believed in treating POWs with respect and dignity. This guy was reprehensible, but this wasn't turning out to be one of those moments upon which you could look back with pride. He reached down and pulled the duct tape off

Accondras' mouth. The man immediately began pleading.

"Please, get me outta here. They're gonna kill me."

"Nobody's gonna kill you," Zerbe said. "Calm down."

He opened the passenger door, and the dome light came on.

The side door slid open, and Wolf saw a familiar face. It was Reynolds, the guy they'd met in Vegas, who'd set this whole thing in motion. He was wearing a black tactical outfit instead of a shirt and tie this time. His sleeves were rolled up over his muscular forearms, and Wolf caught a glimpse of what appeared to be a Glock in a tactical holster strapped to his right leg. The guy didn't look much like an employee of a law firm, even in the investigative division.

He smiled as he looked down at Accondras.

"I see you got him. Good job."

"We got him," McNamara said, looking around. "This don't look much like an airstrip, though. I thought you were going to fly him back to the States."

"They're not," Accondras said. "They're going to kill me. You too, most likely, you stupid idiots."

"The plane's just over the ridge," Reynolds said.

"Can't you see he's lying?" Accondras yelled. "He's a hired killer."

Reynolds raised his right index finger to his lips and made a shushing sound.

"There, there, Mr. Accondras," he said. "It would behoove you to behave yourself and cooperate."

"Cooperate?" Accondras barked a harsh laugh. "The sooner I do that, the sooner you kill me."

Reynolds shook his head and smiled. "If you two gentlemen will be good enough to escort him over to my vehicle, I'll fire up my tablet and transfer the rest of your payment." He shifted his body and gripped the door, sliding it all the way open. That was when Wolf saw the tattoo on the back of Reynolds's right forearm and hand, and not just any tattoo. It was the head and body of a viper. He'd seen one like it over four years ago, back in Iraq. Eagan, the big guy in that PMC, had had one just like it. Wolf remembered staring at it when Eagan was testifying at the court-martial. The head of a snake on the hand of a snake. What did they call themselves?

The Vipers.

Wolf tried to figure the next best move. He had to alert Mac that something was really off, but they were in a totally vulnerable position, crammed into the back of a Mexican van with a dubious ally in the driver's seat and an armed adversary in front of them.

"Where'd you get that tattoo?" Wolf asked.

"This?" Reynolds smiled. "A souvenir from my youth and my old Army days."

"I knew a guy that had one just like it," Wolf said. "The son of a bitch testified against me at my court-martial."

He felt Mac stiffen.

Good. He had been alerted to this new set of circumstances.

Now, if they could just figure out exactly who and what they were up against.

"It's a pretty popular tattoo, I guess," Reynolds said, the smile still fixed on his face.

Wolf detected a flash of movement at the rear of the van. Someone was coming up on them.

Damn. Why did I ditch those guns?

Reno Garth's grinning face appeared next to Reynolds, and right beside him were the broad shoulders and dark visage of Black Hercules. Both of them were holding Glocks and pointing them at Wolf and McNamara.

"Reno!" McNamara said. "What the hell?"

Reno's grin broadened. "Looks like we done scooped you again, Big Mac." He let the words sink in, then the smile faded. "Now, you and Small Fry get your asses out of there so we can collect our pinch."

McNamara seemed too stunned to move. Wolf debated trying to spring out of the van, but with the two of them holding guns on him, it was fruitless.

Zerbe swiveled in the seat, and he was holding a gun as well, although it was a small, cheap-looking revolver.

"You in on this too, huh?" McNamara said. "Looks like we got ourselves involved with some real lowlife sons of bitches, Steve."

"Come on," Reno said, grabbing McNamara's arm and pulling him out of the open door.

"Hey," Wolf said. "Get your hands off of him, asshole."

Reno's smirk regenerated. "Why? You gonna do something if I don't?"

"Put down that gun, and I'll take your fucking pussy-ass apart," Wolf said, praying the insult would engender a lapse in judgment in the burly adversary.

"Come on out of there, sucker." Herc reached into the van. His big fingers sought Wolf's arm, and figuring he had nothing to lose, he slapped it away.

"That goes double for you," Wolf said.

The black man's mouth twisted into a rage-filled grimace. He seemed about to crowd his way into the van to take Wolf on, but another voice intruded.

"Back off. Can't you see he's trying to bait you? Get you close enough so he can make a grab for your gun?"

The voice was all too familiar.

Eagan stepped into view, and next to him was a

swarthy-looking guy who looked like an Arab. The man smiled.

The gold in the guy's front teeth glinted in the illumination from the dome light.

Nasim.

Wolf couldn't believe it. It was like a nightmare vision of Iraq come to life.

He was too stunned to speak.

The back door of the van was jerked open, and two more men, both wearing black BDU outfits and carrying AK-47s, appeared. One pointed his rifle at Wolf and McNamara.

"You'd best get out," Eagan said. "And get that piece of shit out of there and into our vehicle now."

Wolf followed McNamara out of the van, and they watched with their hands on top of their heads POW-style as Reynolds and Nasim carried the now-limp form of Accondras toward the other vehicle. He was sobbing quietly. Wolf heard the doors of their van slam open. He was still in a state of disbelief. Eagan and that Iraqi fucker, Nasim... How in the *hell*?

"Bet you thought you were living a flashback, huh?" Eagan said, sticking his face closer to Wolf. "Huh, boy?"

Wolf said nothing. He debated whether to strike him and then make a break for it. Push them back and run for the shadows of the stone ruins, but with two of them carrying rifles, he'd be cut down in seconds. Plus, he had Mac to think about. Even if he could escape, if something happened to Mac, Wolf would never be able to face Kasey.

Wolf gazed at him. His face was drawn and pasty-white in the moonlight and ambient illumination. One of the other men came up behind them and grabbed Wolf's right arm. Reno still held the Glock on them. Wolf felt his arm being twisted behind his back, then the impact and the unmistakable sound of a handcuff being ratcheted over his wrist. The man brought Wolf's left arm down and secured that one as well, then did the same to Mac.

"Take them over there and guard them," Eagan said. He turned to Zerbe. "Tell your driver here he's going to hitch a ride back to town with his buddy on the motorcycle. We're going to need his van for our scene setup."

Zerbe nodded and went to talk to Paco and José.

Scene setup? What the hell did that mean?

Whatever it was, Wolf didn't like the sound of it.

Zerbe turned. "They'll want to get paid first."

Eagan blew out a loud breath. "Aw, Christ. All right, give me a minute." He glanced at the other van. Nasim and Reynolds had finished placing Accondras in the vehicle. Reynolds walked back over and nodded. Eagan stepped back and pointed at Reno and Herc.

"Might as well cuff these two as well."

"Cuff us?" Reno said, his face registering shock and surprise.

"What you talking about?" Herc asked, then raised the Glock and pointed it at Eagan. "Stay the fuck away from me, motherfucker."

The Viper chuckled.

"You don't think I'd be stupid enough to give you weapons that were fully operational, do you?"

Herc shot a quick look toward Reno, then extended the Glock and pulled the trigger.

It made a loud click, but nothing emerged from the barrel.

Herc racked back the slide, popped the round in the chamber out, and let it slam forward. He pulled the trigger again and was met with the same empty-sounding click.

Reno tried his gun and got the same result.

"The strikers were removed," Eagan said. "Now, drop them and let my boys cuff you, or I'll have them put a couple bullets in you."

Reno and Herc exchanged glances once again and threw down the weapons. One of the Vipers clad in black shouldered his rifle and stepped forward to apply the first new set of cuffs.

"Put your fucking arms together, nigger." The man grunted with effort. "Do it, motherfucker, or we'll put a bullet in you."

More grunts, then he whistled as he snapped the cuffs over Herc's thick wrists.

"Christ, I can only get one click on this big black buck's wrists, they're so huge."

"Keep an extra eye on him, then," Eagan said. "And take them all over there by that low wall to watch them."

Reynolds shoved Reno toward the wall, then he and another black-clad figure herded Herc, Wolf, and McNamara behind him. Reynolds was carrying an AK-47 now as well. The situation looked hopeless.

"Big Jim," Reno said. "You gotta believe me. I had no idea it was gonna turn out like this."

"Reno," McNamara said, "you got shit for brains."

"How the hell did you *think* it was going to go down?" Wolf asked. "That they were gonna let you waltz off with the prize after stealing him from us?"

Reno shot a pained expression at him.

"What's gonna happen now?"

"I don't know," Wolf said. "But you can bet it ain't gonna be good."

His mind was still spinning, but a crazy, half-assed plan was starting to form. This had something to do with Iraq. Why else would Eagan and Nasim be together here in Mexico? He struggled to dredge up the repressed details of that ill-fated raid on the other side of the world. They'd been together back then, and they'd been after something... Something those Iraqis they'd been torturing had.

Wolf shook his head, trying to will himself to remember what had happened. He recalled hearing men screaming, finding one with his throat cut, Spec Four Thompson shaking him awake, the firefight... Everything else was a blur, dancing just out of his mind's reach like a playful nymph teasing and darting away.

It was no use. Trying to remember was like trying to grab smoke.

But another explanation was forming in his mind now.

Accondras had something they wanted. Whatever it was, it was very valuable and most likely related to whatever they had been seeking in Iraq. He'd mentioned somebody's name.

Is Von Dien paying you?

Who the hell was Von Dien?

Whoever he was, he had to be rich. And ultimately, behind this whole elaborate setup.

If this warrant stuff was legit—and Kasey had checked on the veracity before they'd left, so it was— then Eagan had hired both them and Reno and Herc to come down here and grab the guy. But it wasn't to take him back to New York to stand trial. No, they meant to extract information from him. He'd been right when he'd said they were going to kill him.

Most likely, they were going to kill him and Mac too. Reno and Herc were expendable as well.

He remembered Eagan's words: Scene setup.

Wolf looked at the van and saw Zerbe using a rag to wipe down the area where he'd been sitting.

No fingerprints, Wolf thought. A scene setup.

They'd all been brought down here to be patsies, to make it look like they all were after Accondras at the same time, had fought over him, and had ended up killing him and each other.

We'll all be shot and laid out to make it look like a bounty hunting dispute gone bad, he thought.

So they had only as long as it would take Eagan to extract the information from Accondras and retrieve whatever it was they were looking for. He'd want to make sure all the bodies bought it at the same time.

Time... It was fleeting, but they still had a little bit of it.

"Sit down there," Reynolds said, pointing at a patch of brownish dirt and weeds.

The four of them did as instructed. Reynolds and the other two stood about fifteen feet away. One of them took out a pack of cigarettes, and they each grabbed one and lit up. Wolf glanced at the other van and saw three shadowy figures hop into the back. They looked like Zerbe, Nasim, and somebody else, a short, fat guy. Something about him looked vaguely familiar, but Wolf couldn't exactly recall what it was. Eagan strode toward Reynolds and the other two Vipers. "Newman, give me the keys. We're going to take a little ride. We'll be back."

The one called Newman reached into his pocket and gave Eagan a set of keys.

"Where you going?" Reynolds asked.

"Back to the helicopter," Eagan said, his voice lowering to a growl. "Is that fucking all right with you?"

Reynolds shrugged and gestured at Paco and José. "What about them?"

The Mexicans stood expectantly next to the motorcycle.

"Loose ends," Eagan said. "Watch."

He slipped his Glock out of the tactical holster affixed to his leg, brought the weapons up quickly, and fired two rounds in rapid succession. The Mexicans jerked and twisted before collapsing to the ground. Eagan walked over to them, kicked each body, and then put two more rounds in each prone man's head.

The gunshots rang in Wolf's ears, but he could still hear Eagan's laughter.

This was one cold son of a bitch.

Eagan holstered his weapon, walked back over to the idling van, and got in the driver's side. The vehicle started, made a sweeping turn to swing around Paco's van, and left via the exit road.

Wolf shook his head to clear his ears and said in a low voice, "That's what they got planned for us. All of us."

"Oh, shit," Reno said. "Whadda we gonna do?"

Wolf pulled his right foot under his legs and began probing his boot with his fingers.

"I got a handcuff key in my boot," he said. "If I can reach it, I'll unlock my cuffs and slip you the key, top."

McNamara nodded.

"Slip him the key?" Reno said. "What about me and Herc?"

"Shit," Herc said. "Don't need no key. I can bust my way out of these fucking things."

"All right," Wolf said. "But listen. Our only chance is to use the element of surprise. We get at least two of us free, and we all four rush those bastards and knock them down. Whoever's free, the two of us will have to take them out. You up for that?"

The black man's face hardened, and his head jerked up and down.

"Let's try to do it before they finish their smokes," Wolf whispered.

He saw Herc's lips purse, and the huge muscles of the man's arms stood out in bas-relief. Wolf hoped the guy was as strong as he claimed to be. For his part, Wolf continued to probe the inside of his boot with his fingers to ferret out the location of the key.

Gradually, it worked. The ankle bone of his right foot pressed against something hard and obtrusive and about an inch long.

It was the prize.

Wolf shifted his body to give himself a bit more purchase and thrust his fingers farther into the boot. The tip of his longest digit brushed the double-locking pin.

Almost there.

He glanced over to check the progress of the three sentries.

Their cigarettes were more than halfway burned down.

Come on, come on, he told himself.

Herc was sweating profusely. Trying to break handcuffs with them placed in front of your body was the usual strongman trick. It permitted maximum leverage to be applied since the arms could be pulled outward. Wolf had seen a guy do it on TV many years ago, and it had taken him several minutes. Having your arms behind you limited both your leverage and your power.

One of the guards took a long drag and field-stripped his butt.

A second one, Newman, did the same.

Reynolds laughed, also ground his smoke out on the sole of his boot, and began peeling the paper from around the last remnants of tobacco.

Shit, thought Wolf. So close.

His fingers had the key now. He manipulated it so the hollow end was facing upward, then slid it toward the area where he estimated the keyhole was. It slipped over the smooth metal again and again without finding the hole.

Reynolds glanced at them and murmured something, and all three laughed.

Go ahead, Wolf thought. *Laugh, fuckers. Why don't you have yourselves another smoke?*

As if they'd heard him, Reynolds pulled out his pack and passed it around. They each took one, and Reynolds produced a disposable lighter.

Herc let out an audible grunt.

"Got it," he whispered.

Wolf suddenly felt the key slip into the opening. He twisted, and the cuff on his left hand dropped open.

"Me, too," he said.

"They still pretty far away," Herc said. "They'll cut us down we try to move across that space."

Wolf assessed the distance and decided Herc was right. "Let's try to get at least one of them over here then."

"How we gonna do that?" Herc asked.

"I'll think of something," Wolf said. "You guys hit the dirt when I make my move."

"Ain't gonna happen," Herc said. "You grab one, and it'll be enough of a distraction for me to rush 'em."

Wolf said nothing. It didn't appear that a frontal rush would have much chance of success, but if the big man could move fast enough to take advantage of the diversion...

"Hey," Wolf said in a loud voice. "How about giving me one of them smokes?"

"Fuck you," the one called Newman said.

"Come on," Wolf said in a coaxing tone. "I'll pay for it."

Reynolds glanced at the other two. He looked interested.

"Pay with what?"

"I got a couple thousand pesos in my pocket over here," Wolf said. "Buy you some real good grade-A Mexican poontang when you get back in town."

Reynolds drew deeply on his cigarette and blew out a plume of smoke. He wasn't moving.

Wolf debated whether to try to push it further.

No, he told himself. Wait for it.

Reynolds brought the cigarette to his lips once more, and the tip glowed red. He exhaled with a laugh as he exchanged more conversation with his two compatriots.

A nest of vipers, Wolf thought.

He was about to say something more when Reynolds adjusted the shoulder strap of his AK-7 and sauntered over to the four captives.

Wolf felt a surge of adrenaline flooding through every artery and vein.

"Okay, pretty boy," Reynolds said as he walked. "You better not be bullshitting me, or I'll take it out of your hide."

Wolf smiled and threw a quick look at Herc, hoping he wouldn't jump the gun.

Struggling to get to his feet and making it look like he was having a rough time of it, Wolf managed to straighten, still holding his arms behind him.

Reynolds was only a few feet away now. The cigarette's ash was bright crimson, the AK-47 was hanging loosely over his shoulder, and the Glock pistol was in his low-slung tactical holster, secured by a nylon strap.

The pistol is the best target, Wolf thought, noticing that the gun was also held in a black polymer shell. It was level three, the kind where you had to hit the release button and then grip the weapon's handle and twist slightly to free the trigger guard from the internal locking safety. That added another second or two to the snatch.

"All I want's a smoke," Wolf said, stepping forward.

Reynolds was only a foot or so away when Wolf brought his right hand up, fingers extended like a spear, and plunged them into the soft space beneath the Viper's Adam's apple. He jerked forward, his arms rising toward his throat as Wolf grabbed him and spun him around. The bounty hunter's right hand closed over the butt of the Glock.

Press, twist, pull, lift, he thought, praying the gun would come loose.

It did.

As he was bringing it up, Herc rose and charged the other two guards. Newman whipped his rifle around, and a quick burst of flame shot out of the end of the barrel, a flash of yellow in the dark night. The distinctive sound of the Kalashnikov echoed in Wolf's ears, then he heard nothing. Everything proceeded in slow motion.

He acquired the target, centering on the shooter's face, and squeezed the trigger.

The gun jerked back in his hand.

Controlling the recoil, Wolf let the trigger return

forward until he felt the trigger pin make its little click, then squeezed off another two rounds.

The third guard had his rifle pointing at them, and more fire erupted from it.

Wolf felt the rounds zing by his head and directed the gun at him.

Herc's massive body tumbled forward.

Wolf aimed and shot at the third assailant.

Newman crumpled.

So did the third one.

Reynolds' struggling ceased, and he went limp. Wolf let him drop to the ground, then pointed the Glock at the man's face and squeezed off another round.

There was no sound, but he saw a round hole appear in Reynolds's forehead an inch or so from the right temple. The man's eyes stared vacuously with no reaction.

Wolf ran to the other two, gun extended out in front of him, handcuffs still dangling from his right wrist, and bent to check them.

Both of them were dead.

When he turned back, he saw Mac writhing on the ground. Wolf shoved the Glock into the left side of his waistband and rushed over to him. Blood welled from a hole in his right side.

Oh, please don't let it have hit his liver, Wolf thought.

He checked the wound more closely. A ragged exit wound, bleeding copiously, was on the lower right side.

A through-and-through, Wolf thought. Recoverable, depending on how much internal damage there was.

And if I can get Mac to a hospital, he thought.

He looked at Reno, who was grimacing at the two holes in his left thigh and calf. Herc lay about six feet away and was not moving. Wolf saw a trio of holes stitched across the ample back.

In through the chest, out through the back. Non-survivable wounds.

As Wolf scanned the ground for the handcuff key, his hearing returned in stages. The initial sounds, moans from Reno and swearing from McNamara, were swathed in a persistent buzzing. They sounded far away. Gradually, as he uncuffed Mac and then Reno, the buzzing receded.

"Looks like a through-and-through," Wolf said, taking off his blouse and tying it around Mac's waist.

McNamara grunted in pain.

"How bad's Reno look?"

Wolf cinched the knot and placed Mac's hand over the wound site. He pulled Reynolds's body away and checked the bounty hunter. Blood was pouring out of the holes in his leg, but it didn't look arterial.

Reno grabbed his arm. "Herc," he managed to say.

Wolf shook his head. "I'm sorry."

Tears streamed down Reno's face.

Wolf went over and checked Herc's body. His head was twisted to the left, eyes wide open as if he were watching the rest of the scene unfold. No pulse, no breathing. Wolf closed the man's eyelids and stood.

He helped McNamara get to his feet, then reached down and snared his legs, lifting him and carrying him in a run toward the van.

"I can walk, dammit," McNamara said.

"Not fast enough. I got to get you two to a hospital. Plus, we don't know if Eagan heard those shots."

"Eagan?"

"That big fucker that was giving the orders," Wolf said.

"You know him?"

"Yeah. He's one of the guys that set me up in Iraq."

"Set me down here," McNamara said. "By our buddy Paco. Let me look for the keys. You go back and get Reno."

Rather than debate the issue, Wolf gently lowered Mac to the ground feet first. Once he was certain McNamara was capable of standing by leaning against the van, Wolf went back for Reno. He'd crawled over to his fallen partner.

"Oh, God," he was whimpering. "Oh, God."

"Come on, Reno," Wolf said. "There's nothing we can do for him now, and I got to get you guys to a hospital."

Reno grabbed Wolf's forearm.

"Don't just leave him here. Please."

Wolf nodded and lifted the other man, and they began skip-walking toward the van like they were in a three-legged race. The vehicle came barreling toward them and screeched to a halt. McNamara was behind the wheel.

Wolf moved to the still-open side door and helped Reno through it. The big man flopped onto his back and howled in pain. Wolf pulled out his flashlight and checked Reno's leg. The blood was still flowing. Glancing around, Wolf spotted the backpack Accondras had been wearing. Grabbing it, he quickly tied the shoulder straps around Reno's leg to staunch the bleeding, then placed the bag under his leg to elevate it.

"Big Jim," Reno said. "Herc."

"Herc's dead, Reno," McNamara said. "Ain't no helping him now."

"You can't leave him here," Reno said. "Don't. Please."

He coughed.

McNamara glanced at Wolf and waved his arm.

"I'll pull this thing closer," he said. "Can you lift him in here?"

Wolf was about to protest but didn't want to waste time arguing. He ran back to Herc and began dragging him toward the advancing vehicle. The vehicle came to a stop about five feet away, and Wolf managed to lift the dead man into the back of the van, with Reno helping pull the body inside.

He groaned in pain and his head rocked back with a clunk, hitting the metal floor as he reeled from the effort.

Wolf slammed the back doors, then ran around to the right side and slid the other door closed. He then went to the driver's door and pulled the handle, but it didn't open.

McNamara had locked it.

"What are you doing?" Wolf said. "Let me drive."

"Like hell," McNamara said.

"I gotta get you guys to a hospital. *Move.*"

"Huh-uh," McNamara said. "I'm driving me and Reno there. You're going after those sons of bitches and our pinch."

"What?"

"You got to. Take José's motorcycle. You know how to ride one of them things, don't ya?"

"The hell with them. It's you I'm worried about."

"Then let go of that damn door and let me get going before we lose any more blood. It's a straight shot back to the city. There's got to be a hospital open there, as big as that place is. At the very least, I'll find the American Embassy."

"Mac, listen—"

"No, you listen, dammit. You gotta find them guys. Two reasons. One, our fingerprints are on that duct tape.

We get tied to a murder or two down here, they'll lock us up and throw away the key."

"The Mexican police aren't gonna know our fingerprints."

"No, but the feds will. Any time an American citizen dies on foreign soil, the Bureau gets involved."

Wolf started to protest, but Mac cut him off again.

"And two, this whole fucking thing's somehow tied to what happened in Iraq, ain't it? That guy Eagan?"

Wolf hesitated, then nodded.

"Well, it's your last chance to catch him and clear your name."

"No way." Wolf shook his head. "I'm going to get you two to a hospital first."

"Go." Mac shifted the van into gear. "Find them. Grab that skip and turn yourselves in to the American Embassy."

"The embassy?" Wolf said.

"No other option," Mac said. "It'll be up to the state department to turn that sorry asshole over for extradition."

"What are you gonna do?"

"If you ever let me get outta here, I'll get us some damn medical treatment." Wolf felt the strong fingers press into his arm. "Now go. You'll lose their trail."

"You do it, bro," Reno shouted from the back. "Those fuckers killed Herc. Make 'em pay."

Wolf hesitated. He was torn.

"I told you," Mac said. "We can make it. This is your chance to clear your name. Maybe your *only* chance."

Wolf knew that was true. If he lost the trail now, without knowing the whole story of why this had unfolded as it had, he'd probably never know.

"But—"

"No buts, dammit." Mac grimaced. "Take that dead Mexican's bike and go after those fuckers. Their tracks should be easy enough to follow on that dirt road. You can catch them before they take that plane back to the States. You know what to do. You're a Ranger, dammit."

A Ranger. He had been one once.

Yeah, that was what he had to do, and the longer he delayed, the less the chances that Mac and Reno would be able to make the drive, bleeding the way they were. Still, the thought of abandoning them still gnawed at him.

No man left behind.

He repeated the phrase out loud.

"Shit," Mac said. "You ain't *leaving* us. We're the ones leaving you. Now, go do what you gotta do, Ranger."

Hearing the word reminded him of what he had once been.

"How far?" Mac asked.

"All the way," Wolf said, reciting the answer to the Ranger creed.

"That's what I wanted to hear." Mac shifted into gear and the van took off, leaving Wolf standing there watching the dwindling red taillights.

CHAPTER 14

CANCUN AND NORTH OF PUERTO MORELOS

Eagan stood inside a small room, which had ragged stone walls and a dirt floor. The light from a portable lantern illuminated the dank space, casting shadows over the uneven surfaces of the structure. The little cavern in the largest pyramid had proven to be a perfect little interrogation chamber, and although it had been an enjoyable little torture session, it had taken Eagan longer than he'd anticipated to break him, as well as a bit more force than was prudent. Accondras lay in a tangled heap about three feet away, the odors of vomit, piss, and shit permeating the air. The smell of blood was there too, rich and coppery, and Eagan hoped that what had finally been revealed was in fact the truth. If it was, his job had just gotten a whole lot simpler

The backpack. Hopefully, it was in that damn van.

The son of a bitch had had it with him the whole time. But it made sense. Why stash something that's not only your meal ticket but also your ultimate insurance policy?

The fucking backpack…

Cummins stuck his head through the doorway and recoiled quickly. "Oh, shit. He dead?"

Eagan shook his head.

"Christ, what'd you do to him?" Cummins' nose wrinkled. "Smells like a hemorrhoid exploded in here."

"It's a dirty job," Eagan said, "but somebody's got to enjoy it."

"Well, I think something's up. I heard what sounded like distant gunshots. A whole bunch of them."

Shit.

He tried his radio. Several calls went unanswered.

They might be out of range, he thought as he reached into his pocket for the burner phone. "Get that fucking Zerbe in here."

He dialed the number of Reynolds' burner phone. It rang and rang with no answer.

Eagan terminated the call and texted a quick message to Reynolds. **You ok? Call me ASAP.**

He sent the message and waited.

No response.

He had to check that damn van, find out for sure if the backpack was still inside.

"What about the artifact?" Cummins asked. "Fallotti's been texting me like mad."

Eagan looked at him. He started to tell Cummins what Accondras had said but stopped. So far, he was the only one who knew the alleged whereabouts of the artifact. It wouldn't hurt to sit on that until he'd verified it.

"Just get that fucker Zerbe," Eagan said.

The lawyer disappeared from the crude threshold with an audible snort of disgust.

Accondras moaned. "Please. Help me."

Eagan went over to him and knelt by his head, reaching out to pat the man's shoulder.

"Thomas, you did good." Eagan gave him another pat. "Now, are you sure about things?"

"Help me."

"The backpack." Eagan kept his voice even, his tone somewhere between authoritative and non-threatening. "You're sure it's in the van?"

"It was in there the last time I saw it." His voice sounded raspy. "The one guy, the younger one, cut the straps and took it off me."

This concerned Eagan. Had Wolf and his partner found it?

"Why?" Eagan asked. "Why did he take it off you?"

Had Wolf somehow put two and two together?

Eagan prodded further. "Did you tell him what was in it?"

"No."

Eagan spoke again, keeping his voice soft and non-threatening: "Tom, are you sure that they didn't know what it was? Did they open the backpack?"

"They—" Accondras heaved out two gasping breaths, then made a hissing sound. "They don't know. Nobody does. I sealed it in plastic and then had a local artist make the statue."

"The statue?"

"Of a bandito. Plaster. A Mexican bandito."

Eagan took a moment to reflect on that. A priceless artifact encased in a seemingly worthless plaster statue, hiding in plain sight. It was almost laughable.

Behind Eagan, Cummins asked, "That's where it's been the whole time? In a backpack?"

Eagan turned and saw him standing in the doorway. He'd overheard everything.

"I thought I told you to get Zerbe," Eagan said.

"He's on his way. He was just down the hallway having a smoke." Cummins blew out a breath and shook his head. "Where's the backpack now? That other van?"

So he *had* overheard them.

"He says it is."

"What the hell?" Cummins laughed. "Why the fuck didn't we see it in there before and check it?"

Eagan rolled his eyes. The fat fucker had been so worried about Wolf maybe having a gun that he wouldn't go near the vehicle.

Cummins snorted another laugh. "Shit, what a fucking comedy of errors."

A comedy of errors for sure, Eagan thought.

But it won't be so funny if they couldn't get the damn thing back. Or if Accondras hadn't been straight with him. The son of a bitch was leaking a lot of blood and probably wouldn't last much longer.

Eagan tried to remember if he'd seen a backpack in the van when he'd surprised Wolf and his buddy. He thought he remembered seeing something like that but couldn't be sure. Of course, he hadn't known what he was looking for at that time.

Still no reply from Reynolds.

Eagan started to straighten but stopped. He wanted to keep the fear of God in this low-down piece of shit, Accondras.

"Tom, listen to me," Eagan said, letting his voice deepen and sound harsher with each new word. "We're going back there now, and if you're fucking lying to me, you're gonna wish you never were fucking born. Understand?"

Accondras replied with a sob and a whimper.

Zerbe came in.

"What's up?"

Eagan went to the doorway and spoke in a low voice.

"You remember him wearing a backpack when you grabbed him?"

Zerbe's lower lip jutted out, and he looked contemplative, then shook his head. "Yeah, I think so. Why?"

"There's something in it we need."

Zerbe's eyes widened. "Shit. You mean ..."

Eagan checked his phone again for a reply to his text. Still nothing.

He dialed Reynolds' number again.

It rang numerous times, but no one answered.

"You calling Reynolds?" Cummins asked.

"Yeah, and he's not answering."

Cummins blinked twice, and his upper lip twitched.

"Oh, Christ, we gotta get that thing back. We got to. You think something's wrong?"

"What could go wrong?" Zerbe asked. "We had all those fuckers handcuffed, didn't we?"

Eagan keyed his radio and called Wells and Kunish. They both answered.

"Get up here," Eagan said. "We gotta shove off. Immediately."

"Go find Nasim," Eagan said to Cummins. "Meet me by the vehicle."

About thirty yards away, two shadowy forms beginning to make their way up the uneven stone steps toward him. Eagan suddenly regretted having taken Accondras so far up the structure to do the interrogation, but he hadn't wanted everyone to be privy to the conversation.

Or to the methods employed to obtain the information. That was one mistake he wasn't going to make again.

There would be no witnesses this time. Not like Iraq.

And pretty soon, there wouldn't be any remaining witnesses to that fiasco, either.

Better late than never, he told himself.

When Wells and Kunish got there, Eagan swung his arm toward Accondras.

"Pick him up and carry him down to the vehicle," Eagan said. "We gotta go back to the other area."

The backpack, he thought as he strode over to the stone staircase. The fucking backpack.

Then he heard it…a faint buzzing sound.

An airplane?

No, he thought. A motorcycle.

* * *

Wolf downshifted and counter-steered to the left to compensate for centrifugal force as he executed the right turn onto the gravel. He had no eye protection, so the wind was forcing him to squint. It apparently hadn't bothered José, but he wasn't around to provide any advice on how to deal with it, so Wolf kept the speed down. He was more concerned about the noise. He didn't want to ride into an ambush, and he had no idea where Eagan and company had ventured.

I'm flying blind and wearing a dead man's blouse, he thought. It was not exactly a formula for success.

After he'd watched McNamara and Reno take off, Wolf had gathered as much fortification as he could, stripping Reynolds of his BDU blouse and pistol belt. He'd had two extra magazines for his Glock, and Wolf had dropped the used one and taken a fresh one from one of the dead Vipers.

At least, he assumed they were from that same outfit. They all had the serpent's head tattoo on their right hands. After loading his pants pockets as well as those of the blouse with all the extra mags he could carry for the Glock, he grabbed one of the AK-47s and stripped the magazines out of the other two rifles. Each banana clip would give him thirty, so that meant ninety rounds, minus the ones the Viper had fired to kill Herc and wound Mac and Reno. And he had nine mags for the pistols, which roughly gave him about 135 rounds left. Wolf didn't take the time to make an ammo count. He didn't know how many more adversaries he'd be facing, and if he got down to a low-ammo alert, he had no backup en route anyway.

No, it was just him against them, however many that turned out to be.

The whole thing seemed unbelievable, as if he'd dropped into an alternate universe or a time distortion, along with Eagan and Nasim and whatever the hell they were chasing. Accondras had known something about it. He wished now that he'd known all this in advance. He would have gotten the information out of Accondras, even if he'd had to beat him to within an inch of his life. Somehow it was tied to what had happened to him back in Iraq.

But how?

The motorcycle's headlight shone over a six-inch barrier fashioned from dirt and gravel and slim tree branches.

Another *tope*, he thought as he closed his fingers over the front brake and straightened his legs, lifting himself off the seat.

The motorcycle went over the speedbump with a slight bounce.

Wolf's eyes had grown accustomed to the darkness, and three immense shapes materialized before him fifty or so yards away, looking like black hills against a blue velvet sky. Each had a peculiar squared-off top.

Mayan pyramids.

When a cooling breeze blew over him, briny and distinct, he knew he was getting close to the sea.

It can't be much farther, he thought, and he steered the motorcycle to the side of the road to figure out his next move.

Between a crumbling section of wall and the largest pyramid, a pair of headlights suddenly materialized. Wolf immediately cut off the motorcycle's headlight and killed the engine.

It had to be them, and they were coming this way.

He debated his options as he unslung the AK-47 from his shoulder.

Can't let them get past me, he thought.

He snapped the selection lever to the single-round position and nestled the solid butt of the Kalashnikov against his shoulder.

If he took out the radiator and the tires, he'd have them trapped in the area with no means of motorized escape and not much cover. It would then just be a matter of hit and run until he either got them all or they got him. There was no doubt they had him outnumbered, but by how many, he could only guess.

Three men had gotten into the van with Eagan at the other site. That meant it was at least four to one.

No odds like bad odds, he thought as he sighted in low center on the area between the headlights.

Inside his head, Mac's voice came back to him: *You're a Ranger, dammit. Now go do what you need to do.*

Radiator first, then the tires.

He squeezed off the first round, and the sharp crack extinguished his hearing. Lowering his aim, he continued to fire at what he hoped were the tires.

The van zigzagged to an abrupt stop, and the driver's and front passenger-side doors flipped open.

Figuring they'd seen his muzzle flashes, Wolf sprinted toward the first of the three pyramids.

Got to take the high ground.

He was wearing the black BDUs and figured they would help obscure his movements.

Something zipped by his head, splitting the air as only a bullet could.

Wolf dove forward and flattened out, rolling with the rifle held in front of his body.

A pattern of gouges tore the earth next to him.

Night vision. They had night vision.

The ground declined a bit, and Wolf scrambled toward the stone base of the pyramid.

His hearing was still fuzzy, but it seemed to be gradually returning. He reached an outcrop of stacked stones and ducked behind it. There were enough gaps between the stones that he was able to see twin muzzle flashes coming from the area next to the van. Extending the barrel through the opening, Wolf sighted on the muzzle flashes closest to the headlights.

He squeezed off a three-round burst, unable to tell if he'd hit his intended target. Shifting to the side, he wondered who each assailant was and if they all had night-vision capabilities.

Assume the worst, he thought. Hope for the best.

More rounds skittered over the rocks, and he took

another quick peek through the slot-like opening. Only one set of muzzle flashes this time.

That was a good sign.

But he couldn't afford to get pinned down in this location. Glancing upward, he saw that the ancient building sloped upward at a gradual angle. He moved back, snaking behind a prominent ridge of protruding rocks. The ragged wall was almost ladder-like, and Wolf scurried up it as best he could, occasionally having to flatten out and edge upward to the next section using movements reminiscent of intimacy. The rough surface scraped and ripped his skin, and when he finally got to the top, his whole chest burned from the fresh abrasions. A line of once-decorative crenellations like the crest of a storybook castle provided a modicum of cover. Wolf flattened out next to one of them and jammed the end of the rifle through the narrow gap. More muzzle flashes.

Sparks ignited around the section that he'd just left.

They think I'm still down there.

He sighted on the new target and squeezed off more rounds.

The flashes ceased.

Still using the decorative parapet for cover, Wolf scrambled up to the next level. He was just shy of the square box-like section at the peak.

A flicker of movement caught his eye.

Two figures were running down the road, heading back in the direction they'd come. One of them was waddling like a trundling hippopotamus. The other one's upper body glinted white in the moonlight.

Zerbe, Wolf thought, and crouched by a gap to zero in on him.

He hesitated and realized he didn't want to give away his new position. Instead of firing, he took the time to scan the area. While it was moonlit, he didn't have enough visual acuity to determine if he'd neutralized the two threats at the van. He watched and waited, wondering if the others were circling around to flank him.

Staying in one spot was suicide, so he slowly rolled back and began to work his way down the rear of the pyramid. A clear dirt path ran along the back of the building, and he ran to the next one.

Most of his hearing had returned, but he still had the persistent buzzing. He knew it wouldn't last much longer.

After getting to the center area of the second pyramid, he saw two consecutive sets of crudely fashioned stairs leading upward. The first one, the longest, led to a shelf-like platform that surrounded the tapering triangular edifice. The second set led to the squared-off crown. It was too inviting not to try, and the uppermost position would ensure the high ground once again. Wolf moved up the steps as fast as he could manage. Memories of running up the mountain all those weeks in Arizona flashed in his memory. His conditioning was seeing him through. Even though his legs were starting to burn like fire, he had no doubt he'd make it to the apex.

The sound of a muffled voice floated in the air and disappeared.

As far as he could tell, it had been close.

Had his adversaries gotten the same idea about the high ground?

Quickening his pace, he saw he was almost to the top of the first set of stairs.

His lungs were on fire now, too.

Movement in the shadows to his left.

A muzzle flash.

Rounds ricocheted off the steps inches in front of him.

Wolf brought his rifle up as his thumb flicked the selection lever to full auto.

The resulting spray caught a man in black BDUs, and he did a convulsive dance before curling forward and tumbling down the incline. Wolf couldn't tell who it was, and the bolt of his Kalashnikov locked back.

Wolf hit the magazine release button, and the banana clip hit the steps by his feet. He reached for a replacement mag and slammed it home.

In his peripheral vision, he caught a hint of motion on the flattened portion to his right. He whirled, training the muzzle on the movement and jerking the trigger.

Another figure danced in the moonlight, twisting and grabbing, then falling onto the flat shelf. Wolf ran to the prone figure and fired more rounds. The body jerked under the impact, and Wolf kicked a semi-automatic pistol away from the fallen man's hand. Peering around, he saw no one else, then kicked the body over.

Nasim's dead eyes stared up at him.

No answers from him, Wolf thought.

Splinters of rock slapped the left side of his face like red-hot sleet. He closed his eyes and staggered back, starting to lose his grip on the rifle. A massive shadow loomed before him holding a Glock, his face distorted by protruding four-inch tubes in front of his eyes.

It was Eagan. With night-vision goggles.

Wolf tried to swing the rifle barrel around, but the big man deftly kicked it, sending the AK-47 skittering down the sloping rocks. He stepped back, pointed the Glock at Wolf's face, and smiled.

His lips formed words Wolf could not discern.

Too far out of range for me to kick, Wolf thought. He readied himself for the round to go tearing through his skull. For an instant, he wondered if he'd feel the pain or if it would be over too quickly.

A second of cognizance, most likely, he told himself.

A whirlwind of dust stirred accompanied by a blinding beam of light swept over them. Wolf's torn skin felt the syncopation of the rotor blades slicing the air as an orange and white helicopter hovered close to them, training a spotlight downward. Eagan's mouth opened in a silent scream, and he tore off the night-vision goggles. Wolf sprang toward him, reaching out to snare the Glock. He managed to get one hand on the bigger man's wrist and the other on the slide of the weapon.

The helicopter swooped upward and hovered twenty yards away, the spotlight glinting like a midnight sun against the black backdrop of the sky.

Wolf jammed his right hand downward, breaking Eagan's hold on the pistol. The bigger man shifted his substantial body weight in the opposite direction, slamming Wolf into the jutting array of stones that formed the rickety wall.

The air left his lungs, but he brought his knee up, and it struck Eagan's groin. The big man grunted but lurched forward, pulling Wolf into a bear-hug. Wolf snapped his head forward, catching the bridge of Eagan's nose. They staggered to the right in a drunken dancers' embrace, then Wolf felt them tipping over the edge of the flat shelf. He readied himself for the impact as they fell, hoping his huge adversary wouldn't land on him.

In the fleeting seconds before impact, both of them rotated, and Wolf landed in the uppermost position.

Eagan's scream was audible, and his grip on Wolf's body loosened. They rolled slowly down the pyramid, each rotation bringing more pain as their bodies were bludgeoned by the jutting flagstones. It seemed to last forever, then they abruptly stopped. He lay still momentarily, the pain so ubiquitous that he was afraid to move. After a few shallow breaths, he turned his head to the side and saw Eagan continuing to roll down the unforgiving rocks. He reached the bottom and flopped down on his back.

Summoning all the strength he had left, Wolf managed to push himself up and came to a sitting position. The helicopter floated fifty feet away now, its spotlight trained on Eagan's inert form. He wasn't moving.

Wolf caught a glimpse of two heads leaning through the open side door of the chopper.

Zerbe's white sports coat loomed in the opening. Next to him was a man clad in a brown uniform, looking like a head and pair of arms jutting out of a barrel.

Recognition flared in Wolf's memory.

Lieutenant Cummins.

Wolf instinctively reached for the Glock in his tactical holster. After securing his fingers around the handle, he twisted it loose, raised it, and aimed at the chopper. He managed to squeeze off one round before the helicopter zoomed upward and away, disappearing into the velvet night.

CHAPTER 15

AMERICAN EMBASSY
CANCUN MEXICO

Wolf sat alone in the sterile room behind a plastic table, facing what he was certain was a two-way mirror on the white wall in front of him. The air conditioning felt good, although his body didn't. He reviewed the story once more, trying to recall the exact wording he'd used to describe what had happened to the Mexican authorities. Luckily, he'd been able to locate Mac and Reno in the Cancun hospital and relate what had happened. There was no sketchy recall this time.

It came back to him like disjointed scenes from a remembered movie.

As he slid the rest of the way down the pyramid after the helicopter took off, Wolf had used the flashlight to guide his descent.

Finding Eagan just barely alive at the bottom, Wolf shone the light on him. The big Viper had been defiant even on the precipice of death.

"Tell me what this is all about, and I'll get you to a doctor," Wolf had said.

The big man's lips had curled into a feral smile. "Go fuck yourself."

"Eagan, listen to me. I'll go for help, but you've got answers, and I want them. How's this connected to Iraq?"

Eagan coughed, spitting up bubbles of blood that coalesced into a bitter laugh.

"Fuck you, Wolf."

In desperation, Wolf recalled a name Accondras had mentioned.

"Who's Von Dien?"

Eagan turned his head to look at him, an expression of surprise twitching his bloodied face.

"He's..." He stopped and coughed. It sounded wet. "He's your worst nightmare."

Before he could say anything more, his chest heaved and his body gave three convulsive jerks, then ceased moving. Another bubble formed over his gaping mouth, growing to grotesque proportions, then remaining over his parted lips in eerie translucence.

No answers. A Viper to the end.

Wolf found Accondras dead in the van, although it didn't appear he'd been shot.

Beaten to death was a more likely diagnosis, Wolf had surmised as he used the Balisong knife to strip off the incriminating duct tape as Mac had directed.

Two other men in black BDUs lay by the van, their bodies having been perforated during the firefight.

There were signs of a makeshift LZ in the area adjacent to the beach. As far as he could tell, the helicopter had flown south. He didn't think it was going to return and didn't intend to wait around to find out.

After weighting all the weapons, the severed duct tape, and the ragged blouse with rocks from the crumbling wall, Wolf had moved to the edge of a strange opening he'd almost fallen into. It was a hole about twenty feet deep, with waterfalls on each side and a murky pool at the bottom. The gyring water gave off a briny odor. A thick layer of climbing shrubbery had attached itself to the cavern's walls. Wolf didn't know how deep the pool at the bottom was, but it would have to do. He dropped each weighted bundle over the side, then slowly walked to the beach and immersed himself in the frothing waves.

When he'd cleansed himself well enough, he made his way back to the motorcycle and proceeded to town.

Finding the hospital was relatively easy. A mini-fleet of Mexican police cars lined the drive. Inside, the staff was eager to direct him to the injured *Americanos*. A policeman stood guard stood outside the door, and Wolf gave him a Coca Cola and a roll of money to gain entrance to McNamara's room.

"*Un regalo*," Wolf said, curling the pesos around the can.

The cop smiled and nodded, then turned away from the door.

Inside the room, Mac was Mac. He held up his hand, giving Wolf a thumbs-up and a questioning expression.

Wolf did a thumbs-up as well. "How you doing?"

"Shit," Mac said. "I been hurt worse falling off a barstool. Can you believe that they won't let me outta here until I pay them off? Just because I don't have any damn Mexican insurance."

"How about Reno?"

"Aw, that tough son of a bitch is all right, except for

his case of amnesia." McNamara winked. "The cops asked him what happened, but the poor guy's got CRS."

"CRS?"

Mac grinned. "Can't Remember Shit."

"How about you?" Wolf asked. "What do you remember?"

"Not much," Mac said with a mock sigh. "We went out for a drive, and some badass banditos stopped me and Reno and Herc on the road somewhere. Robbed us, shot us up, and took off. Musta stole their passports as well. Other than that, I don't remember nothing." He paused and smiled. "You're mighty lucky you weren't with us."

Wolf chuckled. "Want me to call Kasey to wire the money?"

McNamara shook his head. "No need. I called Ms. Dolly, and the P Patrol is coming down here on a chartered plane to pay the bill and fly me back to the US. Should be here later today. Want me to save you a seat?"

"Absolutely," Wolf said.

That was before two FBI agents arrived and told Wolf they wanted to speak to him. After a quick drive to the American Embassy, they stuck him in a room for over an hour.

He declined the cup of coffee they offered him and sat with his hands in his lap.

Finally, the door opened, and the two of them entered the small room. They both wore blue suits that were impeccably pressed, along with white shirts and conservative power ties. The younger one sat across from him, identified himself as Special Agent Franker, and asked again if he could get him anything. The guy looked like he'd just started shaving last week.

Wolf shook his head.

Special Agent Franker glanced at his partner. That guy was older and heavier and had flecks of gray in a dark-brown Ivy League haircut. He gave a fractional nod.

"Are you sure?" Franker asked. "You look kind of beat up. How'd that happen?"

"I was doing some sightseeing, and I fell down."

"Where at?"

Wolf shook his head. "Can't recall exactly. This is my first trip to Mexico."

And hopefully my last, he thought.

The FBI agents exchanged glances, then Franker turned back to him.

"Mr. Wolf," the agent said, "do you know it's a crime to lie to a federal agent?"

"I guess I do now."

Franker stared at him for the better part of fifteen seconds. Then he leaned forward, placed his elbows on the table, and steepled his fingers.

"Okay, then. I'll get right to the point." Franker lowered his hands. "There was a very serious incident down here involving American citizens, one of whom perished. Two others were injured, one of whom I believe you know quite well."

Wolf nodded. "I was at the hospital when you called me."

Franker pursed his lips. "We have reason to believe that you and your associates were involved in that serious incident, and we need to find out what happened."

Wolf said nothing.

"Well?" the agent asked.

"Well, what?" Wolf replied.

"Are you going to cooperate or not?"

"What do you want to know?" Wolf countered.

The agents exchanged glances a third time, reminding Wolf of a Penn and Teller comedy skit he'd seen.

"Well," Franker said, "who shot your three friends, for one thing."

Wolf nodded. "Good question."

Franker's eyebrows rose. "Do you know?"

"Maybe," Wolf said. He paused while the agent edged forward a bit more.

"We're listening," he said.

"According to what Mac told me," Wolf said, his face devoid of emotion, "it was some very badass Mexican banditos."

* * *

PHOENIX INTERNATIONAL AIRPORT
PHOENIX, ARIZONA
FIVE HOURS LATER

Wolf watched as Ms. Dolly and the P Patrol ceremonially pushed McNamara's wheelchair past the final checkpoint after they'd cleared Customs. Brenda strode alongside, and Yolanda walked next to her. Wolf brought up the rear, carrying both his and Mac's baggage.

Kasey was standing just beyond the barrier with her arms folded. Her face was pulled tight in disapproval. Wolf didn't see Chad anywhere but figured that might be a good thing.

Apparently, Mac didn't think so.

"Where's my grandson?" he asked in a loud voice.

Kasey's frown deepened, but she leaned over and embraced him.

"Rod's watching him." Her eyes darted to the P Patrol. "And I'm glad I didn't bring him."

"Hey, honey," Mac said. "Don't be acting like that. I'd like you to meet Ms. Dolly and the—"

"My associates," Ms. Dolly interrupted. "Brenda Carrera and Yolanda Moore."

Both of them smiled and muttered pleasantries, but Kasey largely ignored them.

"You bring that cashier's check like I told you?" McNamara asked.

Kasey nodded and reached into her purse, which Wolf thought was a Louis Vuitton knockoff.

Wolf set the bags down and stepped closer. Yolanda smiled at him and took his hand. He noticed that Kasey's nostrils flared in disapproval. She thrust an envelope at her father.

"Here," she said. "For the amount you specified."

McNamara held it toward Ms. Dolly, who accepted it and dropped it into her Louis Vuitton purse. That one was *not* a knockoff.

"I appreciate it, sweetie," she said. "But I already told you there was no hurry to pay me back."

"I always pay my debts." McNamara's head tilted, and he looked up at her. "Don't you want to check it, darling?"

Ms. Dolly laughed. "I trust you, honey-bunny. And if it's short, it'll just give me an excuse to come a-looking for you." She punctuated the sentence with a sly wink.

Kasey's face was livid. Once again, she glared at Wolf.

Looks like I'm out of the garage and in the doghouse as far as she's concerned, he thought.

After a few moments of awkward silence, Ms. Dolly said, "As much as we'd all like to draw this out, we got us a plane to catch back to Sin City. Come on, girls."

She and Brenda bent over and planted affectionate kisses on McNamara's cheeks. Yolanda's hand caressed Wolf's head and pulled his face toward her. After their mouths disengaged, she let her fingers linger on his neck for a few moments and said, "Call me, boo."

Wolf watched the three of them saunter off, appreciating the sway of their hips.

"Oh, Dad." Kasey sighed. "How could you?"

"How could I what?" McNamara asked. "They're business associates."

"Yeah," Kasey said. "And I bet I know what *kind* of business."

McNamara clucked and shook his head. "It ain't like that at all."

"Well, I hope you realize that cashier's check wiped out the advance that you got for this stupid endeavor." She held up her index finger and thumb with a quarter-inch separation. "Trackdown, Incorporated is *this* far from being broke."

"Well," McNamara said, "it wasn't a complete loss." He gestured for Wolf to give him the black plastic garbage bag that was on top of his suitcase.

Wolf handed it over and McNamara unwrapped it, displaying Accondras' bloody backpack and something else wrapped in a Mexican newspaper.

"Wait till you see this," McNamara said, pulling the newsprint off. He held up a plaster statue a foot high, painted in vivid primary colors. It was an obese Mexican *vaquero* wearing a huge sombrero and drawing six-guns out of twin holsters.

"What *is* that thing?" Kasey asked.

Mac's brow wrinkled, and he looked at his daughter with a pained expression.

"It's one of them damn banditos we run into down south of the border. Right, Steve?"

Wolf couldn't help but laugh.

"Absolutely," he said.

Kasey said she would pull the car around to the passenger pick-up area before storming off.

McNamara looked up at him and shrugged. "Now, what's she so pissed off about?"

"You know women," Wolf replied.

"Yeah, well, I think this is gonna look *real* good on top of my mantel," Mac said. "Whaddaya think?"

Wolf shook his head and laughed. Exhaustion was settling in, and he was having a hard time hiding his disappointment with the whole ill-fated endeavor.

"Aw, hell," Mac said. "I know we come away with a lot of questions and not a lot of answers, but it ain't like we're empty-handed or nothing. We got something to work on, don't we?"

Something to work on… A name, Von Dien, and now he knew it was all tied to something that had happened in the Sandbox four years ago. Something Wolf couldn't remember. He had a lot of questions but no answers.

"Plus," Mac said, trying to sound upbeat, "we got this fine bandito here as a reminder of this misadventure. I think he's gonna bring us luck."

Wolf looked down on the brightly colored plaster statue. The facial features were finely carved, and for a moment, he could almost believe the figure was staring at him with a sly grin like it was privy to some obscure private joke.

Yeah, we've got the bandito, all right, he thought. *I guess that is something after all.*

A LOOK AT BOOK TWO
DEVIL'S FANCY

Exoneration is the goal. Survival is the challenge.

Former Army Ranger and ex-con Steve Wolf is making a name for himself as a bounty hunter with Trackdown, Inc., but his past still casts a long shadow. Wrongfully convicted of a war crime he didn't commit, Wolf is determined to clear his name —but a critical eight-minute gap in his memory stands between him and the truth.

What he doesn't realize is that his pursuit of justice has put him in the crosshairs of a powerful and ruthless billionaire. This man's deadly treasure hunt has already left a trail of bodies in its wake, and Wolf is the only obstacle standing between him and his ultimate prize—a priceless artifact worth killing for.

As Wolf pieces together the puzzle, the danger escalates. A relentless squad of elite mercenaries has been sent to eliminate him, and they don't miss. Outgunned, outnumbered, and hunted across a battlefield where the rules don't apply, Wolf must rely on his training, instincts, and sheer will to survive.

AVAILABLE APRIL 2025

ACKNOWLEDGMENTS

I wish to thank Dave Case and Shauna Washington, my beta readers, without their advice and assistance, this book would never have gotten off the ground.

ABOUT THE AUTHOR

Michael A. Black is the author of 36 books and over 100 short stories and articles. A decorated police officer in the south suburbs of Chicago, he worked for over thirty-two years in various capacities including patrol supervisor, SWAT team leader, investigations and tactical operations before retiring in April of 2011.

A long time practitioner of the martial arts, Black holds a black belt in Tae Kwon Do from Ki Ka Won Academy in Seoul, Korea. He has a Bachelor of Arts degree in English from Northern Illinois University and a Master of Fine Arts in Fiction Writing from Columbia College, Chicago. In 2010 he was awarded the Cook County Medal of Merit by Cook County Sheriff Tom Dart. Black wrote his first short story in the sixth grade, and credits his then teacher for instilling him with determination to keep writing when she told him never to try writing again.

Black writes under numerous pseudonyms and pens The Executioner series under the name Don Pendleton. His Executioner novel, Fatal Prescription, won the Best Original Novel Scribe Award given by the International Media Tie-In Writers Association in 2018.

He is very active in animal rescue and animal welfare issues and has several cats.

www.MichaelABlack.com